## PRAISE FO

T0275192

"A literary breakthrough. . . [                    ] ssured debut, and we hypothesize it s just the first bit of greatness we'll see from an author who somehow has the audacity to be both an academic powerhouse and [a] divinely talented novelist."

—*Entertainment Weekly*

"Another Hazelwood home run." —*People* on *Bride*

"*Bride* is a delight! Passionate and witty and primal in its intensity, Ali Hazelwood's paranormal debut introduces a world as intriguing as its characters. I absolutely adored this read."

—*New York Times* bestselling author Nalini Singh

"Contemporary romance's unicorn: the elusive marriage of deeply brainy and delightfully escapist. . . . *The Love Hypothesis* has wild commercial appeal, but the quieter secret is that there is a specific audience, made up of all the Olives in the world, who have deeply, ardently waited for this exact book."

—*New York Times* bestselling author Christina Lauren

"It's official. There's nothing Ali Hazelwood can't do brilliantly when it comes to writing. LOVED it."

—#1 *New York Times* bestselling author Jodi Picoult

"Ali Hazelwood is a romance powerhouse and she's put me firmly back in my werewolf era."

—#1 *New York Times* bestselling author Hannah Grace on *Bride*

"Everything I want and more in a paranormal romance novel."

—*New York Times* bestselling author Lauren Asher on *Bride*

"Whenever I want a sexy, witty, delicious romance, told in a fresh and intelligent voice, I read Ali Hazelwood. Prepare to get addicted. Each book is pure joy."

—*New York Times* bestselling author Simone St. James

"Funny, sexy, and smart. Ali Hazelwood did a terrific job with *The Love Hypothesis*."

—*New York Times* bestselling author Mariana Zapata

"Gloriously nerdy and sexy, with on-point commentary about women in STEM."

—*New York Times* bestselling author Helen Hoang
on *Love on the Brain*

"STEMinists, assemble. Your world is about to be rocked."

—*New York Times* bestselling author Elena Armas
on *Love on the Brain*

"This tackles one of my favorite tropes—Grumpy meets Sunshine—in a fun and utterly endearing way. . . . I loved the nods toward fandom and romance novels, and I couldn't put it down. Highly recommended!"

—*New York Times* bestselling author Jessica Clare
on *The Love Hypothesis*

"Ali Hazelwood finally gives us paranormal, with her trademark humor, twisty plot, and spice that doesn't quit—buckle up."

—*New York Times* bestselling author Hannah Whitten on *Bride*

"Hazelwood unleashes her sparkling voice and wit on a paranormal Romeo and Juliet."

—International bestselling author Ruby Dixon on *Bride*

## ALSO BY ALI HAZELWOOD

🔹 🔹 🔹

# DEEP END

# ALI HAZELWOOD

BERKLEY ROMANCE
NEW YORK

BERKLEY ROMANCE
Published by Berkley
An imprint of Penguin Random House LLC
penguinrandomhouse.com

Copyright © 2025 by Ali Hazelwood
Penguin Random House supports copyright. Copyright fuels creativity, encourages diverse
voices, promotes free speech, and creates a vibrant culture. Thank you for buying an authorized
edition of this book and for complying with copyright laws by not reproducing, scanning, or
distributing any part of it in any form without permission. You are supporting writers and
allowing Penguin Random House to continue to publish books for every reader.

BERKLEY and the BERKLEY & B colophon are registered trademarks of
Penguin Random House LLC.

Library of Congress Cataloging-in-Publication Data

Names: Hazelwood, Ali, author.
Title: Deep end / Ali Hazelwood.
Description: First edition. | New York: Berkley Romance, 2025.
Identifiers: LCCN 2024021046 | ISBN 9780593550441 (paperback) |
ISBN 9780593550458 (ebook)
Subjects: LCGFT: Romance fiction. | Novels.
Classification: LCC PS3608.A98845 D44 2025 | DDC 813/.6—dc23/eng/20240510
LC record available at https://lccn.loc.gov/2024021046

First Edition: February 2025

Printed in China
1   3   5   7   9   10   8   6   4   2

Book design by Daniel Brount
Interior art: Water splashes © Vector Tradition/Shutterstock.com

*This one has to be for the AmsterDAMNs.*

Dear Reader,

Once again—thank you so much for choosing one of my books. This one might be my favorite I've ever written, and I'm so happy it's out in the world! Before you dive in, I want you to know that this work contains consensual and negotiated explorations of kink—in particular, of power exchange. If you choose to read it, I hope you enjoy the experience.

Love,
Ali

# DEEP
# END

# PROLOGUE

IT ALL STARTS WHEN PENELOPE ROSS LEANS IN OVER THE restaurant's solid wooden table, lifts her index finger, and declares, "Tenth circle of hell: you find the love of your life, but the sex is intensely *meh*."

In front of the entirety of Stanford's diving roster.

At eleven fifteen in the morning.

During my twenty-first birthday brunch.

Four seconds ago we were oversharing about our digestive issues, and the whiplash is disorienting. I've been taking advantage of my newly acquired legal rights, but no amount of alcohol can prevent me from blurting out, "What?"

Not my most tactful moment. Thankfully, my incredulity is drowned out by the reactions of the rest of the team: Bree's spit take, Bella's scandalized gasp, and Victoria's skeptical "Isn't *Blomqvist* the love of your life?"

"He sure is." Pen nods.

I fill my mouth with mimosa. The taste is far worse than plain orange juice, but the buzz is *very* welcome.

"Pen. Honey." Bree wipes espresso martini off her glasses using the shirt hem of her sister, Bella—who allows it. Twins stuff, I guess. "How many drinks have you had?"

"Like, half of that pitcher."

"Ah. Maybe we should—"

"But *in mimosa veritas.*" Pen leans forward even more. Her voice drops as she makes a sweeping gesture. "I am confiding in you, guys. Being vulnerable. We're having a *moment.*"

Victoria sighs. "Pen, I love you, ride or die, would follow you into the very fires of Mordor and all that shit, but we're not having a *moment.*"

"Why?"

"Because you're making shit up."

"*Why?*"

"Because Blomqvist *fucks.*"

I sit back in a semi-zonked state and force myself to think about Lukas Blomqvist—a rare occurrence for me. People assume that I'm fascinated with everything that goes on in a pool, but nope. The only sports I find remotely interesting are diving and land-diving (or, as the normies call it, gymnastics). The rest is out of my purview. There's just too much stuff going on in aquatics. I can't keep track of Stanford's water polo teams, let alone the swimmers.

And yet, Blomqvist is hard to ignore. Because of the truckload of medals, maybe. The world records. Plus, if the captain of my team is part of an athletics power couple, it behooves me to be aware of its other half. And Pen and Blomqvist have been dating since forever. For all I know, they were betrothed at birth to cement US-Sweden diplomatic relations.

I close my eyes to resurface my spotty memories of him. Black Speedos. Tattoos. Short, choppy brown hair. Above-average wingspan. The majestic and yet improbable build of every other DI swimmer who ever lived.

Victoria is right. We can safely hazard that yes, Blomqvist *does* fuck.

"I didn't say he doesn't. He's great. Just not . . ." Pen winces, and it's such an odd break from her sparkling self-assurance, it slices right through my mimosa haze.

The thing about Pen, she's kinda great. Aspirational. The type of person who instinctively knows how to make someone feel at ease. She'll remind you to drink water. Offer the ponytail holder on her wrist when your hair sticks to your lips. Remember your half birthday. I could take personal development workshops till I turn fifty *and* let a team of data analysts reprogram me, but I still wouldn't have a third of her charm, because charisma like hers sprouts from base pairs nestled in chromosomes. And now she's biting into cuticles like she just discovered social anxiety? I don't love it.

"Just not . . . what I want. And honestly, vice versa," she adds in a low mumble.

"Which would be?" Bless Victoria for asking what I don't have the courage to. The extroverted, filterless member every team needs.

"Oh my god. I just want to . . . you know, sometimes . . ." Pen groans.

I stiffen, suddenly alarmed. "Is Blomqvist forcing you to—"

"No. God *no*." She shakes her head, but I must look unconvinced because she continues, "No. He would never." Everyone else has dropped off the conversation—the twins, bickering over whose drink is whose, Victoria, gesturing toward the server. "Luk's not like that. Just . . . how do you tell a guy that you need something different?"

Why is she asking *me*? Have the lines on my forehead arranged to form the words *previously asked someone to spank her*?

Honestly, it would check out. "Aren't Scandinavians very open-minded?"

"Maybe? He's definitely open-minded when it comes to—" But

she breaks off, because a small posse of out-of-tune waiters interrupt us with a string of *happy birthday to you*s, and many things happen at once.

I blow on the single candle haphazardly plonked on top of a lava cake. A team present of new stretch cords is produced. I am briefly verklempt that someone as chronically introverted as me found people who are, god, so *nice*. Victoria needs to use the restroom. Pen gets a call from her aunt. Bree wants to know which classes I'll be taking in the fall.

It's too much. In too little time. We never end up returning to the topic of Penelope Ross and Lukas Blomqvist's mysteriously imperfect sex life—which is for the best. Whatever issue they're dealing with is probably trivial, anyway. She doesn't like the brand of condoms he uses. He falls asleep without cuddling her. They're tired after practice and squabble over who should be on top. Not my circus and/or monkeys, so I let the matter slip out of my mind, smooth as a longfin eel.

Until a few weeks later, when everything changes.

# CHAPTER 1

THE THING I DREAD THE MOST ABOUT JUNIOR YEAR BEGINS on a Wednesday morning, a couple of weeks before the start of the autumn quarter. It's penciled into my Google Calendar for the ten to eleven slot, a single word that weighs more than the sum of its letters.

*Therapy.*

"This is somewhat unconventional," Sam tells me on our first meeting, no judgment or curiosity in her tone. She appears to have mastered neutrality in all facets of life—her beige pantsuit, the medium grip of a handshake, an ageless, graceful look that could be anywhere between forty and seventy. Is it too early in our acquaintance for me to want to *be* her? "I was under the impression that Stanford Athletics had its own team of licensed sports psychologists."

"They do," I say, letting my eyes skim over the walls of her office. Diplomas outnumber personal photos, four to zero. Sam and I may *already* be the same person. "They're great. I did work with them for the past few months, but . . ." I shrug, hoping to broadcast that it's on me if it didn't work out. "I had some issues a few years ago—unrelated to diving. At the time, cognitive behavioral therapy worked well for me. My coach and I talked it over, and since it's your specialty, I decided to try Counseling Services." I smile like I have full trust in this plan. If only.

"I see. And in the past, when you did cognitive behavioral therapy, what issues did you—"

"Nothing sports related. It was . . . family stuff. My relationship with my dad. But that's all solved now." I realize that I spoke a whit too quickly, and expect Sam to challenge what's obviously a half-baked, still-frozen-in-the-middle truth, but she just stares, assessing and hawkish.

Lots of attention, all on me, all at once. I squirm in the chair, feeling the ache that always clings to my muscles. Her presence is not particularly calming, but I'm here to be *fixed*, not *soothed*.

"I see," she says eventually. Bless CBT and its lack of bullshit. *There is this thing you do that's bad for you. I'll teach you to* not *do it, your insurance will give me money, and we'll each go our merry way. BYO trauma. Tissues are on me.* "And just to be clear, Scarlett, you *want* to be here?"

I nod emphatically. I may not look forward to the agony that comes with exposing the squishy bits of my soul, but I'm not some cliché detective refusing to see a shrink in an eighties crime show. Therapy is a privilege. I'm lucky to have it. Above all, I need it.

"I must admit, I don't know much about diving. It seems like a very complex discipline."

"It is." Lots of competitive sports require a delicate balance of physical and psychological strength, but diving . . . diving has trained long and hard to become the mind-fuckiest of them all.

"Would you be willing to explain?"

"Of course." I clear my throat, glancing down at my joggers and compression shirt. Black and cardinal red. *Stanford Swimming & Diving: Fear the Tree.* Whoever designs our gear clearly wants for our identity to be reduced to our athletic performance. *Never forget:*

*you are what you score.* "We jump off things. Plunge into pools. Do some acrobatics in between."

I mean to make her laugh, but Sam's not prone to amusement. "I'm assuming there's more?"

"Lots of regulations." But I don't want to bore her, or be a difficult client. "I'm an NCAA Division I athlete. I compete in two events. One is from the springboard, that bouncy fiberglass board that . . ." I mimic its up-and-down motion with the flat of my hand. "That's three meters high. About ten feet." *As tall as an ostrich*, the voice of my first coach reminds me.

"What's the other event?"

"The platform. That's ten meters high." Thirty-three feet. Two giraffes.

"No bounce?"

"Static."

She hums. "Does the scoring work like gymnastics?"

"Pretty much. A panel of judges looks for mistakes and subtracts points accordingly."

"And how many dives do you perform per competition?"

"That depends. And it's not . . . it's not really about how many." I bite the inside of my cheek. She lets me take my time, but stays engaged. "It's the group."

"The group?"

"The . . . type of dive, if you will."

"And how many groups are there?"

"Six in total." I fidget with the tip of my ponytail. "Forward. Backward. Reverse. Twist. Armstand."

"I see. And in your email, you mentioned that you've been recovering from an injury?"

Therapy *is* a privilege. I don't like it, though. "Correct."

"When was that?"

"About fifteen months ago. At the end of freshman year." I

clench my fists under my thighs, wait for her to demand the gory details, ready to recite my list.

Sam, though, spares me. "Did you say that there are six groups of dives?"

"Yes." I'm surprised at the topic shift, and let my guard down.

It's a misstep of catastrophic proportions.

"And this injury of yours, Scarlett . . . does it have anything to do with the fact that you only listed five?"

# CHAPTER 2

**Y**OU FUCKED UP," MARYAM SAYS DURING THE FIRST WEEK OF classes, and all I can think past the despair droning in my ears is that I deserve better from my roommate. I've helped her clean bloodstains off countless wrestling singlets—am I really not to be afforded compassion? Or at least disapproval of the more tacit variety?

"I am one whole fourth German," I counter. "My mom was born there. I should be good at this."

"Your mother died when you were two, Vandy. Your step-mommy, who *raised* you, is from Bumfuck, Mississippi."

Harsh. But fair. "My genetic makeup—"

"Is irrelevant and does not predispose you to a passing grade in German," she says with the contempt of someone who grew up bi-lingual. I can't presently recall what part of the brain controls the ability to learn languages, but hers spins beautifully and turbine-like. An excellent source of renewable energy ready to power a small European country.

Meanwhile: "I'm not good at this stuff," I whine. Why *should* I be, though? "It's ridiculous that med schools have foreign language requirements."

"It's not. What if you decide to do Doctors Without Borders, and your ability to save a life depends on knowing whether 'the scalpel' is male or female?"

I scratch my neck. *"Die skalpellen?"*

"Bam, patient's dead." Maryam shakes her head. "You fucked up, my dude."

With a little help from my academic adviser. *Take the premed courses first*, he said. *You'll need the knowledge to pass the Medical College Admission Test*, he added. *It's the right move*, he concluded.

And I listened. Because all I ever wanted was to be *on top of shit*. Because I'm a student athlete, and my schedule is a crossover between a Jenga tower and a shibari tutorial. Spontaneity? Only if prearranged. I made a fifteen-year plan the day I graduated from high school, and always intended to stick to it: upwards of one NCAA title, med school, orthopedics, engagement and marriage, compulsory happiness.

Of course, I screwed up that plan by stuffing chem and bio sequences into my freshman and sophomore years—without considering that science classes were never my weakness. Enter junior year, and my GPA quakes in its boots. Psychology is distressingly vague. The German dative haunts my goriest nightmares. English composition wants me to construct cogent arguments on elusive, slippery topics—poetry, the ethics of pest control, maximum mandates for government officials, do people exist when we cannot see them?

It's easier for me when balls fall neatly into their intended buckets. Black and white, right and wrong, carbon based and inorganic. This year is shades of grays and marbles scattered all over the floor, a German Language 1 oil puddle spilled underneath.

I used to be a straight A student athlete. Used to be in control. Used to live in pursuit of excellence. At this point, I'm just trying to avoid explosive failures. Wouldn't it be lovely if I could manage not to constantly let down the people around me?

"Switch to another language," Maryam suggests, like I haven't already explored every escape route.

"Can't. It's like shingled roofing—they all overlap with something." Such as morning drills. Afternoon practice. Any of the other million activities for which Stanford recruited me. And this is supposed to be the year I fulfill my athletic potential. If I still have it, anyway. If it was ever there.

It sure felt like it, back at Bumfuck High School (Missouri, but I've given up on correcting Maryam). Half a dozen DI coaches aggressively elbowed each other to lure me to their schools, because I was a former junior Olympian, national team member, junior world medalist. Top recruit. Every club coach I'd had since age six had blown smoke up my butt: *You're excellent at this, Vandy. You'll do great things, Vandy. Promising young diver, Vandy.* I frolicked in that smoke like a blissed-out prairie vole—until college, when I finally stood corrected.

In fact, I barely even stood.

My brain must have decided to do me a solid, because I have no memories of the thirty seconds that changed my life. Lucky me, the whole thing is on tape for anyone to watch, because it happened at the NCAA diving finals. It even comes pre-commentated.

*"And that was Scarlett Vandermeer of Stanford University, Junior Olympic bronze. Definitely the big breakout of the season, and on the verge of a new platform record. Before this dive, that is."*

*"Yeah, she was attempting an inward dive with two and a half somersaults in pike position that she managed flawlessly this morning at the prelims. In fact, it got her eights and nines. But this time something went poorly from takeoff."*

It's always those you trust the most.

"*Yeah. That was definitely a failed dive—that's going to be a zero from the judges in terms of scoring. But she also entered the water at the wrong angle, so here's hoping that she isn't hurt.*"

To which my body said, *Fuck hoping.*

It's funny, in a remarkably unfunny way. I clearly remember the anger—at the water, at myself, at my own body—but I have no recollection of the pain. In the video, the girl limping out of the pool is a doppelgänger who stole my body. The long braid roping down her red swimsuit belongs to an impostor. The dimples as she strains her lips into a smile? Uncanny. And why does the little gap between her front teeth look exactly like mine? The camera follows her woozy gait mercilessly, gawking even as Coach Sima and his assistants run to help.

"*Vandy—are you okay?*"

The answer is unintelligible, but Coach loves to recount the story of how the girl said, *Yeah, but I'm going to need an Advil before my next dive.*

Turns out, she was right. She *would* need an Advil before her next dive. And surgeries. And rehab. Her final tally?

Concussion.

Ruptured eardrum.

Twisted neck.

Labral tear of the left shoulder.

Pulmonary contusion.

Sprained wrist.

Sprained ankle.

A heavy, viscous weight lodges in my chest cavity whenever I watch the video and imagine what she must have gone through—till I remember that the girl is *me.*

There isn't a single guy I've matched with on dating apps who hasn't asked me, *Diving is pretty much the same thing as swimming, right?* But much like boxing, ice hockey, and lacrosse, diving is a contact sport. Every time we enter the water, the impact beats through our skeletons, muscles, internal organs.

Eat your heart out, NFL.

"You need to prepare for the very real possibility that you won't be able to dive again," Barb told me before my surgery. So difficult to dismiss what your stepmom says as pessimistic drivel when said stepmom is a brilliant orthopedic surgeon. "We just want your shoulder to regain full mobility."

"I know," I said, and cried like a baby, first in her arms, then alone in my bed.

But Barb was overcautious—and I was lucky. Recovery turned out to be within the realm of possibility. I redshirted during my sophomore year. Rested. Took the meds. Stuck to the anti-inflammatory diet. Focused on the PT and the stretches and the rehab, as zealously as a nun saying her nighttime prayers. I visualized my dives, cradled my aches, showed up for practice anyway, watching the rest of the team train, the smell of the chlorine clinging to my nose, the shimmery blue of the pool just feet away, yet impossibly far.

Then, two months ago, I was cleared for training. And it has been . . .

Well. There's a reason I'm seeing a therapist.

"I think I have an idea to fix your foreign language problem."

I glance suspiciously at Maryam—and yet lean forward, all ears and eyes and hope.

"You're going to tell me to take an acid bath, aren't you?"

"Hear me out: Latin 201."

I push to my feet. "I have to go."

"Think how helpful it'll be when Doctors Without Borders sends you to ancient Rome!"

I slam the door behind me and leave for practice forty minutes early, just to avoid garroting my roommate.

We were paired up during freshman year, and despite Maryam's unflinching meanness and my inability to timely replace empty toilet paper rolls, we have somehow become unwilling to live apart. Last year we (voluntarily?) moved together to a place off campus, and we just (voluntarily?) renewed our lease, condemning ourselves to twenty-four more months of each other. The truth is, being together is simple and requires little emotional labor from either of us. And when you're like me (a goal-oriented, control-focused, overachieving perfectionist), finding someone like Maryam is a gift.

Not a *good* gift, but I'll take it.

The Avery Aquatic Center is the best facility I've ever trained at. It's fully outdoors, with four pools and a diving tower, and it's where all Stanford aquatic teams practice. Today, the women's locker room is blissfully silent. It's a rare Goldilocks zone—swimmers are already off to practice; divers aren't yet getting ready. Water polo players have recently been exiled to another building, and many a thankful tear was shed.

I put on my swimsuit. Slide a tee and shorts over it. Set my alarm and sit on the uncomfortable wooden bench, contemplating my life choices. Exactly ten minutes later my phone vibrates, and I stand, having achieved no clarity or inner peace. I'm walking to Laundry Services for a fresh towel, when I hear a familiar voice.

". . . not okay," Penelope is saying.

She stands in the hallway, a few feet away, but doesn't notice me.

"Not at *all*," she continues, a curl of tears in her words. I recognize it from that dual meet in Utah, when she screwed up a forward pike, belly flopped like a flying squirrel, and slid from first to ninth. "Not for us."

The reply is quieter, deeper. Less distressed. Lukas Blomqvist stands in front of Pen, bare chested and arms crossed, a pair of goggles around his neck and a cap dangling from his fingers. He must have just gotten out of practice, because he's still dripping. The slight frown between his eyes is hard to interpret—could be a glower, or resting Swede face. I can't make out what he's saying, but it doesn't matter, because Pen cuts him off.

". . . there's no reason for that, if . . ."

Another rich, low-pitched response. I retreat. This conversation is not for me. I don't need a towel *that* bad.

"It's for the best." Pen leans closer. "You know it is."

Blomqvist inhales deeply, and his glistening shoulders rise, making him look even taller. I notice the tautness in his jaw, the sudden bend of his head, the bunching of muscles in his upper arm.

*Menacing. Threatening. Scary.* That's what he is. Next to him, Pen looks small and upset, and my brain clicks into a new mode.

I couldn't care less whether it's my business. I stride closer, eyes narrowed on Blomqvist. My fingers tremble, so I fist them at my sides, and even though he is probably four times stronger than Pen and me put together, even though it's a terrible idea, I ask, "Pen, is everything okay?"

# CHAPTER 3

**M**Y VOICE RICOCHETS AGAINST THE TILED FLOORS. PEN AND Lukas look at me, equally taken aback.

I swallow and force myself to ask again, "Do you need anything, Pen?"

"Vandy? I didn't know you were—" Her mouth curves in a puzzled tilt. Then the distrustful way I'm regarding Lukas must register, because her eyes widen, and her lips part. "Oh my god, I . . . oh, no. No, he wasn't—we were just . . ." She lets out a breathy laugh, and turns to her boyfriend to share her amusement at the misunderstanding.

But Lukas's gaze lingers on me. "Everything's fine, Scarlett," he says. I'm not exactly inclined to believe him, but he doesn't sound defensive, or annoyed, or even angry at my obvious assumption that he's a danger to Pen.

Also, he appears to know my first name. Even though I've been Vandy for the entire sports community since I was six. Fascinating.

"I didn't mean to intrude," I say, unrepentant. Maybe I'm hypersensitive when it comes to situations like this one—okay, I'm a stack of hypersensitivities in a trench coat—but I have my reasons, and I'd rather make a fool of myself and err on the side of caution than . . . whatever the alternative is. "Just making sure that—"

"I know," Lukas says quietly, that blue gaze still settled on mine. "Thank you for looking out for Pen."

The soft praise in his tone has my mind shorting for a second. By the time I recover, he's giving Pen's shoulder an affectionate squeeze and brushing past me. I follow the play of muscles on his broad back until he turns the corner, the baby hair drying at his nape, the black-inked outlines rippling on his left shoulder and twisting down his arm. It's a full sleeve, but I can't quite make it out. Trees, maybe?

"Shit," Pen says.

I glance back. Find her wiping a hand down her face.

I *definitely* overstepped. "I'm sorry. I wasn't trying to be nosy—"

"It's not you, Vandy." Her green eyes are shiny, a hairbreadth away from overflowing. I was fully willing to be Pen's meat shield if it came to that, but pulling her back from crying? I doubt I can manage that.

"Do you . . . would you like me to call Victoria?" They're both seniors, and she's Pen's closest friend on the team. Not much of a pool: the twins are very absorbed with each other, and I've barely been around. "Or I could ask Lukas to come back?"

"Call me for what?" Victoria appears—aviator sunglasses, inside. Purple smoothie. That dark, curly mullet that should be an aberration, *spectacular* on her. "I told you, I won't be complicit in the assassination of any more spiders—what the . . . ?"

It all happens so *fast*. Pen's tears bursting free. Victoria's scandalized gasp. The voices of the water polo team, filling the hallway. Before I can excuse myself from whatever the hell is going on, the three of us are barreling into an equipment room.

The door firmly shuts under Victoria's back. "What the hell happened?"

She alternates staring at Pen (with worry) and me (with . . . murder?), and I feel a sudden spark of compassion for Lukas. Maybe people *shouldn't* go about indiscriminately glaring at others, after all.

"I was having a fight with Luk." Pen wipes her cheek with the back of her hand.

"Aww, babe. About what?"

"I'll give you guys some privacy," I murmur, reaching for the doorknob.

Pen's fingers close around my hand. "No, stay. I don't want you to think that Luk could ever . . ." She takes a deep breath. I shift on my feet and think longingly of the locker room, the Epsom salt tub, a creepy porcelain doll factory—*anywhere* but the here and now. "He could never be violent, or mean. He's the best person I've ever . . . We've just been in the process of—"

"Oh, god. Is this about the whole breakup thing?" Victoria asks. Significantly *less* gently.

Not my business. Not my business. Intensely not my business.

But Pen nods tearily.

"Listen." Victoria sighs, like they've been over this. "Babe. Honey. I get it, you and Lukas have been together since you were, like, twelve—"

"Fifteen."

"—and popped each other's cherries and now you're wondering, what would an uncircumcised dick be like?"

A sniffle. "Actually, in Sweden most people don't—"

"TMI. The point is—what the fuck are you doing?"

I've always found Victoria's bluntness delicious, but this seems a bit harsh. And Pen might agree, because the weeping fades into a scowl. "You're supposed to be on *my* side."

"I am. As someone who's on your side *and* has been on the dating scene for the last two years, I'm telling you, you do not want to lose that man. There are lots of assholes out there, and Lukas is a smart, decent, hot guy who puts the toilet seat down and has yet to contract the French disease. That's much rarer than you think."

"But I'm not happy. And he's not getting what he wants from this relationship, either."

"Pen. Come on. If he told you he's okay with not doing that stuff—"

"He's settling. Just like I'm settling. If we stay together, we'll get married, have a house in the suburbs and two point five bilingual kids I cannot understand, and will always wonder what we missed out on. I won't know what being young and free feels like, and he'll be bitter because he had to give up all that kinky shit, like spanking people and tying them up and ordering them what to do."

I freeze. I should really not be here, but I can't leave, because my feet weigh a million pounds, and every drop of blood in my body is flowing up to hang out on my cheeks.

"I get it." Victoria is exasperated. "But you need to decide—"

A hard pounding at the door. We all jolt. "Hey? Is anyone in there?"

Victoria shouts, "Yeah, just a sec!"

"I left my gear bag in there, so if you guys could move your orgy to the showers . . ."

Victoria rolls her eyes but opens the door. We march past Gear Girl—Victoria, with a defiant expression; Pen, wiping residual tears; me, stubbornly refusing to make eye contact. The conversation may have resumed, but the twins are coming our way. "Where were you guys?" Bella asks. I panic, but Victoria makes up something about a missing shammy on the fly, because for her lying doesn't require two to three business days of careful preparation, and we all go warm up, like a big happy family.

I'm still flushed. Aware of my pulse. Cogs turn in my skull. All I can think of is: Pen has always been *so* lovely to me.

After my third surgery, when Barb couldn't take more than a

week off without collapsing the field of medicine, Pen popped by to check on me every day. *To make sure your evil roommate isn't making belts out of your skin*, she'd say with a wink, but she's just a naturally caring person. And there was the time she sat down with me after my first dual meet, to remind me that a few splashy entries didn't make me a bad diver, that sometimes we're just too much in our heads, that she'd been there, too—that chaotic, overthinking feeling that makes the platform feel like a tightrope and turns your body into an unreliable narrator. That moment when your focus dissolves into panic, and the dive is irreparably fucked before it even begins.

It had meant so much to me, back in the fall of freshman year. Everything was new and raw and too big, but Penelope Ross, world and Pan Am medalist, NCAA champion, held my hand and told me that she felt like I did.

I think about it during Pilates, and dryland training, and while climbing up the infinite steps of the diving tower. I think about it as I stretch every muscle I possess, with special care for my tender, stupid shoulder, the one that all my doctors insist is healed, but in my nightmares shatters like a champagne flute at least twice a week.

By the time practice is over, I've made up my mind. And while the rest of the team chatters away in the locker room, I walk to her side, take a deep breath, and ask, "Could we go get coffee after this? Just you and I."

# CHAPTER 4

THOUGHT IT MIGHT BE HARD TO SAY OUT LOUD, MOSTLY BE-
cause I never have, not to anyone who wasn't . . . *intimately* involved in the matter. But the words flow out of me, as smooth as a
perfect dive. No hiccups, no stutters, just a knife-sharp slice
through rippling water. I picture a panel of seven smiling judges,
raising several perfect-ten boards in unison.

*Full points, Ms. Vandermeer. This disclosure of your sexual his-
tory was unimpeachably executed. Now hit the showers.*

Not gonna lie, I'm feeling pretty proud. Unfortunately, Pen isn't
impressed. "You are into *that*?" She blinks and glances around the
Coupa Café. Classes started this week, and campus is too crowded.
Backpack straps wrapped around tanned shoulders, stickered water
bottles, a new cohort of freshmen that comes in two versions: invincible and terrified. I started out the former, but my slide to the latter
was *swift*.

Pen sets her elbows on the small wooden table, satisfied with
our level of privacy. "You're into what Luk's into."

"Well, I can't be sure about that."

"But you said . . . ?"

"There are many, *many* facets to kink and BDSM."

"Right."

"I've never talked with Lukas before this morning. I have no idea what he likes."

"Should I tell you? He—"

"I—no, that's not . . ." I clear my throat. Starting to have some regrets here. "That's beyond the, um, scope of this conversation."

"Ah."

"You shouldn't feel like you have to explain what you guys . . . but I was there"—*unwillingly*—"when you and Victoria were discussing the matter, and she seemed to be lending a slightly less than, um, sympathetic ear—"

"Hall of Fame–worthy understatement. Please, continue."

"I just wanted to offer myself as a resource, as someone who has experience in . . . this."

"And 'this' would be . . . ?"

"An established relationship in which only one party is interested in kink. Figuring out something you can both enjoy and can affirmatively consent to. If that's what you want, of course," I add with a small smile.

She leans back in her chair to study me, and I know what she's seeing: damp dark hair, guarded dark eyes, unexpectedly dark sexual history. I've never navel-gazed too much about what turns me on—she could slap me on a microscope slide and label me *Sexual Deviant*, and I wouldn't bat an eye. Still, it's nice to see more curiosity than judgment in the tilt of her head.

"Luk wants to be in charge. Is that what you want, too, or . . . ?"

I shake my head. "The opposite, actually."

"Ah." She curls a finger in an auburn strand of hair. Pen's coloring was the first thing I noticed about her, back in the varsity circuit. How strikingly beautiful she was—generous, too. In competition, between dives, athletes usually avoid looking at each other. Not Pen, though. Always a kind smile. Never arrogant, even though she was always ahead in our age group, by leaps and bounds. The flag bearer at the Junior Olympics. She'd dive with pink, then blue hair. Friendship bracelets made by her fans. Nail art. I found her impossibly cool. I'll never *not* be intimidated by her, at least a little bit.

"How did you discover it?"

"How did I discover . . . ?"

"That you were into it."

A guy who looks remarkably like Dr. Rodriguez's fascist TA, the one who docked one point off my orgo final for writing the wrong date, walks by. Bet he'd love an earful. "I always knew, to some degree. I mean, I wasn't browsing eBay for deals on PVC masks in middle school, but once I became, um, aware of and interested in sex, I always had . . . fantasies. Ideas." I shrug, and don't add, *It felt right. It* feels *right.*

"I see." Pen nods, thoughtful. "And how did you end up actually, you know, *doing* it?"

"My high school boyfriend and I dated for about three years." I skip the part where we were neighbors, then seventh-grade best friends, then fell in love. I trusted him, and it was an easy conversation, as easy as everything else with Josh. Everything except for that phone call during freshman year. His subdued tone as he explained, *It's not just because of her . . . honestly, the distance is a lot. And maybe our personalities are too different for this to last?* That one, it had been difficult. "I told him what I was interested in."

"And he . . . was he interested, too?"

I workshop the perfect phrasing. "Not in the same things. That's why I thought my experience might be relevant to you and Lukas." Because Lukas Blomqvist is kinky. Lukas "Olympic gold medalist, swim-world darling, record-holding Scandinavian treasure" Blomqvist. What *is* life?

"And how did you approach the situation?"

"I told him what I thought might be hot. Josh did the same. We cross-referenced." The resulting Venn diagram didn't include much, but still.

"This is so *Fifty Shades*, Vandy."

"Right?" Our eyes meet, and we share a smile at the improbability of all of this. But she seems much more at ease.

"Would you be able to explain what you like about letting someone else take charge?"

Would I? "It's lots of things garbled together." The ease of pre-negotiating a social interaction. Having, for once, specific instructions. The stable quiet in the never-ending chaos of my brain. The satisfaction of doing something right, of being told as much. Disconnecting from the rest of the world and going with the flow. And yeah: I'm not sure *why* I'm wired like that, but pain and pleasure have always mixed up in my head, and it feels good when someone I trust pinches my nipples. It's *that* simple, sometimes. "To me, it's about freedom."

She snorts. "The freedom of . . . having someone telling you what to do?"

"I know it sounds counterintuitive, but I'm usually overthinking something. Desperately trying to avoid screwing up and working myself up to a panic." *Am I taking up too much space? Boring you? Disappointing you? Would you rather be somewhere else, with someone else?* "Overwhelmed by the burden of wondering whether I'm doing it right."

"Doing what right?"

I laugh. "I'm not even sure. Sex, but also, more in general, being a human?" I shrug, because that's the problem, isn't it? There is no right or wrong way to exist. Real life doesn't come with an instruction manual. Fortunately, sex can. My kind of sex. "If someone I feel safe with is directing me . . ."

"You like the structure."

"That's a good way of putting it." I smile. "I can't speak for Lukas, or people on the more . . . *dominant* end of it." The word oscillates bizarrely between us. Truth is, I don't feel totally comfortable dol-ing out BDSM terms, either. Like any other community, I cradle an assortment of doubts on whether I have what it takes to truly be-long. Labels have to be earned, and my pockets always seem too empty to pay up. "But clearly they get something out of it."

"Clearly. Are you and your boyfriend still together?" Her gaze sharpens. "I feel like I know so little about you."

*What a coincidence. I, too, know very little about me.* "We broke up."

"And the guy you're seeing now . . . ?"

"I'm not. Seeing anyone, that is."

"But that's not because of what you're into?"

"Not really." At least, not entirely. What I like to tell myself and whoever asks—Barb, mostly—is that I'm too busy and career driven to date. But my celibate phase has been going on so long, I'm not sure it's voluntary anymore, and I'd rather not mention that after what happened with my dad, men can be unsettling to be around.

"I suspect I shouldn't ask it like this, but I truly have no clue how to phrase it, so I'll just . . . Did your ex hurt you? During sex, I mean."

I nod. "Sometimes. A little."

"And you were okay with it?"

"Absolutely. Everything was pre-agreed. We constantly checked in with each other and had a safe word."

"Oh my god, so *Fifty Shades*. Did it ever make you feel . . . ?"

"Feel what?"

"Like you're flushing seventy years of feminism down the toilet?" Her face scrunches in a guilty grimace, but it's nothing I haven't asked myself.

"For me, choosing to be sexually submissive has little to do with gender equality. And I'm not giving up my rights. Josh always stopped when I asked him to—and the other way around." I shrug again. "I understand how vulnerable it can be, discussing this stuff. For you. For Lukas, even. Plus, kinky people sometimes get this bad rap, like we're intrinsically aggressive or predatory—"

"I know you aren't," she hurries out, palms wide open. "I'm not a prude, I swear. I don't think Luk is twisted or disturbed for wanting this."

My relief is genuine. "Good."

"It's more that *I* am not into it."

"That is absolutely your prerogative." I scratch the back of my neck, where I forgot to put on lotion before diving. Hello, chlorine rash, my old friend. "And if you told Lukas that you're not interested in exploring those sexual dynamics and he's insisting on it, that's a *huge* red flag that—"

"That's the thing, he's *not*. We tried. Because it was . . . well, it was obvious that he wanted it. So I offered." She wraps her hand around her untouched iced latte, but doesn't take a sip. "I just hate it. Being told what to do. Asking for permission. I already have Coach Sima's incessant commentary about my diving techniques buzzing in my ear—I don't want to hear 'You're doing this or that so well, Pen' while we're fucking." She rolls her eyes. "Such paternalistic *bullshit*. No offense."

This is, perhaps, the *least* relatable thing anyone has ever said to me. "None taken. Did you tell him you didn't enjoy it?"

"Yup. And he immediately stopped. Never brought it up again. He still wants it, though. I know he does."

This conversation is taking a turn that's less Kink 101, more *GQ* sex advice column. I might be out of my depth. "So he made the conscious decision to put his relationship with you *and* your well-being before his sexual preferences, which is commendable—"

"It's *stupid*." The word is a sibilant, frustrated hiss. She leans closer, her eyes once again that liquid green. "I love him. I really do. But . . ." A bob in her throat. Her posture straightens. "I want other things, too. I want to go to a party and flirt freely. I want to be hit on without feeling like I'm betraying someone. I want to have fun." A deep breath. "I want to sleep with other people. See what that's like."

It all sounds as fun as shaving my armpits with a can opener. But Pen is not me. Pen is outgoing and funny. Pen has work-life balance. Pen knows what to do, and when to do it. Everyone likes Pen. "How does Lukas feel about this? Is he angry? Or jealous?"

She rolls her eyes. "Luk's too self-assured to feel anything as lowly as that."

Wouldn't know what *that's* like. "What about you? Would *you* be jealous if he were to sleep with other people?"

"Not really. Lukas and I have history. We love each other. Honestly, even if we break up, I suspect that we'll find each other in the future. We're kind of meant to be."

Where do these people get their bottomless reservoirs of confidence? From a pot at the end of a rainbow? "Meant to be . . . except for the 'meh' sex?"

"It's not—the sex is good." For the first time in this very flush-worthy conversation, Pen flushes. "Luk is—he's very single-minded. It's more that—" Her phone buzzes, shaking the entire table. Pen glances at it once, mid-sentence, distracted. Then again, lingering. "Fuck."

"Everything okay?"

"My International Trade study group. I forgot we're meeting." She leaps out of her chair and quickly gathers her stuff. Inhales her iced latte in record-eclipsing time and tosses the cup in the recycling bin. "I'm sorry. This is so rude, unloading on you for twenty minutes and—"

"No problem at all. Do your thing."

"Okay. Shit, I have to run all the way to Jackie's place."

Her voice fades as she dashes out of the café, and I'm left alone, contemplating the sheer *weirdness* of the afternoon, the sheer *idiocy* of putting myself in this situation, the sheer *impenetrability* of the relationship between Penelope Ross and Lukas Blomqvist.

Then Pen runs back inside and stops by my chair. "Hey, Vandy?"

I glance up. "Did you forget something?"

"I just wanted to say . . ." Her grin broadens. It helps me realize how strained her earlier smiles have been. "Thank you for taking the time to talk to me. For being cool and not judgy. I'm glad you're all healed and back on the team."

I barely manage a nod, and then she's sprinting out, leaving me to wonder if anyone else ever uttered the word *cool* in relation to me.

# CHAPTER 5

**B**Y THE FOLLOWING WEEK, I'M STARTING TO SEE THE LAY OF the academic land.

English composition is not impossible (my professor doesn't care whether my opinions are valid, only that I argue for them with my whole chest). Psychology, not as wishy-washy as I originally thought (there is a method to the madness of human behavior). Computational biology is a piece of cake (even if Dr. Carlsen's perennial glower *is* a little unsettling). And then there's German. A tentacled, homicidal swamp, infested with sharks and tarantulas and sentient currywurst ready to mangle me.

"Aren't there tutoring programs for people who are . . . less than gifted when it comes to languages?" Barb asks during our weekly call, after I air out my anti-Germanic propaganda speech for thirty minutes of despair.

"Nothing works with my schedule. I should have booked some help sooner." Like back in the womb. "But I think I'll be fine." I got a two out of ten for the first assignment, and a three for the second. Yay for upward trends.

"I'm sure you will, Scar." After she left Dad, after the battle royal that won her custody of me, after our lives became *ours*, Barb moved us to St. Louis, where she rules the division of orthopedic surgery like an autocratic nation-state. Her job is incomprehensibly high-stakes, pays her a semi-sickening amount of money, and keeps her so shockingly busy, one of my middle school teachers suspected I was a runaway secretly living on my own.

She is, without question, the reason I want to be a physician. A bit of a cliché, I know, but it didn't come completely out of left field. I've always gravitated toward science, but it wasn't until I started doing my homework in Barb's office that I realized how admirable her work is. How she makes a difference. The breadth of her knowledge and the depth of her care.

"Why can't Dr. Madden or Dr. Davis take care of your patient?" I once whined when she said she wouldn't be able to come to my meet.

"Because"—she lowered her voice to a whisper—"Dr. Madden is an assho—an *anus*, and Dr. Davis is so spectacularly incompetent, I'm never sure whether he's rooting for the patient or the disease. Mrs. Reyes has been in pain for a long time. She deserves to be treated by someone who's not mediocre and will take her seriously. Would you agree?"

I was fourteen at the time, but it made perfect sense. Not only was I proud of how incredibly badass Barb was, but I wanted nothing more than to be a non-mediocre physician who'd take people seriously.

And now, here I am. Daydreaming of liver failure to escape the MCAT.

"By the way," Barb tells me, "I met Coach Kumar the other day."

I flinch. He's my high school coach. "How is he?"

"Good. He sends his love. Asked me about you."

"And you lied and told him that I'm a twelve-time NCAA champion and Olympic hopeful?"

"I considered that, but then I remembered that there are public records of this stuff. Like, online. A Google search away."

I sigh. "Is he mortified? Am I bestowing dishonor upon my old club?"

"What? No. You're not a white-collar defense attorney on the Sacklers' payroll, Scarlett. You had a bad injury. Everyone's rooting for you."

*I cannot wait to disappoint them once again.* "How's the love of my life?"

"Currently occupied with her prescheduled junk licking."

"Important business."

"Hang on, I think she wants to talk to you."

Pipsqueak, the husky-pug mix who was once up on Facebook Marketplace because of "a bad temperament" (falsehoods, slander) and "an unbreakable scooting habit" (yet to be broken), howls her love for me and tries to lick my face over Barb's phone. I baby-talk at her for fifteen minutes, then leave for practice.

It's preseason, which means conditioning. Skill refinement. Takeoffs, entries, body positions, rotations, corrections—hours in the gym, the diving well, the weight room, and then more hours at home, in class, in bed, the nagging worry that all this training won't be *enough* poking at the back of my skull.

I'm a good athlete. I've TiVoed my dives enough times to know that. My body is strong and healthy at last. My mind . . .

My mind hates me, sometimes. Especially when I'm on a platform, ten meters above the rest of my life.

Because ten meters is *high*, but people don't realize how high until it takes them over fifty steps to climb a tower. They reach the top, look down, and suddenly get that queasy feeling in their stomach. It's a three-story building. A whole McMansion, stretching between you and the water. Lots of things can happen in ten meters—including a body accelerating to thirty miles per hour, and the water becoming as difficult to crack as the universe's hardest eggshell.

On the platform, punishments are swift and merciless. Room for error, nonexistent. A bad dive is not just ungainly and humiliating—a bad dive is the end of an athlete's career. A bad dive is the last dive.

"The pool closes at eight, but take your time, Vandy," Coach Sima yells up at me.

I smile, palms flush against the coarse edge, and slowly lift my legs in a headstand. My shoulders, core, thighs, they all ache in that good, clenched way that means *control*. I linger there, a perfect straight line, just to prove to myself that I'm capable of it. I have what it takes. It's a relief, seeing the world resized. Liberating how insignificant everyone else looks from here, small and irrelevant.

"No hurry at all! I'm not bored out of my mind here!"

I huff and let the rest of the dive flow out of me: pike. Half twist. A somersault. Another. I enter the water with just a handful of bubbles. When I resurface, Coach is crouching poolside. "Vandy."

I lift myself on the edge, clutching my shoulder. Doesn't hurt. Doesn't bleed. Still intact. "Yeah?"

"That is NCAA material there."

I squeeze water out of my braid.

"Problem is—that's not the dive I asked you to do."

I look around. Where did I throw my shammy?

"Vandy. Look at me."

I do. I have to.

"You can keep doing your emotional support dives, yes. But we have other issues we need to be focusing on." He taps the spot between my eyes with his knuckles, like he's inspecting coconuts at the grocery store. "You have to work on what's in here."

"I know."

"Then do as I say, and don't change the damn dive when you're up there." He sighs and shakes his head. "It's okay, kid. We got time. Go get changed. Y'all are coming over tonight." The cookout. Yearly team-building tradition. He winks at me, crow's feet multiplying by a factor of ten. "Ain't no party like a Coach Sima party."

Tragically true. Because a Coach Sima party is compulsory.

I head for the locker room, sparing one last glance at the forward tuck the twins are practicing together on the springboard. I used to do synchronized diving, too, back in St. Louis, but there's only five of us in the Stanford team, which makes me the odd girl out. Bella and Bree compete together (two athletes who simultaneously perform the exact same dive *and* look identical? Judges eat that shit up). Pen and Victoria have been partners for three years, and have a good thing going on. Maybe next year a new recruit will pair up with me. Or maybe I'll die alone in a vale of tears, clutching German present perfect flash cards. Who can say?

I catch a ride to the Simas' with Victoria, who spends it updating me on a recently confirmed human case of the bubonic plague. We're the last to get there, and the only two losers to show up without a plus-one. "Love this taste of what my Thanksgivings are gonna be like for the next fifty years," she grumbles, pasting a smile on her face and reaching out to hug Mrs. Sima.

I chat with Leo, Coach's thirteen-year-old son, who's about as awkward as I am, until he pretends to remember outstanding homework and ducks back into the house. Then I go in search of something to drink—and run into a wall.

And by wall I mean, Lukas Blomqvist.

When it comes to DI college swimmers, he's not too much of a standout. Most of them are tall. Most of them are muscular. Lots of them are handsome. His proportions—broad shoulders, long arms and torso, huge hands and feet—are basically an instructional drawing. That is to say: it's not because of his *looks* that my thoughts swerve to a halt.

"Sorry." I am physically unable to produce a smile. Temporary cranial nerve VII paresis. It's okay, though, because he doesn't smile, either.

His eyes pin me in place. "No problem."

He has a nice voice, deep and resonant. Familiar, but only vaguely, like an ad in the middle of a podcast: heard it before, but tuned it out. Must be a by-product of his orbiting the periphery of my life for the past two years, since the pool where the swimmers train is across from the diving well.

"Where did you get that?" I point at a sports drink that looks oddly kid-sized in his hand. He gestures with his chin to a cooler that I could have easily located on my own. If only I wasn't an idiot. "Right. Thanks."

Lukas nods, only once. I wonder if he came with Pen, if they ended up solving their issues, but she's nowhere in sight. He and I are, kind of hilariously, both wearing jeans and the same gray Stanford Swimming and Diving tees—except, he's *barefoot. Why* is he barefoot in my coach's backyard? Also, why is he staring at me? Why am I staring back?

I can't tear my gaze away, and I think it's because of his eyes. They're studious. Focused. Dialed in. Preternaturally blue. Somewhere in the Baltic Sea, a cod splashes through a patch of water that precise color, and—

Did Pen tell him about *me*? Did Pen tell him that she told *me* about *him*? Is that why Lukas looks so . . . I don't know. Curious? Absorbed? *Something.*

"What were you saying about the Swedish Open, dear?" Mrs. Sima asks. Lukas turns back to her, and I realize that I crashed right in the middle of their conversation. Or, most likely, her interrogation of Lukas. I've been on the receiving end of a few of those through the years, and they're no picnic. "When is that happening?"

"Next year. The week after the NCAAs."

"Oh my goodness. And you'll need to attend to qualify for the Melbourne Olympics, right?"

"Not after the world championship." He has an accent, in that faint, northern European way. I'm not even sure what letters it coats, but I occasionally pick up on it.

"Right, earlier this year. And you won that, so you're officially going to Australia next year?"

He nods, indifferent, like being an Olympian is not a big deal. His face is . . . that jaw has me thinking of diving cliffs, and the cleft in his chin—textbook movie-star shit. He could be Captain America.

Captain Sweden. Whatever.

"That is fantastic, dear. Now, here's hoping that Penelope qualifies, too. She *was* bronze at the Pan Am games last summer, but with so many mistakes." Typical Mrs. Sima jab. She loves to imply that the diving team is an untalented bunch, chronically unworthy of her husband's coaching skills. I'd challenge her on this, but when it comes to me, I'm not sure she's wrong.

Lukas, thankfully, has no such qualms. "She was still recovering from injury."

"Oh, yes. Yes, of course." A nervous laugh. "Well, still. *You* won all your races, didn't you?"

His reply is a noncommittal grunt.

"I bet your mother's *so* proud of you."

No reply at all, but the ink on Lukas's skin shifts, like he's flexing his muscles. Maybe his relationship with his mom is as lovely and uncontentious as mine with Dad?

"Will she be in Melbourne, too?"

Lukas's face could be a megalith on Easter Island.

"I bet she cannot wait to cheer you on."

Sudden twitch in his jaw, like he's a single question away from a rampage. *Come on, Mrs. Sima. Read the Swede.*

"If it was one of my children, I would take my whole extended family—"

"By the way, Lukas," I interrupt, "Pen was looking for you a minute ago."

His eyes fix mine. "Was she." He's not really asking. He knows it's a lie.

"Yup." *Fly, little bird. Be free.*

"Excuse me," he says in the general direction of Mrs. Sima. I help myself to some coconut milk, but when I glance to make sure he escaped safely, his attention is once again on me, and—

Maybe Pen did tell him about me, and that's why he's so interested. Does he want to chat with me? Vent? Find someone who'll sympathize? Does he want a heart-to-heart, kinkster to kinkster?

Maybe I should become a couples counselor. Nice alternative to med school. They might waive the foreign language requirement.

"First batch is ready," Coach yells from the grilling area. "Everyone, help yourself!"

I eat my chicken burger slowly, quietly, while conversations flow. Pen sits in front of me, the center of attention, dispensing funny stories and warm feelings. Lukas is next to her, arms crossed on his chest, saying little, smiling rarely. He seems like a quiet, reserved guy. Together they are viciously, comprehension-defyingly good-looking. I don't consider myself ugly by any means, but I had my years of braces and constant breakouts, which are not too far off. These two were clearly never less than radiant. Hard to stomach, really.

For the first time, everyone on the team is over twenty-one. Coach hands out his home brew, muttering something about how this better be our last sip of alcohol for the season. I picture him stirring and fermenting in the same bathtub where Leo discovered masturbation, and give it a pass. Lukas and Victoria, who both drove here, stop after the first bottle. The twins have two each, and comment on how much stronger than regular beer they are. Pen . . . I don't know. Maybe she doesn't, either. Her laugh is a little loud, but she's still her charming self.

After dinner I move to the patio with Bree, Bella, Devin, and Dale, where I struggle not to show how mind-boggled I am that two monozygotic twins are dating *another* set of monozygotic twins.

Was this preplanned? How did they meet? Did one couple find true love, then force the other into a relationship? Is kinky stuff involved? And, why am I so goddamn curious about other people's private lives? Bold of someone who enjoys being tied up like a mesh bag full of limes. It's a big relief when Pen wobbles over to "steal Vandy for a sec" and whispers at me, "Kinda weird, right? Twins dating twins?"

"I was thinking the exact same, and felt so bad about it."

"I know, me too."

"It's inappropriate that this even occurred to me, but if each couple has a kid—"

"They'd be fraternal brothers!"

"Oh my god, yes!"

We high-five like we cracked the human genome and end up in the back of the house, toward a set of swings Coach must have installed when his kids were little.

"Is everything okay?" I ask when we sit. I rock a little, testing the sturdiness of this setup.

"Yup." She giggles. Her eyes are glassy. "Except that Coach's toilet beer is hitting me hard. I just needed a bit of quiet. You looked like you might, too."

*When do I not?* "Want me to find Lukas and ask him to take you home?"

"God, that's a great idea." I make to stand, but she stops me. Taps at her phone. "I'll just text him. He only came because I'd already told Coach that he would, anyway."

"Oh. Did you two end up . . ."

"Breaking up? Yup. I'm free as a bird." Her words slur, just a bit. She doesn't look particularly happy.

"Do you want to, um, talk about it?" I'm not sure I'm equipped for it, but the idea of Pen wanting to confide in me is a warm, pleasant weight in my chest. Between my injury and my inability to stop working until I achieve perfection (i.e., never), I haven't made many friends in college. Or before.

"Do I?" A shaky, forced laugh. Then her gaze fixes somewhere beyond me and she repeats, louder, "Do I?"

I turn around. Lukas is walking toward us, and my first thought is he didn't need to come here. I was going to deliver Pen to him. In front of his car.

But his barefoot stride never falters. The sun is a fuzzy halo around his short hair when he asks, "Should I drive you home?"

Pen regards him lovingly for a long, sluggish while—so long, I start wondering whether she's much drunker than I originally believed. "Vandy, you've never formally met my *ex-boyfriend*, have you?"

And there is my *second* thought: this is clearly a messy breakup, a sore one that's still being negotiated. And I want no part in it.

"She did." Lukas's impassible gaze flits to mine. "During her recruitment trip."

No memory of it, but I nod anyway, glad I didn't stand to shake his hand.

"Oh, that's cool." She shrugs. "Yeah, Luk, you can take me ho—"

Pen stops suddenly, with a gasp that turns into a smile so manic, unease slithers down my nape. "Oh my god, you guys. I just had the best idea in the fucking universe!" She glances at Lukas, at me, at Lukas again. She's going to bring up something ridiculous that only sounds good to a drunk person. *Let's go to Taco Bell. Let's prank call our middle school teachers. Let's shave our eyebrows.* I'm desperately looking for a gentle way to talk her out of karaoke—and then stop.

Because what Pen actually says is, "You two should have sex!"

# CHAPTER 6

GRIP THE SWING'S CHAIN HARD ENOUGH TO PERMANENTLY print it on my palm.

I gawk at Pen, slack-jawed. Then turn to Lukas, who seems as taken aback as me.

But he recovers quickly. His arms cross on his chest, and the corner of his lip curls upward. "Pen," he chides calmly, like his ex is an unruly toddler. A kitten caught breaking into the treat drawer. "I'm taking you home."

She ignores him. "No, no—it's *genius*!"

"Is it."

"Yes. Yes! How do you not see it? Oh my god. *Of course* you don't. It's because you don't *know*." She laughs and gestures inchoately. Her cheeks glow bright pink on her post-practice, scrubbed-clean face. Maybe Coach puts MDMA in his beer? "Luk, please don't be mad, but . . . I had to tell Vandy about the stuff you're into. Because it was all a mess, and I needed to talk about it with someone. I'm *sorry*, okay?" she cries, even though Lukas doesn't seem particularly upset at the thought of me knowing his private business. Until: "But here's the thing . . . Vandy's into the same exact stuff as you!"

And that's when I realize that, no.

Pen had *not* told Lukas about me. Because he turns to me and stares *infinitely*, lips parted, like I've suddenly shape-shifted into something new. Something instantly comprehensible to him.

I stare back, unable to breathe.

Even as Pen continues, "So you two *should*—well, no one *should* have sex. But since we're all single here, I thought that . . ."

Lukas tears his eyes from mine. "Pen," he says, firm, exuding a tolerant, condescending sort of patience. "Let's go."

Her eyebrows knit. "What? I think it's a great idea!"

"Of course." Lukas sounds so unperturbed, it actively adds to my distress. Why is *he* not experiencing mortification? Am I exhausting the North American supply? "I'm taking you home."

"No! Luk, she is it. She's the *sandwich*."

He sighs. I don't follow—then I do.

Sandwich. *Sub.*

Christ. I should *not* be witnessing the inside sex jokes of the golden couple of college swimming.

"It makes sense," she insists, unsteady on her swing. "Think it through!"

"Okay. Let's." He nods like he's actually contemplating the whole thing. "You and I break up, and a week later you come to me with recommendations on *who* I should be fucking next." His eyes settle on me. Cold. Evaluating. "And you do the same for Scarlett. Out of the kindness of your heart."

"I just thought it would be nice if we could all—"

"Be happily paired with our government-mandated fuck buddy?"

"Luk," Pen bristles. "As the current holder of half a dozen world records, you're a recognizable public figure who can't just make a profile on a dating app and write a bucket list of kinky stuff."

"But you fixed the issue by getting wasted and offering me your teammate. Who, by the way, hasn't breathed in over a minute."

He's right. I suck in some air.

"Come on, Luk. I know you think she's hot. You said so."

Silence.

"And I see the way you look at her."

A buzz of unease bursts in the back of my skull.

"How do I look at her?"

"You *know* how."

He folds his arms on his chest. "Anything else I should know about future directions of my sex life? Where are Scarlett and I going to meet? What will we do first?"

Pen bolts to her feet. Sways her way to Lukas to press an index finger to his pecs.

"Luk, if you can't understand my *vision* . . ." She bursts into laughter. "Whatever. Let's go home." She brushes past, but after about fifty feet she plops on Coach's yard and lies on her back to sunbathe. "You guys, I love this time of the day!"

Lukas shakes his head and sighs deeply, long feet peeking through the grass. And there, in the rise and fall of his shoulders, I finally see it. The strain that comes with a splintering relationship. I picture the late-night conversations, the incessant texting, the fights that led to their breakup.

"She shouldn't have told me about your . . . not without your permission," I say. "You might want to ask her to stop doing it." A bit presumptive, to assume that this classically handsome athlete with citizenship in a universal-healthcare country might need my advice. But I remember the way Dad used to be with Barb and me. How he'd gnaw at us and strip away even the thinnest of layers, until what we wanted was of no importance and the world revolved around him. It's not something I'll ever take for granted, the ability to say no.

"I don't mind," he says, almost reassuringly. The *don't worry* is implied. He has a steady, calming, problem-shouldering presence that tells me everything I need to know about how good he'd be at . . . well. All that stuff that got us in this mortifying situation to begin with.

"I had no idea she'd say any of this," I blurt out.

"I figured. You looked about to faint."

"It was a close call."

We exchange a tired, soft-edged smile. Just our eyes, really. "I doubt Pen knew she'd say it, either. Or that she'll remember tomorrow."

"Still . . . I'm sorry. I told Pen about my experience, thinking it would help, but I didn't mean to be up in your business or—"

"Luuuk, can we go home now?" she interrupts.

He bites the inside of his lip. Gives me one last look. "Goodbye, Scarlett."

I wave and watch him leave, his steps relaxed, his brown hair almost golden in the setting sun. Once he and Pen disappear behind the house, I tip my head back to look up at the sky. Push that *Where are Scarlett and I going to meet?*—the near-perfect pronunciation, the closed *o*'s, the telltale *s*'s—out of my mind. Let my heart slow to a normal speed, and tell myself that decades from now, when I'm frail and prune-hearted in the retirement home, and the AI nurse feeding me steamed brussels sprouts asks, *What is the most bonkers thing that ever happened to you?* my mind will instantly zero in on this conversation.

I don't even know how wrong I am.

# CHAPTER 7

"I'M SORRY, WHAT WAS THAT?"

For every session, there are a lot of silences between Sam and me. Because she asks hard questions that I cannot answer, and doesn't move on until she has received some kind of reply.

I guess it's how therapy works.

"I said, has this ever happened to you before?"

"And by 'this,' you mean . . . ?"

"This block of yours."

"Right." I shake my head. "No. No, it hasn't."

"Not even at a smaller scale?"

"Not really."

She glances down at her notebook. "I did some research. It appears that lost move syndrome is a typical phenomenon in athletes. A sudden inability to perform a skill you had previously mastered." She recites the last bit, like it's a definition she's quoting. Her eyes find mine through horn-rimmed glasses. "Does this description match what you are experiencing?"

I take as long as I can before nodding. Maybe the more I delay this, the less true it will become.

"Twisties," I say eventually. "Or yips. That's what we divers call them."

# CHAPTER 8

PENELOPE: Funny story.

PENELOPE: I woke up this morning with a huge headache. Couldn't figure out why. Then I remembered what happened last night and started praying for my bones to turn into lava.

PENELOPE: I have no words for how dumb I was. I think I only had two drinks—I have no clue how I got that drunk. And it's not an excuse. I'm so sorry, Vandy.

As she should be.

SCARLETT: I think Coach's home brew might be stronger than regular beer. The twins were pretty wasted, too, and I ended up driving Victoria's car back home.

PENELOPE: Bet the NCAA would LOVE to hear that.

SCARLETT: Moving forward, though, please don't blurt out facts about my sex life.

PENELOPE: God, I promise I won't! I swear I'm not usually that shitty. And honestly, I'm your captain. What I did was totally sexual harassment, and you have every right to report me.

SCARLETT: It's okay. You're forgiven, this once. Plus, this whole thing will give us both an edge in future Never have I ever games.

PENELOPE: LMAO two truths and a lie, too.

PENELOPE: "I pee in the pool." "I hate tomatoes." "I once got so wasted that I tried to get my ex and my teammate to fuck each other."

SCARLETT: Very worried atm since I've seen you eat tomatoes with my own two eyes.

PENELOPE: They pump so much chlorine in there!

SCARLETT: I'm officially making myself unknow this about you. Never mention it again.

SCARLETT: Is Lukas mad?

PENELOPE: I called him this morning to grovel, but he just shrugged it off. It's impossible to make Lukas mad. He's literally the most unfazed human in the universe.

A few days ago I'd have guessed the opposite—that he'd be the silent treatment type, surly and prone to anger. But that was just a hunch, based on my general assumption that men can be scary and unpredictable.

Not all men, I'm sure. Maybe not even most men. But with my past, I cannot help distrusting them until they give me reason not to. Lukas Blomqvist, though, seems fairly unobjectionable.

I have no real insight into his personality, but following Coach's cookout he becomes something of an intrusive thought for me, and I find myself taking time out of pondering the German sentence structure, to . . . gather information about him. Mostly, through my own recollections.

Try as I might, I can't remember meeting him during my recruitment trip. There are snippets of him here and there, though, like confetti stuck to my hair after a New Year's Eve ball drop. I didn't mean to take them home, but still get to examine them, and I'm glad for that.

Freshman year, Halloween, when some kids broke into the diving well to egg and toilet paper the pool. Lukas, who was already captain, volunteered the men's team to clean it up. When they started bitching, a twitch of his eyebrow was all they needed to fall quiet.

Or that time some guy mistook the pool cover for pavement and fell inside, backpack and clothes and all. An image resurfaces: Lukas's inked arm, fishing him out. The same arm that last year separated those two seniors who got in a fight, shoved them apart, pinned them to the wall for stern talking-tos.

And then, the bits Pen threw out in passing. Something about how he'd been offered sponsorship deals, but declined to "peddle shampoo and high-fructose corn syrup." Anniversary posts on her Instagram, photos of the two of them through the years, Lukas's serious bulk, Pen's wide smile. The careless way she mentioned never having been to Sweden to visit him—*Too busy, you know?*

That's the extent of my memories, but it doesn't matter. Because now that Pen has tried to squish us into this odd triangle, now that I'm aware of him, I notice him *everywhere*. Padding over the deck. With the PTs in the recovery room. Lifting truly ludicrous weights. At those annoying Saturday meetings that happen behind the diving tower—though he's quiet there. The swimmers take turns celebrating each other and announcing their weekly achievements, but Lukas Blomqvist, five-time Olympic gold medalist (two are relays, which makes him slightly less humbling), never has anything to share.

Maybe he's in a rut. Maybe he hates public speaking. Maybe it's a Swedish thing.

I've never cared much about mapping the aquatics social network, but he seems to get along with his teammates. "Sweedy," they call him—not *sweetie*, as I originally thought. The realization hits me while doing pull-ups, and I dangle in the strength room for a few seconds, exhaling breathless chuckles until Bree asks if I'm having a mental breakdown.

I catch him pushing the other Swedish guy on the team into the pool, and snort when the only thing that pops out of the water is a middle finger.

I see him walk around campus with two other seniors who are also Olympians—Hasan, a nice English guy who asked me out freshman year, and Kyle, one of the hopes and dreams of US swimming, who looks like twenty stereotypical frat bros chucked in a blender and spread over a slice of Wonder Bread.

I watch Lukas swim. At first, out of curiosity. Later, because I cannot stop, in utter disbelief that he and I are made of the same stuff—carbon, hydrogen, oxygen—and yet his body can do *that*.

He's probably a good guy—or person, leader, swimmer, whatever's the NCAA buzzwordy pick of the day. Sometimes we'll pass each other and exchange a nod. A sardonic smile. A shared moment of *remember when your ex wanted us to fuck?* understanding. For the most part, though, he seems too focused on training to pay attention to me.

And so am I. Twenty hours of practice a week plus classes, homework, MCAT prep, and this thing I've been told people should really do if their plans include staying alive for longer than a couple of months. "Sleeping," Coach calls it. I hear great things. Would love to try it someday.

"We didn't even choose good sports," Maryam reminds me during dinner. We're staring lifelessly into our plates of spaghetti, fully aware that we have at least three hours of schoolwork ahead of us. "Wrestling? *Diving?* Poorly funded *and* spectated. No chance at fame and glory. My fucking *eyeballs* hurt, and what for?"

"At least you have the WWE option."

"Maybe. I'd need a pro wrestler name, though."

"What about the Rock?"

"Isn't it taken?"

"Nope. All yours."

But the grind pays off. The plyometrics. The strenuous arm, ab, leg workouts. The visualization exercises. I'm in good shape, especially considering how little I dove last year. I'm really—

"Are you jerking me around, Vandy?" Coach Sima asks me on Friday night, a week after his cookout. He appears out of the blue while I'm toweling off, giving me a cardiac event. "What was that last dive?"

"My back two and a half—"

"And what did I ask you to do?"

I take a step back. I'm not scared of Coach Sima—he's gruff, rough-edged, but kind. I am, however, terrified of what he's about to say. "I'm sorry." I glance away for a beat. When I look back, his eyes have softened.

"How's it going with that psychologist?"

"We've . . ." I fist my towel. "We're getting there. I promise."

He scans my face, on the hunt for lies. "Okay. Okay." He nods, not fully convinced. "Make sure you keep on keepin' on, okay? Anything I can do, alright?"

I slacken in relief when he turns to Pen and Victoria's synchro dives. Their hurdles are different heights. Their twists are poorly timed. And they're both doing whatever the opposite of *nailing* is to that pike.

"Just to be clear, you two *are* attempting the same dive, right?" Coach yells.

I spare myself the roast comedy, change into dry clothes, grab a protein bar from the snack shed, and go stretch.

My PT gave me a list of exercises that should keep my injured shoulder from crapping on me again. Three times a week, over one hour. When she told me that skipping them would equal certain reinjury, I wished for a swift death, but they've grown on me. They are gentle, slow, an excuse to be kind to my body. To *not* push it past its physical boundaries and instead follow its lead. It's after sunset by the time I'm done. Avery is deserted, and when I swipe my ID, the locker room door won't open, no matter how many times I try.

And it's *many* times.

My house keys, my laptop, my wallet, are all in there. Maryam's out of town for a wrestling meet. I feel bad about calling Pen, but team captains have physical, old-fashioned keys.

"Hey," I say when she picks up. There's noise in the background. Hopefully she's still on campus.

"Hey! Everything okay?"

"Kind of." I think I can hear music. "The locker room door is doing that thing again, and I can't find any staff."

"Oh, shit. Hang on—I'll . . . give me a second."

What comes next is muffled, like her phone mic is pressed against the fabric of her shirt. I pick up a brief exchange between Pen and a deep, male voice, but only make out two words: *someone* and *else.*

"Vandy? Hey, could you . . . could you call Luk? Or any of the other captains? We all have keys."

*But isn't Lukas with you?* I almost ask. Before I can, everything clicks into place.

"Oh." I pause for too long. "Sure, I will," I say, with no intention of doing so. First of all, I don't have his number. Secondly—fuck *that.* My nonconsensual involvement in this relationship is maxed out. I'm not calling Lukas because Pen is—

"Actually, I'll text him your number and tell him myself, okay?"

Shit. "I don't want to bother him."

"He's the captain. Part of the job description. Just sit tight, he'll be there ASAP."

Thirty seconds later, I'm considering drowning myself in the pool, when my phone pings with a text from an unsaved number.

# CHAPTER 9

**U**NKNOWN: On my way

I stare into the abyss of those three words—and boy, does the abyss stare back.

Does Lukas know why Pen won't come herself?

I close my eyes and lean back against the wall, taking several deep breaths. This will be over soon. A pinch of discomfort is well worth the obscene amount of lo mein I'll stuff inside my face once I'm home.

I can be brave. I can be *anything* for noodles.

Lukas arrives less than ten minutes later, damp hair falling on his forehead, a single pair of keys dangling from his index finger. He approaches with the relaxed, long-legged gait of someone who's at peace with the universe. I stare at him staring at me, not quite sure how to make myself stop.

Notable fact of the day: he's wearing shoes.

It occurs to me that one of us should probably say something—*hi* or *how are you* or *you ruined my night, shithead*—but for indecipherable reasons that don't fully have to do with nerves or discomfort, neither of us speaks for too many seconds. Until:

"Want to get it out of the way?" he asks.

Rich. That's what I'd call his voice. Rumbly, maybe. "Get what out of the way?"

"The elephant in the room."

I swallow. Is he referring to . . . ?

"The one with the ball gag in his mouth."

Laughter pops out of me. "Wow. Ball gags?"

He shrugs. "Not really my thing, actually."

I stop myself from saying, *Not mine, either*, because—it's not like he *cares*. Still, the knot of tension between us loosens. "Maybe the elephant's just . . . blindfolded?"

He nods slowly. "And tied up."

"And doing as it's told."

He looks like he might find that more appealing. "What a good elephant."

Blood rushes to my cheeks. I tear myself away from the weight of his eyes. "Okay. Well. I'm glad we got over the awkwardness of barely having had a conversation and yet somehow knowing the kinky sex stuff the other's into."

"I don't know what you're into," he says. It almost feels like something's being withheld. A *yet*. A *but I'd like to*. An *unfortunately*. Or it could just be his intonation. English is not his first language.

I clear my throat. "Thank you for coming."

"No problem." He unlocks and holds the door open for me, careful to keep his distance—which I appreciate. Deserted hallway. Big man. Not a huge fan. "I'll wait till you're out."

"You don't have to."

"The doors have been jamming both ways."

"It's okay. I'll be fine."

He stares at me, doesn't move, and . . . okay. Fine. Thank you. Polite, decent people who care about your safety—gotta hate them. I hurry to pick up my stuff. *Dinner*, I tell myself. *My reward. The promised land.*

As it turns out, he was right. The door won't open from the inside, either. I have to knock. Ask to please be let out, like he's my own personal warden. "I hate this," I mutter.

"I'll email maintenance again," he says. So much more graceful than *told you so.*

I set my backpack on the floor to tie my hair in a ponytail, and when I lift my head, I find him staring at me. Shouldering my bag. "You don't have to . . ."

"Let's go."

We walk toward the exit. I'm usually comfortable with silences—have to be, since I never really know how to break them—but this one prods at me. Maybe because I cannot stop thinking about Pen. The male voice. What Lukas might not know. "I'm sorry, I would have called one of the other captains, but—"

"It's all right, Scarlett."

His tone is simple and firm and doesn't brook any further genuflecting on my part, so I shut the hell up and steal a glance at his profile. The fuzz of his jaw, like he hasn't shaved in a while—typical preseason swimmer stuff, but instead of sloppy it looks kind of *GQ* on him. And those freckles that shouldn't work, but really do. I wonder whether he's considered handsome in Sweden, or just your run-of-the-mill ordinary guy. Is it a favorable exchange rate—a Stockholm three translating to a US ten?

"What's wrong with your shoulder?" he asks.

"*Nothing.*" It's a knee-jerk reaction—a bit of manifesting, mixed with some old student athlete denial. Calmer, I add, "How can you tell that there's something wrong with it?"

He gives me a half-puzzled, half-contemptuous look. Then the corner of his mouth twitches. "Right. I forgot."

"Forgot what?"

"That you have no memory of meeting me."

I flush. Was I that obvious?

"I should have introduced myself," he continues. "I'm a swimmer."

"Oh. I know?"

"Same team as yours actually."

"I know."

"One of those people with caps and Speedos."

"I *know.*"

My glare doesn't faze him. "Why do you keep massaging your shoulder?"

*Do I?*

"I thought your surgeries went well and you were healed."

How does he—Pen must have told him. "It did. I am."

We step out of Avery, and Lukas keeps his distance, just a bit more space than is customary, like he knows that I'm easily spooked. Maybe he doesn't want me to feel threatened—out and about with a *known sexual deviant* past sundown. But I'm just as deviant, and the plaza teems with people strolling past us, headed for what are undoubtedly fun plans.

I watch them a little enviously, but putting on makeup to drag myself to a bar sounds more exhausting than a decathlon—a normal feeling, surely appropriate for a twenty-one-year-old.

Meanwhile, Lukas could be anywhere. The world is his oyster, and I stole his Friday night pearl.

"Labral tear, right?" he asks.

I nod. "It's mostly rehabbed. I overdid it today, though." It's hard, getting used to a new body. New limits. New rules. "What about you? Any injuries?"

"My back, a while ago. Nothing big yet." *Yet.* Like it's just a matter of time. Water's a cruel mistress, and all that. "Come closer," he orders.

Lukas stopped a step behind me. I turn and frown up at him. "Why?"

"Because I just asked you to, Scarlett."

It might seem a bit out of character, given my . . . proclivities, but I really don't like people who order me around with no authority to do so. There's something about Lukas's serious, no-nonsense tone, though, that works on me like the opposite of a red flag. So I go for it and take a step closer. His scent envelops me, soap and chlorine and something warm.

*What now?*

His hands descend on me—one on my wrist, the other on my shoulder. They're unyielding and other things I'm *not* going to think about. He shuffles me with ease, turning me away from him, pinning my wrist against my lower back, gently but ruthlessly making sure that my spine stays straight, and . . .

God, the extension feels good on my muscles. Really, *really* good.

I close my eyes and let out a small moan. This might set a new gold standard for partner stretches—while Lukas's former partner is out there, *stretching* with—

"Why are you so nervous, Scarlett?"

"Me? I'm not." Lie.

"Is it because you feel uncomfortable around me—"

"No, I—"

"Or because you think I don't know where Pen is?"

My stomach plummets. I try to look at him, but his hold stays strong.

"Calm down." His voice is even-keeled. "You know you don't have to feel guilty about any of this, right? It's something you were dragged into. I'm just glad that cutting out your air supply last week didn't kill any brain cells."

A breathless laugh bursts out of me. He's just so blunt. Direct. Difficult, to not be direct back.

"Do you know where she is?" I ask quietly. How did she meet the guy? We're DI athletes. Perennially exhausted. Not stellar at socializing with other students. Maybe she's on dating apps? Maybe she's hooking up with other swimmers?

"I didn't ask," Lukas says.

"Don't you want to know?"

"No."

"And are you . . . okay with that?"

"My ex sleeping with someone else? Why should it matter whether *I* am okay with it?" He could stuff so much recrimination and self-pity in the words, but he's a straight arrow. I detect only genuine puzzlement.

He and Pen really were perfect for each other. Extroverted and reserved. Grumpy and sunshine. Warm and frosty. They remind me a bit of Josh and me—except that *I* was the Lukas of the relationship. "You just recently broke up. Are you really not jealous?"

"Nope."

"Is it a Swedish thing?"

"Maybe? I'll ask my brothers. They might have some insight."

I catch a small smile with the corner of my eye, and it relaxes me just enough to ask, "Do you still have feelings for her?"

It's *so* not my business. He tells me, though. "Sure. We've been through a lot."

It's not really an answer, but it echoes what Pen said. I wonder what it is that ties them together. Blood pacts? Body in the trunk of their car? Same sleeper cell?

I should tell him that I'm better, that he can let go of me, but my shoulder is in the throes of a hundred little orgasms. Which must be why I blurt out the question that has been buzzing in my head for days. "If Pen hadn't . . . if you guys hadn't broken up, would you have just gone with vanilla sex for the rest of your life?"

He mutters something under his breath. "Put like that, it sounds . . ." He exhales a laugh. His grip remains steady.

"Sad?"

"Frustrating." A pause. "But yes, I would have."

"Because you love that much?"

"Because I made a commitment to her."

*That's more stubborn than noble*, I think. Or maybe I say it out loud, because a soft laugh slides out of him, and my cheeks burn. "What I meant is, I don't think that settling for an unsatisfying sex life because you take your commitments seriously automatically makes you a better person than Pen, who—"

"I know what you meant, Scarlett." His thumb digging into my trapezium feels so good, I lose track of my mortification.

The thing is, I love reading Mafia erotica as much as the next girl with daddy issues, and my attraction for fictional guys making scenes in iconic, over-the-top ways is among my most virulent traits. But jealousy is born less of love and more of insecurity. And it intrigues me, the way Lukas obviously cares about Pen without being possessive of her.

His quiet self-assurance seems surprisingly mature. Boys around me, they feel like . . . well. Boys. But Lukas might already be a man.

"So," I ask, "are you going to . . ." He finally lets go. My shoulder begs me to whine at him to continue, but I shut it up and turn to him. "Start seeing other people? Ball gag them, or . . . whatever it is that you prefer."

His smile sits there, at the corner of his lip. "Still considering."

"Why?"

"It's complicated."

"You're single. Isn't it simple?"

"I don't know. Is it?"

"You can probably go to a bar tonight and find five hundred options."

"Five hundred."

"Well . . . many. Several."

He nods like I'm making a good point, but then asks, "What about you?"

"Me?"

"Are you seeing someone?"

"Oh. No."

"Then you're free to fuck whoever you like."

A sparkling, unusual sort of heat drips into my stomach. Spreads all over my chest. "I guess I am."

"You could go to a bar. Find some options."

"Five hundred?" I smile.

He doesn't. "Realistically, no. But several. Many. You could look for someone who'll give you what you need."

Drip. Drip. "Yeah. I could."

"Will you?"

"It's not so . . ."

"Simple?"

I face-planted right into that one. I rock on my heels and try to think of a witty comeback, but my brain is a rotting wasteland.

His mouth curves. "I don't think Pen's date was the real reason you were anxious."

"Yeah. I think it was."

"We cleared that out, and you're not any less nervous." He cocks his head. "Is it me? Or men, in general?"

Jesus. Does he always just—*say* what he *thinks*? Narrate the world as he sees it? Shouldn't some things stay unspoken?

"I need to go," I say, holding my hand out until Lukas returns my backpack. But even then, I stand rooted in front of him for several beats, until the realization hits me that I'm hoping he'll say something else.

Ask me another question, maybe.

Ask me to . . .

Oh my *god*. Pen's drunken ramblings must have wormed their way into my prefrontal cortex.

"Thank you again. I really appreciate you coming out."

"I'll walk you home."

And what? We chat amiably about the rigors of collegiate sports? I don't think that's what I want. I'd rather not think about what *he* wants. "No, thank you. Have a good night, Lukas." I walk away— and after a few steps I look over my shoulder and he's still there, hands in the pockets of his jeans, haloed against the streetlights. He's invincible. And golden. And focused wholly on me.

"I really do hope you have a good night," I murmur. It's too low for him to hear me, but I still wish him something . . . nice. So odd, the sense of kinship I feel toward this man with whom I've exchanged no more than a couple hundred words.

I turn around, head home, fall asleep before I can eat dinner. And wake up early the following morning, ravenous, to an email delivered a little after midnight. The subject line just reads *What you need*. The body:

*If you decide to go for it, I think it should be me.*

# CHAPTER 10

ON MONDAY MORNING, WE'RE TORTURED WITH STRENGTH training. Pen's giddiness hums throughout the locker room. Victoria is not an early bird, and her bad mood is an ugly, tangible thing.

"It's six fifteen a.m.," she grunts. "Let's keep unconscionable displays of happiness at a minimum."

"Oh, come on. It's such a good day."

"You mispronounced *heinous*."

"But we have synchro practice." Pen sneaks up to Victoria, pressing a surprise kiss to her cheek. "I know you like it."

"What I *like* is being on the couch feeling my atoms rot as I succumb to entropy."

On paper, Victoria and I are the same person: two promising athletes who sold Coach Sima a bill of goods, then merrily proceeded to never fulfill their potential. I was injured, but Victoria's talent simply . . . fizzled. Bad luck, competition anxiety, skills that never quite turned out right—it all conspired together, and she never qualified for the NCAA championship. Her perennially crotchety state is the mask she put on when her diving started going south. I know this because a few weeks ago I overheard her admit to Pen how much she *needed* a successful senior season to go out with a bang.

As for Pen . . . she's always cheerful, but I'm not going to try to guess where today's extra spark comes from, because it's none of my business. I stuff the thought in the same corner of my head where I painstakingly shoved Lukas's email—*it's a bad idea, he's my captain's ex, maybe he just wants to get back at her, make her jealous, bad idea, what is he into, what do I need, bad idea.*

I focus on training. Field questions from Coach Sima about my "issues," and his demand that I "stop changing those dives at the last minute. What is this, improv class?" Listen to Pen and Victoria's golden retriever and black cat banter throughout lifting and drills, marveling at their unlikely friendship.

I wonder what that's like. My old synchro partner and I had a good relationship, but she was older than me. We dove together for only a year or so, and outside of that we had little in common. I've never been bullied or maliciously isolated, and I hardly ever *don't* get along with people. Unfortunately, I rarely ever get along with them enough to qualify as more than an acquaintance. And, of course, my *best friend*, Josh, hasn't talked to me in over a year.

I spend the next hour focused on my lecture, but find myself scowling at the end, when Otis, Dr. Carlsen's TA, returns last week's homework. Comp bio was supposed to be my safe place this semester, but here I am, leafing through the pages, finding no letter grade. I covertly eye the guy sitting in front of me, the one with the cowlick the size of an orca.

*D*, his paper says in red ink. Below: *You still have time to drop this course. AC*

Orca Cowlick buries his face in his hand. I frantically look for a similarly inspirational quote on my own paper, and find it at the bottom of the second to last page.

*See me after class. AC*

My entire body goes hot, then cold, then damp. Every student knows that there is only one infraction egregious enough to warrant a summons.

Plagiarism.

The Great Expellable Offense.

I'm about to be accused of *plagiarism*. Which I am *not* guilty of. Which I can *prove*.

I still have the Word file. I can run it through the plagiarism detection software. I already would have, if Dr. Ozone-Hating Triassic Dinosaur Carlsen didn't demand hard copies.

I power walk to his office. Every door in biology is wide open— except the one of Dr. Adam J. (Jackass?) Carlsen, which is just ajar enough to not be considered closed. Clearly a department policy loophole.

I knock with trembling hands, a little belligerent, mostly terrified. My diving, my other courses, my MCAT, my lack of meaningful social connections, my mean roommate, my long-distance dog—everything in my life is fucked up, or painful, or beyond my control, *except for comp fucking bio*. I can't be kicked out of this class.

Dr. Carlsen spares me a three-nanosecond glance and turns back to his monitor. "My office hours are Thursday from—"

"I'm Scarlett Vandermeer."

His look is a barely disguised *and I should give a fuck, because?*

"You asked me to come see you."

*And I should give a fuck about* that, *because?*

"From your computational biology class?"

"Ah. Come in, please. Take a seat."

I don't want to be alone with this inflexible, bloodcurdling man. I leave the door wide open and park my butt on a chair. "I can prove it," I say.

"Prove what?"

"That I didn't plagiarize the essay."

His brow furrows. "Of course you didn't."

*Oh?*

"I do need to know, however, if you wrote it on your own."

"What do you mean?"

"I asked you to choose a science problem and solve it using computational biology. You proposed to classify different types of pancreatic cells using deep learning, *and* detailed the appropriate neural networks. Was it your idea? It's a simple yes or no question. Don't waste my time."

I scowl at his audacity. Hot blood rushes to my cheeks. *Of course* it was my idea. Who the hell would I even ask to—

"I see that it was." He seems . . . pleased? "Would you be interested in pursuing it further?"

"What?"

"The deep learning algorithm. Would you like to participate in a research project?"

"So it's . . . is this why you asked me to come here?"

He nods.

I sink back into my chair, and must spend too long savoring my relief at having escaped plagiarism jail, because he prods: "The research project."

"Oh, right." Would I? In my carefully and anally crafted academic plan, I was going to get some research experience next summer, just in time to ask my mentor to write me a rec letter. Med schools love that stuff. "Maybe?"

"Maybe." A puzzled eyebrow lifts, like he's encountering the concept of indecision for the first time.

"Well, I'm a student athlete, and this semester is . . ."

His eyebrow demands to know, *Did I ask?*

*Nope, you did not. My bad.* "It would be amazing. But I'm not sure I'm quite good enough to . . ." I drift off, because he's now writing something on a Post-it, then handing it over.

It's an orange square. The printed message in the top corner reads *Pumpkin Spice Life.* The bottom is a smiling coffee cup, little hearts orbiting around the lid. Scribbled in the middle is an email.

"If you decide you're interested, contact my colleague."

"Will they know who I am?"

"Yes," he says. No explanation. I have so many questions, it must take me too long to decide on which. "You may go now," he says, sterner than a Victorian governess.

I quickly scurry to the door—then stop. "Dr. Carlsen?"

He types away, giving no sign of having heard me.

"There was no grade. On the paper."

His eyes settle on me again, and he looks genuinely confused.

"Will I receive one?"

"Ms. Vandermeer, you planned a graduate-level study and extensively described its pitfalls and possible solutions, showing a command of the topic that eighty percent of my fellow faculty members will never achieve. Most of your peers copy-pasted their projects from Wikipedia and neglected to remove the hyperlinks. If your topic weren't much more in line with my colleague's research, and if my colleague wasn't incredibly . . . persuasive, I would be recruiting you into my lab."

"Oh." Wow. Just . . . wow.

"Believe me when I say that the grade is . . ." I sense despair in him. I bet he'd *love* to slug off the mortal coil of scoring rubrics. "Irrelevant."

"If you don't care either way, I'd like an A plus."

His mouth twitches. "I will let Otis know."

I grin. This time, Dr. Carlsen nods his goodbyes. The overall effect is stilted, like he pulled an item off a How to Act Politely list that someone scribbled for him on an orange Post-it, but I'll take it.

I'm starving, but my walk to the athlete dining hall is slow, because I'm busy writing an email to one Dr. Olive Smith.

# CHAPTER 11

LET'S GO BACK FOR A SECOND TO THAT DIVE GROUP YOU MEN-tioned. Inverse."

"Inward?"

"Yes." Sam sighs, like she's starting to lose patience with herself for not having the lingo memorized. It's endearing, I must say. "Once again, sorry."

"No problem. The names are weird."

"So, when your injury occurred, you were performing an inward dive. Correct?"

I make a deliberate effort to avoid squirming. Sam, I suspect, takes note of that kind of stuff. "Correct."

"As I understand it, your injury is fully healed."

"It is."

"Are there any remnants of it that make inward dives particularly challenging for you?"

I wish I could nod. So, *so* bad. Instead I drag out saying, "No," for as long as I can, and this time, I cannot help fidgeting.

# CHAPTER 12

"HATED PICTURE DAY IN ELEMENTARY SCHOOL, HATE MEDIA day in college. I'm nothing if not consistent."

I doubt Victoria, or anyone else, has ever uttered words worthier of my endorsement, even if Pen shrugs cheerfully and says, "I think it's fun."

It's Thursday after practice. The entire team wears black meet suits and crowds around the locker room mirror—the unflattering one that magically spotlights all our pores at the same time. We have one reflective surface, two harsh ceiling lamps, three poorly placed outlets, four curling irons, five divers, and twenty minutes to fool the world into believing we're more than chlorine-soaked hair tangles.

"If this is fun, I fucking hate fun," Victoria mutters. She turns to Bree and Bella, who are fighting over eyeliner techniques. "Can't you two ever do your own individual thing?" she snaps. The twins look so fiercely outraged, I'm surprised she doesn't collapse into a pile of elastane blend.

"Okay, well, what are *you* doing with makeup?" she asks Pen and me. I have hairpins held between my teeth, but point at my mascara.

"I did consider all-body galaxy glitter, just to see Coach's face,"

Pen says, "but I think I'll replicate the natural look I did last weekend when I went out."

"Date with Blomqvist?"

"Uh . . . yup. Yeah."

"Nice to see the end of your breakup delusions."

"Yeah." Pen clears her throat.

Bree gasps. "Hang on—were you about to break up with Lukas?" I see they went for the cat eye.

"I . . . briefly considered it."

"Why?"

She shrugs. "The joy of being single. The thrill of being chased, you know?"

"Maybe in your next life you'll be a mallard duck," Victoria mutters.

"Quack, quack." Pen grins and sneaks a quick, secretive glance at me. She's not a particularly good liar, and I'm not sure what surprises me the most: that she's hiding something, or that the others can't tell.

Truthfully, given Victoria's reaction a couple of weeks ago, I understand her choice. Plus, she and Lukas are kind of a big deal on campus. Maybe they're working their way to making an announcement.

As usual, Pen manages to be the first to get ready, help everyone else with their full-coverage foundation, *and* herd us to the media team on time. I stand between the green screen and the baking-hot studio lights, palms clammy, doing as the photographer instructs. *Smile, show your biceps, spread your arms, kick your legs back, jump.* It'll give the underpaid social media managers something to work with if I ever win a competition—unlikely, considering that the inward dive I attempted this morning morphed into a cannonball in midair. Under Coach's displeased scowl.

Maybe they'll write a human-interest piece about the bucket of slop that is my athletic career. My photo will end up in one of the glossy magazines they send to all Stanford alumni to promote school spirit and solicit donations. *Meet the girl who has been diagnosed with dumpster fire brain by a team of board-certified neurologists. And give us money.*

Even after I step out of the strobes, I still feel uncomfortably vulnerable. Most of my awake time is spent in wedgie-prone swimsuits, and self-consciousness has little space in aquatic sports, where athletes constantly pad across the deck in the bright, unforgiving sunlight, every imperfection up for inspection. But in the pool, my body is a machine—all that matters is what it can accomplish. Here, I feel almost obscenely exposed. Something that could be sectioned and poked and stripped for parts.

Not to mention that of late, my body has accomplished very little. Being a good athlete, a good student, reaching for perfect—those were the building blocks of *me*. Now that I'm struggling with almost everything, do I still have a fully fleshed identity? Or am I just an assembly of meat pieces, to be sold separately on clearance?

"Vandy?" Pen's hand slides into mine, cardinal-red nail polish dark against my skin. She tugs me back in front of the green screen and hands everyone on the team heart-shaped sunglasses. My pair, she slips right onto my nose. "Team pics!"

The photographer clears his throat. "We already—"

"But not *fun* ones."

He scratches his neck. "I don't think props were approved . . ." Pen, though, is an avalanche of charm—hard to resist, harder to say no to. The sunglasses pics are followed by sequined hats, Charlie's Angels poses, "Another one like we're a nineties boy band, please," and by the end we're all laughing, photographer included, and I feel more at ease.

*If you spent more time with your friends*, Barb's gentle voice echoes in my ears, *you'd be less in your head about stuff.*

Okay. Sure. Fine.

"Vandy, wanna get dinner with me after?" Pen asks. "They're filming captain interviews, but it'll be fifteen minutes, tops."

"Did something happen?"

"Why?" She smiles, kindly amused. "Because I want to hang out?"

"No, just . . ." I guess that gave away the status of my social life. "I have a meeting, and . . ." I check my phone. Time flies when you're re-creating the *Abbey Road* pic. "I'm already late, actually." I'm genuinely disappointed to decline, but Pen's smile doesn't waver.

"What about tomorrow, after practice?"

It's probably a tad pitiful, how the simplest overture warms my heart. "I'd love to."

On the other side of the room, the men's swimming team is going through its own media ordeal. When I pass them on my way out: There's an animated scuffle going on, laughter, "You go on the right" and "We got him, we got him." Lukas is in the thick of it, with three other swimmers trying to restrain him while a fourth holds the US flag behind him. The Swedish one, bright yellow and baby blue, is on the floor.

The camera clicks, and a USA chant erupts. Everyone laughs, Lukas included. A sophomore—Colby?—teams up with Kyle to wrap the flag around Lukas's shoulders. More laughter, more scuffle. Rough play and loud voices can be a trigger for me, so I take a step back. A deep breath.

"How much to make that disappear?" Lukas asks the photographer's assistant, freeing himself.

"How much would one gold Olympic medal get me if I were to melt it?"

"I don't know, man, but it's yours."

"Deal."

Lukas shakes his head. In the movement, the blue of his eyes catches mine.

Time slows.

Curious, patient, it stops.

My breath lodges somewhere in my trachea.

*It should be me.*

I force a brief smile and turn around to run across campus, heart pounding from more than effort. I make it to my meeting with two minutes to spare, but when I peek inside the office door, the conversation is already animated.

Dr. Smith—*Olive*, as I'll never call her despite her repeated invitations—*looks* not much older than me, but *sounds* like the repository of hundreds of years of knowledge on the biology of pancreatic cancer cells. Her office is a mix of gentle chaos and early fall scents, the same Post-its I spied on Dr. Carlsen's desk stuck on most surfaces, scribbled with barely sensical handwriting. Lancet review. Upload 405 assign. Anh baby shower. Insurance paperwork. Vet appt. SBD abstract. Call program officer. What if cobwebs???

They must be the official stationery of the Biology Department.

"I feel like I know you already—because of your paper!" she says excitedly before quoting entire passages of it and introducing me to one of her grad students, Ezekiel. ("If you call me anything other than Zach, I will report you to HR.") He's cheerful, easygoing. Charming. Dr. Smith will guide my project, but her calendar sounds like a nightmare. "So if you can't get a hold of me, Zach is here for you."

"Feel free to stop by my office whenever. I'm always there. It's like I have no life." His smile is kind. The "unfamiliar man, solo meeting" combo is not my favorite, though.

"I'm a student athlete, so I'll probably do most of the work alone at night? My schedule can be a little inflexible."

Dr. Smith grins. "A student athlete! That makes two of you."

I turn to Zach. "Are you . . . ?"

"The undergrad working on this project is. He's been harvesting and classifying the initial cell samples. Done some preliminary work on the algorithms, too." She cocks her head. "Do you happen to be a swimmer?"

My stomach churns. "Diver."

"Those are different sports, right? You two will get along great, though. He's—" A single, soft knock. Dr. Smith swivels her chair. "Come in."

The door opens, and I watch Dr. Smith's eyes rise—and rise, and rise, and *rise*. She grins, just as a familiar whiff of sandalwood soap and chlorine registers.

"Lukas, we were just talking about you. May I introduce you to Scarlett Vandermeer?"

# CHAPTER 13

THE HALLWAY OUTSIDE DR. SMITH'S OFFICE IS QUIET. I SHIFT on my feet and glance at the white walls papered in old conference posters, the corkboard pinned with study abroad opportunities and *Participants Needed* flyers. The glow of the sunset spreads over them from the closest window.

All in all, the four of us just had a pretty good conversation. My mild "Lukas and I already know each other." His low "Swimming and diving are the same team." Dr. Smith's delighted "This works so well, then!" Zach's amused "Must be something in the water turning people into biologists, huh?"

"Chlorine-induced brain damage," I mumbled.

Everyone laughed.

Except for Lukas, who just stared.

The three of us linger outside for a few minutes. At first we make plans for our first research meeting, then it's just Zach, chitchatting with Lukas. He reminds me of Josh—that adorable mix of good-looking and nerd. Thick-rimmed glasses. Tall, wiry physique. Mop of black hair. Heavy, self-effacing sarcasm. He must be a handful of years older than us, but he feels like a *boy* next to Lukas, and none of it has to do with Lukas's size.

I walk beside them, silent as they talk about some obscure sport. Lukas must notice the landscape of blurry nothingness in my eyes. "Fantasy Premier League," he supplies. I nod, pretending the words make sense together. Then Zach leaves, and we are alone.

We're both in our picture-day glory—black joggers, red hoodie, Stanford Tree. We're even zipped up to the same height, and I'd love to crack a joke about it, but I'm not sure even *I* find it funny, so I just tilt my chin up and stare at him staring at me, much longer than society rules would deem acceptable.

A pleasant heat spills throughout my entire body. Coalesces in my belly. "Well," I say.

"Well," he repeats.

"So . . ."

"So." There is amusement at the edge of his voice. In the crinkles cornering his eyes.

How did we go from avoiding even the slightest passing interaction for two whole years to *this*? His presence feels so . . . brutal. I'm not sure how to phrase it any better—he's just aggressively, unyieldingly here. A command to pay attention.

Any trace of humor clears from his face. "The email I wrote."

My heart trips in my chest.

*It should be me.*

"I had no idea we'd need to collaborate on a project, or I wouldn't have sent it. If you're uncomfortable, I can pull out. We can tell Olive—"

*Olive.* I nearly wince.

He notices. "What's wrong?"

"Just—you said her name."

A confused look.

"Her first name."

His head tilts. "Are you planning to call her Dr. Smith for the rest of the semester?"

"Of course." The corner of his mouth curls like he's entertained. Me: a spectacle. "What?" I ask, defensive.

"You really *do* like your authority figures, don't you?"

I gasp in outrage. And then . . . then I laugh. "Seriously?"

He shrugs, all height and mass, and rests against the wall behind him, one calf crossed comfortably over the other. The shape of his shoulders, his hands in his pockets—he's the picture of relaxation. It's *almost* a slouch.

On my side of the hallway, I lean back. Mirror his pose. It's the third time we are alone together, and I think I'll graduate him to Only Slightly Intimidating. Takes me longer, usually. "So," I ask evenly, "we're just . . . doing this?"

"Doing what?"

"Openly acknowledging that we know way too much about each other's sexual preferences every time we meet?"

"Unless it bothers you. Would you like me to pretend I don't know about your perversions?"

"You're just as much of a perv as I am."

"Oh, no."

My eyebrow lifts.

"Way more," he adds. "I guarantee it."

I laugh. Slip my hands in my joggers, just like him. Our gazes catch, weighty, tethered. "You know, you're right. Let's just own it."

"Let's."

"One of us gets off to . . . flogs?"

"The other, to calling people 'Doctor.'"

"Just two regular freaks."

"Nothing to see here."

A small smile, exchanged. Private. "Maybe Pen was right," I muse.

"And we're made for each other?"

I nod. It's a joke, but his eyes darken.

"Won't know till we try," he says quietly, low, and that warmth inside my belly rekindles, slinks up my spine, pinkens my cheek.

*It should be me.*

I hang my head, suddenly enraptured by my own frayed shoe-laces. "How long have you been doing research?"

"I've been working with Olive—*Dr. Smith*—for a couple of years."

"Really? What's your major?"

"Human bio."

"Premed?"

He nods. I'd have guessed business, or accounting—it's what lots of swimmers seem to go for. An interesting Venn diagram.

"Me, too," I volunteer. Then regret it—is he supposed to care?

"I figured."

How? Did he see me drool all over my MCAT prep text at Avery the other night? Snoring may have been involved.

"Relax," he says, reading my mind. "You took my physics class last year. Orgo, too. We were constantly in the same lectures."

"Are you sure?"

He just smiles, like he's charmed by my total lack of recollection.

"I never . . . I didn't notice you."

"I know." A small, self-deprecating laugh. His expression softens. "You were going through it, weren't you?"

"What do you mean?"

"You were struggling."

"No, I wasn't." I'm an excellent student. Or I used to be. "I got As in both classes—"

"I'm not talking about grades, Scarlett."

I wrap my arms around my torso. "I was fine." The words slip out reflexively, from the part of me that can't bear to admit how many times in the past year I needed to lock myself inside bathroom stalls and just *breathe.* But Lukas looks at me with something that resembles understanding. Like he's *gone through it,* too, and gets it.

"What about you?" I ask. "Would *you* feel weird, working together? I'm friends with Pen. And I know of your . . ."

"Sexual deviancy?"

The words sound so *good,* rumbling out of him. "Hmm. That."

"Nah." He shakes his head, without having to think about it. No hesitation. "She's great, by the way."

"Pen?"

His smile pulls at the edge of his mouth. "Her, too. But I meant Olive. She's the best at what she does. Helped me quite a bit when I applied for med school."

He's a senior. Must have started the application process earlier this year—on top of the swimming, the competitions, the classes, the research project, the girlfriend. On top of being Lukas Blomqvist, freestyle god, he's also some kind of premed semi-deity. How annoying of him.

"Where do you find the time to do all this stuff *and* train?" I half think out loud.

"Where do *you?*"

I huff. "I'm not an Olympic medalist."

"Medals have little to do with how hard one trains."

Do they? It feels like they should. Like my inability to secure any can only be due to a moral failure of mine. I didn't do enough, therefore I fell short.

But it's hard to ponder the matter now, with him so dialed into me, gaze shifting across my face like he sees *all.* In the last of the day's light, we study each other, unblinking, sucked in our respective corners. A woman walks between us, muttering, "Excuse me." Our eyes don't follow her.

"It's not," I say at last.

Lukas swallows. Straightens a little. "What?"

"Uncomfortable. For me. Doing the project together. If it's not too weird for you?"

A beat. He pushes from the wall, and I hurry to do the same. "Come on," he says. "Let's get dinner. I'll catch you up with what I have so far."

"You don't have to. I'm sure you have better things to do."

"Actually." I feel the ghost of his hand between my shoulder blades. The soft brush of his thumb at the top of my spine. It's barely there, but it guides me in the direction of the stairs. Whispers at me exactly where to go. "I have absolutely *nothing* better to do."

# CHAPTER 14

STANFORD HAS A DEDICATED ATHLETIC DINING HALL, BUT there's enough of us that it barely matters. We're right in the middle of dinner rush, which means crowds and loud noises. Lukas, a head and some change taller than most, spots a free table, tells me to hang on to him, and leads us there, our plates and drinks stuffed on his tray.

I look down at my fingers, how they fist the fabric at the hem of his hoodie for dear life. It's like we're friends. Like I have the right to orbit around him. I briefly disassociate and picture myself narrating this moment to the swimming coaches at my old club. *Then Lukas Blomqvist ordered stir-fry with rice, thanked the lady who gave him extra, and when the crowds parted for him like the waters of the Red Sea during the exodus—*

"You okay?" he asks.

I nod, taking a seat across from him and grabbing my plate. I'm a voracious eater—the alternative is not sustainable under my training regimen—but I find myself blinking at the mountain of food on his plate, then glancing away. I bet journalists ask him about his diet all the time. It must be annoying, people's curiosity about the honing and maintaining of his speed machine of a body. Intrusive at best, objectifying at worst.

"You don't look okay," he points out.

I force myself to spear a few penne. "What were you saying about the cell line?"

We talk about the project for twenty minutes. He's very passionate about it, and it's clear that it's been a labor of love for him—but it's just as clear that he's stuck, and that building algorithms is not his forte.

"It's because you're using a recurrent network," I tell him.

"There is a sequential element—"

"But it's spatial data."

He leans back, drumming his fingers on the table. "What would you do, then?"

"Convolutional neural network, for sure. It'll be a million times better."

"A million."

"I—*many* times better. It's feedforward. And the filter and pooling layers would . . ." His knit eyebrows tell me he's not following. "Hang on." I fish into my belt bag for something to write with, then look around for a flyer or a scrap of paper. Find none. I consider using the back of *my* hand.

Lukas's, though, is so much larger.

"Here." I reach across the table and grab his wrist. "You have your input, right?" I start drawing under his thumb and follow with the rest of the model. "You move to your first layer, the convolutional one, that picks up spatial features. Then pooling. Then there's another—"

Booming voices, the rasp of scraping chairs, and I instinctively pull back. When I look up, three people have joined our table, and Kyle Jessup is sitting next to me.

"Luk, you piece of elk shit." He steals one of my grapes from

Lukas's tray. "You left for your *thing*. I had to deal with Coach Urso and the lane-separator saga."

"He told me smooth separators were a go."

"He told *you*. Second you disappeared, went back on it."

Lukas massages the bridge of his nose. "I'll talk to him tomorrow."

"While you're at it, mention the touch pad issue . . ." He cuts off and turns to the swimmer who sat next to Lukas, Hunter something or other. He's coughing so loud, people around us are staring. "The fuck is wrong with you, H?"

"I drank a gallon of water during that bucket set. My tummy *and* my nuts hurt."

Lukas pats him forcefully on the back. "An elite athlete." It's directed at *me*, a hint of complicity in his eyes, like I'm a friend he shares jokes with. It has the unfortunate side effect of making the others notice me.

The shift of attention is a physical, tangible thing. "Who do we have here?" Kyle asks. "I thought you were Pen."

It's not inconceivable. She and I have similar builds—platform divers, like us, tend to be on the taller, leaner side. We both have long hair. That's about it, though.

I sip on my water to temporize. Over the rim, I say, "Surprise."

"Little Scarlett Vandermeer. Long time no see."

I make myself smile. Kyle is loud, but has never been anything but nice. "Hello."

"How are you, Vandy? I missed those dimples."

*Don't stiffen.* "And I missed that . . ." I search his Midwest-wholesome face for something of note. "Nose?"

Hunter convulses into laughter. "Your fucking *nose*." He claps at me and nearly rolls off his chair, like I'm the jester that keeps on giving.

God, they're loud. It's all I can do not to jolt.

"She meant that my nose is beautiful, you moron." Kyle laughs, too, but kicks Hunter under the table.

"Dude, maybe that's why you're so slow in the water. Your nose *drags.*"

"I'm faster than *you.*"

"Not this morning you weren't."

"I've been *injured*—"

"Hey." Lukas cuts through the squabble. "Could you sad sacks go eat elsewhere?" It's phrased as a request, but he's not *asking.*

They begin to stand, even as Kyle mutters, "Why?"

"Scarlett and I have stuff to talk about."

"And we can't be here?"

"Nope."

Kyle faux pouts. "This really hurts my feelings, bro."

"I'll kiss it better later, *bro.*"

"Cannot wait, b—"

"What do you guys have to talk about?" a female voice asks. I look up, and—Rachel, I believe. The third swimmer. She was sitting on the other side of Kyle, that's why I didn't notice her. I vaguely remember her from my recruiting trip. Backstroke. Long distance. Used to have long, blond hair, now cut pixie-style.

I think she's friendly with Pen. Her smile doesn't reach her eyes.

"Biology," Lukas replies.

"You're doing a project together or something?"

"Or something."

"Huh." Her eyes slide to the back of his hand. The model I drew. "And where *is* Pen?"

Her tone is . . . not quite insinuating, but it has my cheeks burning, and I pause mid-sip and open my mouth to explain myself. But before I can blurt out something socially destroying (*It's not what it looks like and even if it were they broke up and it was Pen's idea and also I didn't ask to be born just leave me alone okay*), Lukas shrugs. "No idea."

Rachel wants to press it, but Kyle swings an arm over her shoulders. "Come on, we've been dismissed. See you at home, Sweedy." He leads her away. Hunter points silently at his nose, gives me an overenthusiastic thumbs-up, blows a kiss to Lukas, and goes on their heels.

I swallow a sigh of relief. Grip my fork. "So, you and Kyle live together?" I ask into my food. When Lukas doesn't reply, I glance up.

He sits back, his plate forgotten, studying me. The quiet weight of his gaze is familiar. So is the curve that sets in his mouth: he's observing something; coming to conclusions. My belly feels tight and warm. "I thought it was just me," he says. "But it's men in general, isn't it?"

"What?"

"We make you nervous."

My fork hits my plate with a clink, swallowed by the background chatter. "How did you . . . ?"

"Earlier, in the hallway, you kept putting barriers between you and Zach—me, mostly. Then your face, with Kyle and Hunter. It's not hard to guess, if one cares enough to pay attention."

My heart beats in my throat. *And do you? Care?* It's a fair question. He and I have had so few interactions, all of them products of force majeure—malfunctioning doors, academic coincidences, Penelope Ross. *What the hell are we even doing here?* seems like something we should ask each other. Instead, to my horror, I say, "I had some issues with my dad, growing up. I'm not—it wasn't *that* bad, but . . ." I suck in a deep breath. Silence the voice in my head that cringes and yells, *Stop. Unloading. On Lukas. Blomqvist.* "I just don't like loud noises. And too-crowded spaces. And . . ."

It's not that women can't be noisy, but boys feel so unpredictable, with their deep voices and abrupt movements and boisterous attitudes. Male athletes, on top of that, tend to take up so much space. I know it's unfair of me, but my issues are not rational. My high school therapist kept using words like *trauma response* and *PTSD*, words that feel too *big*, like I don't have a right to them. They belong to war reporters and ER doctors, not girls with shitty dads who bossed them around and told them they'd never amount to anything.

*In the end*, the therapist said, *the measure of whether you're doing well is: Is your condition preventing you from living a fulfilling life?* And I know the answer to that.

"I function fine," I say, chin tilted up, a hint of challenge.

It's unnecessary. "I don't doubt it."

"Okay. Good."

He resumes eating, quick but meticulous, but his eyes stay on me.

"I know it seems . . ." I start. Do I wanna go there?

"Seems what?"

"Like someone who's into what I'm into, shouldn't be all . . . fearful." It never ceased to puzzle Josh. *You have issues with authoritarian, aggressive men in everyday life, but you want to have authoritarian, aggressive sex?* He never judged me, but he did *not* get it.

Lukas finishes chewing, wipes his mouth with a napkin. "Actually, I still don't know what you're into," he points out.

My belly swoops.

"Aside from your *doctor* fetish, that is."

I turn away to hide my smile.

"Regardless, no. I don't think it makes sense to conflate everyday violence with the kind of stuff you—*we*—are into. In fact, I don't think the two things are related at all." His gaze is steady. "What you and I want, it's all about trust. We decide to be part of it. It sounds like whatever happened to you had little to do with you making any decisions, right?"

*Right.* That thick warmth flares up again, this time in the hollow of my chest. *You get it. Thank you for getting it.* And: "Thank you for asking your friends to leave so that I wouldn't be uncomfortable."

He nods. Doesn't pretend that it isn't exactly what he did. "Thank you for getting Mrs. Sima off my back at the barbecue so that I wouldn't have to talk about my mother."

*All about trust,* he said. I won't betray his by asking why he doesn't want to do that. "First exit diversion is on me, but the next will cost you."

I hear his amused exhale, and let a comfortable silence wrap around us for the rest of the meal.

# CHAPTER 15

THAT WEEK, FOLLOWING THE CALENDAR GUIDELINES KINDLY provided by my courageous forebears (i.e., people who got into med school and lived to tell the tale), I finish writing the first draft of my personal statement.

And promptly right-click it into the trash can. I also consider deep-frying myself straight to the gates of hell. According to Maryam, it's *that* bad.

"'I desire to follow the footsteps of my heroes, such as Hippocrates of Kos . . . which is how I realized that my favorite bacterium was *Bordetella parapertussis* . . . and as I looked at Queen Amidala dying on the screen, I decided that I would become a doctor to help people like her survive to see their Force sensitive twins thrive . . .'" Maryam is bulge-eyed. "Who *are* you?"

I grab a throw pillow and hand it to her. "Will you please hold this against my respiratory airways for the next sixty to ninety seconds?"

"Seriously, what is this word soup? Did you kidnap a middle school dropout and force him to write this at gunpoint? Is it AI generated? What was the prompt? 'What if crotch smell was an essay?'"

I groan and let myself fall back onto the couch. "Is it that hard to believe that I'm just that bad with words?"

"You could be an illiterate praying mantis, and my answer would still be a resounding *yes*." She scoffs. "None of this is true, anyway. Just be honest. 'Hi, my name is Vandy McVandermeer and I'm a neurotic, perfectionist, overachieving student athlete who memorized the workings of the musculoskeletal system by the age of nine but is still unable to timely replace toilet paper rolls. Hobbies include staring at the As on my student transcripts. I want to become a physician because I love my stepmommy. And because I'm a control freak and this job is as close as I'll ever get to mastering life and death. Aside from maybe holding the nuclear codes. Do you happen to know if there are any openings for *that* position?'"

I *could* do that. I *could* be honest. But if I went that route, I'd have to admit to the low C I'm currently pulling in German, to how *under* I've been *achieving*, to my inability to exert control over *anything*.

I bemoan my language constipation on Saturday, on my way to practice. There are student services I could use for help, but they're for fine-tuning and wordsmithing, not the nuclear makeover I need. I should ask Barb, but she got into med school nearly three decades ago. Maybe Lukas would be willing to share his essay with me? I have his number. And his email, of course.

*It should be me.*

Nah. Better not.

Avery is larger than my entire high school used to be—one diving well, three pools, a million satellite structures—and today it's packed full. I follow the cheers and music to the competition pool until I spot Coach Sima, who's glaring resentfully at the crowd.

"What's going on?" I ask him.

"Pool Wars."

"Oh, right. I always forget that it's a thing."

"As you should. It's damn unnecessary." Coach's resentment for the swimming team is legendary, and mostly due to how many more resources they get compared to diving. He has a point, though: intramural competitions *are* a waste of time.

"Is it almost done?"

"It's a damn pentathlon."

It means, I think, that all swimmers race one hundred yards for every stroke, plus individual medleys. Not sure, though. Also: don't care. "When does it end?"

"Daylong infestation, apparently."

I pat his shoulder. "There, there."

"The rest of the diving team is over there." He points to under the stands. "They wanted to watch the medley race. And apparently it would be too much of a tyrant move for me *to demand we begin practice on time.*" He raises his voice, as though anyone but me could hear him. "We'll start dryland once it's over, which cannot be *soon enough.*" I give him one last pat and head toward the others. "If any of you is late, I'm making y'all run laps!" he yells after me—a frequent threat with zero percent follow-through.

Pen is delighted to see me, in a way I'm not used to experiencing from anyone but Barb or Pipsqueak. She asks the swimmer next to her to scoot over to make space for me, then twines her arm with mine. We had dinner yesterday, just me and her. We talked for hours without mentioning diving or Lukas Blomqvist. Nothing special, but it'll go down in my top five Stanford moments.

Who am I kidding? Top three.

"I think it's the first time I've seen you at a swim meet," Pen says.

"I think it's the first time I've been to one since I was in high school, and my ride home was the mom of one of the backstroke guys."

She laughs. "In your defense, you're always taking so many classes and—" She stops, as if recalling something. "I heard about the project with Luk! That's going to look so nice on your CV when you apply for med school!"

"I hope so." A pair of distrustful eyes flashes into my head. "I . . . did Rachel tell you?"

"Rachel? Which Rachel, Hale or Adrian?" Her brow furrows. "Either way, Luk told me. Why do you ask?"

*No reason*, I almost say. But this is Pen, and . . . I don't know. I trust her. It's a gut feeling. "The other night Lukas and I were together in the dining hall, and she looked at me like I was doing something wrong."

"Wrong in what way—oh." Pen's eyes widen. Then she laughs. "Nah, Rachel's just chilly. Freshman year she'd treat me like I was crashing swimmers' parties or distracting Luk just by *existing*." She bumps her shoulder against mine. "Plus, he's single. And *I'm* the one who got wasted and cosplayed a Tinder algorithm to set you two up, remember?"

"Hmmm." I squint. "Nope. I'd forgotten. It's definitely *not* seared into my mind."

She laughs. "Don't worry about Rachel. She has no idea what's going on."

A lump of tension I wasn't quite aware of dissolves. "Will she, though?" I remember Victoria's questions on media day. "Are you and Lukas planning on telling people that you broke up?"

She sighs. "For now, you're the only one who knows. We're still trying to figure out the logistics of not being a couple, you know? People have this weirdly idealized view of us, and I know they're going to make such a big fucking deal out of it. You know how invasive the gossip is in the athletic village." She rolls her eyes. "Plus, our social circles overlap. We don't want to make things weird with that, especially since he and I are still best friends and together all the time. And I won't lie . . . it's nice, being seen as Luk's girlfriend. During freshman year, before people knew about it, so many guys would hit on me and get aggressive when I rejected them. Luk's existence is like an instant repellent."

I understand it would be a problem, when one looks like Pen and is that widely beloved.

"Not to mention," she continues, "he's very Swedish about this stuff."

"What's that?"

"Just, private. Pretty hard-core about not disclosing. Like that time an ESPN journalist asked him whether he had a girlfriend."

"What'd he say?"

"He just calmly asked, *Do you have any other sports questions for me, given that you are a sports journalist?*" Her impression is spot-on, down to the faint accent. She knows him inside out, and then some. "He was sixteen, and that was the last time anyone asked him about his private life. So *awkward*."

Appealing, too. I know Lukas is our age, but he seems to have skipped the self-doubt stage. Resolute. Strong-willed. Knows what and where and when he wants to be. I bet he wrote his med school essay in twenty minutes.

"He's a good guy," she adds, more serious, eyes toward the pool. "I know he seems . . . distant, and rarely bothers to switch on the charm, but he's great." I'm not sure *distant* matches my impression of him, but before I can point it out, Pen adds, "He deserves to live his best sexy, depraved, dungeony life."

The athletes are walking to the starting blocks, and people around us start clapping. I ask, "Are you, um, living your best sexy, undepraved, aboveground life?"

She turns to me. Leans closer. "There is this guy—"

A piercing whistle. Pen springs to her feet. Her screams of "Go, Luk! Go, go, *go!*" fade in the cheers of the crowd. The sudden noise startles me, and I take a deep breath to collect myself.

Lukas wins, though he doesn't beat Kyle by a lot. He doesn't slap the water, dance on the lane separator, or do any of the icky things that I was forced to witness in my club youth and turned me off swimmers forever. He just evades Kyle's (playful?) attempt to drown him and slides out of the pool. Pen takes my hand to head to dry-land training, and—

Nope. We're turning for the pool deck. "There he is." Pen waves a hand. "Luk!"

Lukas is talking with another swimmer, but he's wrapped it up with a one-armed hug by the time we've reached him. Pen beams at him. "Congrats!"

He nods. If he's happy to have won, I can't tell.

"Could you stop consistently being the best at what you do?" Pen teases, lifting her arms to hug him.

"I'm dripping."

"Since when do you care?"

He doesn't lean down, so it's up to Pen to reach up for him. My gaze reflexively flicks away, cheeks heating. I'm intruding on this non-couple, again. I shouldn't be here. *Leave for practice. Pen'll be right behind you.* But she brought me here. And she's my friend. And I'm doing a project with Lukas, and—*No reason to be so damn weird all the time, Scarlett.*

I give it a couple of seconds, then glance at them again, clearly underestimating the duration of their hug. Pen's arms are looped around Lukas's neck, but he's not reciprocating. Instead, over her shoulder, I find him looking at me.

There is no smile on his face. His eyes are dark, and serious, and heavy, and I—

"You goddamn *machine.*" The men's head coach gives Lukas's shoulder a weighty slap. Pen breaks apart from him, and I exhale in relief. "Have you seen the splits? Can't believe this is *unsuited.* Pen, whatever you're feeding him, do more of that."

"He feeds himself, Coach Urso."

"Am housebroken, too," Lukas deadpans.

I take a step back as the coach pulls out an iPad and starts critiquing every micro-aspect of Lukas's stroke, not wanting to crash the conversation, and take the opportunity to study Lukas, for once *without* being studied in return.

Swimming and diving are only sister sports out of convenience. They both require pools, locker rooms, and yards of polyester, but that's where the similarities end—and all it takes to figure it out is a good look at the athletes.

Diving necessitates balance and control of powerful bursts of movement. Swimming is all about reducing drag through the water to increase speed. We are all muscular, but the sports have different demands, and swimmers' bodies tend to be cut in a way divers' aren't. And Lukas . . . well. Lukas is one of the fastest swimmers in the world. He looks the part.

I know, rationally, that it's nothing to write home about. I grew up in pools, surrounded by rippling lats and arching trapezii since before I fully understood what sex was. *That guy's ass in a Speedo belongs in MOMA*, someone would say, and I'd nod, unimpressed, wanting the attraction but not feeling it in my stomach.

But with Lukas I think I see it. His hair tousled by the peeled-off cap, the width of his wrist as he wraps his goggles around it, the play of the tattoos on his shoulder, triceps, forearm. It's a forest, I think. Stars in the night sky. Snow. Something flying around the hill of a biceps. No sign of five interlaced links, unlike one hundred percent of the other Olympians I've met. He nods at something the head coach says, thoughtful, a palm rubbing the slope of his jaw, and yes.

I really do get it.

But maybe it's just this kinship I feel for him. Maybe Pen hacked my head, and I'm imagining what he could use all that strength for. Maybe I finally reached puberty at the geriatric age of twenty-one.

*It should be me.*

"Bottom line," Coach Urso tells Pen, "this guy just shaved nearly a second off his medley best from the summer—fastest progress he's ever made."

Pen grins without missing a beat. Squeezes Lukas's arm.

"What's that?" Coach Urso asks him, pointing at the back of Lukas's hand. He's a portly middle-aged man valiantly holding on to what little hair he has left. Widely beloved, and considered something of a talent-fostering genius. He is also, according to Pen, absolutely unhinged.

Which must be the reason Lukas looks like he's bracing for impact. He catches the towel a sophomore tosses at him and nods his thanks. "That's my hand, Coach. Nothing to see here."

"No—what did you write on it?"

"Can't recall."

It's not the model I drew, right? No. Can't be. It was *days* ago.

"Well, kid, try to recall," Coach Urso insists. "This is it."

"It's what?" Lukas dries his midriff, puzzled. *Kid*, I think, bemused, noticing the V muscling down his abdomen.

"The perfect circumstances. To re-create. To win."

"Ah. Of course."

"Remember last season's lucky routine?"

"You mean, putting a Disney princesses Band-Aid on my toe for an entire year?"

"It's how you won the NCAA and the world championship."

"Nothing to do with training."

"Are you sassing me, Blomqvist? You know I can't tell. Either way, we're set. We got our lucky routine. Our work here is done. *Ad majora*, kid." Coach salutes him and walks away—then turns around to finger-gun him. "The hand. Make sure you take a picture."

Lukas shakes his head and dries his face with the towel.

"He's going to make sure you have a whole-ass painting on your hand every meet," Pen says.

"Yup."

"What even is it? Looks like boxes and scribbles?"

"Pretty much."

Oh, shit.

"Well, good luck with that." On her tippy-toes, hand on his stomach to balance herself, she presses a kiss to his jaw. Lukas, I notice, doesn't bend down to make it easier. "We gotta go, or Coach Sima's gonna get angina."

Lukas nods. His eyes lift to mine. "Bye, Scarlett."

I'm flushing. Not sure why. "Yeah. Bye. And . . . congrats."

His smile is faint, and crooked, and almost intimate. Short-lived. But it sticks to me through the afternoon, like adhesive tape under the sole of my shoe, and I don't want it. There's no reason for it. I try to concentrate on Pen's chatter, on warming up, on my core exercises, but I'm distracted. Dryland practice is my least favorite, and somersaults in a foam pit get old surprisingly fast. Focusing on the aerial parts of a skill definitely has benefits—but at what *cost*.

"If I'd wanted to jump off of a springboard and land on my feet on top of a crash mat, I'd have become a gymnast," Victoria mumbles when I'm done with my set of reverse somersaults, nose scrunched up in disgust.

"At least Coach didn't bust out the spotting rope."

"Or the twisting belt." She makes a gagging sound and goes in for her turn. We only have four dive stands, which gives me a compulsory break. I sip on some water. Take out my phone. Write a text to an unsaved number.

SCARLETT: Please tell me that someone else drew a convolutional neural network on your hand in the past two days.

Immediate reply.

UNKNOWN: Are you calling me a computational slut?

SCARLETT: How has it not faded?

UNKNOWN: Someone used indelible marker.

Shit.

UNKNOWN: Looks like I'll need you around this year.

And: fuck.

SCARLETT: As in, I'm in charge of drawing a CNN on your hand before every meet?

UNKNOWN: Nah.

Thank god.

UNKNOWN: Just the international ones. And Pac 12. NCAA.

Jesus.

SCARLETT: Do you really want to be reminded of my computational superiority that often?

UNKNOWN: I do. I have a thing for women who are smarter than me.

My heart hiccups.

SCARLETT: I'm not ready for the responsibility of being part of your lucky routine. If you lose, will the King of Sweden get mad at me?

UNKNOWN: My country is a parliamentary democracy.

SCARLETT: You're a man of science. You're not really superstitious, are you?

UNKNOWN: Maybe I am.

I sigh.

SCARLETT: On the one hand, I want to shame you for it. On the other, my worst dive ever happened the day after someone stole my tie dye shammy.

I'm ready to admit that as far as evidence supporting the efficacy of competition-adjacent rituals goes, it's pretty thin—until a scream startles me.

I drop my phone and run toward the sound. When I reach the portable board farthest from me, my heart drops into my stomach. Because Victoria is lying on the floor. Her eyes are full of tears, and her ankle is bent at an unnatural angle.

# CHAPTER 16

**W**HAT CLINGS TO ME LIKE SMOKE THROUGH THE NEXT FEW days is something Bella says right after Coach Sima disappears inside the aquatic center, carrying a sobbing Victoria in his arms.

*She'd just bought that new chlorine treatment for her hair. Was so excited about it not looking like hay this year.*

I think about it throughout my workouts, my meals, my German homework, my fight with Maryam over washer cycles. Bella's resigned, despondent tone. The way she sat on the coaches' bench next to Bree, cheek on her sister's shoulder. I sat, too, hugged my legs and rested my chin on top of my knees, stared at the empty diving well while the obnoxious cheers of the Pool Wars and the late afternoon breeze made my skin break into goose bumps.

"And how is she now?" Sam asks on Wednesday morning. I feel guilty, filling our session with chatter of something that has nothing to do with inward dives. This is what's on my mind, though.

"I don't know. Her family's in town. Coach Sima has been vague. I . . . she is a senior."

And that's that. Lots left unspoken behind those four words, most of which has to be lost on Sam, but sits heavily on the team.

Yesterday, in the gloom of practice. Today, in the too-quiet locker room.

"Are you concerned that it might be a season-ending injury for her?"

"I hope not." Even at her best, Victoria never excelled. She's no Pen, who'll almost certainly go pro after graduation. All she could do was cling to the prospect that next season would be better. But if there's no next season . . .

"I hope not," I repeat.

"She's a good friend of yours?"

"I don't know if she'd consider me a friend. I like her a lot."

Sam blinks like she's putting a pin in that, a mental note of something for later. More to unpack—how excellent. "How does her injury make you feel?"

"It just . . . sucks."

"It does," she agrees. "But you didn't answer my question. How does it make *you* feel?"

I dislike the Use Your Words part of therapy. A problem, since it's *all* of it. "Sad that she might be in pain. Angry that it happened to her. Anxious for her recovery."

"What about fear?"

"Of what?"

"You have been severely injured. Now the same has happened to a friend. Does this validate your fears?"

"Our situations are completely different. Victoria wasn't even in the pool."

"But doesn't this solidify that diving is inherently dangerous?"

"Victoria tripped over a mat—the same could have happened walking over cobblestone."

"What you're saying is that you are *not* afraid of diving and the dangers it presents?"

I'm starting to get a little impatient with this line of questioning.

"Diving comes with risks. What I'm saying is, I knew those risks long before my or Victoria's injury."

"However, before your injury, you did not have a mental block. Something must have changed between then and now."

"I know, but . . ." But? My mouth hovers open for a few seconds and then snaps shut. I glare at Sam, tight-lipped. Ambushed, like I'm some born-yesterday brothers Grimm orphan, led to a slaughterhouse by a trail of stale breadcrumbs. "I don't dive in constant fear of injury," I say firmly, knowing it to be true.

"I don't doubt it, Scarlett. I believe that fear of injury is *not* a motivating factor in your issues." Sam cocks her head. "But then I have to ask—if you're not afraid of getting hurt, what *are* you afraid of?"

# CHAPTER 17

THE FIRST MEETING FOR DR. SMITH'S PROJECT IS THAT NIGHT, in the Green Library. When I arrive I pull up Lukas's emails to double-check the location, and two results appear: the thread we've been using to make plans with Zach, and the *other*.

*What you need*

A hazy flush spreads over my cheeks.

I haven't reread the email since it was delivered. I don't need to, because it's branded into my occipital cortex. I didn't *mean* to memorize it, but it was one and done. I can't revert it to unread—it would drive me bananas, as I cannot dwell in this plane of existence unless *all* my notifications across *all* my devices are cleared. I could archive it. Trash it. Mark it as spam.

It's not like I'm ever going to *reply* to it. It would be so weird, and—

A knuckle bumps softly against the fleshy part of my arm. "Room's this way, troll," says a deep voice above my left ear. Lukas's long legs don't slow down, and by the time we're upstairs, I'm winded—and trying to figure out whether I hallucinated that last word.

"Huh," he says, holding the door open.

"What?"

"A surprising amount of panting for someone who spends her day climbing stairs." His eyes are warm, gently teasing. Heat blooms inside me as I wave at Zach and enter the small room. It has three chairs, one desk, and one projector. I'm not sure what it says about the fun house of horrors that is my social life, but the meeting that follows is the most fun I've had in a while.

"You really know your neural networks," Zach tells me during a break. It could be the glossy patina of the deep learning algorithms, but my brain has classified him as Fairly Unthreatening. I'm relaxed enough to kick off my shoes and genuinely laugh at his terrible non-parametric statistics joke. Lukas is at the fountain right outside, re-filling our water bottles. He conspicuously left the door open, and he made sure I was aware that he could see me through the glass doors.

Ah, the frazzling ordeal of being known.

"I took a couple of online classes," I explain to Zach, lifting my bare feet on Lukas's chair to stretch my hamstrings. "And was in the bioinformatics club in high school. And went to a comp bio re-search camp in my junior year."

"Wow. A jock *and* a nerd."

I laugh into my shins and deepen my stretch, closing my fingers around my toes. "Collecting archetypes is my passion."

"Don't stop on my account. You're clearly great at it." He points at the whiteboard, where I drew the forward and backward passes of my network. "You're a senior?"

"Junior."

"What are your plans for after?" He laughs at my pained expression. "Are you going pro?"

"With diving? I don't think so. I'm trying to get into med school."

"Have you taken the MCAT?"

"This weekend."

"You're on top of it."

"Not really. My essays are a shitshow. And I think the German homework I've been turning in might be the written equivalent of burning a German flag?"

Lukas returns and hands me my water bottle. "You're taking German?"

"Regrettably for everyone."

Before I can vacate his seat, one of his hands wraps around both my ankles. He lifts them, holds them up as he sits down, and then lowers my bare feet in his lap.

I blink at him. Then at his hand. His grip softens against my left calf, its circumference loose. He has short, blunt nails. Long, enveloping fingers.

A wave of heat irradiates up my legs.

"Why?" he asks.

My eyes rocket up to his. *What are you doing?*

"Why German?" he repeats, imperturbable.

My cheeks burn. "Just . . ."

*Move your legs*, I order myself. *He's* not *pinning you.* He is, in fact, fully relaxed in his chair. Only mildly interested in my tales of academic mistakes. The pad of a chlorine-roughened thumb unhurriedly sweeps back and forth over the ball of my anklebone. Is he even *aware* of what he's doing? "Med schools like foreign languages," I say. It's raspy. More of a dry-mouthed croak, really.

"Do *you* like foreign languages?" His eyes are on me. The weight of his hand settles on my skin like it belongs there, unchallenged.

I manage a fuzzy headshake. *No, I don't like learning foreign languages* is as beyond me as the Cartwheel Galaxy. My pulse thuds, sticky in my ears. Between my legs.

"Maybe you should take Norwegian," Zach jokes. With the table between us, he can't see what's happening. "That way Lukas could help you."

"Swedish," I correct reflexively. Lukas's hand wraps against the heel of my foot in a lingering caress.

"Oh, shit—sorry about that, man."

"You're fine. Same peninsula." His thumb presses into my arch, strong, capable. I bite my lower lip. Hard.

Zach, whose hobby appears to be inquiring upon the five-year plan of everyone he meets, asks, "You going to move back there when you're done with school?"

"We'll see."

"Your girlfriend lives here, right? Wait—weren't you dating a diver?" His eyes dart to mine. "It wasn't you, right?"

"No." I clear my throat. Consciously slow down my breathing as Lukas's grip trails upward, under the hem of my leggings.

Zach nods anyway. "Gotcha." He laughs. And after an awkward beat: "What about you?" He points a pencil at me. "Are you dating a swimmer?"

"Me? I—"

Suddenly, Lukas's hand is a manacle around my ankle, like I'm something for him to hold and control and restrain. My brain trips. I'm sure everyone—Lukas, Zach, the front desk librarian downstairs—can hear the erratic pound of my heart.

"She's not," Lukas replies, eyes steady, fixing mine. Voice rumbly and calm. His hand is a vise, and—

It's just the way I'm wired. It's written in my neurons, how much I enjoy the strength behind his grip. His size. The ease with which he could overpower me. He could *make* me do things, and knowing that stokes a hollow ache in my abdomen. But he will not, not unless I give him the go-ahead, and *that's* the kind of belly-warming knowledge that makes that ache even sharper.

It's not morally *wrong*. It doesn't hurt anyone. There are no victims here, but maybe it's messed up? At the very least it's so fucking—I don't even know, heteronormative of me. Gender conforming. Regressive. Stereotypical. *Banal.* I hate it.

I *love* it.

"A diver, then?" Zach jokes, somewhat clumsy, and I need to re-thread the conversation, find its lost stitches. Whether I'm dating a swimmer. Or a . . . ah.

"Nope," I say, and Zach nods, like I've given the correct answer. He excuses himself with a soft "be right back," and Lukas and I are alone, his touch light again. I open my mouth to ask him what he's doing, why now, why *here*, but—I haven't opened my mouth at all.

I'm just staring, lungs and heart not quite steady.

"He was trying to figure out if you're single," he tells me. His casual stroking continues in small, light patterns.

I swallow. Collect myself. "I knew that."

"Did you? Really?"

Truthfully, no. But it has nothing to do with me being oblivious, and everything with his hands. "I'm not clueless."

He hums low in his throat. By now, I know him better than to believe it's in agreement. "Do you remember Kent Wu?"

"I don't—wait. Swimmer?"

"Butterfly. Distance. He was a senior when you joined the team."

"I think I do?"

"He tried to ask you out twice."

"What?" I frown. "How do you—how would *you* even know that?"

"We were good friends. Still are." He drums his fingers over the back of my foot. "He noticed you. We talked about it."

*Talked* about it? What does that even mean? Lukas is probably thinking of someone else. Swimming and Diving are more incestuous than we like to admit, mostly because our chaotic schedules match well enough to allow the penciling in of some fucking. "You're mixing him up with Hasan. He asked me out when I was still with my ex, a million years ago—"

"A million?"

"Two. *Two* years ago." I bite the inside of my mouth. "You are very literal."

A twitch of his lips. "And you are prone to exaggerations."

"It's a rhetorical figure also known as—"

"Hyperbole, yes." He thumbs my skin, and I nearly shiver. He seems to weigh me like I'm a pound of meat. "Kent was after Hasan. Toward the end of the season."

"I don't—"

"Remember. Because you never noticed. Don't worry, Kent's happily engaged, I just got his save the date."

I glance away. Lukas's flesh is still warm against mine, and so is that liquid feeling traveling down my spine, but the implications of what he said sit heavy in my gut. "I'm not clueless," I repeat.

"You're not. You just keep your head down. Focus on what you can control, and cut the rest out as much as you can without letting your world collapse. Right?"

I exhale. "Just because Pen shared something about me she should never have, it doesn't mean that you know me." It comes out nicely firm. I'm proud of it. Except that Lukas's reaction is not contrition, but amusement, the beginning of that crooked smile on his lips, and I don't—

"Ready to start again?" Zach asks.

I do what I should have five minutes ago—pull my feet away and fold them underneath me.

"Yeah." I smile at Zach without glancing at Lukas or waiting for him to echo me.

# CHAPTER 18

**D**URING THURSDAY MORNING DRILLS, AFTER I HAVE EX-
hausted every other group of basic dives, I stand on the edge
of the three-meter springboard, head hanging, eyes closed, two
words beating against the wall of my skull.

*Inward.*

*Tuck.*

*Inward.*

*Tuck.*

It's an overcast day. A little foggy. The early breeze brushes
against my too-tight muscles and breaks me into shivers.

I lift my arms above my head and let them fall again, limp as
noodles. I rotate the tension out of my shoulders, and after a deep
breath I arrange myself into position again. Backward press.

The number is 401C.

One of the most boring, simple dives.

I first learned it when I was seven or eight, barely heavy enough
to get the elevation I needed to fit my tuck in. Its degree of difficulty
is low enough that I retired it from my dive sheet somewhere in
high school. *It'd be leaving points on the judges' table*, Coach Kumar
had said.

And now, here I am. Deltoids shaking. Heart in my throat. Too close to tears.

*If you're not afraid of getting hurt, what are you afraid of?*

Sam's voice is needling and insistent and so loud, only one thing will shut it up: I take off, the rush of the air drowning every other sound, the water swallowing all my doubts.

When I lift myself out of the pool, Bree is there, holding out my shammy. "That looked great. Seriously, Scarlett, your rip entry is one of the best I've ever seen. Barely any splash."

I smile as I dry my face. She's the most easygoing twin. Bella remains a shrouded, aloof mystery to me.

"Toes were so pointed, too. I love your back tuck."

*Back.*

*Tuck.*

I almost say it. *Almost* admit to her that it's not the dive I was going for. There's several of us in the pool at any given time, training is hectic, and I'm not sure whether anyone but the coaches is aware that in the sixteen months since my injury, I haven't managed a single inward dive.

"Vandy, come here." Coach Sima motions for me, and I head over, bracing myself for a (gentle?) reminder that if I don't figure out my inward dive before the season, I might as well not bother competing, *I ain't trying to put pressure on you, 'cause the pressure's already there . . . How's that therapy going?*

*If you're not afraid of getting hurt, what are you afraid of?*

"You done with drills? Come to my office for a minute."

My heart jumps in my throat. Coach is not the type to request privacy. He lives to make fun of us, put us on the spot and watch us squirm. Every correction, criticism, conversation, is public.

The office is for the *bad* ones.

I nod helplessly, wrap a towel around my body, and follow him inside, taking the chair he points at. I squeeze my eyes shut while he walks around his desk. By the time he's sitting, I'm almost collected.

"Listen, Vandy. This is gonna be hard to hear."

I swallow, but my mouth is dry. "I know," I say. "I know, and—I'm working on it. My therapist gave me some mental exercises that—"

"Exercises? Ah, *that*. No, it's fine. It's not what this is about."

I frown. "What, then?"

"Victoria's out. It's official."

I look at my lap and take a deep breath, blinking against the pressure at the back of my eyes. I knew this was a possibility, but there's something about the words being said out loud that's so devastating, I stop breathing for a handful of seconds.

"Is she redshirting?"

Coach shakes his head. I'm not surprised. Victoria *could* take the season off and come back for a fifth year with NCAA eligibility, but she'd have to delay graduation, and she already has a job offer from the startup where she interned in the summer. "It's a bad injury, Vandy."

It's over, then. Victoria spent her entire life training, hours every day, every week, every month of every year. Traveling for meets. A constantly bruised body, and early mornings, and *Sorry, I cannot hang out this weekend*. A damn gap between a portable board and a crash mat, and it's all over.

I blink fast. I have no right to cry. It's not *my* injury to cry about. "Do the others know?"

"Pen's telling the twins right now."

The twins, and . . . that's it. Because there's only four of us left. Like a shark bit a limb off. I clench my jaw. "It's so fucking *unfair*."

"Language, Vandy." He slouches back in his chair, rubbing his face with one hand, and I wonder how many other times this has happened to him. How many careers, interrupted. Heartbroken divers and unfulfilled talents. "And yes, it's *very* fucking unfair."

I swallow and pull myself together. This is not about *me*. "Do you know where she is? I'd love to see her—"

"Vandy, there's a reason I'm telling you separately. I want you to consider pairing up with Pen on the synchro."

"What?"

"You two won't have much time to train together, but this could work. You're both stronger on the platform than on the board, and your height and body types are nearly identical—judges love that."

"My inward—"

"Listen." He gives me a level stare. "If you haven't recovered your inward dives by the start of the season, we have other, more serious problems than the synchro."

He's painfully right.

"You don't have to say yes. As you know, Pen is very strong in all her individual events, and doesn't need to be doing synchro. But I think there is potential here."

"What about . . . I don't like the idea of replacing Victoria."

"This is not a tribute band situation. You and Pen will have your own dive sheet and partnership. You're not filling anyone's shoes— you're starting from scratch."

I rub my temple. "Still, how will *Victoria* feel about this?"

His round, scraggly face curves into a small, sad smile. "It's not you or Victoria, Vandy. It's you, or nobody else."

# CHAPTER 19

**O**N SATURDAY, I TAKE THE MCAT.

Or maybe the MCAT takes *me*. I'm no linguist, but afterward I lie face down on the couch while Maryam stacks an increasingly tall pile of textbooks on my butt. ("JengAss, this fall's hottest game.") There seems to be little agency in what I was put through.

I won't get the results for a month, but my brain zapped so many times during the test, I don't think I did well. I *could* retake, but med schools will still get to see my bad scores, and the next testing opportunity will be in January, during the season, and—why do I have no memories of my critical analysis and reasoning part? A fugue state, clearly. I blacked out and rubbed against the proctor to scrounge up a couple more points.

My skull feels like oatmeal, the instant, microwavable kind. And in a shocking turn of events, I have plans for the night.

"It's a good thing, it'll take your mind off the test," Maryam says, an evil glint in her eyes, a cackle when I scowl. She knows that compounding my academic exhaustion with social exhaustion is only going to drive me even closer to the edge of lucidity. She just wants to catch me making out with the spin mop in our closet.

"Why do you look like you just donated a chunk of your pancreas to the organs museum?" Pen asks when I sit in the passenger seat of her car.

"That is such a *good* summary of what I feel like right now."

She flips her hair. "Why, yes, I *am* minoring in creative writing." We're going to the twins' birthday party, which is happening at the house of the Shapiro twins, whom they are *still* dating. Pen's car is a cozy mess of slushy cups, protein bar wrappers, and about twelve poorly crocheted animals hanging from the rearview mirror. "My baby cousin makes them for me, and yes, I'm aware they're a driving hazard, Luk has been very vocal about it." She grins at me over the warm beats of a K-pop playlist. "Are you sick?"

"Nope. Just took the MCAT."

"What's the—hang on, is that the seven-hour test for med schools?"

"Yup."

"Oh my god. Lukas took it last year." She pulls out of the parking lot. "He was *toast* after that."

"I'm starting to suspect it's part of a Big Pharma conspiracy to force us to seek psychiatric care." I sink back against the headrest, and have no reason to ask, but still do: "Did Lukas do well?"

"I think so?" She glances at the directions. "He was *satisfied*, which is unheard of. I think the score was 525."

I almost choke on my tongue. Screw Lukas Blomqvist and his 525. Is it too much to ask for a bilingual Olympic gold medalist to *not* be in the ninety-ninth percentile for the test I've bombed?

"Actually, I'm sure that's what it was. Because we celebrated and, um, Hershey's syrup was involved. *My* idea, of course." She shoots me a proud side-look, and I cannot help huffing out a laugh, even as my insides twist at something I can't quite name—a primordial, swampy blend of academic jealousy, vague horniness, wistfulness at the memory of having someone to share victories with.

"Hey, can I tell you something?"

If she's going to detail her threesome with Lukas and sundae ingredients, I might have to ask her to pull over.

"Synchro partner to synchro partner?" she adds.

Ah, right. I now have a new item to add to my bulleted list titled Things I'll Probably Fail At. I feel like a total impostor, but still nod.

"I have a date," she tells me. Her fingers drum excitedly against the wheel. "Tomorrow."

"With . . . ?"

"This guy I know from my advanced microeconomics class. He's a NARP."

The acronym takes a second to click—non-athletic regular person. "First date?"

Her lips press together. "We've been seeing each other, actually. Mostly as friends. Off campus—I'm trying to, you know, be a little circumspect."

"To avoid your and Lukas's friends?"

"Um. That, too." She fidgets a little with her hair.

"Is he a senior?"

Her silence stretches so long, I half wonder whether she didn't hear me. I'm about to repeat my question, when she says, "He was actually my TA." She rushes to add, "*But* he's a PhD student and, like, only three years older, and that class is over, and he's really cute and has, like, a man bun, which is *totally* my weakness for some reason that I cannot even fathom, and—" She stops and gives me a pleading look, as if expecting me to tell her that it's not a big deal.

I remain quiet. Pick up her phone.

"Vandy? Please, say something?"

I don't. Instead, I scroll down her Spotify app.

"I don't think I'm doing anything, like, unethical." Her voice is unusually high-pitched. "I've always liked him. *I* approached him. It's not like I'm milking him for better grades or . . ."

I set the phone down just as the drums of "Hot for Teacher" by Van Halen fill the cabin.

"Oh my god." She turns to me, exhaling an outraged laugh. "Vandy, I hate you so much."

I pout. "Is it because I cannot grade your macroeconomics homework?"

"It's micro and—" She slaps me on the arm. "Oh my *god*."

I sigh dramatically and tap my chin. "Maybe I should give Mrs. Sima a heads-up."

"About *what*?"

"Your insatiable hunger for older pedagogues, of course."

She shouts a new peal of laughter, and by the time we make it to the party, the song has played twice, and we both have tears rolling from our eyes.

# CHAPTER 20

SOME STUDENT ATHLETES ARE ABLE TO HAVE HIGH GPAS, sport their little hearts out, and maintain fulfilling and exciting social calendars that yield solid lifelong friendships.

I am *not* one of them.

In high school, my catchphrase was "Sorry, I'm busy"—to the point that a bunch of people in Josh's friend group *gasped* when I showed up for prom with him. I still remember the icy slither in my stomach when I overheard them from the bathroom stall, something giggled like *Did she not have to throw herself from a cliff tonight?*

I didn't take it personally. Josh was outgoing and kind and had lots of buddies I never bothered to get to know. They probably thought I was just another athlete with a god complex, and maybe they weren't wrong. At the time, I felt invincible, like all I had to do was put in the work, and I'd reap the rewards. I felt *in control*, tungsten coated, and the people making fun of my dedication to diving or studying or *overachieving* were never going to scratch my shell.

But that armor is long gone, stripped off by time, injury, and the painful realization that deserving and obtaining are two vastly different things. When I trail after Pen inside the Shapiros' hallway, and Kyle's eyes widen in shock, I feel a little tender.

"ScarVan?" he booms over the generic pop music. "Showing up for a *party*?" He sounds like a children's librarian seeing Judy Blume show up unannounced: happy, but nonetheless baffled.

"Is that a thing people call me?" I murmur in Pen's ear.

"People? No. Kyle? I was PenRo for half of sophomore year. Don't let him see that you don't like it, or it'll stick forever and he'll use it at your eulogy—at which, yes, he'll manage to book a speaking engagement. He's *that* good."

I take that advice to heart and produce my most unbothered smile. "Hey, Kyle."

"Look at you." His eyes travel down my sweater and shorts. "Haven't seen you in civilian clothes in years."

"She was observing the period of mourning that is customary for her religion," Pen says solemnly.

Kyle lifts a hand to his nape, taken aback. "Oh, man, I'm sorry. Who did you, um, lose, if I may—"

"No, you may not," Pen scolds.

He winces, steals an unopened can of Budweiser from a passing freshman, and presses it into my hand. "Here. Feel better, ScarVan."

"Don't laugh," Pen mutters in my ear, pinching my hip. "Kyle, where's Luk?"

"He and Hasan are talking about soccer—sorry, *football*—somewhere in the living room. It's so European in there, I had to get out before my dick turned into a bidet."

"See you later, KyJess." Pen takes my hand and drags me deeper into the house. There must be thirty or forty people here, and while I'd probably be able to name only a fifth, most faces are familiar. "All the swimmers came," she tells me with a smile, like it's a *good* thing. And it is, I guess. They're tight-knit. Hang out every preseason weekend. It's nice, just . . .

"There's Luk," she adds, pulling me through the throng of too-hot bodies. He's on the couch with Rachel and a few others, fingers closed around a dark glass bottle, wholly focused on what Hasan is saying. He laughs and shakes his head, gesturing as he explains something. The memory of his hand on me is so visceral, my heart explodes in my stomach.

"Restroom," I tell Pen. "Be right back."

I'm just not in the mood for this. And by *this*, I mean the way Lukas looks at me, like he can see the little crumpled-up piece of paper tucked in a corner of my head, the one where I wrote down my secrets. Like he could easily flatten it and read every last word.

He's unnerving. And other things I'd rather not deal with.

I wander into the kitchen. Lots of swimmers smile and say hi, but I can tell that they either can't fully place me, or they're surprised to see me. I sip on my beer, trying to avoid creating fanfiction of people's smallest facial expressions until I'm certain that they despise me. If only googling whether someone hates me were a possibility.

When was the last house party I went to? Maybe on my recruitment trip, when an upperclassman shoved a White Claw in my hands and left me terrified—half that someone would snitch to the coaches that I'd drunk it, half that they'd . . . still snitch to them, that I was too lame to drink.

Bree finds me a minute later, and I wish her a happy birthday, clumsily returning her hug. "I'm so happy you came," she tells me. "Bella's devastated that Victoria won't."

"I'm so happy to be here, too."

It's not true, but spending the next twenty minutes chatting with her helps. For the following fifteen it's a swimmer who shadowed me in a chem class last year during his recruitment trip, but he's clearly looking to hook up with another guy on the team, and when it becomes obvious that I'm in their way, I whip out another restroom excuse. Upstairs I find a small sunroom, and slump on an IKEA Poäng chair—the exact copy of the one Maryam and I assembled last year, during a macabre comedy of errors that nearly became a fatal, mutual murder. Can't believe we managed to move past that one.

I check my phone, and boy it's a mistake. Herr Karl-Heinz's social life must be as active as mine, because four minutes ago he posted the results of our latest German test. I know better than to check, but I do just that and ruin what's left of my day.

Because it's a C. With a message.

*Scarlett—may I call you Scharlach? Let me know if you'd like to talk about ways to improve your performance. I'd love to see you succeed, and there is no shame in asking for help. Viel Glück!*

I cross my legs on Poäng and sink my face into my hands.

Once upon a time, not so long ago, I didn't *need* help.

I was a competent diver.

I had a boyfriend and good grades.

Once upon a time, I had shit under control. And then I must have pulled the wrong book from the JengAss tower, because everything is collapsing and—

"Not a good night?"

I don't need to look up to know it's Lukas, but I do it anyway, hating the flush that immediately hits my cheek. He fills the doorframe in a way I struggle to comprehend, ominous, backlit, the strong lines of his face destructively handsome. His muscular arms hold both jambs, and he's once again barefoot, even though no such request was made of guests upon arrival.

"It's good, I just . . ."

His eyebrow lifts, inquisitive, and I fall quiet. "Pen was looking for you," he says.

"Oh? Does she—are we leaving?"

"Just checking in." His lips curve a little. "She's protective of you."

She has been lovely, really. Taking me under her wing. I'm wondering why *Lukas* came to find me, but as usual he's reading my mind.

"Just trying to escape being offered coke for the third time."

"The doping officers would love that."

"I considered doing a line, just to give them something to talk about."

I laugh quietly. Some of the tension relaxes. "I was going to return downstairs in a minute. I just . . . I'm tired, I think."

"MCAT'll do that to you."

How does he . . . ? "Did Pen tell you?"

"You did."

"When—oh." On Wednesday. The Day. The Day of the Touch. "It's so *barbaric*."

"Yup."

"I feel like I could sleep for a hundred hours."

"Hyperbole?"

I snort. "Not this time."

"I figured. You think you did well?"

"I think I'd rather carve out my liver like Prometheus than retake it, so I better have. But I doubt it. And then I got a C on my German test," I add, even though I shouldn't—because he didn't ask. I try to sound self-deprecating, like I don't care too much about my recently developed inability to . . . to *function*.

Of course, he reads right through it. "Lots of med schools don't have foreign language requirements, Scarlett."

So unnervingly compelling, the way my name is distorted through his accent, *inside* his mouth. "It looks good, though."

"So does a near-perfect GPA."

"I don't have—"

"Yes, you do."

I pinch my lips. "How do you even—"

"I don't. But you're not the type to leave that to chance."

I nod, wishing he left—or came all the way in. It's confounding, the way he's just on the edge. *He* is confounding. "Why did you do that? On Wednesday." As far as questions go, this is the Budweiser's more than mine. But once it floats between us, I realize how much I need to know. If he pretends not to understand what I mean, I will scream. Something wild and vicious will come out of my throat, and it'll have every single person in this house stop by the knife block and then stampede upstairs. It will be so liberating.

Lukas, though, doesn't give me the satisfaction. "Because you seemed . . . touch starved."

I blink at him once. Maybe twice.

"And lonely."

He pushes away from the frame, *finally* inside. My brain hums, then blanks.

"A little hungry, too." He's not talking about food.

"You—" I shake my head. Where *is* his filter? Was he born without one? How did Pen ever get used to this? "You don't even know me."

"I don't. But no one else here does, either, which proves my point." He stops a few feet from me, and the room shrinks to half its original size.

I'm at a bit of a bifurcation. I could play the outraged, derisive, *Who the fuck do you think you are?* card, and it would be wholly within my rights. As tired as I am, though, I just want to understand him. "The way you're acting with me. What you did on Wednesday. Is it some kind of game? I can't figure out if you're hitting on me, or just . . . Is it because I didn't take you up on your offer when you emailed? Are you trying to convince me that I made a mistake?"

"I have no interest in that." I must look skeptical, because he continues. "What I want from you requires enthusiastic consent, not *convincing*."

I rub my thumb against my eyes, trying to untangle this mess. "Are you trying to use me to get back at Pen for breaking up with you?"

He seems amused. "It would be a very ineffective way to go about it, since she's the one who first suggested we do this."

"Is it an ego thing, then? Am I the first person to ever reject you? I know that with all the medals, and the way you look . . . but the thing is, not *every* girl is attracted to you—"

"You are, though."

This time, an affronted gasp makes its way out of me.

"Come on." His smile is faint. "You're always flushing or fidgeting. You either do your best to not look at me, or you stare."

"I'm just a generally awkward person who—"

"You are. You're also uncomfortable with men. This, though, is different. It doesn't take a stratospheric ego to figure it out, not when your face is . . . You're not good at hiding anything, Scarlett. I could tell when you didn't know I existed, and I could tell when you became aware of me."

My stomach sinks, and I want to deny it so, *so* bad, my throat itches. Instead I bury my face in my hands and pretend that this, the last two weeks, the last two *years*, didn't happen. I'm going to fall asleep here, cradled within Poäng's loving embrace, and wake up as a freshman, on the day of the NCAA finals.

A redo. I won't mess up that inward, get those unmanageable curtain bangs, or *ever* acknowledge the existence of Lukas Blomqvist.

Who's currently taking my wrists and pulling my hands down. He kneels in front of me, still managing to be imposing. I'm not a thin-boned, birdlike creature, but his hands swallow my entire forearms, and liquid heat crawls up my spine. It gets worse when he transfers his hold to the right, and the knuckle of his free index finger slides to tilt up my chin, forcing me to meet his eyes.

I expect triumph, maybe some gloating. Not a genuinely puzzled, "Why are you embarrassed about this?"

I groan. "Maybe I just don't want to shovel more fuel into some guy's already overactive hubris furnace?"

"That's not it."

I squeeze my eyes shut. "It's just never happened to me."

"What has never happened?"

I swallow. This whole conversation is so . . . *baring.* "I've just never been attracted to someone that nearly everyone else in the universe seems to be attracted to."

"You think I *care* whether people are attracted to me?" He sounds almost offended at the idea. But . . .

"Yes?"

"Why would I?"

"I . . . because?"

"No, seriously." His accent seems to be a little thicker. "Why would I care about *everyone in the universe* being attracted to me? What would I get from that?"

"The certainty that the sack of skin and meat you're saddled with as you walk god's green earth is pleasing to them, and that they will . . . I don't know, have sex with you, if you want?"

His palm shifts upward, gripping the side of my face, the hinge of my jaw. His thumb rests right below my lower lip.

"Come on, Scarlett." His mouth twitches. "You know who I want to have sex with."

His low voice makes my entire body spark, and brooks no misunderstanding.

"Look at you." His expression softens to something almost tender. "Is it so hard to believe that I saw you, and thought that you needed touching?"

I cannot breathe. "How?"

"I have no idea. But I saw you, and you made sense to me. And the more I looked, the more I knew how hard you work. How it paid off until it didn't. How little you like chaos. You want to maintain control in every aspect of your life, and yet you are unraveling. And that was *before* I knew that you're kinky as shit."

The pad of his thumb presses against my bottom lip, a shock of heat to my system. I inhale, sandalwood and chlorine and beer flooding my lungs and my brain.

"You know what fucks with my head?" It must be a rhetorical question, because he continues: "You're at ease with me. I don't think you realize it, but you tend to move closer when others are around. Sometimes you look to me, for reassurance maybe. And we're alone right now and there are no signs of distress, and—at some point you chose to *trust* me, and you get why that gets me going so hard, right?" His voice is a slow roll that starts in his chest, travels through our limbs, ends in the red of my cheeks, the spill between my legs.

For people like me, like him—like *us*—trust is the real currency. I nod, hazy.

"Thank fuck," he exhales, and my lips part against his thumb without meaning to.

It gives him an idea, or maybe it was his plan all along. His finger slips inside, hooks just behind my teeth, hot and big and salty over the flat of my tongue. I let out a choked gasp and feel it inside me, electric, syrupy. Lukas could do whatever he wants to me, and I'd welcome it. Push the pad of his thumb deeper inside my mouth. Stand, undo his belt and his pants, grab the back of my head and—

He pulls back, and it's like the first dive of every morning practice—freezing water slapping against my skin, jerking me awake. He stands and walks away, leaning against the doorframe. His arms fold on his chest, casual, unaffected. I was, maybe still am, ready to do pretty unspeakable things for him. In an open room. With thirty to forty people downstairs. If only he were to ask.

The shame eats at the arousal in my belly.

I guess I'm *that* desperate. I guess I could walk myself into interstate traffic.

"Okay." Lukas's voice snaps me out of my self-flagellating party. He looks authoritative. Making decisions. Laying out timelines. "We have to . . . this is what we're going to do. You have two options. Say nothing, and I won't ever bring up anything like this again. You and I meet at Avery, we work together on Olive's project, whatever you want. But this conversation and the ones before never happened. Pen never got drunk, never told me about you. I never noticed you. I never touched you."

*Anything like this*, he said. *This.* So vague. I understand exactly what he's talking about. "The alternative?" I ask, surprised at how firm my voice is.

"Say the word, and . . ." His jaw tightens. I marvel at the play of lights on the hollow of his cheekbones. "We're going to find a time and place to meet." It's a subtle shift, but his fist tightens under the elbow, knuckles bleeding white. It's a sign, a *promise*. Goose bumps chill my skin. "And we're going to negotiate."

He gives me all the time I need to reply, and then some. He slouches, lazy, composed, and I'm struck by how much I want to say something, by how difficult it is. I can't think clearly around the pounding of my heart. Around the odd mix of fear of making a mistake, fear of *not* making a mistake, and just pure fear lodged behind my sternum.

He gives me all the time I need, and when I stare in helpless silence, he's true to his word. There is a moment of twitching tension, but it fades immediately. His smile is warm. "I'll see you around, Scarlett." Then he's gone, padding away barefoot, as confident as when he arrived.

I, however, am a coward.

I beat myself up about it for five minutes, and it takes me ten more to collect myself enough to return downstairs. The lights have dimmed, and the party has gathered in the living room, around a sheet cake decorated with too many lit candles.

". . . the thought process behind it?" someone is asking.

"I dunno—since Bree's turning twenty-two, and Bella's turning twenty-two—"

"You put *forty-four* candles on their cake?"

"That's just not how it goddamn works, Devin."

Kyle pats Devin on the back. "C'mon, Dale, let the kid show off his math."

"Is it time to cut into that *amazing* cake yet?" a girl next to me yells. There aren't enough seats for everybody, and Pen is perched on one of Lukas's legs, leaning forward as she chats with Rachel. Behind, Lukas is once again talking with Hasan. It's like he never left.

*Stupid*, I tell myself. *Stupid, stupid, stupid.*

"There's actually a surprise we've been working on for a while." Devin clears out some space at the center of the room and looks at Kyle, whose phone is at the ready. "We have a *choreography* for you," Dale declares.

The room fills—cheers, groans, whistles, claps. Bree shoots to her feet, almost flipping the cake over. "Oh my god, is it BTS?"

More excited screams.

"Can't wait for when Coach asks me *how* they pulled a quad and are out for the season," Lukas says.

"Just don't drag BTS into this," Hasan suggests. "Say they were giving a lap dance."

"Shut up, you losers," Pen commands. "This is gonna be the best!"

"Thank you, Pen." Dale salutes her. "For your support, and for helping us refine this over countless sessions. You're a true friend, unlike your boyfriend and *his* boyfriend."

"You guys, it was my pleasure."

Lukas and Hasan exchange amused headshakes, and—

I'm always on the sidelines, always detached from what's happening around me. I never mind. But tonight, watching Lukas laugh with others, something greedy opens up in my stomach.

*A little hungry, too*, he said upstairs. But I think it's more than a little.

I think I might be *ravenous*.

The music starts, and so do some questionable body rolls. Laughter. Nearly everyone takes their phones out, and I do the same. Except, I'm not filming. I'm not even watching. Instead I pull up an old email, type three words, and hit reply.

*When and where?*

Devin and Dale gyrate their hips. Lukas's phone lights up on the coffee table. I see him glance at it once, distractedly. Then again when the message registers.

He doesn't even have to search the crowd. His eyes lift up to meet mine, and when he nods, I finally manage a true, genuine smile.

# CHAPTER 21

**M**ONDAY MORNINGS AT THE POOL ARE USUALLY RELAXED, full of athletes slowly rebooting after their day off. *This* Monday morning, however, the atmosphere around the aquatics center is thicker than the fog.

"Cuts for the swim team," Bree tells me, pale face scrunched together as she wraps tape around her wrist. "They're finalizing the roster."

"Already?"

"Creeps up on me every year, too."

In the locker room, the swimmers' cheerfulness feels forced, and I wonder how they cope. Am I the only one who cries in the shower, and can never find enough air to properly breathe, and opens the fridge hoping to discover a magic portal leading to a Narnia-like society in which competitive sports have been banned?

German, too.

On my way to breakfast, I hear, "Scarlett. A minute?"

It's Lukas—of course it is. No one else calls me by my name. I pause in the Avery lobby and try not to blush, or to remember how many times I checked my phone, email, and physical mailbox yesterday, waiting for him to contact me. Maryam asked me if I was high on glue, which led to a twenty-minute fight over whether the USA Anti-Doping Agency would find that objectionable.

I *could* pretend that in the twenty-four hours he spent ignoring me I changed my mind, but it would probably just give him a chuckle. "Sure." I walk over. Take in his hair, still wet from practice. The freckles hugging his nose and cheekbones. The compression shirt he's wearing does great things for his thick arms, and even more for his chest. "Everything okay?"

"Have you met Johan?" He points at the guy next to him, whom I recognize as The Other Swede. He looks like he could be Lukas's cousin, just blond.

"I'm Scarlett, nice to meet you." I smile and hold out my hand.

Which he takes, even as he says, "It's also very nice to see you, but we already met."

*Shit.* "Oh. Um, right, of course, I—"

"Don't take it personally, Johan. She didn't remember meeting me, either." Lukas's smile, somewhere between teasing and tender, has me flushing. He and Johan have a brief Swedish conversation that ends with Johan nodding, and then smiling at me like we're more than one—no, *two*-time acquaintances. Like he knows *things* about me.

I look up at them, neck craning. They could be talking about the stock market economies, their favorite dactylic pentameters, or the size of my boobs—I have no way of telling. Did I hear the word *troll*?

"What was that?" I ask Lukas after Johan leaves.

"He asked me if we're together."

Does he know Lukas broke up with Pen? "And what did you say?"

"The truth."

"Which is?"

I'm beginning to suspect that a conversation is over when Lukas

Blomqvist decides he's had enough, because he doesn't reply. Instead he reaches into his pocket and hands me a sheet of paper, folded once and then again. I open it out, and—

*Oh my god.*

Cheeks on fire, I hug it to my chest. Where my heart is *racing* against my ribs.

"You know what that is?" he asks casually, like he's talking about calculating a molecular orbital and not—

"Bye, Luk!" A small group of swimmers walks by us. "See you later, Sweedy," another adds, trailing behind them.

"Great job today, everyone," Lukas says. Then, still looking at his teammates, but lower: "Breathe, Scarlett."

I'm trying. I'm *trying*, but it's not easy.

"We're going to need to work on this," he says.

"On w-what?" I scrape out.

"Your tendency to let your vital organs shut down whenever something unexpected happens. Your neurons can only take so many anoxic events." We're in the middle of the lobby of our place of employment. Lukas's voice is low and warm. And in my hand . . .

In my hand there is a list of the filthiest things two people can do to each other.

"Do you know what that is?" he repeats, patient.

I nod, forcing myself to inhale deeply. *Here, brain, have some oxygen and glucose and . . . porn?* "I am familiar, yes." It just caught me by surprise. And it's not my fault if the first thing I read on it was *cum play*. It's a dramatic sea change—from talking about sex in the vaguest of terms, to holding a piece of paper that proudly proclaims DDLG.

"Ever used one of these?"

"Not really. I . . ." Truthfully, I researched them. And I read them through. And I debated showing them to Josh. And then I realized someone who balked at the idea of nipple clamps would probably not enjoy reading a BDSM checklist that included stuff like *anal fisting, cross mounting,* and *chastity gear.* "No."

"Are you okay with using it now?"

"Yes. I am." *Very* Fifty Shades, Pen would say with a smirk.

*Pen.* God. Will sober Pen still be okay with this?

"Text me when you're done filling it in," he says. All business.

"What about yours?"

"I'm done with mine."

"Can I see it?"

One of those crooked smiles. "Are you trying to copy my homework?"

"Well, it would help."

"And it would save you the ordeal of having to admit to your own wants, wouldn't it?"

He's *absolutely* right. And I am mortified that I even asked. "Okay. I . . . thank you for giving this to me. I'll let you know when I'm done." I make to leave, but a finger slides in the belt loop of my jeans and pulls me back. Close.

"Hey," he says, soft. "I need to know what you need, Scarlett. And whether I can provide it for you."

*It should be me.*

"What if . . ."

"Listen." His thumb and forefinger find my chin and lift it. His eyes are a level, impossibly pretty blue. "I spent the last few years with someone who had no interest in any of this, and have lots of experience with mismatched sex drives. I can handle you not wanting the same things as I do, and I'll never judge you for what you're into. Fuck, some of the things that *I* want—" His laugh is an unamused huff. His hand runs through his hair, tousling it a little.

It occurs to me that maybe it's hard for him, too, coming clean about this. That we both have some baggage when it comes to being honest about what turns us on. And more importantly, that I *want* to know everything about his desires, and it's natural for him to want the same.

"Okay." My smile is small, but sincere. "I'll do it as soon as possible."

"Take your time. Think it through."

I snort. "I feel like the weak link in a group project. Last to do her part."

"Hmm. That's not incorrect."

I poke at him. My index finger finds the side of his stomach, and for a moment I cannot process the *everything* of what I'm feeling. The solid muscle of his obliques, the lack of yield, the shock of warmth.

Because he may have touched me, but *I* never touched *him* before. And he knows that, too, because the following silence stretches long, as thick as molasses.

"How's German going?" he asks quietly.

I let my head hang low. Listen to his soft, deep chuckle. "About as well as my other classes. I'm not good at this stuff."

"What stuff?"

I gesture vaguely. "Pronouncing Foucault? Diving into the marketplace of ideas? Telling apart different waves of feminism? *Opining.*" I shrug. "Textual analysis is way harder than logarithmic differentiation."

He stares down at me like I'm—god. Like I'm *cute*? I'm not a fan of that patronizing look. At least I shouldn't be. *All messed up.* Yup, that's me.

"Anything I can do?" he offers.

"I don't know. Do you speak German?"

"Despite what you Americans believe, Europe is not a single country where everyone speaks—"

I quietly flip him off, and he laughs like I handed him the exact thing he wanted. Then there's another silence, smaller, lighter, until he says, "You'll text me, then." Not a question, but I nod, feeling a warm, pulsating sort of anticipation spread through me, one that has as much to do with the list as with . . . I'm not sure.

"Go, Scarlett. You need to eat breakfast."

Right. Yup. Did I tell him where I was heading? Doesn't matter.

I feel the heft of his eyes on me all the way to the dining hall, even after it becomes a physical impossibility.

◆　◆　◆

My first synchro practice is that afternoon.

I try to play it cool, like it's not a big deal, but last year, while Pen and Victoria placed sixth at the Pac-12 finals, I was . . . home, probably trimming my toenails. Binge-watching *The Great British Bake Off* was likely part of it, too. I'm the new kid here, and I'm painfully aware of it as I stand between Pen, Coach Sima, and two volunteer coaches who I really wish had not decided to stick around to witness my unavoidable screwups.

I bet they wish the same, especially thirty minutes and fifty takeoffs later, after Pen and I have been working on matching the simplest of hurdles without the blippiest trace of success. It doesn't help that we've started with dryland, and that we cannot look at the fourth portable board without seeing Victoria and her sheared ligaments.

I know she asked for space, and I get not wanting to be inundated by condolences while still mourning the loss of her sport, but I can't help wishing she were here to make some snide comments on the futility of carbon-based life-forms.

"Pen," Coach Sima says between disapproving sighs, "you're too fast. Your hurdle is about five inches too high, and ugly to boot. Vandy, you're too . . ."

"Slow?"

Coach rubs his temple. "I'm not even sure what's wrong with

your technique. Let's say everything and just start from scratch, okay? Take ten, you two. Have some water. Think about your ancestors and ask yourself whether they'd be proud of your performance today."

Synchro is a scary, three-headed beast. Pairs aren't scored just on the success of the individual dives, but also on how well they harmonize. There are *so many ways* to lose points, and Pen seems to be thinking the same. We sit side by side on the deck, heads bent over our water bottles, and I want to apologize to her. I want to tell her that I'm a mess, and it's my fault. That I'm sorry I'm not Victoria, and I'll try harder, and to please not hate me.

But she's silent, and I'm silent, too. I try not to stare as she takes out her phone and begins tapping at it, wondering if she's mad at me, wondering if—

The first few notes of "Hot for Teacher" fill the air.

My snort is so sudden, I choke on my sip of water.

Everyone turns to give us curious looks, but Pen's eyes are fixed on me, and after a couple of seconds, we're laughing like we haven't just been laid into within an inch of our lives.

Coach is not amused, but the weight in my chest feels a thousand pounds lighter.

# CHAPTER 22

**I**T TAKES ME TWO DAYS TO GO THROUGH THE LIST.

I'd love to say that it's because some of the items are things I've never heard of and require a large amount of research, but there are only a handful I'm not already familiar with. I may have to spend some time on Google to figure out what shrimping is—and come away with no more clarity than when I started—but I've known what a sybian is since I figured out how to use the incognito tab on my browser.

Sexual deviant, and all that.

The reason I spend so long on each item is that they require an almost ridiculous amount of introspection. I've never been in the position to be fully sincere about my fantasies, and as a result I don't yet know what they are. My sex life with Josh was great: he made sure I had all the orgasms I could ever want, helped me feel beautiful and sexy, and we laughed *a lot*. That time I was too mortified to tell him outright that I was on my period and used so many euphemisms, he thought I had terminal cancer. When he accidentally got Minions novelty condoms. His harrowing screech of pain after I tried to give him a hand job seconds after hand sanitizing. That kind of stuff.

But when I asked him to be rougher with me, he suggested that I bring it up in therapy and get my psychologist's take on "whether it's a good idea, or, um, something oedipal that'll fuck you up for the next decade?" After that, I tried to pretend I didn't have certain desires, and he half-heartedly slapped my butt a couple of times.

So it takes forty-eight hours, but on Wednesday night, I text Lukas: Done.

And, at last, save his name on my phone.

We decide to meet up that night. Then the following morning. Then the following night. Every time, he cancels at the last minute. The only explanation: Something urgent.

I see him at practice, which means that he's not ill, injured, or expelled from Stanford for crimes against public decency. I'm starting to suspect he's changed his mind—and then he skips our meeting with Zach and Dr. Smith.

"He won't be joining us," she tells me. "He mentioned something about . . . captain stuff? Not Crunch, sadly. God, I haven't had those in a while." She chews her lower lip for a moment, writes Buy Cap'n Crunch on one of her Post-its, and then proceeds to slay at cancer biology nonstop for forty-five minutes.

I don't hear from Lukas until Friday night, after a difficult practice that leaves me in a bad mood. Pen and I are alone in the locker room, and I've been trying to untangle my hair for so long, my entire upper body aches.

"Any plans for tonight?" she asks.

I shake my head. Then say, "I have these . . . exercises that my therapist is making me do."

"Oh?" Her eyes catch mine in the mirror. She's putting on foundation, which is an unusual post-practice level of grooming. "For what?"

"My most ingrate children." Her brow knits in confusion, so I sigh. "My inward dives."

Her eyes widen in understanding. I haven't discussed my issues with anyone on the team, but Pen is my synchro partner, and she must have noticed that we haven't practiced a single inward dive.

I don't mind. I know she gets it—the way our brains cannot help hiccuping. "What are the exercises like?"

"Visualization, mostly. The purpose is to . . . rewire my brain. Overwrite the negative feelings I automatically associate with certain dives with more neutral ones." All I need is the most basic, *shittiest* inward dive. The bar is so low, it's underground with the turnips.

Pen puts down her brush. Her hand reaches out to squeeze mine, and I love, love, *love* that she doesn't say shit like *You can do it. Believe in yourself. It'll be a piece of cake. Positive thinking.* She's just quietly there for me, green eyes full of understanding and a compassion that's not pity, and that's all I need.

I squeeze back. There's something in my throat, and I have to swallow past it before asking, "What about you? Any plans?"

"Actually." Her lips twitch. "I'm meeting Hot Teacher. He's . . . making dinner for me—Vandy, please, regain control of your jaw."

I try. It's not easy. "How was last weekend?"

"Good. Great. We chatted. Talked about our lives. We made out. You know, that kind of stuff."

I half gasp, half laugh, delighted. "You *made out.*"

"Way to focus on the one single non-PG item on my list." But she's giggling, clearly elated. We both lean our shoulders against the mirror, facing each other. "I really, *really* like being with him," she tells me, low, serious. Her smile dims a little, but she's not sad. "I think it was a good choice, breaking up with Lukas."

It's my turn to reach for her hand. "I'm so glad you're happy."

When her phone rings, she frantically gathers her stuff and stops for a short hug, and then she disappears in a burst of energy that's so *her*, I cannot stop smiling even after she's gone.

And, once again, I have *not* told her about Lukas and me.

I tried it on Monday, with the list burning in the pocket of my shorts. On Wednesday, when we lingered in front of Avery and exchanged high school diving stories. This morning at breakfast, after I helped her out with orgo homework while she read through my English essay.

*Tell her*, I ordered myself.

But tell her *what*? That Lukas and I might be exchanging A4 papers? In order to *maybe* initiate a sexual relationship, *if* we are compatible, *if* it works with our schedules, *if* he hasn't changed his mind, *if* he doesn't find someone else? It's all so hypothetical, talking about it so early in the process just seems like courting trouble.

I head home, wondering whether Maryam will do her usual bit if she catches me mid–visualization exercise: cut two cucumber slices and slap them over my closed eyes. The text I receive stops me in the middle of the sidewalk on Stanford Way.

Free? It's Lukas. My pulse trips, but quickly steadies. I tilt my head and type:

SCARLETT: In Sweden, when you text, do they charge you by the word?

LUKAS: There's an emoji surcharge, but I'll make an exception for you:

LUKAS: 👆

I laugh out loud—a yappy sound that has me glancing around to make sure no one noticed.

LUKAS: Are you free tonight, Scarlett Vandermeer?

SCARLETT: For someone with proper grammar? Always.

LUKAS: Meet me at Green in ten.

Why does he want to meet in the library? Is this for Dr. Smith's project? Am I . . . misunderstanding?

When I arrive, he's already leaning against the wall by the elevator—eyes closed, thick neck, incongruous freckles. He's wearing black joggers and a red T-shirt, once again an almost exact replica of the outfit *I* have on, and he looks . . . tired. Something that lives between curiosity and admiration has me stopping to observe him—*him*, and the energy that flows in his surroundings.

"That's the guy who won the Olympics—the swimmer?" a boy whispers to a friend. Three girls walk past him in the opposite direction, sneaking glances that become progressively less covert.

I'd love an NCAA title or two, let alone the Olympics, but I don't think I envy this facet of Lukas's success. Being singled out. Generic appreciation from people who remember that swimming exists once every four years.

"Hey," I say.

His eyes open slowly, as though whirring to life. For a moment he looks so exhausted, my instinct is to scream, *Go home, to bed, right now.* Then his lips curve, just because *I* am *here*, and my heart beats in my belly.

"Come on."

I follow him in silence to a study room. It doesn't provide much privacy, not with glass walls. They're all built like that—because, I assume, librarians have graduate degrees and better things to do than walk into teenagers groping each other. Or cleaning up used condoms.

I linger next to a chair, not yet taking a seat. Watch Lukas pull a folded piece of paper out of his backpack, toss it over the table in my direction, and stand kitty-corner from me.

I feel, instantly, very hot. Or cold.

"Why the library?" I ask, eyes fixed on the paper.

"We could go to my place, but I figured you wouldn't want Kyle and Hasan overhearing."

I nod, trying to come to terms with the fact that his list is right *there*. I could reach out and pick it up and *know*.

"Scarlett." Lukas leans forward, clearly amused. "We talked about this."

"About what?"

"You need to breathe."

I inhale sharply. Fill my lungs. "Right, yes, I'm fine. I . . . what should I . . . ?"

"Before we start, I'd like to know something."

I sneak another glance at the folded paper. "Yes?"

"What happened with your father?"

My eyes bounce to his. I feel like he grabbed me by the neck without warning. "My father? How is this relevant?" An atrocious possibility occurs to me. "Please, don't tell me that you're looking for some deep-seated past trauma to explain what I like."

His eyebrow arches. "I think you can give me a little more credit than that."

"Then why?"

"You don't have to tell me. It's not a deal-breaker. But you clearly have triggers, and understanding what happened might help me steer away."

Lukas doesn't need the whole story for that. But he and I have already been so open with each other, I don't mind him knowing. *And*, I have no reason to be embarrassed. So I square my shoulders, hold his eyes, and try to be as factual as possible. "Over the years, my dad became increasingly abusive of both me and my stepmother. By the end, he was tracking all our movements, monitoring our interactions, isolating us from the rest of the world and from each other. He'd belittle us. Criticize us. Yell for no reason. He was financially controlling. I'm not sure how it got so bad, only that it was gradual. Barb and I were both very good at pretending that it was all normal, and that Dad was just having a string of bad days. Then, when I was thirteen, Barb picked me up from school. I began crying and begging her to not take me home, and she decided to put an end to it. She left Dad, managed to get custody, put us both in therapy." Years of terror, condensed into a few dozen words. Years in which my sole happy place was diving. "I can usually work through my triggers. I don't like raised voices, but it's not a hard limit. And I actually *like* being handled roughly. Control. Discipline. As long as it's within specific contexts." I can tell from his eyes that he understands what I mean. It makes sense in his gut as much as in mine. "The one thing Dad did . . ." I look away. "Degradation kink is a thing, and I'm never going to judge . . . but if you want to call me ugly, or disgusting, or worthless—"

"Jesus, Scarlett."

"—then we're probably not going to be able to—"

"Hey." He lifts my chin. "Look at me."

*I am*, I want to say. Except, I lowered my gaze to my feet without realizing it.

"I'm not interested in demeaning you in any way. Okay?" In his eyes I find no disappointment—just a promise. He doesn't let go until I nod, and once I'm free, I swallow. Take my phone out of my pocket. Gently, hoping he won't notice my trembling hands, I pop its case off.

When he sees the piece of paper lodged inside, he smiles faintly. "Guarding it closely, huh?"

I drop it on the table, next to his. I'm not sure how to explain the sticky, toe-curling, happiness-creating heat that spreads through my limbs whenever I think about the list being *there*. All my secrets. All his questions. The potential for this improbable, dizzying, sharp thing between us, never too far from my body.

"How do you want to do this?" I ask, a little too breathless to sound businesslike. "Do you want to put them next to each other and compare, or . . . ?"

He reaches out and grabs mine, stretching it out before I'm even done formulating the thought, eyes scanning horizontally across the page. There's nothing jerky or hurried about his movements, but watching him feels like a natural disaster, something unstoppable that I'm allowed to witness but not interfere with.

I rock on my heels as he reads, the little room shrinking around us. The air swelters, as hot as my cheeks.

*Pick his list up*, I tell myself. *And read it. Even out the playing field.* But I can't. It's the same brand of bloodcurdling, muscle-freezing paralysis that seizes me when I attempt an inward dive.

*What if*—it doesn't work.

*What if*—I mess up again.

*What if*—I'm being given a chance, and I squander it.

*What if I'm not good enough.*

"I haven't—" I fidget with my hair. "I experimented a bit with my ex, but haven't done much of this stuff." He knows. There is a column on the sheet dedicated to that, which I filled. I completed my assignment. Yet I power through. "There are a couple of things that . . . They'd depend on how you want to approach them. I put asterisks next to them." He lowers the paper and stares at me from over it, unsettlingly undecipherable. I shift on my feet. "And I couldn't understand what—"

I don't get to finish that sentence. Because Lukas Blomqvist takes a long step, pushes me into the wall, and kisses me.

# CHAPTER 23

FIRST FEEL IT IN MY SHOULDER BLADES, SUDDENLY PRESSED against the wall with too much strength. The back of my head could have suffered the same fate, but Lukas's hand cushioned the impact, one palm wrapped against my nape as the other curls around my jaw.

It starts simple enough—lips crushed together, his chest as flush to me as it can physically be, given the differences in our heights. When his tongue brushes against mine, there's an explosion at the base of my spine. Tentative, testing, gentle.

Then, instantly, not at all.

All at once it's filthy. Deep. Sharp. Lukas's lips are hot. His tongue is hot. His fingers, framing my face, are hot.

My entire body is on fire.

He hears the catch of my breath and takes advantage of it, tilting my head farther, an impossible angle that allows him to control the kiss, to lick inside my mouth and leave no place untouched.

It's all-consuming. My mind whites out. I loop my arms around his neck, fuzzy brained and blurry edged, and he finds a way to pull me even closer. He rumbles *something*, but it's not in English. So I focus on his hand traveling down my backbone, palm wide, like he wants to use all of it to feel me, won't miss a single inch of flesh. It reaches the place where the hem of my shirt brushes against my lower back, gently lifts it, and his skin finally—*finally*—touches mine.

I fist my nails in his shoulder.

A whiny sound crawls up my throat. A needy grunt punches out of his.

We breathe fast and loud in each other's mouths, and his grip shifts to my hip, rough and demanding, slipping under the waistband of my joggers—until noise seeps in from the outside.

A cart being pulled. Stacks of books falling. Hushed apologies. We both freeze, coil-muscled, long enough to regain some common sense.

Or at least, for *me* to do that. I unwind my arms from his shoulders, inching back against the wall to put space between us. Lukas seems to have a harder time letting go. Even after his hands leave my waist and my cheeks, he's still unwilling to pull away. He remains there, hulking into me, a cage of bone and muscles and hungry eyes, fists white-knuckled against the wall, on either side of my head. His tattoos clench and release.

He's trying to get himself under control, but he's not quite there.

I reach up to touch the freckles that fill the hollow under his cheekbone, and he exhales a slow laugh, no more than a puff of breath against my temple, stymied and hot. A smile builds inside me in response, and I lift my chin to kiss him again. This time it's a slow thing, even as his heart races against my skin. His lips slip against mine, quiet, almost sweet, and my hand closes in the fabric of his shirt, a silent, reassuring *I'm here, I've got you.*

I savor his face buried in my neck, the tickle of his stubble, the rough, throaty groan as he inhales my skin. His warmth and scent and sheer size, pressing into me. Odd, how this started out frenzied and wild, but evolved into something languid. Just easy.

"We need to stop," I say evenly, running a hand through the

short hair at the back of his head. When he draws away, his eyes are open and earnest.

He pulls a chair back, hair a little tousled. It's an invitation to sit down and give him space.

"You okay?" I ask when we're both at the table.

His nod is quick. When I smile, he smiles back. Tense, maybe, but sincere.

"Do I have to read your list?" I ask, eyeing the still-folded sheet. "Can we just . . . skip that part?"

His eyebrows knit. "No."

"No, I don't have to read it—?"

"No, you cannot skip it."

"Says who?"

"The rules."

I tilt my head. "Who made the rules?"

"Me."

Tilt it more.

"I think you're okay with that, Scarlett," he says.

Tilt it *more.*

"Hard for me to buy that you don't like me taking charge, given what I just read." His words are calm, but my cheeks glow. He's right. In a sense, he might know me better than anyone in the entire world.

I'm not sure how to deal with that.

"You know I'm not some kind of pushover, right? This is about sex. I'm not looking for some kind of twenty-four seven arrangement."

His eyes harden. "Scarlett, you *need* to read my list, because the only way we can do this in a healthy and sane way is if we both know what to expect." His stare is measuring. "What are you afraid of? That there will be things *I* want and *you* don't want, and I'll ask you to do them anyway?"

I glance away.

"The opposite, then." He sighs, and it's tender, the way his fingers move across the table, knuckles brushing my own. An electric spark, liquid, searing, travels through my nerve endings. I'm convinced he'll take my hand, but he pulls back almost immediately.

A wise move, all things considered. Maybe we shouldn't be left alone at all.

He leans back in his chair, the line of his shoulders once again uncompromising. "Scarlett, you—"

A phone—*Lukas's* phone—rings. He checks the caller ID and tilts his head back with a muttered, exhausted word. Once again, not English.

"Are you okay?"

He mutes the call. "I have to go."

"Oh." A mix of disappointment and relief flickers in my stomach. On the one hand, respite. On the other . . . I'm not sure I want to *not* be with him right now. "Anything I can do?"

He shakes his head, massaging his left eye with the heel of his hand. "Eighteen people were cut from the team this week."

*"Eighteen?"*

"I know, it's a fucking mess. Some of the guys were preferred walk-ons and are not happy about it. The coaches are the bad guys, so they've been talking to us to figure out options."

All his cancellations. *Captain stuff.* "I'm sorry."

He nods and leans forward, elbow on the table. "Listen, keep my list. You can take your time, but you're going to have to read it before we . . ."

He doesn't finish. I understand, anyway. "Okay."

"I don't know when the cuts shitshow will clear up, but I need you to know two things."

I force myself not to squirm under his gaze.

"You say *stop*, I stop."

I nod. Nice of him, to remind me that—

"No, Scarlett. There's going to be some trial and error, for sure, but I need you to understand that it doesn't matter how or when. You say *stop*, I stop."

My mouth is dry.

"Repeat it back to me," he orders.

I may have forgotten how to breathe, but still manage to say, "When I say *stop*, you stop."

He nods, pleased. "Do you want another safe word?"

I think about it, then shake my head. I know safe words tend to be unique, and this may not be best practice, but I'm confident that I won't say *stop* unless that's what I want from him. "What's the second thing?" I ask, hiding my trembling hands in my lap.

He exhales a small laugh and stands, grip tightening around the strap of his backpack. "The second thing is that I've read your list. And there is *not* a single thing you want that I don't want more." He leans into me for a kiss that's at once chaste and clinging. By the time he pulls away I'm off-balance, confounded by his heat and his smell. "No need to repeat this one to me."

I watch him walk away. Something occurs to me only when his hand closes around the door handle. "Lukas?"

He turns.

"What about Pen?"

His expression is blank. "What about Pen?"

"Will she mind?"

"You *do* have a terrible memory." His eyebrow lifts, amused. "Pen and I are no longer together."

"I know, but she's also my friend. I need to be sure that she's okay with this. I need her to know that I'm not trying to . . . this is going to be just sex. I'm not trying to start a serious relationship with my friend's ex."

For a moment, I think he will protest. But right as my heart is about to sink, his face an inscrutable mask, he promises, "I'll take care of it."

◆  ◆  ◆

It's not until much, much later that night—after dinner, and my mental exercises, and two hours spent watching one of those political thriller movies that only middle-aged Republican men and Maryam seem to truly enjoy—that I allow myself to think about Lukas's list again.

I lie in my bed, the mint of the toothpaste sweet in my mouth, the day's exhaustion dragging me into sleep, and . . . it's nice, being too tired to work myself up to a panic. Shaking the piece of paper open and reading through Lukas's sharp, neat handwriting doesn't seem like a big deal. In fact, it's almost fun.

He took my sheet when he left, which means that I cannot stretch the two lists side by side and spend hours on an in-depth comparison. But that's not necessary, because I remember every single thing I wrote. And Lukas's—it could be the mirror image of mine.

What I want done to me, he wants to be the one doing it.

*Oh*, I think.

Oh.

Suddenly, the kiss in the library makes lots of sense. I roll into my pillow, smile, and fall asleep that way.

# CHAPTER 24

T HE HIGHLIGHT OF MY SATURDAY MORNING PRACTICE IS
Coach Sima's applause after my back three-and-a-half-
somersault tuck, one of my most difficult dives.

"This might be the best goddamn dive I've seen in my collegiate
coaching career," he tells me from the deck while I'm still in the
pool, wiping droplets from my eyes.

I smile up at him, a burst of the pride I haven't let myself savor
in months neutralizing the too-cold water.

"Which is nice," Coach continues, "since you gotta make up for
the line of zeros you'll get for your inward dives."

"Wow." I elbow myself out of the water. "Can't believe I fell
for it."

"Me neither, Vandy. Me neither."

He scheduled individual corrections for today, which means
that the twins arrive right as I'm leaving Avery. I wonder if Pen's
turn will be after theirs—and then get a single text from her.

PENELOPE: We need to talk.

The period at the end of the sentence does *not* sound affable. I
must have done something terribly wrong, and it could only be one

thing—which happens to be several inches over six feet and rhyme with Bukas Llomqvist. I stare at Pipsqueak's pic on my screen saver and forbid myself to spiral.

*Send me strength, Pip.*

Pen is sitting on the green-despite-the-droughts grass outside the dining hall, eating a red apple. Her sunglasses make her unreadable, but the line of her mouth is somber.

"Hey." I try for a smile and plop down next to her, canting my face toward the sun. "How are you—"

"Vandy."

She won't look at me, but her grip on the apple tightens. Her tone is . . . not promising.

"I'm not sure how to say this without sounding like a total asshole."

Shit.

"I know it's probably unfair of me, but I can't move on until I say my piece." She turns to me. "And you owe it to me to listen." Lowers her sunglasses, stone-faced. "Because . . ." She shakes her head, and my heart is so heavy it'll drag me underground, deep down to the center of the earth, where I'll deservedly burn, because Pen, whom I'm starting to consider a dear friend, is . . .

Grinning?

"I told you so. I told you so. I told you so—*I told you so.* Who told you so? Me. Moi. Penelope Fucking Diana Fucking Ross, ladies and gentlemen and nonbinary friends, *that's who!*" She breaks into the most uncoordinated dance I've ever had the displeasure of witnessing.

I'm going to kill her. "I hate you *so much,*" I hiss, high on relief.

"No, you don't, you *loooove* me."

"I just lost twelve years of my life!"

"It's for the best. Climate change will ravage the earth, and the machine czars will subjugate us to harvest our toes. Anyway, not to repeat myself, but—I told you so."

I groan and bury my face in my hands. "Did Lukas tell you?"

"Yup. He called me early this morning. Said, *You got your drunken wish, Penelope*, and guess how I replied?"

"'I told you so,' seventy-three times?"

"Precisely."

I let a cautious smile stretch my lips. "Are you really okay with the idea of your ex having sex with *your synchro partner*?"

"Put like that, it does sound weird." She giggles. "Can I be honest with you? Like fully, one hundred percent, 'please don't judge me' honest?"

I nod. A new weight threatening to expand in my stomach, but Pen's smile is serene.

"I was the one who initiated our breakup, and I've been worrying about him. It's hard for him to date freely, but I hate the idea of him pining alone while I'm out there having fun. He's a great guy. When no one else wanted anything to do with me, and I thought that my diving career was over, he stood by me. He's loyal. Kind. He's still my best friend. But I have to admit that he's not exactly . . . passionate. It can be hard, for someone as cold as he is. But it sounds like you're mostly interested in him for the sex, and the stuff you guys like"—her voice lowers—"it's hard to romanticize being flogged, right?"

I blink. Did she just—

"I love that you two are gonna get to be all horny and pervy together. Congrats, my friend."

Honestly, she's right. I really like Lukas, and I definitely don't perceive him as cold, but I don't have the emotional bandwidth to catch feelings for him. Not beyond lust, anyway.

"Anyway," she says, "while we're on the matter of horny and pervy . . . as you know, I, too, have taken a lover."

I wince. "*Terrible* phrasing."

"Right? Since Luk is my best friend, you're the only person I can tell about my sexual skylarking."

I savor it, the quiet pleasure of someone wanting to confide in me. "And how's that going?"

She lies back in the grass, and I follow. We stare at the sky for a minute, silent, until she rolls over on her elbows. The glare of the sun beats against my eyes, and I lift my hand like a visor.

"When Lukas and I first started having sex, we were young and had no idea what we were doing. There was a learning curve, you know? But with Theo—"

"Theo the Hot Teacher!"

"Yup. Theo the Hot Teacher." She grins. "It just kind of fell into place. I really like that he's a little more . . ." She sighs. "I really like him. Luk is so *overwhelming* sometimes. Even when he's actively trying *not* to be. Sometimes he'll just be sitting there doing readings for class and still manage to suck up all the air in the room, and I—I kind of get lost in it. I forget about myself. I forget to be my own planet and just start orbiting around him. And I think it feels right to him, to be this monolith of *forbidding* energy, but Theo is so much softer, and . . ." She bites her lower lip. "He calls me honey."

"Oh. Is that a good thing?"

She shrugs, a little embarrassed. "It's trite, I know, but Luk never calls me anything but *Penelope*." She works in a slight Swedish accent. "He's just not naturally affectionate. Theo the Hot Teacher is. And, I slept, as in, actually *slept*, at his place."

"You didn't sleep at Lukas's?"

"Not really. Not if we could help it. We're both fussy sleepers. With Theo it was nice, though."

I nod. I'm happy for her. I'm happy that she got what she wanted. We stare at each other for a while, her elbow brushing my shoulder, the quiet of a Saturday afternoon on campus balmy against our skins. Laughter in the distance, birds, the rustling of trees.

And then something occurs to me.

I sit up. Almost choke on my saliva. "Your name is Penelope *Diana* Ross?"

# CHAPTER 25

**I**T'S A NICE SATURDAY—BECAUSE I HAVE NO PLANS.

After lunch with Pen, I go home, shower until I fool my skin and hair into believing that I wasn't spawned inside a puddle of chlorine, and then catch up with laundry and assignments. Herr Karl-Heinz, may both sides of his pillow always be cold and his favorite fanfiction update every night, shed some light on German's obscure sentence structure. I walked out of his office last week feeling . . . in deep shit, but less alone.

Look at me. Acknowledging my deficiencies. Accepting help.

*It's difficult even for native speakers*, he told me. *You're a STEM major, right? Try to see the rules as basic laws of biology. Sometimes you just have to accept them. And I can help you.*

I managed not to burst into tears at the far-reaching, existential implications of his words, but decided to make a mental note for future me. *Highly susceptible to inspirational messaging. Must NOT join cult.*

I do my readings for Dr. Carlsen's class. Finish an English composition essay, expanding my opinion that teachers should be paid more from *because yes, duh*, to a semi-cogent, multi-paragraph argument. Slog through my visualization exercises. By late afternoon, I decide to reward myself with some work on the bio project.

It sounds deeply uncool, but there's nothing I'd rather be doing. It'd be nice if Lukas texted, but he's obviously been putting out fires for the past week, and anyway, I haven't had much of a sex life in the last year and a half. I can wait a few more days for . . . whatever comes next.

Zach kept his promises, and my student ID grants me access to Dr. Smith's deserted lab. It makes me like her more, that none of her grad students seem to feel like they should be hard-core pipetting on a Saturday afternoon. I move through the benches, remembering the feeling of being in a lab—my favorite part of organic chemistry. Working with compounds. Chromatography. Synthesizing aspirin. Follow experiment protocols, see what happened. I cannot wait to become a capable, badass, life-changing physician like Barb, but I hope I'll get to do some research on the side. Watching things explode and crystallize will never *not* be fun.

At the back of the lab, I find the computer Zach pointed me to. Before I can power it up, I hear a noise behind me and whirl around.

Lukas sits on a stool at the end of a bench, for once looking like he's not coming *from*, going *to*, or currently *at* practice. Hair chlorine lightened, but not tousled. No goggles marks around his eyes. Jeans and a dark Henley with no Stanford logo in sight.

It's . . . disrupting. He's an athlete, and most of our interactions have in some shape revolved around that. But he's also a person with interests and hobbies and a life, and I know so little about *that* Lukas.

And yet, I feel myself smile. "Hi?"

"Hi."

"Where did you—did you come in behind me?"

He shakes his head.

"Um, okay. I'm here to . . ." I point at the computer behind me.

"Get the pictures for the input dataset?"

I nod.

He lifts his left hand, showing me the USB lodged between his thumb and pointer finger.

"Ah. Great. We're going to need to—"

"Reorient the pics."

"And—"

"Resize them."

He completes my sentences unhurriedly, like finishing my thoughts is a natural thing for him. We assess each other for a silent beat. It feels like a contest, and when my lips curl first, I realize that he won.

"Maybe Pen has a point," I muse.

"I'm sure she has many," Lukas says. "What's this specific one about?"

"You *are* a bit overwhelming."

He laughs, low, amused. "Just a bit?"

"She may have been downplaying it. So I wouldn't run."

"She's a great wingwoman, then."

"Seems like it." *Why does she think you're distant? Why can't I reconcile the Lukas she talks about with the one I know?* I ask none of this. Instead I idly step toward him, slowly glancing around the lab. It's so wide. And we're so alone. "What were you going to do with the flash drive?"

"Check your phone."

I take it out of my pocket and find a text from him, delivered a few minutes ago.

LUKAS: Free?

I smile. "Is it over? Emotional support duties, I mean."

"I hope so. Kyle and Nate took a couple of meetings today."

Right. His cocaptains. I move closer, stopping when I notice a photo, pinned with a magnet on the upper edge of the bench. "Is that you?"

He follows my gaze to the boy with the windblown hair. There are three other men in the picture, all tall and strong-limbed, wrapping long arms around each other's shoulders. "Yeah."

"And the others?"

"My brothers."

I grin and push on my toes to study it. Lukas's siblings seem to be very similar to him in height, size, and bone structure, with occasional exceptions. Dark, long hair. A blond beard. A rounder face and fuller upper lip. Lines carved deep around a strong nose.

He is, undoubtedly, the most handsome.

I am, undoubtedly, biased.

"You have three?"

"Yup."

"All older?"

"Quite a bit."

"How much?"

"The second youngest is Jan, born eleven years before me. I was a surprise baby."

"Do you get along? Do you miss them?" I don't know why I want to gobble up crumbs of Lukas-related information. He seems willing to oblige, though.

"They're great. And annoying, although there's a range. Jan and I are closest—he's the one who got me into swimming. We travel together often. Oskar, the eldest, thinks that I'm still a minor. Gives me a bedtime when I stay at his house. His kids are cute, though, so I forgive him. And Leif . . . Leif once convinced me that I had Dutch elm disease." He shakes his head when I laugh. "I do miss them, but when I'm with them, I sometimes contemplate violence."

"Isn't that what being siblings is about?" Not that I would know. "How come you get your own bench as an undergrad?"

"I've been working with Olive for a while. Plus, she recently started out her lab, so she doesn't have many grads."

"Are you planning on working with her past graduation?" A thought hits me. "Did you apply for Stanford Med?"

He nods. "It's where I hope to end up."

"Interview?"

Another nod, but an Olympic medalist with a high MCAT score and computational biology experience? It's a given. Thank god I don't know his GPA, or I'd have to chug down a bottle of mercury.

"When?"

"Back in August."

"Did you wear a suit?"

"And a fucking tie." I laugh, and he seems to enjoy that. "Figuring out what to wear was more labor-intensive than putting on a tech suit."

"Aww. Did you get a coach to help you?"

He fights a smile. "That's a lot of cackling from someone who'll go through the same process—in *heels*."

"First of all, not cackling. More like gentle chortling. Second . . . how did it go?"

"I don't know." He notices my skeptical gaze and shrugs. "Worrying is pointless. I'll either get in, or I won't."

I wish I could be as at peace as he about . . . anything, really. "And if you stay, you'll want to keep on working with Dr. Smith?"

"If she'll have me. I like her style. She's hands-off, but involved. Trusts us to get shit done."

"And I bet you *hate* being micromanaged."

"You have no idea." He cocks his head and studies me. "I bet you would, too. In the lab."

The subtext—*but not* everywhere *else*—is loud, but it leads us into a warm patch of silence. And after that . . .

I'm not sure how it happens. Maybe he's the one pulling me between his thighs. Maybe I step into him. All I know is that I'm in his arms, my face buried in him, his hand splayed wide on my lower back, a soothing caress above my shirt.

He inhales deeply, purposefully—looking for something he's already familiar with, revisiting a beaten path. His skin is sandalwood. Sun. Grass. The faintest trace of chlorine. *Where were you today? What did you do?*

"You read the list?" he asks against the shell of my ear.

I nod into his chest. His palm slides up, to the top of my spine, a slab of heat and touch, until his thumb finds the pulse at the base of my neck, wipes back and forth over it. "Good girl."

I close my eyes. Dissolve into the gratification of knowing that I've done something right. The simple pleasure of pleasing someone.

Maybe I'm fucked up. A victim of the sexist power structures that society has imposed on me. If being praised by some guy I barely know gets me going this fast, I must have internalized the same patriarchal shit that I despise outside of the bedroom. Or maybe I just *am*, and should stop beating myself up about this.

"Anything you want to say about that?"

I think about it in earnest, but it's like Lukas said: there is nothing he wants that I don't want more.

"Can you just . . ." I free my arms from between our bodies and loop them around his waist. It might be the most intimate hug I've ever been part of.

"Just what?"

I swallow. "I just want to be told what to do. For once."

His fingers slide through the hair at my temple. He pulls back my head. Catches my eyes. "Will you do what I ask, then?"

I nod eagerly, feeling the slight remodeling of the energy in the lab, an empty heat inside me. A new *us*. This—it's not who we are when he tells me about his med school applications, when we discuss deep learning, when we wave at each other from across the pool. This is him and me, yes, but a variation on our theme.

Outside, very little stitches us together. Here, we couldn't be more perfect for each other.

"Can I trust you to say *stop* if you want me to stop?" he asks.

I nod again.

"Scarlett."

I know exactly what he's asking for. "You can trust me to say *stop*, if I want you to stop." I swallow. My body is a vague haze of arousal, longing, of hot, liquid eagerness. "Otherwise . . ."

His eyes crease with a smile. "That's lovely of you." His kiss is light, sweet on my mouth. "In that case, I want you to get on your knees and go down on me."

A scattered thought occurs to me, that Lukas might be testing me. *Does she really mean it? How far is she willing to go?* But it's fleeting and immediately discarded, because in this moment only one thing matters.

He asked me to do something. And I cannot imagine anything better than to follow his instructions.

So I lower myself between the spread of his legs, letting my bare knees prop against the footrest until I'm at the perfect height. I reach for the opening of his jeans, but he stops me, one of his hands closing around both of mine as they work on a button. I freeze—*I'm already messing up*—but he lifts my chin and pushes back my hair to study my face at his leisure, and after a handful of seconds murmurs, "You are beautiful, Scarlett."

They don't sound like empty words. More like something he wanted me to know. I smile, and when he frees my hands, I get back to work, one button after the other after the other, the snapping loud in the silent lab, the fabric rustling as I reach inside his boxer briefs.

I couldn't be less surprised by the size of him. He's already fully hard, smells like soap and shower and skin, and I'm more turned on than I remember ever being. The seam of my shorts digs against my clit, and it feels nice—it feels *good*, really—but it doesn't matter.

This is the one thing in my life that's not about *me*.

Lukas's hand cups my face, thumb pressing against the corner of my mouth. "Still okay with this?"

Another eager nod. Truth is, I don't want him to check in on me. I want to be free of it. I want him to—

"You just want to be told exactly what to do, don't you?" he says quietly, with a small smile. Because he *truly* understands. "Right now, you just want to be a mouth, huh?"

I push past the lump in my throat. "I think I do."

His thumb slips past my lips, large, testing. He leans forward for a kiss that's just tongue—his meeting mine over the place where his finger holds my mouth open, filthy and mind-wipingly good.

"We can make that happen, Scarlett." He straightens back up. When he looks down at me, I think of Nordic deities and sky-sent mandates. "Open up."

Lukas wants to be in control, and I get to do very little about it. He takes the base of his straining cock, flattens the underside against my mouth, brushes the head across my lips. He grunts as he starts feeding me the first inch, and the second, and—

"Oh, fuck." His palm is around my jaw, controlling every move-ment. All I can do is keep myself open and soft for him. "I need a minute to . . ." He pulls out. Another groan. A deep inhale. He ca-resses my cheek gently, sweetly, like his cock is not dripping pre-come on the side of my mouth. "I'm going to teach you the way I like it. You want to learn, don't you?"

It's my purpose in life. It won't be one hour from now, and I had no clue I cared twenty minutes ago, but now—I want nothing as intensely as this. Fuck diving, fuck med school, fuck being a pro-ductive member of society. "Please."

He lets out a half-cursed, hushed word. I'm ready to do whatever he asks of me, but he hesitates. Takes a moment to push back the dark locks falling on my cheek, his touch kind and almost reverential. "You're so fucking . . ."

"What?" I ask. My lips brush against his foreskin. He exhales.

"I don't even know." His eyes are amused, but his voice is hoarse and hungry, and then his fingers are knotting in my hair and I'm sucking around his length, an easy rhythm completely guided by him, the speed and depth his choice alone. A brief moment of adjustment as I get used to his size, to the way his hands give directions, to how easy it would be to choke on him.

"Eyes up here, Scarlett."

My mind is a buoyant, soft space. My underwear so sticky, it'll have to be peeled off. It's everything I asked for. Maybe not out loud, but I doubt I could ever fully explain how much I enjoy discovering what he likes.

Lukas gets it, though. His gaze flicks between my lips and my eyes, and he understands *everything* about what's happening here. "You're doing so well." His accent is thicker, as hefty as the wet slide of his cock on my tongue. "I thought about this a lot, and it was a great mental image, but *Christ*." One finger traces my cheek, the imprint he creates from within my mouth. He mutters something in Swedish, raspy and furious and definitely *filthy*, desperate enough to annihilate the language barrier. "You love this, don't you?"

His hold slackens just enough to allow a verbal response. "I do." His thighs tense under my hands, as though he wanted to hear it as badly as I wanted to say it.

My jaw is a little sore, but I can barely feel it when he says, "That's good. Because you look fantastic with my cock in your mouth." He pulls me back to it, and maybe it's my one true calling, because he's rougher now, the strokes deeper and not as restrained. He's too big to do anything pornographic with, but he's willing to try, and to let me do the same. The head of his cock bumps against the inside of my cheek, then moves farther inside, a nudge, just the edge of it trying to make its way down my throat.

"Don't worry, we're going to—*fuck*—work on this. You're doing great. So good to me," he reassures me when I don't have enough experience to make myself lax, like this is precisely what he wanted.

Me, trying.

And I do try. A slight push, like I can fit him inside just by will, and it must catch him off guard. There are more Swedish words, and an unsteady quality to his grip on my nape, and then he's on the edge of coming.

"Fuck, Scarlett—"

For a second, I'm sure he'll hold my gaze throughout. Then, just before his orgasm tears through him, his eyes close, his head tips back, and his lost expression has me moaning around his flesh. His grip strengthens around both sides of my face, and I'm convinced that there is a universe in which I could come just from this—from how much he's enjoying it, from knowing that I did this for him, the lightness of being in my *body*, and not in my *head*.

I do my best to swallow, work convulsively, but there's too much, the positioning's wrong, and Lukas has to use his thumb to press what's left of his come in my mouth. He's slow and patient and thorough, glassy eyes and flushed freckles, and every time I suck on the pad of his finger, he lets out silent groans and something foreign that could be *perfect*.

I'm high-strung. Floating. Burning up. He lifts me like I weigh less than a feather, settles me on the edge of the bench. I'm almost— *almost*—aware of my surroundings: The pungent, chemical smells of the lab. Lukas's biceps, steel around me. The loud tempo of his breathing.

I once learned that the fastest sprinters don't bother taking a single breath across the entire pool. Something about the head rotations being inefficient, and the oxygen not having enough time to reach the muscles. They go totally anaerobic for twenty seconds, which means that their lung capacity must be a work of art.

And Lukas Blomqvist, the fastest person to ever swim fifty meters, is panting against the curve of my throat like there isn't enough air in the universe to fill him up. And it takes him a while to recover, before he's able to cup the back of my head again, his tongue in my mouth almost obscenely deep.

He's still hard against my stomach. My arms are wedged between our torsos, as though he wants to burrow me into him. "You did really well, Scarlett." He sounds shaken but steady. Slowly regaining control. His fingers slide down my flanks, travel down to my thighs, and . . . the hem of my shorts comes up so high, it's easy for him to slide one hand underneath and meet the elastic of my cotton panties.

I gasp.

He smiles.

"And you know what girls who did good get?"

His thumb, the same that was in my mouth moments ago, taps faintly against my clit through my soaked underwear. I'm so swollen, so oversensitive, my whine echoes throughout the lab.

"You're really wet, Scarlett. Aren't you?"

I hide my moan in his neck, but he pulls me back, forcing me to meet his gaze. I know that my face is red and blotchy. I felt the tears sliding down the corners of my eyes as he came. I am mortified. Also, trembling with want.

And he knows it.

"You did so well. You *deserve* to come. I would love to make you come. I would pay a not insignificant amount of money to go down on you. Though you could probably come just from this." Another slow stroke, this time against the drenched seam of my underwear. I lean in, whimper, sink my teeth into the hard muscles of his lats, but he doesn't mind. His palm cradles the back of my head, gathering me into his skin. "The problem is, I'm not sure you want it enough yet."

I shut my eyes and barely, *barely* stop myself from begging. I'm not sure I've earned the right to do *that* yet.

"Come on."

He pulls me down from the bench. Adjusts my shorts. Straightens my tank top, pausing to swipe a finger over my hard nipple, where it sticks out against the ribbed cotton. When my breath hitches, he presses a kiss to my cheek. "So sweet," he murmurs, and then, "let's go."

"Where—" I have to clear my throat. "Where are we going?"

He smiles and takes the USB out of his pocket.

"Did you forget? We have a project to work on."

# CHAPTER 26

**I**'M FAWN-LEGGED AS WE WALK DOWN THE MAIN QUAD, WOB-blier than after a week with the flu. The fresh air does little to clear out the haze, or to ease the throbbing between my legs.

I lift my chin, trying to look like I'm not still processing the ins and outs of what just happened, like it wasn't a bit of a religious, existence-defining experience.

*Scenes*, that's what people call what we did. Pockets of time in which power is exchanged. They have a beginning and an end. They can be broken with safe words. They can be structured and formalized as much as their participants like—in my case, not too much, at least for now. Words like *dom* and *sub* feel a little cumbersome. Unwieldy. I wrote on my list that at this stage I'd rather explore than constrain, and Lukas seemed . . . eager. For now, we're just two kinky people, checking in with each other and figuring it out.

I wonder if something like this birthed the expression *fuck around and find out.*

I take deep breaths, squinting at the glare of the late-afternoon sun, until a pair of sunglasses is pushed up the bridge of my nose. Lukas looks formidable against the suddenly dark sky, but his eyes are very much bare.

"You—"

"That way," he instructs, tapping my nape and taking a right turn.

My lips are tender and pouty. Earlier, in the elevator, he traced them with his thumb over and over, the soft hint of a pleased smile obvious in the creases at the corners of his eyes. He took my hand and held it—out of the lab, the hallway, the building, until I wiggled free.

It's disarming, how a five-minute walk through campus results in several eyeballs slipping in his direction. But Stanford is the alma mater of dozens of Olympians, many of whom end up medaling, and Lukas is by no means unique. *Basically a public figure*, Pen said, and maybe she wasn't wrong.

"Do you mind?" I ask him. I am slowly winding down. Not quite steady yet.

"Mind what?"

"Just, you know, the people. The attention."

He gives me an empty look. "What attention, and what people?"

A laugh bubbles out of me, and I picture bringing this up with Pen. *He doesn't realize! I told you—constantly unfazed!*

"You still doing okay?" he checks in, and I nod.

I feel used, deliciously so. But not like one might use a thing, only to discard it. I feel precious, something able to bring pleasure, a product of enthusiasm and instructions well carried out. And that, really, is the crux of it. When I'm following commands, my shoulders are bare of any weight. I'm sure there are many reasons people like what I like, but for me—this is it. The quiet. The grind, stopped. Knowing that for a brief moment, someone else has me. No decisions, no responsibilities.

When that's over, though, reality seeps back in. Classes. Practice. Projects.

"I've been working on the pooling layers for the neural network," I tell Lukas.

"You said max pooling, right?"

"Zach did."

"Ah. What do *you* think?"

I pause. Chew my lower lip. "Zach is a grad student. I'm just an undergrad."

"Uh-huh. And you can still disagree with him."

"The average value would be better." I glance up at him, sideways. "What do *you* think?"

"I think you're better than me, or Zach, at this."

I don't strictly *need* Lukas to tell me that I'm good at something, especially when I already know that, but it's still nice. A quiet warmth. My knees no longer shake, but I'm empty. Electrified. "Love the trust."

"It's a hell of a drug." We exchange a knowing look. "I'm going to write a script to prepare the training dataset for the model."

"Can you?"

His eyebrow quirks. "Are you doubting my coding ability?"

"No, no. I'd rather do it, though."

"Why?"

"Well, I don't know what coding languages you know, for one."

"And?"

"I'm concerned that you'll say, I don't know, MATLAB."

He scoffs. "*MATLAB.*"

"Your indignation *is* a relief." I catch the twitch of his lips as he nudges me into a left turn. We're slowly heading toward the outskirts of campus—maybe another library I don't know about? "You may write the script."

"How generous of you. How's German going, troll?"

I glare at his smug, self-satisfied face. "Okay, first: *troll*? And, that was *low*."

"But warranted. *MATLAB.*"

"Uh-huh. Next thing you're gonna ask me about my inward dives."

"Hmm. Which ones are those?"

I halt in the middle of the sidewalk.

"What?" he asks.

"Did you just . . . do you not know what an inward dive is?"

He shrugs. "I get them mixed up."

"But . . . Pen." He stares at me like I should elaborate. "Your ex is a diving prodigy." More blank stares. "You can tell different dive groups apart, right?"

"Well, I did notice the difference between the short, bouncy board and the tall, stiff board—"

"You mean the *platform*?"

"Is that what it's called?"

I cover my mouth with both hands to prevent a clamor of harpies from slipping out of my trachea and attacking him—and then realize he's messing with me. "I hate you."

He smiles and reaches out, pushing a strand behind my ear. Then tugs me till I resume walking. "I do get the diving groups confused. I couldn't pick out an inward dive."

Unacceptable. "Maybe if you did she wouldn't . . ." I stop myself mid-mumble, and cast about for a not wound-salting way of ending the sentence.

But Lukas is already grinning. "Have dumped me?"

"I didn't mean to . . . I'm sorry."

"Don't be. I could memorize every item in the diving book by degree of difficulty, and it would change nothing."

"Are you sure? It's a bit of a red-flaggy, deadbeat boyfriend move, not knowing the basics of your girlfriend's sport. Maybe she feels neglected?"

He chuckles. "Sufficiently supporting each other was the one issue we did *not* have, Scarlett." Then continues, more serious. "Pen and I got together when we both needed something—*someone* outside of our disciplines. Knowing little about each other's sports was part of the draw."

I guess it's not too outlandish. "Josh once said that splashier dives were prettier because they reminded him of fountains, and that judges should score them higher."

"Josh?"

"My ex."

We take another turn. Lukas's arm brushes against mine, his elbow grazing my shoulder. "The one you experimented with?"

"The one and only." I huff a laugh. "Quite literally 'the only.'"

"Is he here?"

"You mean at Stanford? Nope, he's at WashU. St. Louis."

"Is that where you're from?"

"Where my stepmom's from."

He nods. "Did you break it off because of the distance?"

It's more questions than Lukas has produced in the entirety of our acquaintance—all in the space of about ten seconds. Maybe he's sussing out whether I'm a weirdo. "The opposite, actually. He broke up with me." Lukas's forehead curls into a scowl. "What's that face?"

The scowl remains. "Nothing."

"It wasn't because—it wasn't a sex thing," I reassure him.

Lukas seems baffled. "I never assumed it was."

I'm not convinced. "If anything, it's more because of the way I am."

"The way you are?"

"Just—my personality. Overachiever. Obsessive with wanting things to go my way. Hyper-controlled. Distant, sometimes. Basically, I know I come across as a stone-cold bitch, but—"

He laughs. Lukas straight-up, outright laughs. A rumbling, deep sound that's louder than anything I've heard from him. I'm not sure what to do, except keep walking and stare, perplexed.

"What?" I ask.

He shakes his head. "You're not cold, Scarlett," he says. "You're . . . soft."

"I'm not soft."

"You are with me." His eyes meet mine. A dark, unflinching look that sands layer upon layer off me. "Maybe *I* make you soft."

Heat rushes to my cheeks, and I force my gaze away, down to our shoes, his legs that are so much longer than mine, he must be matching our paces, or I'd have run out of breath a while ago. "Josh met someone he liked better." The truth is not the sucker punch it used to be, back when just hearing his name made me feel alone and unwanted. "But he wasn't really . . . like us. We weren't well matched in that sense."

He stops in front of a white Spanish Colonial house just outside campus. I do the same, trying not to be intimidated by the serious way he's studying me. "Are you still in love with him?" he asks quietly.

The question takes me by surprise. So does the ease of my reply. "No. I haven't been pining for him. It's been a million years, and—"

"A million."

I roll my eyes. Smile. "One and a half years." It's a more helpful answer than the one he gave me when I asked if he still had feelings for Pen. *Do you, Lukas?*

"And there hasn't been anyone else?"

I shake my head. "Not because I'm hung up on Josh. It has more to do with being premed and practice schedules. Plus, with my luck, I'd swipe right on someone who stormed the Capitol and hates routine vaccinations. So . . . yeah. Just Josh." *And now you* pulsates sweetly between us. I want to squirm against it, this heat in my stomach he left burning, this frustrating but pleasant reminder that Lukas *is* like me.

I shrug. Chew on my lower lip before finding the courage to ask, "What about you?"

"Me, what?" He gives me an expectant look. A Norse god granting an audience to his subject. It's more than a slight turn-on, because I'm twisted like that.

"Has there been anyone else aside from Pen?"

He hesitates, then tilts his head, gesturing toward the entrance of the house, and says, "It's complicated. We can discuss it inside the house."

# CHAPTER 27

**A**SKING WHETHER I SHOULD TAKE OFF MY SHOES BEFORE stepping in seems like a fairly normal question, and I don't understand why Lukas recoils as though I offered to smear badger turds all over his guest bathroom.

"Is there an alternative?" he asks, like there is a right answer, before shaking his head, and mouthing something under his breath. *Americans*, I believe it is.

I cannot help laughing as I follow him down an uncannily spotless hallway.

Sadly, my perfectionism never quite extended to cleanliness. Maryam and I have quarterly household meetings that share a tried-and-true agenda: we start by blaming each other for the pigsty-like quality of our place, continue with some superficial stress cleaning that temporarily assuages the heft of our shame, and conclude by swearing on what's dearest to us—my dog, her Cthulhu funko pop—that we'll procure coasters and never again let entropy conquer us.

Pipsqueak and Cthulhu are fucked.

"Your house is so much tidier than mine," I say, hating the awe in my voice. Lukas looks at me over his shoulder, a little judgmental.

"That's our closet." He points at a wooden door. "You may borrow cleaning supplies."

I snort. "You're officially *never* coming over."

"Fine by me." He guides me into the kitchen, which looks like something a realtor might show to clients in the hope that they'll buy the house in cash.

"Lukas, when do you even find the time to—"

"Mate, I didn't know Pen was—oh." Hasan appears under an arch and stops in his tracks, eyes settling on me. "Hey, Vandy."

"Hasan," I say. He's British, tall and broad and deep voiced, and while I've never seen him be anything but kind, I instinctively shuffle closer to Lukas. My flank meets his heat, and I find that he's already done the same.

"Sorry. I heard a female voice and assumed you were Pen."

I glance at Lukas, waiting for him to explain to *his* roommate why I'm here, but he's busy selecting a Fuji apple from the most pleasingly arranged bowl of fruit I've seen outside of a nineteenth-century still life painting. The burden of half-truthing must fall upon me. "Lukas and I are working on a project together."

"Ah." He smiles in something that looks a bit like relief. His expression clears. "You done with rehab?"

Last year, we'd often be in the PT room at the same time. "Yeah. And your right knee?"

"Good. It was just some MCL strain."

"You're breaststroke, right?"

"Yup." We exchange a smile. I already feel more comfortable—till he adds, "That was a bad injury. Yours, I mean."

"Oh . . . yeah. I guess."

"It wasn't just a tear, right? There was other stuff?"

"Oh, um . . . a concussion. Some lung stuff. Sprains." I shrug, tense. I doubt Hasan notices.

Lukas, though . . . "Why did you tell me not to ask you about inward dives?" His voice takes me by surprise. I turn to him, admiring the way he's nonchalantly peeling the apple with a knife—a perfect, continuous spiral, like it's *easy*, when I've tried a million times and always mess it up. Then his question falls into place.

"I didn't say that."

"Close enough."

"Not really."

"You said, 'Next you're going to ask me about my inward dives.'" He finishes peeling, eyes never letting mine go.

Ugh. "They're just hard."

"Ah." Hasan nods knowingly. "Like mini max sets with double ups?"

"Exactly." No idea what that is, but I nod, relieved. Lukas's eyes on me are still sharper than I'd like. I glance around the kitchen, desperate for a change of topic. "By the way, I love your pristine and—I can only assume—weekly pasteurized home."

Hasan grimaces. "We've got a bit of a regime situation going on." He shoots a heavily insinuating stare at Lukas—who settles apple wedges on a plate, unbothered. "A full-on dictatorship, some would say," Hasan adds.

I drum my fingers over the immaculate counter. "That's not very collegial of you, Lukas."

"We are adult men," he simply says, sliding the plate toward me.

Did he . . . did he make me a *snack*? Is it a thank-you for the—

"Adulthood is not necessarily incompatible with the occasional crumb in the sink," Hasan says.

"And Kyle's or your head are not necessarily incompatible with the toilet," Lukas counters benignly.

I nearly choke on my apple, and ask, "Did you—was that a threat?"

"I don't know." Lukas's eyes remain on Hasan, serene and challenging. "Would you like to test me?"

*Dictatorship*, Hasan mouths at me. *Regime.*

"Is it a Swedish thing?" I mock-whisper at Hasan, biting into another slice. Sweet and crispy. Perfect.

"He also cooks extremely healthy meals, does laundry every weekend at the same time, and probably uses a protractor to fold his underwear. Maybe it *is* a Swedish thing."

"It's a not-a-manchild thing," Lukas counters. He hasn't eaten any apple yet. Is this just for *me*?

"How long have you two been living here together?"

"Since sophomore year," Hasan explains. "Caleb moved out last year after he graduated. Kyle took over."

"Is Kyle as enthusiastic a, um, cleaner as you are?"

"He's as terrified of Lukas and susceptible to his authority as I am, yes."

"Is he home?" Lukas asks casually, as though we're not discussing his most despotic personality traits.

"Upstairs, I think."

He nods and turns to me. "Want more?"

I must have been hungry, because I scarfed down the entire apple. "No, thank you. Want to go work on that project?"

He nods. "I have a desktop computer upstairs."

"Awesome."

I smile my goodbyes at Hasan, chuckle silently when he mouths, *Tyrant*, and then follow Lukas up the stairs. His room is on the eastern corner—must be nice, especially in the summer, when sunrise and practice come about at the same time. I'm still not sure why he brought me here instead of the library, but—

A strong hand shoves me inside his room.

And a second later, when I'm about to trip over my own feet, an equally strong arm catches me around the waist and pulls me back to his chest.

The door closes behind us. Lukas's face buries in my throat with a long, sharp inhale. "You always smell so fucking good," he murmurs against my neck, and my heart breaks into a race.

The bed is not close to the door, but it doesn't matter. Lukas is twice as big as me, a million times stronger, and—it does a lot for me, I guess, the way he picks me up with no difficulty, like I'm a doll, a pet. When he lands me on his mattress, I feel like I do after failing a dive with several twists.

Disoriented. Out of breath. Lost.

He gives me no time to get my bearings. His fingers hook into the elastic of my shorts and pull them down my legs, together with my underwear. I must offer no resistance at all, because a moment later he's there, on his knees next to his low bed staring down at what he uncovered.

My bare cunt.

He's not much for preambles. And maybe he doesn't want to make me suffer more than I already have, because he touches me without hesitation. His thumb is a gentle, firm pressure against my sticky slit, teasing me apart. Starting just below my clit and swiping down, once, twice, until on the third pass it hooks inside of my opening.

I gasp.

He doesn't.

He stares at the place where a small part of him is barely inside me, and I think he's unaffected, as in control as I could *never* be, but when he speaks . . .

"Do you want to know a secret?" His voice is like nothing I've heard. A low hum. Hard-edged. Foreign.

I nod.

"I dreamt about fucking you."

I swallow. His thumb moves up again, and this time—this time he lets it graze my clit.

I arch up, biting a moan into my lower lip.

"Several times. Too many, probably."

I feel myself clench around nothing.

"The first was about two years ago."

My heart pounds. I'm right on the verge of—of *something*, but his thumb is gone. I could come so hard. If he only touched me. Anywhere, with anything. But he doesn't, and it's not outside the realm of possibilities that I might burst into tears.

"Scarlett."

"Yes?" I didn't think I'd be capable of speaking, but his voice is that authoritative.

"If you want me to stop, what do you do?"

"I say *stop*." I *can* say it. I know I can, and he will. I've just never wanted anything less.

"You are even wetter than in the lab. Is it because I didn't let you come? Because I'm in charge?"

It seems to be a genuine question, something he needs to know for sure. I nod, desperate. Flutter greedily around air.

"You want to be ordered around by someone you trust, is that it? You want rules, to be told what's good for you."

It's so patronizing, and I—I nod like my life depends on it, half ashamed of the loud moan that slips out of my throat.

"Hey. Hey, baby." One of his hands comes up, fingers brushing against my lips, circling my jaw. "Kyle's room is just down the hallway. You're going to have to be quiet. *Can* you be quiet?"

I'm lost for a second. Unable to fully grasp the magnitude of—this. The way he talks to me. His grip. The mix of violence and control and tenderness. So close to what I've always wanted and never managed to ask for, it's hard to believe it's not a fantasy.

"Scarlett. Can you be good?"

I nod against his hand while the other pins my wrists to my belly. His pleased smile works me up that much higher. "If you can't, just bite," he says, his palm right by my lips, his long fingers caging my cheeks, and I want to tell him that it's okay, that I can be good for him, that he doesn't need to worry, but it turns out to be a lie.

The first time, it takes him less than ten seconds to make me come. It's just his tongue on my clit, flat, relentless, and when my orgasm rushes over, Lukas grunts like it's happening to him.

I thought I could be quiet. Instead, I keen into the fleshy part of his hand.

"You are *so fucking good*," he tells me. I'm not sure how, but a handful of moments later, I come again. "Already? You *are* perfect, huh?" He continues to suck and lick and hum against my clit, eating at me like I'm made of air and water. Quickly, the pleasure shifts from something to chase, to an avalanche that I want to run from. Tears slide hotly down the corners of my eyes. "Lukas, Lukas—I—" My voice breaks into a sob. I arch again, head tilted back, convulsing. It's too much, too intense, too new to be defined by something as uncomplicated as *good*. It is, however, thought-annihilating. My bouncy mind and my racing anxieties sit still, as though Lukas knows exactly how to bend them to his will.

I squirm away from his mouth, but he knows it's not what I need. "Shh. It's okay. You're doing great." My heels push against the muscles in his upper back. He presses my wrists more firmly against my stomach, avoids the hypersensitive, over-touched parts of my cunt, and still manages to make me come again.

"More?" he asks after I float down, like the past ten minutes have not just been a glorious assortment of *more*s, like I don't twitch every time his breath puffs against my flesh. I'm hot. Heavy. Made of sparks. I watch him watch my clenching hole, on display for him.

"I . . ." My throat is raw, scraped from the inside. His palm, marked with my teeth. "It's not up to me." I say it because we're both thinking it, anyway.

"You sweet thing. You were made for this, weren't you?" His

hand leaves my face and comes down to spread my legs. Pin my right knee to the bed. When his teeth bite into my inner thigh, my whole body jerks. It hurts a little, more than that, but I'm cross-wired, neurally confused, and the pain and pleasure are impossible to tease apart. "You're so right."

I wonder if I'm going to get used to his strength. The rational part of me knows that his physique is a simple product of training, discipline, and questionable priorities. The other part, the one that just wants a minute of rest, loves the ease with which he flips me around until I'm all the way on the bed, belly down on the covers, my cheek pressed against a pillow that smells so much like him, I cannot help grabbing two fistfuls.

*Mine.*

"I really want to fuck you," he says from behind me. I'm still quivering. Wearing nothing but a white tank top that has long ridden up to my rib cage. Lukas is on his knees, my thighs trapped in the spread of his. He must be looking at my ass, and if this was anyone else, I'd be fretting over it. Am I pretty enough? Have I disappointed him with my body?

Except, *he's* the one who gets to decide what happens. And if he didn't like me, he simply wouldn't continue. My worries quiet down, and I smile into the comforter.

I could live *here*, in the quiet of this moment, forever.

"You'd let me, right?"

His hand comes up to the valley between my shoulder blades. Pushes down. My head has little range of movement, but I try to nod.

"That's so sweet of you." He leans forward. Kisses the first vertebra of my spine, slow and patient. "Then again, I really *don't* want to fuck you with a condom."

His voice pierces through the dense fog in my brain. I recall the list. *On birth control, to avoid periods*, scribbled in the margins of mine.

*If you're up for it, let's both get tested and exchange results*, he wrote.

I sent mine.

He got busy, and didn't send his.

"We'll have to do something else," he says.

I groan into the mattress. *"Please."*

He licks the trails of my tears. The stubble on his jaw brushes deliciously against my ear, and he lets out something that resembles a regretful, strained laugh. "You're pretty when you beg." Another kiss on my cheek. "You always are."

I let out a second, frustrated groan, but he's unbuttoning his jeans, pushing layers of fabric down his hips, his weight infinite as he lowers himself against my back, presses my legs together with his knees, and—

Oh my god.

He grunts. I gasp. The first glide of his cock between my thighs is choppy, too rough. Unlubricated. But then his thrust slides up, where he made me plenty wet just a minute ago.

"Jesus, you feel—" His hips find a steady rhythm, and it all works like a dream.

And that's when I realize, he *is* fucking me. Not the way I want him to, maybe, but his head bumps my clit on every push. I can feel the hot length of him against my folds, and it's good enough for me to beg for it.

"It's like I made you up in my head, Scarlett."

I'm babbling, wild and inappropriate, and he has to shush me again. He laughs once, a little rough. "You just can't be quiet, can you?" This time it's the palm of his hand wrapped against the lower side of my face, and biting into it is not an option.

I shouldn't moan this loudly. I should be able to choke these sounds back. But I'm not and it's okay, because for once the responsibility is not on me. This time, *Lukas* decided, and I don't get to be heard. Fresh air is hard to come by, his fingers span my entire jaw, and I wholly forget the burden of being myself for a few moments.

"Next time," he promises in my ear, heavy and urgent and raspy, "I'm going to fuck you properly."

I nod and roll my spine, trying to get closer to him. Failing. I have no control over this, and I hear myself whine, high-pitched and reedy.

"What am I gonna do next time? C'mon, Scarlett. Say it."

He's not unreasonable. Kind, really. His hand on my mouth loosens just enough to allow me to speak. Cool air fills my lungs. I open my mouth to whisper, shaky, "Next time, you're going to—" A silent hitch when the head of his cock hits a perfect spot. I gasp, a hairbreadth from coming. If only he was to do it again, just once. Even stay *there*.

But he *knows*. And pulls back right before I slip over the edge.

"Not until you say it. Come on."

I am so close. So *close*. "You're going to . . . to fuck me properly."

"It's a promise, Scarlett." He resumes thrusting, and I'm so wet now that the sounds are filthy, the slapping of his body against mine faster, and the noises I make—his palm seals against my mouth, a tight grip that I never want to lose. His movements stop. "And you'll fucking take it."

He bites a deep, guttural groan in the tender flesh of my shoulder, and when I feel the thick ropes of his come painting my cunt, I start convulsing against him. For long moments, I'm just pleasure and sensation, no awareness of anything else.

When I can breathe and think and *be* again, Lukas has shifted us so that he's spooning me, held to his chest with both arms—at once precious cargo *and* a flight risk.

"Okay?" he asks.

His voice is so shaken, I wonder if that should be my line. I turn a little and lift my hand, letting it run through the soft hair at the side of his head, where it's shorter than the top. He leans into it like a pet, still trying to catch his breath. "Yeah. You?"

He doesn't say yes. What he *does* say is, "Fuck," which means nothing and everything at once.

I nod in agreement, because yeah. Fuck.

*Fuck, we're really doing this.*

*Fuck, your roommates are here, and I'm sure I lost consciousness at some point, and I hope they had headphones on.*

*Fuck, I thought it would be good, and it still felt so much better than it should have.*

"God, you are so . . ." Lukas pants, but never finishes the sentence. He presses sweet, open-mouthed, almost involuntary kisses to my neck and temple and collarbone. He licks my tears dry. His hands are—well, still strong, but his grip is nothing like before. He caresses me like I'm crystal, follows the line of my arm and my hips and my belly, a little desperate, a little hungry, a little incredulous, a little satisfied. "I'm going to clean you up in a minute. Just let me . . . I just want to touch you. Okay?"

I nod with a happy, sated smile.

And a handful of seconds later I fall asleep.

# CHAPTER 28

**W**HEN I WAKE UP THE ROOM IS DARK, AND LUKAS'S HOLD ON me is as tight as in my last memory, which must have been several hours ago.

My phone reads 9:39 p.m. when I manage to wriggle myself free and retrieve my shorts. I have a single text, from Maryam, asking me whether I stole her jasmine rice. (I did, months ago, and forgot to replace it; I'll never hear the end of this.)

Lukas is a heavy sleeper. He never stirs, not even when I elbow his nightstand while putting my clothes back on. I'm much cleaner than I'd have expected, which tells me that he must have followed through with his promise—and that I must be as heavy a sleeper as he is.

I smile fondly. Try to sneak one last glance at him as I step out, but the hallway lights are out, too. I listen for noises, not wanting to get caught leaving, but when I walk past the kitchen, all I can hear is the whirring of the refrigerator. Hasan and Kyle must be either out or asleep. Student athletes love both resting *and* partying, so I guess it's fifty-fifty.

Campus is by no means deserted. I walk back to my place, body still buzzing with sleep and orgasms. I grin as I let myself into my apartment. My own bed feels small, weirdly soft.

It was good.

Really good.

Lukas is exactly . . . when I say I wanted . . . the list was just a bunch of words, but the way he . . . perfect, and . . .

My cheeks are hot. I brush my teeth and get ready for bed, and then it occurs to me that I should probably tell Lukas that I'm not the victim of a UFO kidnapping.

SCARLETT: Sorry I snuck out—you looked like you needed the rest.

I fall asleep wondering what his reply will look like tomorrow morning.

As it turns out, I shouldn't have bothered.

# CHAPTER 29

*H*E LEFT A MARK ON ME.
　　　　Several, in fact.

The largest, the one I believe was intentional—but how can I know for certain?—is on my inner thigh, close to the place where the leg meets the abdomen. It aches and hums just below my skin, a slight discomfort that *reminds* and *promises*, and I spend my Sunday alternating between studying and pressing into it, just to reassure myself that *yes, yes it happened*.

The other marks I don't find until Monday after practice. Peeling off my suit in a corner that's reflected by the mirror reveals thumb-sized bruises on both sides of my waistline, angled toward my spine. They look perfectly symmetrical. A depraved twist on angel wings. I do *not* remember pain. I do, however, remember Lukas gripping my waist and holding me still as he—

Why has he not contacted me?

"Everything okay?" Bree asks. "You seem distracted."

"Oh, yeah. I just have a test this week."

"For what?"

"Psych."

"Oh, right. Let me tell you what my questions were like last year."

Pen is out, sick with some virus that's been making her "puke my soul out," which means that it's just me and the twins—which means, in turn, lots of one-on-one time with Coach Sima, corrections, dryland.

"How are your exercises going, Scarlett?" Sam asks on Wednesday.

"Honestly, I think they're helping," I say. *Not* honestly.

Because I may have been rewriting neural pathways, but I'm no closer to inward diving, and that's . . . pretty fucking crucial. "Do you think . . . is there any chance that I'll just be able to, you know, do my dives at our first dual meet?"

She cocks her head. "What's a dual meet?"

"When two universities compete against each other, during the preseason. It's informal, but good practice."

"And when is yours?"

"Two weekends from now."

"I see."

"Maybe what I really need to get over my block is to be put on the spot?" I swallow. "Maybe if I just *have* to do it, my brain will bypass the fear . . ."

She just looks—not dismissive, but measuring. "Fear of what, Scarlett? You have not answered my question."

*What* are *you afraid of?*

I curb the urge to roll my eyes. This—this needling psychoanalytic digging—is *not* helping. *I need to be able to do an inward dive in ten days*, I nearly scream. *Can we focus on that?*

On the upside, I get a whole-ass seven out of ten on my next German assignment—*Ich bin so stolz auf dich, Scharlach!* Herr Karl-Heinz writes. It requires some googling to figure out that he's proud of me, but once I do I'm a bit teary-eyed. I do my conditioning. I call Barb and ask her to put Pipsqueak on the phone. I bring Pen a batch of homemade soup, watch comfort rom-coms with her, and hug her when she comes back on Friday, looking pale but whole. I restart my med school essays. I fight with Maryam, eat plenty of lean proteins, and by the following weekend, when it looks like the bruises Lukas left behind might fade, I press hard into them, biting my tongue, hoping the trick will make them last.

I always wear one-pieces for training, mostly out of an irrational terror that a bikini top will come off. I could keep these marks forever, and no one would see. Not even Lukas, because as it becomes obvious by Friday, he has no interest in further contact with me.

I text him once more over the weekend, short and to the point (Let me know if you'd like to meet this weekend) and the reply I receive is: I will.

That's it.

He has dropped the (perfectly processed) input dataset on Dr. Smith's server for me, and I find out only because Zach emails me. All signs point to *Leave me the fuck alone, Scarlett.*

I guess I have failed at sex. It's nothing new (my first blow job to Josh ended with us debating whether I should drive him to the ER). Tragically, this time I failed at the kind of sex I hoped to be good at.

Since I'm also failing, ranging from moderately to spectacularly, at diving, school, applying to med school, *and* hanging out with my dog as much as I'd like, I should be used to it—but I have failed at *that*, too. After Saturday practice I let out a half-miserable, half-amused laugh into the jet of the shower. It gets me puzzled looks from two freshman swimmers, and I summon my most *nothing to see here* smile.

I used to define myself by how well I could perform. I used to flail myself alive when I got less than nines for my dives, or wasn't first in my class. Now, I'd just like to not crash and burn.

It doesn't help that I see Lukas around all the time—a painful reminder that I should be . . . different. Because Lukas is not dead, not kidnapped, not too swamped. I catch sight of him around Avery. In the dining hall with Johan and other people I don't recognize. In the weight room as he hands Pen his water bottle, busy with a thick, low conversation that ends in laughter. Part of me wants to feel the rage of having been used and discarded and bedpost-notched, but it doesn't add up. Lukas is not the kind of asshole who'd leave me on read out of boredom.

I *could* confront him. But I don't, and it stems from more than my well-cultivated conflict avoidance. Stuff like what we did—the potential to hurt the other person goes both ways. Boundaries are important. So I quietly step out of Lukas's way whenever it looks like we might be thrown together. It works so well, I have to wonder if he's doing the same.

By Sunday night, I'm knee-deep in the cognitive restructuring of what happened: a Manna-like, onetime event that confirmed something about myself. I'd been wondering if I'd like the real thing as much as the fantasies of it, and . . . it was the best sex of my life, and it did what I hoped it would: Gathered my scattered thoughts. Stilled me. Quieted my mind for a few hours.

It doesn't make Lukas's rejection less painful, but it's at least worth it. *He's probably pining after Pen, anyway*, I tell myself. *It was never going to be anything serious.* I do my best to shrug it off and re-download my old dating apps, as well as a couple more sex-forward ones.

"Want me to start with the good news or the bad?" Coach Sima asks Pen and me on Monday, at synchro practice.

My "Bad," fully overlaps with Pen's "Good." We burst into laughter.

"Glad to see y'all are having a jolly time, since your dives clearly are not."

Pen fights a smile. I pretend to look for my shammy.

"Today's practice wasn't as bad as last week's." Coach wags his finger in our direction. "But it better be heaps worse than the next."

Pen bats her eyes. "No need to spare our feelings, Coach."

"Hush. You"—he points at Pen—"splashed like the fountain on Trevi, and your arm circle looked like a parallelogram, and"—he turns to me—"you came out of that pike position way too late, and did you hear that *tu-tum*?"

"Do the synchro judges even listen for that?"

"Are you serious? The judges' only purpose on this overheated rock of a planet is to take points off for the inanest reason. You think, *Oh, our hurdles didn't match but we caught up in the air, they won't mind.*" His impression of me is high-pitched and a little breathy. Do I sound like that? "They are drooling for every little point-ducking splatter."

"Doesn't sound paranoid at all," Pen mutters, which earns her a tundra-blazing glare.

"Wanna try the backward pike again?" I ask her.

"*I* tell you what to do next," Coach grunts. "Go try that backward pike again."

Pen and I exchange a grin. It's fun, bearing together the brunt of Coach Sima's grumpiness. "I'm going to try to get my hurdle a bit higher," I tell her, walking by her side.

"Can you?"

"Honestly, changing the fulcrum—"

"Actually," Coach yells after us. "Since your dives are hopeless, you may as well come back here."

We turn, and my heart trips in my chest.

Coach is pointing at Victoria, who stands next to him and glances around wide-eyed, as though while she was gone the pool went through a full remodeling.

On her foot, I spot a cast.

My first instinct is to run to her for a hug, but I stop myself because I'm wet—and because we never really did that before her injury. Do I even have the right?

I quickly glance at Pen. I know they've been in contact the entire time, but she seems surprised to see her here. "Vic!" She smiles, dragging me back. She forces Victoria into something that looks like a choke hold, clearly aiming for maximum dripping on her dry clothes. When she pulls away, Victoria is staring at me, a small smile on her lips.

"So, you stole my spot."

My heart sinks, but I point at Coach. "Please, direct your complaints to HR."

She motions me closer like she really, truly wants a hug, and . . .

"I'm so happy you're here," I whisper in her ear. I wish to go back to before she got hurt. A simpler, more balanced time.

"Me, too, Vandy." We move back at the same time. She glances between Pen and me, sighs dramatically, and says, "You two really suck at synchro."

I flinch.

"Ouch," Pen says.

"Here's the deal. I'm never going to dive competitively again, synchro *or* individual. And it's fucking horrible. And I've spent the last two weeks sobbing into the *Get Well Soon* hedgehog stuffie my cousin Cece sent me. *But.*"

I cock my head.

"The magnitude of which you both suck is larger than I ever suspected, and it's my civic duty to reduce it. And there is an open volunteer coach position . . ."

I'm nodding desperately.

Next to me, Pen seems to be tearing up. "God, please. Save us from ourselves."

"Then it's settled. I mean—" She shrugs. "It's not like you could have said no after a fucking three-centimeter gap between crash mats ravaged my lifelong hopes and dreams." Victoria widens her arms, and Pen and I walk into what could very well be the first three-way hug of my life. "And hey," she mumbles into my hair—or Pen's. "Maybe I'll get a Nobel Prize or something, if I help create the world in which you two suck a bit less."

# CHAPTER 30

OUR FIRST DUAL MEET OF THE SEASON IS AT HOME, AGAINST UT Austin.

It's a huge relief: traveling is fun in theory but exhausting in practice, and usually requires us to skip classes. I'm "too much of type A dictator freak" (Maryam's words; probably the truth) to rely on other people's notes, and "too much of an antisocial turd monkey" (also Maryam's words; certainly the truth) to have made reliable friends within my major, which makes every absence a huge hassle.

In preparation for the meet, practice has been ramping up, and I'm pleased with how much my body has recuperated and its ability to produce clean dives and controlled entries. Still, it's hard to be optimistic when I know that an inward dive will be required, and that my failures will reflect on Pen during synchro.

"Did you discuss it with her directly?" Barb asks me when we FaceTime.

"Yeah. Well, kind of." Pen has been nothing but great, and I feel even more guilty for dragging her down like a giant anvil wrapped around her neck.

*It's just preseason, Vandy.*

*Dual meets don't mean that much.*

*The last thing I want is for you to feel like you're disappointing me.*

"I had this idea," I tell Barb. "You know how people who suffer from insomnia are told *not* to toss and turn, and instead to get out of bed? To avoid forming negative associations with it?"

"I did *not* know that."

"You're a doctor."

"Must not have come up in my orthopedic surgery residency."

"*Well*, I've decided to stop trying to force my inward dives for a few days. Avoid negative associations with the platform. Might help, like a factory reset?"

"What does your therapist say about this?"

"She's not against it." Because she doesn't know. In fact, I had to cancel our session because of a lab this week, and never bothered rescheduling.

I'm doing to my therapist what Lukas is doing to me. I'm just not sure Sam and I are going anywhere.

"I've always hated this preseason malaise," Pen says on Tuesday night in the dining hall. "The constant reminder that we're *about* to start something. Like a pimple that's ripe but cannot be popped yet."

"What *delightful* imagery." Victoria drops her fork into her mashed potatoes.

"What I'm saying is, I'm ready to squeeze that white goo out of my body, and I'm glad UT's coming."

"I beg you. Less pimple-popping philosophy and higher hurdles, okay?"

Pen's right, though. Exhaustion and anticipation are in the air. Everybody's training harder, and Avery is full of wincing steps, athletes guzzling post-workout coconut water, overworked PTs. I'm not immune: my shoulder is holding up, but my back seems to be in a May-December relationship with the rest of my body. Cold baths help, but they're hell in liquid form, and I can only stomach them if they're followed by hot ones. Bree and I usually take them together, but the more strenuous training gets, the more I find myself lingering afterward. "I'm pruning," she tells me on Wednesday morning, stepping out of the Epsom salt tub. "You're really staying longer? Are you sure you're not going to . . . deliquesce?"

I laugh. "How's that chemistry class going?"

"Like shit. Did I use that word right?"

"Almost."

She sticks her tongue out, and I'm left alone in the recovery room.

The tub is a medium-sized, rectangular sunken pool. I turn, leaning my elbows on the deck and leaving the lower two-thirds of my body submerged. I put on my AirPods and spend about ten minutes looking through the PowerPoint for my psych lecture. Once I'm done, I turn off the music, roll around, and nearly drop my phone in the water.

"Vandy!" Kyle's loud voice freezes my blood. "Haven't seen you in a while."

"Oh." I glance around. The landscape of the tub has changed. Vastly. It's me, Kyle, Hunter, and four more male swimmers. Jared, one of them, was in my freshman math class. He waves at me. I try to wave back, but I'm overwhelmed.

It's a lot of men. And me.

"What's up?"

*Breathe. Breathe.* "Not much."

"We've been calling you," another swimmer says. I'm certain I've never talked to him in my life.

"I d-didn't hear you." I point at my earbuds.

"Makes sense. We thought you were ignoring us."

"Yeah, like—what did we do to piss Vandy off?"

Their laughter echoes off the walls. It's just—there's six of them, and they take up a lot of space, and they're between me and the ladder, and I'm . . .

Low-key terrified.

"I'm sorry." I try for a smile, but my cheeks won't behave. *Calm down.* "I better go . . ."

"Nah, stay," Kyle says.

"Some company would be nice," Jared adds. "Kinda bored of these losers."

"Asshole, who did you call a loser?"

"Shut up—Vandy, stay in my mojo dojo Epsom tub."

In the steaming heat, I shiver. "That's lovely, but I have class."

"What class?"

Shit. What class? "It's—" No class. *Think.* "Psych."

"Wait." One of the guys scowls. "Is there a psych class on Wednesday afternoons? My adviser told me that—"

"Come on," a deep voice says from behind me.

Two strong hands slide under my armpits. I clutch my phone, and for a second I'm suspended in the air, a toddler in floaties plucked out of a pool. My feet touch the floor, but I don't turn around to see who my rescuer is.

It's not a touch I could ever forget.

"Sweedy." Hunter frowns. "Did you just, like, steal her from us?"

"You okay?" Lukas asks me. When I nod, he adds, louder, "We have to go. We're working on something."

"Ah, yeah." Kyle nods wisely. "That physics project."

"Bio," Lukas corrects.

"Same difference!"

Next thing I know Lukas is ordering his teammates to behave and pushing me out of the room, his hand hot on my lower back, not too far from where the bruises have started to fade, no matter my—deranged?—attempts at keeping them alive. In the hallway, his fingers close around my shoulder. He turns me around. "You okay?" he asks again.

I'm really, *really* relieved to not be in the tub anymore. So much so, I don't care if it's a bit awkward, seeing him after nearly two weeks, wearing joggers and nothing else, smelling like soap and *him*. He looks at once like Lukas Blomqvist, Pen's ex, the Greatest Swimmer in the World or Whatever, and like *my* Lukas, who printed out a checklist and peels apples and hates rhetorical figures, and it's all . . . confusing.

I shush the odd pang in my chest. "Thank you. I was feeling a bit overwhelmed there." Not that Kyle & Co. would have done anything. But my gut isn't always aware.

"I'm going to talk to Kyle," Lukas says. His mouth is a straight, displeased line.

"What?"

"He needs to give you space."

"There's no need—"

"I won't tell him why. He's not a bad guy, but he has no idea how he comes across. He, Hunter, and a few of the others move in a pack. It'll be good for him to know."

I want to tell him not to bother, but—why not? It'll be a ten-second conversation between them. Saves future unpleasantness. "Okay. Thank you." I give Lukas one last smile and turn around to leave.

He stops me with a hand around my wrist. "Where are you going?"

"Oh." I squeeze out one more smile, and that's it. I'm all out for the day. "I appreciate your help, but I'd rather not make this weird."

His eyes close, like he's gathering the strength of a dozen Valkyries. He slowly exhales from his nostrils and says, "Scarlett."

"It's fine. I'm not—"

"Scarlett," he repeats. It's a harsh, frustrated command. I'm lost as to what he might want from me.

"Lukas, I'm not sure what the protocol is." I'm unable and, frankly, unwilling, to be anything but honest. "We had sex, or—or whatever, and you didn't call me back. I'm trying to take my cues from you, and I *think* you want to pretend it never happened?" I shrug one shoulder, the one not attached to the arm he's still holding. "This is baby's first ghosting, I'm going to need some direction," I add, just to lighten the mood.

Lukas's mood, though, is nothing but dark. The more I speak, the angrier he looks. *Always unfazed*, Pen said. She was wrong, but I can't pinpoint the object of this rage.

Unless there was a breakdown in communication? I hate the hopeful little spark that lights up my chest. "Is that an inaccurate read of what happened between us?"

"No." He finally lets go of me. "It isn't." That impatience, though, is still there. The set of his shoulders, the lines in his brow.

"Is there a good reason you didn't contact me?"

He looks away, jaw clenching. Then back to me. "No."

Irritation pops through me. "Then I—"

"Lukas!" a man calls. He's walking toward us, at once familiar and unknown. His eyes settle on me, inquisitive, and when I notice the unique blue of his eyes, something clicks in my brain.

"Jan, right?" I ask. "Lukas's brother?"

I *immediately* regret it. Is it pathetic that I recognized him after one single photo? Does Lukas think that I've been sequestered in my room, drawing his genealogical tree, making collages out of used Q-tips pilfered from his trash can?

Hard to beat myself up about it with Jan grinning at me. "I am *flattered*." He throws an arm around his brother's shoulders, delighted. He has the body of a retired athlete—big frame softened by time and real life. There may be over a decade between them, but with Lukas having put off shaving for a while and Jan's full beard, they look like they could be twins. "Does he talk about me all the time? Scrapbook about our imaginary lives together?"

"I only ever saw one picture, but it was prominently displayed on his lab bench."

"I knew it."

"It's not a giant picture of your ugly face," Lukas says flatly. The tension of whatever was happening between us has relaxed. "This is Scarlett, Jan. Do leave her alone."

"Swimmer?"

"Almost," I reply. I don't feel intimidated by Jan, probably because of his similarity to Lukas. "Diver."

"Wow. Those things you guys jump off of, they terrify me."

"Me, too." I keep my laughter as non-bitter as possible. "Were you a swimmer?"

"Almost." He winks at me. "I came to the US on a water polo scholarship, back when you weren't even born."

"Jan, she's twenty-one."

"Or conceived."

"Jan."

"Not even an idea in god's beautiful mind."

A deep sigh. "Scarlett, you do not have to listen to this."

"Of course she does. Hey"—Jan turns to me—"did he mention that I taught him everything he knows about swimming?"

"He taught me to play dead in the pool to scare the lifeguard."

"And it was *hilarious*. Scarlett, do you hike?"

I blink at the abrupt change of topic. "Yeah?"

"Have you ever hiked around this area?"

"Oh, yes. Several times. I'm happy to give you some recs, if—"

"Nah, we know where we're going. Would love for you to come with us, though."

Oh. *Oh.* "Thank you, that's really lovely, but . . ." Does he think I'm Lukas's girlfriend?

"But?"

*Say that you have class. A date. Say something about being allergic to the sun.* But when I sneak a glance at Lukas and find him staring, all I feel is a frisson of annoyance that *he's* not the one put in the unpleasant position of lying to his kind brother, and what comes out of my mouth is "I doubt Lukas wants me to go with you guys." It's, at least, the truth.

Which is why I'm taken aback by the deep laughter that pops out of Jan. "I'm no mind reader, but I know my brother, and he very much wants you to come. And even if he didn't . . ." His smile is a bottomless pool of charm. "*I* want you to come. That's what matters."

# CHAPTER 31

*L*UKAS'S NAME SOUNDS DIFFERENT IN HIS BROTHER'S MOUTH.
Jan's English is more accented, the grammar a bit stiffer, as
though he began learning it too late to hit the perfect window of
opportunity. I listen to their bickering—*You're a reckless driver. I'm
not, Jan. Scarlett, is he not a reckless driver? I'm just glad he didn't
get a vanity plate.*—and don't bother hiding my smile. Every once in
a while, when they're talking about practical matters that don't involve me, they break into Swedish.

It's lovely to hear. Pitchy, melodic. An interesting combination
of pillows and sharp edges. Sounds I could never reproduce, not
even if I took daily classes on tongue positioning for the rest of my
life. Peaks and dips. Songlike and calm.

The difference between Jan's *Lukas* and mine is mostly in the *u*
and *s*, and it makes me almost morbidly eager to find out how Lukas
pronounces his own name. Is it weird, the way we all twist it into
something else? What's it like, living in a second language? Maybe
I'll ask, if it ever comes up. If we ever talk again.

And perhaps we will, because as awkward as being here is, he
seems genuinely happy to have me along for the ride. It's nice to be

off campus in the middle of the week, in a place that's never been touched by chlorine. On Wednesdays, I usually catch up on school-work, but the rolling hills and chaparral of the City of Palo Alto parks department couldn't care less about my outstanding MCAT scores and inward dives.

I needed this break. A moment to recalibrate my perspective. I used to come here all the time as a freshman. When did I stop?

"Turn back," I order from the bottom of a hill. Jan and Lukas do—two almost identical handsome, sweaty, freckled faces—and I snap a pic with my phone. "I'll send it, and you can forward it to the rest of your family."

Lukas snorts. "You think Dad's gonna cry, Jan?"

Jan laughs. "He's gonna send us a four-paragraph autocorrected wall of text about how proud he is of us. Because we went for a walk."

"He sounds nice," I say, hurrying behind them. When a misstep almost has me tripping, Lukas's fingers are suddenly under my arm. They stay long after I've regained my footing.

"Dad's great," Jan agrees. His eyes stay on Lukas's hand, and I hastily free myself. "But . . ."

"But?" I ask.

"We think he read too many parenting books," Lukas explains. He trails right after me, as if keeping tabs. Making sure I don't slip again. "Especially too many stressing the importance of praising your children for their smallest accomplishments."

"And doting on all of them equally. Oskar's a woodcutter, and Leif's a human rights lawyer. Dad performs the same enthusiasm for a finished Adirondack chair and a granted asylum."

"We should really have a talk with him."

Jan scoffs. "Not until you win another Olympic medal and he equates it to me publishing a blog post." During the drive he ex-plained that he's a Victorianist. He's visiting Lukas after attending a conference down in LA, and tomorrow will return to Paris, where he lives with his partner and *four cats*.

"How many of you are based in Sweden?" I ask.

"Only Oskar."

"Source of big pain for Dad," Lukas adds.

"*Biiiiig* pain. But he'll never admit it."

Lukas nods. "If you love something, set it free."

"He sounds kinda . . . perfect?"

"He is," Jan says. We stop at the top of the hill and turn around. The Dish is there, ready to be plucked. "Decent and caring. None of us will ever measure up."

"Might as well not even try," Lukas adds, wiping his brow with the side of his T-shirt. When he drops it, it's wet and nearly see-through.

"Sorry the weather is so unseasonably warm while you visit," I tell Jan. "The heat is rough."

"Oh, not at all. We're Swedish. There's no such thing as bad weather—"

"—just bad clothes," he and Lukas finish together.

They exchange a grin above my head.

🌢 🌢 🌢

After, Jan insists on buying us food.

"We can have dinner for free at the cafeteria later," I point out, but he waves me off and leads us to a quaint coffee shop.

"Let him pay," Lukas tells me. "He still owes me six thousand kronor from when he broke my Xbox in a fit of rage."

"That was, like, eight years ago."

"Good point." Lukas pulls back a chair, and waits patiently until I lower myself into it. "I'll calculate the accrued interests while you buy us coffee."

Lukas and I are briefly left alone. I take my phone out of my pocket and pretend to check my messages as I brainstorm a topic of conversation with a low land mine density. Jan returns with three coffees and an assortment of pastries.

"Are you divers the kind of athletes who need tens of thousands of calories per day?" he asks.

I laugh. "I'm not sure anyone is?"

"This one eats as much as all of Luxembourg." He points at Lukas with his thumb. "We have this tradition, in Sweden. Every afternoon we sit down for coffee and snacks. We relax."

"Oh, yes. *Fika*, right?" I flush the instant the words are out. Because I'm probably butchering the pronunciation, and because . . .

Jan turns to his brother. "Did you teach her?"

"I don't believe so." Lukas sits back in his chair and casually drapes a long arm around the back of mine, somehow managing not to touch me. He stares over the rim of his cup, like he caught me with a hand in the stalking jar. "She must have learned about it all by herself."

I lower my gaze to my lap, trying to look less mortified than I feel. But—why? Why should *I* be mortified? Maybe I did open up Google and look up Swedish customs. Maybe I turned on the close captions and watched a couple of YouTube videos while brushing my teeth. Maybe I discovered that Swedish people have real ice hotels, and their cheesecake is completely different from ours.

I lift my chin and meet Lukas's eyes, a little combative. *Maybe I thought about you after what we did. Maybe I find you interesting. Maybe I like you without being liked back. I refuse to be ashamed.*

"*Fika* is usually with sweet things," Jan says, oblivious to the two-sided argument inside my head. "But Lukas"—*so Scandinavian*—"refuses to eat sweets, so . . ." He gestures toward a pretzel.

"I don't refuse to eat them," Lukas counters, tearing off a piece. "I don't like them."

Jan's *pshhh* is very older-brotherly. "He *does* like them. He just lies to himself about it."

Lukas rolls his eyes. "Not this again."

"Please, Jan." I prop my chin over my palm. "Tell me everything about his self-deception."

"Well, I'm sure you already know how good he is at denying himself. The more he wants something, the less he'll let himself have it." My curiosity must come through, because he continues, "Like when he was twelve, and he slept on the wooden floor for three months."

I glance at Lukas, who's drinking his coffee with a put-upon air. "Why?"

"No reason whatsoever." Jan throws a hand up. "He'd gotten a new bed, and it was really comfortable, and he liked sleeping in it, and he needed to *prove to himself* that he could do without it. When he was eleven? Only cold showers. For a whole year."

Lukas sighs. "Jan, could you tone it down with the whole 'grandma pulling out a photo album' bit? I doubt Scarlett cares."

"Oh, Scarlett *cares*," I counter.

"See? She's a rapt audience. For two whole years he didn't season his food. Not even salt. Before that, he would wake up an hour earlier than he needed to."

"Jan," Lukas warns.

"It's his thing. His way of feeling in control. But it's foolish— we are humans. We are not in control. Self-determination is a myth."

An icy, heavy weight sinks to the bottom of my stomach. I turn to Lukas. "Do you still do that?" I ask, as if from a distance.

"Well," Jan interjects, "by now he's successfully proven that he is capable of divesting himself of *aaall* worldly attachments—"

Lukas snaps something in Swedish. It doesn't sound melodic or soft, and it has Jan falling silent, then replying in the same language.

A short back-and-forth ensues, but Jan's eyes remain calm, and he looks at Lukas with something that can only be affection.

When Jan turns to me again, his voice is kind, and the topic is over. "Eat up," he tells me.

I don't put a single bite in my mouth.

# CHAPTER 32

*L*ATER.

After Jan hugs me, gives me his email, and makes me promise to stay in touch.

After Lukas drops him off at his hotel.

After it is agreed upon, without any conversation, that he'll drive me home.

After I tell him my address and ask, "Should I type it into the GPS?"

After he shakes his head and remains silent for several minutes.

After he kills the engine in front of my apartment building, unbuckles his seat belt, unbuckles *mine*, and then sits back half against the door so that he can look at me.

After he patiently waits for me to speak for a long stretch of silence that seems to claw at my throat and expand within my body.

I ask, "How long?"

He knows what I mean.

*How long were you going to deny yourself, this time?*

*How long till you planned to reach out to me again?*

"Fifteen days." There is no shame in his voice. And maybe there shouldn't be. He was on track to make it, after all.

I nod. "Just a few more, then."

His arms cross on his chest. I wish I could read his expression, but his face is blank. When he finally talks, a million moments later, it's *to* me, but I'm not sure it's *for* me.

"That first day, the Sunday, I almost called you a dozen times. It was . . . difficult. Last week Pen mentioned that you two were having lunch together, and I went to the dining hall just to—I don't fucking know. Look?" He shrugs, detached. It's like he's reporting the results of an experiment. On me. On *himself.* "On day seven Jan arrived. He's good at taking up every free second of a person's day with no regard for their schedule."

"How nice of him."

"I thought the same."

I bite the inside of my cheek. "Did you consider that I'm not a bed, or a condiment. I'm not hot water." I try to sound as disengaged as he seems to be, but I doubt I'm succeeding. "Did you consider that I might be the type to hold a grudge? Or self-respecting enough to pick up the phone on the fifteenth day and say, 'Fuck off'?"

He nods, like I'm being nothing but reasonable. The quiet, impersonal civility of this conversation is . . . devastating, actually. "I think part of me hoped you would."

"Why?"

It takes him a while to answer. When he does, he's not looking at me. "Because sometimes I can't breathe when you're around."

"Well, I . . ." I shake my head. Huff bitterly. "I'm sorry."

He laughs, silent. "It's not a bad feeling, actually. Just overwhelming." He shakes his head, as if to get rid of bad thoughts. "I had no frame of reference for how much I . . ."

I can fill in the blanks. *I liked it more than I thought I would, and it scared me.*

He bites the inside of his lip. "I'm . . . not sure I enjoy it. Not being in control."

*Welcome to the club, Lukas.* "Well, if it makes you feel any better, I doubt it has anything to do with *me*. I'm just the first not-vanilla girl you've ever been with."

A long, icy stare. He doesn't reply.

"The thing is, Lukas, I understand how you feel. I really do. And I don't blame you, but . . ."

I'm silent for so long, trying to put my thoughts together, feeling the clammy weight of this press down on me. Lukas never rushes me, and at last I have my words.

"Even if it's just sex, it's not a good idea for me to be with some-one who resents wanting me."

It's just for a blip, a gaping, voracious, rioting moment, that I can see a hint of how he really feels about this. But it lasts so little, I'm not even sure. Whether he cares. Whether he's happy to be free of me. Whether he heard what I'm saying.

I swallow around the off-kilter heartbeat in my throat, and then I reach out to squeeze his hand one last time. The marks of my teeth, I notice, are still there. Like those, too, weren't allowed to fade.

"Bye, Lukas," I say.

He doesn't try to stop me, and I never look back.

# CHAPTER 33

**A**S I ONCE EXPLAINED TO BARB, DUAL MEETS ARE OFFICIAL
and regulated by the NCAA, but "not, like, too much."

"What you just said makes absolutely no sense," she pointed out,
and she was right.

The most important swimming and diving competitions are
clustered in the spring. That's when our regional conference, the
Pac-12, happens, when the NCAA trials and finals happen, and, in
a year like this one, when we fight it out to see who'll get to go to the
Olympic Games. Preseason meets are much smaller in size, and it's
understood that no athlete is expected to be in tip-top shape yet.
Records or personal bests are unlikely, they are not televised, and
the atmosphere more convivial. If we win, good. If we lose: *See you
in March.*

"No synchro for you on this meet. You're just not good enough
yet," Coach tells Pen and me on Friday night, sounding ready to
combat our counterarguments.

Pen and I, though, both slump in relief. "You're right," she says.
"No need for public humiliation."

I nod. "We should definitely spare the Texans our shame."

"Someone could even TiVo us and post us somewhere."

I scrunch my nose, Pen faux shudders, and we leave a perplexed Coach Sima behind.

Basically, this meet is no big deal. It might even be a *small* deal—if not for two reasons.

One: this is my first time competing since my injury, and the thought has been making every cell in my body want to puke since I woke up.

Two is, of course: The. Inward. Issue.

"It's normal to be nervous," Pen says, holding my eyes in the mirror as I part my hair to French braid it.

I half exhale a laugh. "Is it that obvious?"

"Just to me." She smiles. "Because I know you."

She does. Maybe our relationship started as circumstantial, but lately we've been together so often, it'd be hard not to describe what we have as friendship—even for someone like me, who strives to avoid overestimating her emotional significance in other people's lives. "I just need to get through the first dive, I think. Then I'll calm down."

She lays her head on my shoulder. "I'll be there, Vandy. If you need anything."

We march out of the locker room with the women's swimming team, and there's so many of them, all so powerfully upbeat, it's hard not to be infected with their enthusiasm. Last night, in preparation for UT's arrival, someone put up a bunch of MEET THE ATHLETE posters. They're plastered on the hallway leading out to the exhibition pool, and I pass by a few familiar faces. Kyle, Niko, Rachel, Cherry, Hasan. Lukas.

He's the only unsmiling swimmer, and boy, is it fitting.

I stare at his picture, unsurprised by the stomach squeeze that hits me, an odd mix of wistfulness, anger, sadness—and irritation at myself.

In the last few days, he tried to call me. Twice. Then texted me. Once.

"I forgot that Lukas is trying two hundred freestyle, too," Bree says, tapping at his poster.

Pen nods. "Sweden's head coach told him that they don't have anyone fast at it on the Olympic team."

"Is he just, you know." Bella shrugs. "Against anyone else medaling?"

"Oh, shit." Pen winces. "I forgot that two hundred freestyle is Devin's and Dale's main, too! But don't worry—it's not going to be one of Lukas's NCAA events."

"Oh, yeah." Bree snorts. "'Cause otherwise Devin and Dale were *totally* gonna win that race."

"Hey!"

"I'm just trying to be realistic about who we're dating, Bella." Bree sighs. "See, the difference between me and you? That's how you know that clear-sightedness is *not* genetic."

"Then basic human decency must not be, either."

"Excuse me?"

"They're so scary when they argue," I whisper at Pen, hurrying outside ahead of them.

"They grew up together and are basically the same person. They *know* how to strike the chakra that'll hurt the most."

"You make an excellent argument for lifelong solitude."

One of UT's most recent recruits is Sunny, a girl I trained with back in St. Louis. "I can't believe I'm in my first college competition!" she tells me on the deck, hugging me once and then again. "And you're in it, too! You've always been *goals* for me."

*You sure about that?* I don't let myself say. I smile, pretending to be excited and not full of worms crawling over my internal organs, and go sit next to Pen to begin the time-consuming process of putting on wrist guards and taping my joints. In the pool across the diving well, the swimmers are warming up. Lukas is there, speaking with his coach and Rachel as he stretches, and I recall his text.

LUKAS: I owe you an apology.

"Pen?"

"Yup."

"Can I ask you something about Lukas?"

"You mean, my ex whom you're currently doing? Sure."

*Not currently.* "The other day I met his brother, and—"

"What brother?" Her eyes widen.

"Jan."

"Wait—which one is Jan?"

"The next youngest."

"With kids? The lawyer?"

"Those would be Oskar and Leif, the two oldest."

"Right, right." She shrugs. "What about Luk?"

"You know how he . . . tries to prove to himself he's above wanting things?"

She gives me a baffled look, like I just announced that I'm moving to a farm in Vermont to tend to pygmy goats. "Lukas Blomqvist? Are you sure—holy *shit*." Pen slaps my forearm, staring somewhere into the stands.

"What happened?"

"He's here."

I squint into the distance, looking for a non-otherwise-specified he. "Who?"

"Theo. Teacher. The teacher I'm hot for!"

I gape. "Is he here to see you?"

"I—maybe?"

"Did you invite him?"

"No! No? I mentioned in passing that I had a meet and now he's over there . . ."

Pen sinks her obviously delighted smile into her knees, and I bite my lower lip to avoid laughing.

◊  ◊  ◊

My first competing dive after my (forced) hiatus is a thing of beauty, and the judges agree. I get eight point fives and a nine, and for a moment—a beautiful, brilliant, blooming moment—I allow myself to cradle the hope that I might be back.

"That was the most elegant reverse two-and-a-half-somersault tuck I've ever seen," one of the UT coaches tells me while I stare up at the scoreboard from under the shower. Austin tried to recruit me, and she and I met when I visited their campus.

"Thank you," I say, feeling—wow. I might actually be *proud* of myself. What a concept.

"Hope to see many more from you."

Pen goes after me, but her entry is not the cleanest. Sunny's good, but her degree of difficulty is low, which reflects on the score. The twins don't compete from the platform, which means that with the UT divers, there's seven of us overall.

The second round—forward three and a half—goes even better, as do my twist, my armstand, and my backward dives. By the time the fifth round is done, I'm second on the board, trailing Pen by just two points, but am fifteen ahead of Hailey, a UT sophomore.

"And *this* is where I get fucked," I mutter, trying to keep my shoulder warmed up.

"No. Nope." Pen steps in front of me. "This is diving, Vandy. *Negative thinking* is how you get fucked."

I take a deep breath. Force myself to nod. "You're right."

"I'm *always* right. And listen." She takes both my hands. "Taking a break from trying inward dives was a great strategy. You're gonna go up and get that inward pike done, because you are amazing. And if you don't, I'm going to . . . I don't know, beat you up? So you better."

I laugh. Accept her hug. When the referee gestures at me to start climbing the tower, I do that, lingering halfway, waiting for the two girls before me to complete their dives. When I hear the second splash, I dry whatever droplets are left on my skin, throw down my shammy, and walk toward the end of the platform.

It always feels momentous, stepping toward that edge—throwing one's body off a cliff can never be a light decision—but today the ten meters between me and the water are absolutely life-changing.

I visualize. Not the *dive*, this time, but the way I'll feel after I manage an inward pike. Waking up tomorrow morning and leaving what plagued me in the past few months firmly behind. Going to practice without being defined by the one thing I cannot do—once again among peers, instead of an intruder. Returning to St. Louis for the holidays and not having to skulk around in the hope I won't meet any of my former teammates—or, even worse, Coach Kumar.

Feeling *whole* again.

I visualize all the good things that will come from me flying through these ten meters in the right way, and none of what will happen if I don't. Because Pen is right, and a defeatist mentality has no place in diving.

My eyes slide to Coach Sima, Pen, Victoria, the twins, all rooting for me. A few thousand miles away, so are Barb and Pipsqueak. On the far end of the pool, leaning one arm against the wall, a towering, cap-tousled figure in sunglasses stares up at me.

"One minute," the referee yells.

A time warning, but it's okay. I'm fucking *ready* to bury the last two years of my life.

I turn around.

Close my eyes.

Bend my knees. Lift my arms up. Press my back into the shape I learned as a kid.

Take a single deep breath, and *go*.

Divers are in the air for less than a second, but sometimes the process of twisting our muscles and angling our body is so arduous, it seems to stretch for years. Today, that's not the case. My waist bends easily into a pike that's as much second nature as photosynthesis is for plants. And the rest . . . it just works. I'm not sure how, or why, but it does. I'm in the water sooner than I can worry about *failing*, and before I reemerge, I take a moment.

Squeeze my eyes shut.

Savor the relief.

Then I burst out, barely holding back a grin, wipe the water from my eyes, and—

I don't even need to see the scoreboard. Pen's frown tells me everything I need to know.

I may have done a pike. And maybe it was a good one. But I did *not* manage an inward dive.

# CHAPTER 34

'M ON WATERED-DOWN DRINK NUMBER TWO, OR THREE, OR whatever the fuck imaginary complex real rational integer, when it occurs to me that I should probably let the UT guy who's been trying to pick me up for the last twenty minutes know that I'm not going to consent to making out, having sex, or exchanging physical contact of any kind with him.

Trevor (Travis?) is nice, and as far as men go, I don't find him particularly threatening. But that might be the most positive thing I can say about him. His square, handsome face does nothing for me, and his monologue on his silver at the Pan Am games needs some serious workshopping.

"You don't live in this house, do you?" he asks.

I have a headache. Or maybe *he's* a headache. "Nope." In fact, I have no idea where we are. Some swimmer's living room, probably. There's always some kind of celebration after a dual, to show our guests that Stanford has a fantastic party scene.

It might be true. I wouldn't know.

"Too bad. Would be nice if your bed was nearby."

I want to leave. I want to no longer have his muzzle this close to mine. But Pen left a while ago to go meet with Teacher, and upon a cursory glance around the crowded room, I cannot spot any friendly faces. It means that if I leave Trevor and this couch, I'll be all alone. And if I'm alone, I'll think about the things everyone said to me after my dive, the pitying looks, the slimy layers of disappointments coating my stomach.

*Next time.* (Barb)

*Vandy, you placed third out of seven, even with a failed dive. You're fucking amazing.* (Pen)

*Omg, it sucks. It happened to me, too, once. Got the twisties, did the wrong dive. It's just a brain glitch.* (Sunny)

*It's okay, kid.* (An upsettingly conciliatory Coach Sima, whose uncharacteristic kindness made me feel even worse)

A silent hug. (Bree and Bella)

What I need is more alcohol. Once I'm drunk, my neurons will be too drenched in ethanol to process their own firing. The ouroboros of defeat that is my life will fade into the great unknown.

"You know," Trevor says, "my ex was a diver."

"Were they?" I look around, hoping to locate a primary source of rum and Coke.

"She only kind of was my ex. She was more into me than I was into her."

Upon further consideration, alone with my thoughts *is* better than with this guy. *Anywhere* would be, including the back of a refuse collection vehicle or a falling Sumerian city-state. "Poor girl," I say flatly.

"Yeah, it was sad. I'm sensitive, hate saying no to people."

"I bet."

"But we still had fun. That's just to say, I know how you divers are, and . . ." He trails off, and for that I credit the vehemence with which I picture sticking toothpicks into his eye sockets. I've unlocked a hitherto forgotten power. It might even look good on med school applications.

But no. Even in the dim fairy lights, Trevor's eyes shine as he tilts his head up. "Holy shit, Lukas Fucking Blomqvist. Hey, man!"

He holds out a hand. Lukas ignores it and takes a seat in front of us, on a wooden coffee table that looks way too tired for this shit. I'm certain it's going to break. I should probably record it for *Sweden's Funniest Home Videos*.

"You okay, Scarlett?" he asks, ignoring his fanbro's excitement.

"Yup."

He studies me, silent, probing, like what I say cannot be taken at face value, and has deeper meanings that can only be discovered under the layers of my skin.

Meanwhile: "Man, I cannot tell you how amazing it was racing next to you today," Trevor fawns. Which leads me to the shocking discovery that I am, in fact, able to find him even *less* attractive.

Lukas tilts his head toward him. "You want him to stick around?"

"Hell yeah, she wants me around. We're having fun. Aren't you having fun?"

"Not really," I say—alcohol, the ultimate truth serum. Trevor's face crunches into a hurt crumple, and . . . Shit. "But it's not"—*wholly*—"because of you. I just had a crappy diving day."

"Aww." He clearly finds my athletic failures cute—like a capybara bathing, or a child who says *aminal*. He scoots closer, one hand wrapping around my bare knee, and . . . yikes. It's an unpleasant, too-tight heat that has me nauseated—until Lukas leans forward, grips Trevor's wrist, and forcibly moves it back to his lap.

Trevor gives him a confused look. "Am I overstepping here? Are you two . . . ?"

"No." I shift away. I can't take him touching me again.

"Why do you care, then?"

He's asking Lukas, who informs him, "She's my sister."

I almost choke on my spit.

"What?" Trevor blinks at me. "For real?"

I must be a terrible person. Because I nod.

"But isn't your last name . . ."

"Half sister," I improvise.

Lukas nods. "Different dad."

"Seriously? I had no idea. Is it pretty well known, or . . . ?"

I shrug. "It's not a secret."

"Right. You guys must be pretty close in age."

"Yeah." I inspect my nails. "Not to slut shame, but our mom got around."

Lukas tries to hide a smile. Fails. Hangs his head.

"Oh, wow." Trevor sounds impressed. "My mom's kind of a slut, too. Had an affair with one of her colleagues out of revenge for my dad fucking her cousin. So petty."

Lukas and I freeze. Exchange a bewildered look. "Thank you for sharing this . . . powerful autobiographical story," he tells Trevor, finally sparing him a crumb of attention. "Could you go get my sister a glass of water?"

"Oh." Trevor scratches the back of his head. "Um, yeah, sure."

"Thanks, man." Lukas focuses on me.

I sit back, trying not to squirm under the weight of his stare, and once Trevor's far enough, I say, "I'm not drinking a drop of anything coming from that guy."

He holds out the red Solo cup in his hand. I take it, bring it to my nose. Briefly consider pretending that I don't trust *him*, either. I take a sip, though. It's water, and I only realize how thirsty I was after I down the entire thing.

"Are you drunk?" he asks, accepting the cup back.

I sigh. "Not nearly as much as I'd like."

"Don't go anywhere with McKee."

"Who's Mc—oh. What's his name, by the way?"

"Trevor." He frowns into the distance. "Travis? I don't fucking know."

I snort. "He was right, though."

"I doubt that asshole has ever been right about a single thing."

"Last week I learned a German proverb. 'Even a blind chicken finds a piece of corn every once in a while.' Or something." I shrug. "And Trevor did ask a fair question."

"Which is?"

"Why *do* you care?"

Lukas doesn't answer, doesn't tense up, doesn't show a single ounce of discomfort. Typical.

"By process of elimination . . ." I lift my index finger. "You're not warning him off out of *jealousy*, because that's not a feeling you are capable of entertaining."

He watches me, unknowable.

"It's not because you want to get laid. I mean, you have other options. You won what, four, five races today?" His lack of reply tells me it might be more. Whatever. Middle finger: up. "You contributed more to Stanford winning the meet than the entire diving team. Maybe for competition purposes, you should be considered an institution. Get a .org domain, save on taxes—"

"Scarlett," he says simply, like he wants me to stop rambling. But not because he finds me annoying. It is, I think, because he wants to say, "I'm sorry."

I cock my head. *How novel*, I think. In my personal experience, men rarely apologize.

"You and I," he continues, "agreed to trust each other, did one of the most intimate things two people like us can—"

"Wasn't that big a deal. It was just sex—"

"Scarlett." He waits until I'm looking him in the eye. "I'm sorry. I couldn't immediately process what happened. I felt out of control, and panicked. I acted like an asshole. I put *my* own fear before *your* feelings, and that's . . . the most fucked-up thing I've ever done, without a doubt."

My plan was to write him off. Still is.

Except, having him acknowledge how bad he screwed up is blowing a bit of a hole in that.

"None of this is an excuse," he continues, disarmingly earnest. "But what Jan said was true. When I'd felt out of control before, it was always . . ." His Adam's apple moves. I get the sense that this is hard for him—not because he hates admitting his guilt, but because he has disappointed himself. "It was never with another person involved."

*What about Pen?* is on the tip of my tongue, itching to burst out, but I won't let it. It's not my business. "You don't owe me anything," I start, but he's already shaking his head.

"I owe you respect, I owe you care, and I owe you the truth. You, on the other hand, do not owe me forgiveness. But if you ever enter this kind of relationship with someone else . . ." His jaw grinds, tense. I don't think he likes the idea. "These are the things you should demand."

I look down into my lap, gathering his apology, my feelings, the fear and eagerness, all mixed up at the bottom of my belly.

"It's okay," I say at last. This time it's a decision, not an automatic response. I mean it. "I'm also not the best with . . ." I make an all-encompassing, hyper-vague gesture before letting my hand drop on my knee.

"With?"

"Emotions. Mine or otherwise."

His laugh is huffed out, like he shares the pain. "Everything I said about McKee remains true. He doesn't deserve to be within a five-mile radius of you."

"I'm deeply hurt that you'd think I'd go for him."

"You seemed to be considering it."

"I was *not*." I take stock of my body and my brain. I'm mostly sober. Clear thinking. Tired, but when am I not? "I had a shit day, and he was there."

"A shit day?"

It occurs to me that from his standpoint, I did well. I medaled, after all. He doesn't know about my issues—and I'll keep it that way. I've had my fill of pity. "No reason. But he was taking my mind off stuff. As good as anything."

"I'm sure you can find something better."

"I *have* heard great things about being stuck in traffic?"

"Vacuuming is excellent, too."

I laugh. "Sadly, I don't have a car. Or—and you're not going to like this—a vacuum cleaner."

He looks genuinely worried. "What conditions do you live in?"

"My point is, I don't have other options available to me." My heart races. *Slow down*, I order, trying to breathe around the heavy *thump*. "Unless you have other ideas."

He must have expected to have to work much harder for my forgiveness, because it takes a long while to get the gist of what I'm offering. Once he does, though, there's no hesitation. He nods, tosses the Solo cup in the closest bin, and takes my hand to lead me outside.

# CHAPTER 35

*L*UKAS'S ROOM IS STILL IMMACULATE. I INSPECT IT AFTER HE turns on the bedside lamp, and study the military neatness, unsurprised to note the presence of a headboard and the lack of navy sheets. He sits at his desk, and I ponder shuffling his books out of alphabetical order, just to make a forehead vein twitch.

"So, is the bed here just for the sex, or do you actually sleep on it?"

He pulls me into his lap, unamused. I noticed that he has turned on his desktop.

"Are we working on the bio project?" I ask, angling my knees into his spread legs.

His lips twitch, but he doesn't reply. Instead he strokes up and down my thigh, presses one soft kiss and a less-than-soft bite into my throat, and when I shiver, he takes his hands away and begins typing.

His healthcare portal is the same as mine. He clicks through a handful of lab results, and I lean toward the screen.

"Okay?" he asks once I'm done.

"Okay," I reply. I want it to be like last time: my mind wiped, and my body on fire.

Lukas takes my chin between his index and thumb. "After," he starts. "Don't just leave."

My brow wrinkles.

"Wake me up if you need to. But don't leave without saying anything."

There are so many objections I could raise. None seems important, though. "Okay," I say, and after that I hold my breath, ready to be once again reminded of how *in control* he can be.

"You're so good at doing what I ask you, aren't you?"

I nod eagerly, bracing. But Lukas just kisses me lightly on the mouth, so sweet and gentle that his hand slips around my inner thigh almost undetected. He parts my legs, shifts me deeper into his lap. Strokes me lightly, just outside my underwear.

I can't hold in a needy whimper. His knuckles moving under the fabric of my skirt are unspeakably *dirty*, and the second he finds me wet, his tongue clicks, like I'm exactly what he expected and also—

"Fucking out of this world," he rumbles against my throat. His middle finger begins rubbing, and I let out a grateful, pleading exhale. *Thank god he's not making me wait*, I tell myself. Thirteen minutes later, I'm still on the edge, and the clock on the monitor laughs at me.

It starts when Lukas pulls down my top none too gently and tells me, "Your tits are spectacular—has anyone told you?"

Something pleased and proud grows inside me. I shake my head.

"What about your idiot ex?" he asks with a frown.

*He wasn't an idiot*, I want to protest, but there's a time and a place to defend a guy who's in love with someone else. I shake my head again.

Lukas is bewildered. Angry. "I can't wrap my head around it, Scarlett," he says, touching my nipple and my clit at the same time, both grazes, both promising *more*. "He had a treasure and he just . . ." He sounds like he'd like to take it out on someone, but it doesn't occur to me who that *someone* will be until his lips curve. "I despise him. I should just be grateful, though. If he wasn't a world-class asshole, I wouldn't be able to do this—"

He pinches one of my nipples so hard, I forget how to breathe. Then his finger circles around my clit until I can get the stimulation I *need*, and—

"You love it, don't you?"

He twists my nipple, and I come for the first time. He bites the side of my breasts, and—the second. The third happens a little later, when he starts sucking on my puffy, achy peaks, his middle finger knuckle deep inside my cunt. After that . . . it doesn't matter anymore, and not much is required of me. If I wriggle in his arms, if my ass rubs against his erection, he'll still me with his teeth and a stern word, his hand heavy against my belly. All I need to do is take the pleasure. Do as I'm told. Listen to the way he whispers soft commands into my ear, like *Just one more* and *You can do it* and fragments of sentences that include words like *perfect*, and *just for me*, and *beautiful tears*.

He kisses the corners of my eyes, licking away this delicious pain *he* is giving. I've never felt so hollow. "Please," I beg. I'm a mess of quivers and aftershocks, trying to burrow into him. His arms and voice are the only things holding me together.

"Not yet," he says, kind and firm and everything I've ever craved. I just didn't know that someone's voice could be at once tender and cruel-edged. "You can take some more. My good girl."

He's never wrong, not once, and after a while I'm sure that he knows my body better than I do, and what he doesn't know he'll teach himself. This time, when he lays me on his bed, he takes off *all* my clothes. He's patient with them, patient with how boneless and lazy I am, sprawled, looking up with an awestruck smile, too orgasmed out to help. He folds my skirt, and my top, and even my bra, but tosses my panties somewhere to the back of the room, and it's so un-Lukas of him, I cannot help the giggle bubbling out of me. "That's littering *and* theft."

He takes off his T-shirt. His pants. "In Sweden you'd be arrested and sentenced to hard time for it." He lowers himself on top of me, a blanket of heat and flesh, and adds into the soft skin behind my ear, "For littering, I mean."

I didn't expect to laugh with him. Sex was fun and carefree with Josh, but I always assumed it to be a by-product of being in love with one's partner. And yet here I am, giggling my amusement into the throat of a man who, for all I know, might still be in love with another woman.

He breathes me in. Tells me how good I feel under him. Soft. *Pretty*—a ridiculous word that has me arching closer. "I should stretch you out with my fingers, before," he says, the rumble of his chest vibrating against my breast. "How I usually do it. Barest courtesy. But with you, I'm not going to. I'm going to make you take me without."

I shiver. Let him spread me out and gasp at the shock of it. Diving and flexibility go hand in hand, but I feel it in my muscles, the way he pins each of my thighs to the sides, palms hooking under my knees. The strain of forcing my hips to stay *that* wide open for him.

"So obedient," he tells me, pleased, and I smile, the pleasure of his praise warming me from deep within. He dips his fingers in the absolute mess between my legs, letting out a breath that's followed by a foreign, melodic word, and uses it to slick himself.

I consider reaching out. Being a more active participant. But with Lukas, the rules under which I've operated most of my life don't hold true. I lie back, watch him watch me, feel the heavy weight of his cock on my pubic bone, as he uses the palm of his hand to press the underside of it into my abdomen, my cunt. I'm light. I'm eager. I'm ready, because he said so. Malleable.

Floating.

I once read somewhere that power-exchange sex is a farce. Scenes and plays. Scripted shit. Acting. To me, though, this buoyant feeling of soaring is the definition of honesty. Knowing that he's in charge, my wrists pinned above my head by his hand, I can be simple. Artless. My true self, away from blame and judgment.

"Look at you." Lukas presses a sliding kiss into my lower lip, adjusts himself with a hand between our bodies. "A fucking dream." His hips push, and after a few tries, the round head of his cock slips inside me.

He lets out a hot gasp, somewhere around my cheekbone.

My breath hitches as I tip back my neck.

He's inside a couple of inches, but there's nowhere else to go. "Relax," he orders. I nod. Make myself pliant. He thrusts again and advances, just a little. The burn of the stretch is terrible. Everything I ever wanted. "Deep breaths, Scarlett."

We make some progress. I struggle. Lukas watches my face for every second of it, drinking in my bitten lips and my choppy breathing and the winces that slip out of me.

"Too much?" he asks.

I nod, a little desperately.

He halts, pulling out a bit. Instant panic spreads through my stomach. I didn't say *stop*. I didn't ask him to stop. We agreed that he wouldn't—

"That's too bad," he says, his voice at once mean and fond, like he contains every multitude I'll ever need. "Since you'll take what I fucking give you." He rocks back inside, knocking any sense of self out of me. My entire body tightens around him, around his words, and I think that maybe I'm—"Oh, sweetheart. Already? Just from this?"

A few contractions. Low-pitched laughter. He manages to get farther in, and there is no space, but he's *making* it, creating something that wasn't there.

"Lukas," I exhale.

"I know, baby." His voice is taut, like being *that* hard and taking it *that* slow is difficult for him, too. He bends down to kiss me, open mouthed and dirty. "What did I say, Scarlett? Deep breaths."

I don't think he ever gets all the way in, but he starts thrusting anyway, and I'm not sure what I like best about it. His exhale, loud in my ear. The tinge of hurt that makes the pleasure that much sharper. The rhythm, unhurried but purposeful.

I want to touch him, bury my nails in his shoulders, but he's holding my wrists above my head, and all I can do is feel him move inside me, feet limply bouncing with every thrust, blindly biting into his jaw as I feel a surge of heat low in my belly.

I come once, like that, slow contractions that are so good, they almost hurt. If he, we, *this* was normal, I'd assume that this would be it. Faster thrusts, a choked grunt, Lukas's orgasm, the end. But he likes to dictate when things start and when they end. He kisses, then licks the tear spilling out of my eye, tells me how tight and good my cunt feels to him. He throbs inside me but doesn't yet come. Instead he tells me, "A little more. You have to take a little more, okay?" and then he's impossibly deeper and I'm arching my chest and coming again, so hard that on the tail end of it I hear music in my head. Voices. Bells.

Except they're not in my head.

"Abysmal timing," Lukas groans before closing his teeth around my collarbone. "Coming home while I'm having the best fuck of my life."

His roommates. They're back from the party.

Are we going to stop? God, *no*. I want to whine. I *do* whine.

"Can you be quiet?"

He wouldn't believe a lie, so I shake my head.

His smile twitches. "We're gonna have to train you to come a bit more silently, Scarlett. In the meantime." His hand wraps around my mouth like last time, and my brain swims. Yes. *Yes.* Is it sick that I like it this much, knowing he controls my ability to breathe and scream? "I'm going to fuck you for real now, okay? All the way?"

I nod, my eyes a supplicating *yes*, and that's when I realize how little it would have taken him to just shove in through my muscles from the very start. He lets out a hiss of pure, undiluted pleasure, so deep my legs tremble. I feel invaded beyond comprehension, and wish I could tell him the truth, that this is something I've wanted since before I could put my desires into words.

"I knew you could do it," he growls in my ear, and that's enough for me to come again, his praise and his fingers wrapped around my cheeks and the sound of him bottoming out, hips slapping against mine. *Lukas*, I try to say against his palm, but I'm lightheaded and I cannot think about anything but him, him, *him.*

One thrust forward and his muscles tense aggressively, like he's fighting his own orgasm, but he freezes. His face twists. When he comes, he lets go of my wrists and scoops me up, holds me even closer, and none of the rough things he chants in my ear are in English—except for my name.

It takes centuries for my heart to go back to normal. Hasan and Kyle talk as they make their way upstairs. Doors opening and shutting, a hushed phone call, running water mark the passage of time. I burrow under Lukas, his arms that won't unwrap, my cooling sweat and labored breath mirrored in him. Blood that beats steadily against mine. I could fall asleep. I could stay here forever.

When he finally rises on his palms, he looks like I feel: wobbly, shell-shocked. A little humbled. We look at each other with the vague surprise of two people who have had sex before, *good* sex. And yet.

"Okay?" he asks me, deep, raspy. I should say something witty— *That's* my *line*—because he looks undone. But what feels natural is reaching up, cupping his face, lingering until he turns his head to press a hot kiss against my palm.

It hurts a little when he pulls out. Lukas notices in the frown of my brows, the twist of my face, but this time he soothes me, checks my wrists for bruises, runs his mouth along them. "Relax." He folds over to kiss my abdomen, once, sweet. One of his hands finds mine, palm to palm. "Deep breaths."

There is a bathroom attached to his room. I lie on the bed while he disappears inside. The faucet runs, and he comes back with a washcloth that he wipes across my cheeks. They feel ravaged, sticky with tears, and the warmth is a balm.

He spreads my legs gently, but I wince anyway. He comforts me with a hushed, foreign word, but what he finds there has him breathing deeper and putting the washcloth aside, mostly unused.

He stares and stares, and I try to imagine what he's seeing. When he's looked his fill, he closes my legs together again, as if to trap it there. "Will you spend the night?" A hoarse rumble—a request, this time. How easy it is, to transition from the animals we can be into the frequency of civilization. From hierarchy to equals.

"I would like to, yes."

He almost smiles. I almost do, too. It's so easy, slipping under the duvet, burying my face into his neck, savoring his sigh of relief as I settle in his arms. He surrounds me, contains me, presses me into himself, like he needs to hold me as much as I need to be held.

I should pee. Bathroom's right there. It's just so warm, here with Lukas, and there's so little peer-reviewed evidence supporting a link between peeing after sex and UTIs. There should be more studies investigating the matter. *I* could do a study.

And a few minutes later, in the middle of plotting it, I fall asleep.

# CHAPTER 36

SOMETHING WAKES ME UP—NOT SURE WHAT, BUT IT MUST BE outside my own head, because the second I open my eyes, I feel Lukas stir behind me, and the slow glide of his warm body against mine under the covers.

I'm tucked into him, his heavy body wrapped around mine like I'm a pillow or a beloved stuffed animal, something for him to use, a means to a better rest. One of his legs is thrown over both of mine, and his chest is hot against my spine, pressing the right half of me into the mattress. Even in sleep, his arm is clinched around my waist, making deep breaths impossible. I can't recall ever being this *close* to anyone. Objectively, I am uncomfortable, overheated, and held within an inch of my life.

I *love* it.

So much so that my first coherent thought is for Pen: When, how, *why* was she okay with giving Lukas up?

Lukas, who's slowly coming awake. He kisses the curve of my neck, ticklish against my tender skin. *Beard burns*, I think. He left those behind last night, and I'm going to have to do something about that before anyone sees me in a swimsuit—but that's not until twenty-four hours from now.

"You always smell so good." It's a low murmur that purrs through his chest, directly into my bones. He inhales deeply, doesn't loosen his grip.

The opposite, really.

"I smell like you." I'm boneless. Lazy, as though coming out from centuries of hibernation. "And the stuff we did."

"Exactly my point." Another soft nuzzle. His arms tighten around my torso, crossed, pulling me deeper even though there's no air left to fill. "Do you always thrash around in your sleep?"

"I thrash around?"

I feel his nod against my nape, followed by a light kiss, followed by a scrape of teeth, followed by a mumbled "Had to restrain you."

"I had no idea." Josh never mentioned it. "It does explain the state of my bed every morning, though." I attempt to turn. Lukas won't allow it, but I feel how hard and warm he is against the lower curve of my ass. He doesn't seem impatient about it—nothing about the way he's holding me broadcasts anything but a hug, but . . . Are we going to have sex again? Do I want to have sex with him ag—

Yes.

Undisputedly, *yes*.

Before, though, I should clean up. "May I go to the restroom?" I ask jokingly.

He pretends to think it through. "If you must," he says, a low, put-upon rumble that has me laughing, and him kissing my cheek again, and then, after a too-lingering moment, letting go. I sit up on the edge of the bed, facing away from him, and—

*Ouch.*

I twist my fists into the sheets, because it *hurts*. There's a sharp ache right behind my belly button, and where my thighs meet my abdomen. Muscles worked too hard and too long.

I hide the flinch in my step and close the door behind me, cheeks burning. The thing is, I'd *hate* for Lukas to decide to hold back next time. I need him to spare me no quarter and never hesitate. But when I look at my naked body in the mirror, I nearly gasp. I trace the map of what we did last night on my skin like it's a pilgrimage: the red abrasions of his stubble; the bluish bruises on the edge of my left breast; a purple coin blooming on my hip bone; chapped, swollen lips.

Wrecked.

I look absolutely *wrecked*. I look like I'm something that belongs to Lukas, something he handled with strength, something *used* in precisely the way I asked for in that damn list. No more, no less. Brought to the edge and no further.

Warm satisfaction blossoms in my stomach. *This* is it, the feeling I've been chasing. Not just the orgasms and the pleasure, but this sense of compatibility. My needs, met by Lukas's. *We match*, I think. The relief of knowing that the things I want are complementary to someone else's almost overwhelms me.

When I collect myself enough to go back, I find Lukas right outside, leaning against the wall. He put on a pair of gray joggers, and holds a glass of water in one hand, a gel capsule in the other.

I recognize it from decades of muscle soreness: Advil.

So much for hiding *anything* from him.

I make no comment and swallow it. He looks at my naked body, at what he's done to me, like I'm some kind of Olympic medal. Hungry, proud, eager. Other things I can't disentangle from the intensity of his focus.

His hand lifts to brush against the bruise on the side of my breast. "Is this the point where you look contrite and say that you're sorry?" I ask neutrally. Truth is, I'm afraid. *What if he regrets it? What if I'm too much?*

He says nothing. His thumb presses into the mark at my waist— a perfect match. Lock and key. "Should I apologize about these, too?"

I huff a small laugh. "You don't *sound* apologetic."

"Because I'm not." He shrugs, and it hits me like a freight train, how *attractive* he is—not because of the muscles and the bone structure, not *in general*, but to *me*. Because of who he is, and who I am. "You love to be hurt, Scarlett. Just enough pain that you won't even *think* about not doing what I ask." He leans down. His skin is rough against my cheek. "I love giving that to you, and I'm going to for as long as you'll let me."

I shiver. *Not* in fear.

"Drink all of that," he orders, and after the glass is drained, he picks me up and sets me on the edge of the bed.

"I should leave before your roommates wake up."

His lips tighten, displeased, but he nods and plucks my top from the floor. "Arms up," he instructs. I obey, trying to remember the last time someone dressed me. It feels nice.

"Lukas?"

He glances at me.

"Am I doing it right? This whole . . . thing."

He knows exactly what I'm asking, but he continues shaking out my skirt. His reply is unrushed. "I don't know if it's right, but this is . . ." His mouth flattens. "*You* are exactly what I wanted." The skirt drops, forgotten. "I think . . ." He's so rarely hesitant, or lost for words, I almost don't recognize his confusion for what it is. "I'd imagined it a lot. Ever since I became aware of sex, before I had a name for it. And I'd hoped that it would feel good, but *this* . . . I just didn't know it could be like this." His jaw works, like there are words he wants to say that won't come out.

"The stuff on the list." My tongue is too thick in my mouth. "You can do it. All of it. You don't have to hold back."

He looks down at my body, amused. "Does it *feel* like I'm holding back?" It's gentle but fast, the way he presses me down on the mattress, one wide palm warm against my sternum, hot through the thin cloth of my shirt.

"I just don't want you to—"

"Does it?" His fingers stretch my legs open, find bruises I over-looked, press into them like pegs into holes. The pleasure of the pain licks up my spine and quickens my breath. "Am I taking it too easy on you, Scarlett?" Teeth scrape against my jaw. "Am I being too *nice*?" His bite tightens, and—oh my god.

The tentative Lukas of a minute ago is gone. I stare up at him and can only say, "Please."

"Please, what? Please, stop?"

I shake my head.

"Please, make me come?"

I bite my lower lip, suddenly embarrassed.

"Please, fuck me? In your sore little cunt?"

The nod erupts out of me, urgent, unplanned. It surprises both of us.

He frowns. "Come on, Scarlett. You need a break—"

"*Please.*"

It wars on his face for a split second, the question of what to do, but he trusts me to know what I can take. He takes himself out of his joggers. Straddles me. Pulls up my shirt and sucks on my tender nipples till I'm squirming from wanting more and less at once. His knees press against the outsides of my thighs, knocking my legs to-gether, and I whimper, about to protest that this is not . . . I really want him to . . . why is he—

But then he hushes me and I feel it. The fat head of his cock bumping against my clit, a forceful push, a hot, burning, immense stretch that makes me tense like a bowstring, and then he's inside and—yes. The walls of my cunt start fluttering around him. The ache gives the pleasure a cruel, beautiful edge.

"Christ, you're tight." His face buries against my neck. "Like I didn't spend last night fucking you."

He moves slowly, like wading through water, teasing sharp

breaths out of me. It hurts. It feels better than good. I can't take it anymore. If he stops, I'll die. It's not enough.

"Deeper," I plead, because his strokes are too shallow, just a couple of inches filling and then emptying me again. I try to angle myself to get what I need, stilted little rolls up against his cock, but his palms pin mine above my head, fingers twined together, and my thighs are crammed between his, pressed together by his knees. He controls every movement, every glance, every exit route.

"Lukas," I sob. He ignores me. I try to open my legs, but he's stronger. The display of force only revs me up higher. "Deeper," I beg. "All the way."

"Not this time." His teeth close around my earlobe, a threat, a mean little warning. I moan. "Quiet. You'll take what you're given and thank me for it. Won't you, baby?"

I nod. I'm so, *so* close—because of the things he says, the way he moves, his unyielding hold on me. I'm a wet mess of tears and slick and the tightrope of all my muscles.

"You know I'm going to fuck you whenever and however I want," he says against my ear. "Just be patient. You can be patient, right?"

I nod, desperate.

"You can be good?" I clench around him, gripping the end of his cock. His response is a half-groaned laugh. He has to collect himself and pull back from the brink. "You're going to come already, aren't you?"

God, I hope not. I hope I can make this last. Who knows when the next time will be.

"That list, Scarlett?" His mouth slides against mine, messy, uncoordinated, sharing air that feels dangerously thin and hard to come by. "I'm going to do it all to you. All of it. And when I'm done, I'll do it again. And if you don't ask me to stop, I'll do it *again*—"

I come with a soft warble, echoed by the deep rumble of his grunt, and it lasts a long time—me, trembling against him, the loud rhythm of his breathing, the slow, reverential kisses all over my face and shoulders once he slips out and arranges us more comfortably on the bed. The clock on his nightstand reads eight thirty-seven, the light glows yellow through the open shades, and his arms are warm around me.

"I should leave," I force myself to say.

I wait for Lukas to let me go. All he does is dip his face in my neck and inhale me like I'm some kind of drug. "I'll come with. Put some breakfast in you."

Oh. That sounds . . . "Okay." *Nice.* "I should shower first."

He shakes his head before I'm done talking and then pulls back to meet my eyes. His hand cups my nape, holding my head still. "Scarlett, if I want you showered after we fuck, I'll do it myself. Okay?"

I shiver. It'd be gross. Right? I don't know. If it is, I'm not sure that I care. "Okay."

His smile is small, but it makes my entire chest flutter with happiness.

# CHAPTER 37

I WAIT IN THE CAR WHILE HE PROCURES FOOD—BECAUSE I'M NOT sure I want us to be seen together, because I'm not presentable, because he confiscated my damn underwear and it's sequestered somewhere in the kingdom of his bedroom, as accessible to me as the *Curiosity* rover.

When I ask, "How much do I owe you?" he looks at me like I asked him to join me on a hunt to exterminate the harpy eagle. "I can Venmo you," I add, but he glances away and proceeds to pretend that his auditory cortex leaked out of his nostrils.

Whatever.

We drive a few minutes out of campus, stop at a small clearing off the road, and sit on the hood of his car to eat, listening to the chirps of the birds. The sun warms my cheeks; Lukas's legs are impossibly long; when he slides off his shoes, I do the same, wiggling my toes, letting the breeze run through them.

My mind slips to yesterday's competition, my latest-but-probably-not-last failure, but I leash it back, forcing myself to stay in the moment, savor the comfortable silence that's been stretching almost uninterrupted ever since we left his home.

I bite into my egg-and-cheese bagel, moaning like it's being shot up my veins. I haven't eaten anything since well before the meet. *After*, I just wasn't sure I *deserved* food. Maybe this is what I need—to be harsher with myself, punish my body and brain for the things it cannot accomplish, train the weakness and the failure out of—

*No.* I'm not thinking about that *now.*

I focus on each bite. The rustling of the trees. Lukas's steady presence. We exchange a few glances—me, smiling, and him inscrutable. When I finish my breakfast, he picks up his second bagel and holds it out to me.

"Oh, no, I—"

"Scarlett," he says. Just a word. Not an order. Still, it contains so much: *I know you're still hungry. I'd rather you eat it. Make me happy. Be full.* I have no clue how I can read all of it, but when I close my hand around the still-wrapped bagel, he looks so satisfied, I know I'm right.

I eat two-thirds, then hand him the rest. He scans my face, measuring, curious, and then accepts it and finishes in a single bite.

I cannot help but marvel how quiet and stoic Lukas can be when he's not bossing me around. How relaxed I feel with him, content to just be silent. How many fewer words we exchange while sharing a meal than while having sex. That last thought coaxes a small laugh out of me.

"What?" he asks.

I shake my head. "So . . . does this"—I gesture between us—"fall under the umbrella of *fika*?"

"This is breakfast."

"But we're having coffee. And a snack."

He frowns. "Still breakfast. *Fika* is midmorning."

"Well, it's nine thirty, and we usually wake up at five."

"*Fika* is between meals."

"We are between meals—dinner last night and lunch later today. If you think about it, every meal is between other meals—"

"This is *not fika*," he says, final. Arbitrary.

He might be getting mad. I might love it. "But why?"

"Because I say so."

"So just because you're Swedish, you get to decide—"

"Correct."

I hide my smile into my knees. "I never get to use the only Swedish word I know. Just because you *say* so."

He snorts a laugh, and mutters something under his breath—something that sounds a lot like *troll.*

"Hey, why do you keep calling me a—"

"I'll teach you another."

"Another what?"

"Swedish word."

I give him an expectant look.

"*Mysig.*"

"*Mysig,*" I repeat slowly, and he chuckles. "What?"

"You really aren't great at foreign languages, are you?" I glare. "*Me-sig,*" he says again. His smile tells me that my second attempt is no better. "Still sounds a bit like an intestinal parasite."

"Hey," I say mildly, "if you can't handle me at my xenoglossophobic worst, you sure as hell don't deserve me at my best. What's *m* . . . that word?"

He waves his hand at something that encompasses us, the trees, this moment in time. "This is *mysig.*"

"But what does it *mean*?"

"I'm sure whatever website taught you *fika* will be happy to clarify that for you."

"So *mean.*" I steal a long sip of his juice. The link between excellent sex and appetite must have a titanium core. "Did Jan get home okay?"

Lukas nods. "Asks me to send you his regards every time he texts—and he texts a lot."

"Oh. Did you tell him that we . . . ?"

"He figured it out all by himself."

"When?"

He shrugs. "About two and a half seconds into seeing the way I look at you, according to him."

"Oh." A hot flush hits my face. "I'm sorry for coming along. I didn't mean to intrude on your brotherly time."

He laughs. "Brotherly time?"

"Isn't that what you people with siblings call it?"

"Maybe monks do?" We exchange a long, intimate, too-full glance. "I'm glad you joined us," he adds eventually, quiet in the outdoor morning. My heart . . . it doesn't *skip*, but tripping is involved.

"Yeah?"

"I like spending time with you."

The beats completely unravel, one after the other. "Thanks," I say, instead of what I'm actually thinking. *Maybe we could be friends. Aside from the sex, I mean. I don't have many. And you and I—we get along, right?* Instead, I opt for the most milquetoast thing I can find. "I like hiking. Never get to go."

"How come?"

"No one to do it with. I should go alone, but . . ." I shrug. "I'm going to ask Pen if she wants to join me sometimes."

"She doesn't enjoy it much."

"Really?"

"Something about the bugs. She's more of an indoor rock climber."

I remember her mentioning that. "Oh, well."

"I'll go with you."

I blink at the offer. At his clear blue eyes. At his unsmiling face. "Don't you have to . . . win medals, or something?"

"Don't *you*?"

I groan. "Do you really have the time?"

"I make the time to do stuff outside of swimming and school, or I'm going to get burned out. Maybe you should, too."

"I have hobbies," I counter weakly. Sometimes, when I'm done with homework at a decent hour, I read Mafia erotica until I fall asleep. Eat crackers in bed. Consider calling 911, just to talk to someone.

Okay, I need pastimes that can be brought up in polite company. "Let's do it," I say impulsively. "Let's go hiking."

"Now?" He sounds skeptical.

"Unless you . . ." Maybe he wasn't serious, and I'm putting him on the spot. "If you've changed your mind—"

"Scarlett, you can barely stand. I was on you *hard* last night."

I am, impossibly, blushing. And he's not wrong, I'm not in peak physical shape, but what's the alternative? Go home and wallow in the emotional turmoil that comes with the prospect of spending the upcoming season producing a series of malignantly ugly dives? "I feel better, actually."

"You sure?"

I nod, a spark lighting in my stomach.

"Okay." He seems . . . not excited—he's Lukas Blomqvist—but *pleased*.

"I'll need to get changed before." *And shower*, I don't add, but he must read between the lines.

"I'll help you clean up." His gaze is intense for a moment. Then he palms his keys. "Your place okay?"

"Yes." With some luck, Maryam won't be home. And if she is . . . who cares? It's not like I don't put up with the mooing videos she watches to relax.

He jumps off the hood, and then lifts me off it even though I could easily do it on my own. I'm in the passenger seat, waiting for Lukas to start the car, contemplating the possibility of a nice day, not spent collapsing under the pressure I put on myself, when his phone rings.

I find it odd, because it hasn't made a peep for the past twelve hours. Emergency bypass, I suspect. More so when he picks up and asks, "Everything okay?"

On the other side is Pen, but I cannot make out her words. She's doing most of the talking. Lukas's questions are short and to the point.

"Where? Are you alone? Is there anyone else who could . . . ? Okay. I'll be right there."

He hangs up after a minute. When he turns to me, his jaw is tense. "Pen needs a ride," he says tersely. No longer sounding pleased. "Her car broke down in Menlo Park."

My stomach sinks. Twice.

Initially, with disappointment.

Then, *harder*, when I realize that *disappointment* was my instinctive reaction to a friend calling and asking for help—a supportive, generous friend, who always makes sure I don't have globs of sunscreen on my back, who grabs me protein bars from the snack shed before they run out, who held my hand after I fucked up my first meet of the season and said nothing, just like I needed her to.

It shames me. So much so, I can't look Lukas in the eye.

"Of course," I say, glancing out of the window.

"Scarlett—"

"It's totally okay." I turn back to him with a forced smile. "We can hike whenever." Or never. That would probably be for the best, actually. What the fuck am I even doing, organizing cutesy excursions with Lukas Blomqvist? "Just drop me off around campus, since it's on the way. I can make my way home." I try to sound ab-solving, but he doesn't return my smile. "Hey, can I tell you about the progress I've made for Dr. Smith's model? It's exciting stuff."

It takes him a while to nod, and he says next to nothing until we pull into the parking lot of my apartment building.

# CHAPTER 38

THE FOLLOWING WEDNESDAY SAM IS OUT SICK—HEART-swooping relief *and* unspeakable tragedy.

Inevitably, no Sam equals no progress. Then again, the discipline of psychology may have done all it could for me, and it's hard not to see therapy as the squillionth thing I'm failing, especially after the mutterings I overhear through Coach Sima's ajar door.

I'm stopping by his office to let him know that I'll be late for afternoon practice, when something in his tone halts my knuckles just inches from knocking.

". . . a waste," he's saying. "But it's out of her control."

"For real." It's Coach Urso. "It sounds like her shape is otherwise pretty good? There *might* still be some hope for higher levels of competition, since only five groups of dives are required."

"She ain't qualifying for nationals, though," an assistant says.

A few more mumbles I cannot make out. Then: ". . . that she'll just grow out of it?" It's Bradley. The conditioning director.

"Well," Coach Sima says, "mental blocks are common, but this long-lasting . . ." More unintelligible words, and I should leave. It's not good that I'm here. ". . . great talent that's just . . . I feel for her . . . bad injury, but physically she's fully recovered. There are no excuses."

"She's seeing a professional?"

"The second in six months. No progress."

". . . a junior, right?"

"Yup."

"We'll have to think long and hard if she should continue taking up a spot on the team—"

I push away, hands trembling, throat full of something that could be tears or bile.

I hate it—I fucking hate it.

I hate *them*, these men talking about me like I'm a malfunctioning waffle maker that should be harvested for parts and landfilled.

Most of all, I hate *myself*, because—what choice have my constant failures given them?

"Hey."

I nearly walk face-first into Pen. I must have autopiloted my way to the locker room. "Oh. Hey." I push my knot of self-loathing under the surface. "Hi." I sound high-pitched and way too cheerful. Definitely overcompensating. "Did you get everything sorted out?"

"Everything?"

She seems confused. It occurs to me that the last time she saw me, she'd been hopping off a podium after a stellar diving performance. She probably has no idea that I was with Lukas when she called, and that he dropped everything—dropped *me*, to go help her. She simply reached out to her ex, with whom she still has a great relationship. For all I know, the two of them are still—

"Vandy? You okay?"

"Yup." My smile stretches. "Ready for synchro training?"

"No. But does it matter?"

I take several deep, calming breaths, and change into my suit. I may be at my worst, but I *can* masquerade as someone who's doing perfectly fucking fine.

◈ ◈ ◈

In the following days I'm at once despondent and jittery. Messed up. All wrong, like I've lost all say in the person that I'm supposed to be. Entropy personified—just a tangled skein, unraveling, impossible to rescue.

I try not to think about Lukas too much, but the universe seems to be conspiring against me, because while I'm endlessly doom-scrolling before bed, the algorithm feeds me a video that has me slapping a palm against my mouth.

It's simply . . . adorable. The boy adjusting his goggles is *Lukas*—the serious set of his brow, his full, downturned lips, those cheekbones—but a miniaturized version. Skinnier. Long torsoed, long armed, strong legged. The proportions are there, and he was probably already taller than I am now, but he seems so . . . *young*.

The video is in Swedish, so I find another. One hundred meter. Freestyle. Semifinal. World championship in France—no, Montreal, Canada. Lukas is a bit older. He must have broken a speed record, because when his hand reaches the touch pad the audience explodes out of their seats. *"Fourteen-year-old Lukas Blomqvist looks positively shocked by how fast he swam,"* the commentators inform me. Lukas just takes off his goggles and stares at the board, as if to make sure it really happened. The camera pans to a group of people in the stands, and—oh my god, Jan, looking so *different* but also the *same*. His other brothers are there, too, applauding, clapping each other's backs. A man who's a middle-aged template of them wraps an arm around the shoulders of . . .

Lukas's mom.

She doesn't look too much like him, but I know it's her, I just *do*. The image zooms in on her, shows tears brimming in her eyes, and then—she leans in, over the plastic barrier, and lets two glistening shoulders envelop her in a strong hug.

Fourteen-year-old Lukas. Breaking records. Celebrating with

his mom. I'm trying to wrap my head around it, until another video starts, leading me down twisted paths.

It's the individual medley at the last Olympics, a race I know he'll win from sniffing around his Wikipedia. Lukas would have been eighteen or so, the summer before enrolling at Stanford, but the video could have been taken this morning at practice. Except for the sleeve of tattoos, which is not yet complete.

He doesn't really go for most of the pre-competition gimmicks the other swimmers seem to like—large headphones, shaking triceps, meditating breaths, random words written on his palms to show to the camera. Just takes off his warm-ups and sits, quietly focused, unbothered by the chaos. He's in lane four, and whoever's directing this airing . . . they *try* to care about the other athletes, but Lukas is so obviously the favorite, the video keeps traveling back to him. Then it shifts to the bleachers, and there's another familiar sight. Jan. A woman next to him, and then another, holding a beaming toddler in her arms. Lukas's two eldest brothers. His dad, and . . .

That's it.

I click out of the video, wondering why my heart feels wrapped in stone. I can't *assume*. I have no idea. It's not my business. Why am I even . . .

"Idiot," I chastise myself, and switch to Google, remembering something I've been meaning to look up. The word Lukas taught me. *Mi? My?* I cycle through ten or so spellings, and then I find it.

*Mysig.*

*Swedish adjective. Cozy. Warm. Soothing. The quality of sharing a comfortable moment with a person whose company one enjoys.*

"*Mysig,*" I whisper at my phone, like I'm the kind of person who has meaningful tête-à-têtes with fire hydrants. "*Mysig,*" I repeat with a small smile.

I'm a mess. A failure. A ball of anxiety. All twisted. But also cozy.

At least, one person in the universe seems to think so.

# CHAPTER 39

IT'S HOMECOMING WEEKEND, AND THE ANNUAL ALUMNI MEET IS scheduled for that Friday night at five.

I never enjoyed it. Seems pointless, being pitted against old-timers, most of whom last dove competitively before I was born. More of a canine agility exhibition than real sport. It always has me wondering whether I'm supposed to respect my elders enough to let them win, or peacock my skills in the name of institutional pride. Not to mention the pseudo-mandatory post-meet tailgating that always follows.

So on Friday afternoon, I don't head for the aquatic center anticipating to have fun. Still, my expectations aren't low enough, and need to be dunked further down the toilet bowl.

The first blow is the email I get around four, informing me that my MCAT results are available. I stare at it, letting my thumb hover on the link, trying to come to terms with the bed-wetting prospects that the scores might be even lower than I've prepared myself for.

*Rip the Band-Aid*, I order myself. *Click on it.*

But I can't. That simple tap is as impossible as all the inward dives in the world, and fifteen minutes later, when Bella asks if I'm "having a special moment with your phone, or something," I shake my head and stuff it in my duffel bag. It's a problem for later—unlike my *other* one, which is present in flesh and blood.

Mr. Kumar.

My high school coach.

Who is married to Clara Katz.

Who, a couple of decades ago, dove for Stanford.

They were instrumental in me getting on the team, which means that I should have known that this would be a possibility—and yet.

Stupid, stupid, *stupid.*

I'm still wearing my warm-ups when I see them enter the un-usually crowded diving well. They pause to shake a few hands, then head straight toward me.

It's been two years since we last met in person. Coach Kumar's hair is grayer than I remember. Mrs. Katz's, blonder. They have al-ways believed in me. So much.

And I . . .

"Vandy!"

I hug them one after the other, exchanging pleasantries, barely aware of my mouth and arms moving. Did I know they were going to be here? Did Coach Sima say anything about it? So glad it could be a surprise. Do I like Stanford? Am I recovered? Has the presea-son been treating me well? Did my stepmom relay their well-wishes? Do I miss Missouri? It's okay if I don't, we all become California girls when we're in college, don't we?

"I cannot wait to see you dive, Scarlett," Mrs. Katz says, both hands cupping my shoulders. "You remind me so much of myself."

"I'm so glad your surgery was successful," Coach Kumar adds. "We kept saying how a talent like yours would have been a catas-trophic loss."

"Oh," Mrs. Katz interrupts, glancing behind my shoulder, "I know you! Penelope Ross, right? You dove beautifully at the NCAA last year. That gold medal was *earned.*"

"Oh my god, thank you!" Pen comes closer, giving me a curious look, expecting to be told who her fan is, but I'm too sluggish with surprise, and panic, and something that feels too much like shame.

Mrs. Katz picks up the slack and introduces herself, and then Bree and Bella join, and the more people are around us, the easier it becomes to make myself small.

A drop of water, lost in the chlorine.

And that's when I murmur a low "Excuse me," even though everyone around me is too busy laughing and joking and commemorating to hear, and march to the chair where Coach Sima sits with a couple of assistants, cross-referencing diving sheets and lists of names.

It's the most cowardly thing I've ever done; I know it even before opening my mouth.

But I cannot, truly *cannot* go through with this.

"Coach?"

"Yeah, Vandy?"

"I . . . don't feel well," I say, not meeting his gaze. I should have planned my excuse. Come up with an ailment that's equally sudden and debilitating. I'm not ready to field any kind of question, but it turns out that I don't need to.

Because Coach Sima gives me a single glance, a glance that feels like his voice sounded a few days ago, in his office. All he tells me is "Then you should go home, kid."

My heart is full of thanks, but I cannot bear to say even one before I leave.

# CHAPTER 40

WISH I COULD SAY I'M DOING MY HOMEWORK, OR EVEN squinting at my puzzling app. The pathetic truth is that when Maryam's voice reaches into my room, I'm lying face down on my bed, slowly breathing into the damp cotton of my duvet.

"A male underwear model is here to see you," she yells.

I make the managerial decision to ignore her.

A minute later, my door opens. "Dude. Do I need to uncork your earwax?"

I lift my head. "What do you want?"

"There's a guy here to see you."

I blink at her. "Who?"

"Tall. Wearing Stanford Athletics gear. Looks like he'd be a good source of protein."

Another blink.

"Shall I tell the gentleman you are at home for him?" she adds with a tetchy, butchered Jane Austen accent. I nod, confused. A little later, Lukas closes the door of my room and leans against it.

I pull up to my knees and sit on my heels, self-conscious about my wild hair, cotton underwear, plaid baby tee, like I'm a parody of some mid-2000s Victoria's Secret sex kitten ad. His attention is on my face, though.

He's barefoot, even though state-of-the-art microbial analysis would reveal that our floors are a biohazard worthy of Godzilla's atomic breath. He crosses his arms, pins me with his eyes, and asks, "What happened?" in that blunt, northern European way I can't put up with right now.

Should he not be tailgating? There's no way the party is over. The alumni are probably sobbing in the punch. "Is this going to be a thing?" I ask flatly. "Where you offer to pity fuck me after every competition I don't win?"

"Sure. I'm selfless like that. Right now, though, I'm more interested in figuring you out."

I scowl. "I'm not a five-year budgeting plan."

"What happened, Scarlett?" His eyes are laser focused. "You disappeared."

"I'm fine. Just wasn't feeling well. Not sure why it's a big deal."

"Because you came to Avery, started warming up, and then left. A suspiciously drastic turn for your health to take."

"How do you even know that I was at Avery? Did you GPS me, or something?"

"Oh, sweetheart." My belly swoops at the endearment. His tone lives somewhere between sympathy and amusement. "If you don't think that I'm *very* aware of your presence, always, you have no idea what's going on."

A rush of blood hits my cheeks, and I—*can't*. "Listen, Lukas, thank you very much for the . . . welfare check, but I'm not doing great, and I'm not sure I'm in the mood for being manhandled, so—"

"That's not why I'm here, and you know it." He reads through my bullshit so well, he's not even offended. "I want to talk. You can tell me to leave, and I'll leave—"

"Leave," I blurt out.

His nod is unhesitant. He pushes away from the door, crosses my small room in one and a half steps, and bends down to murmur against my temple, "If you need anything, anything *at all*, you have my number. Use it." He presses a kiss to my forehead. Then his back fills the doorway, and I—

"Don't," I say. Why am I being like *this*, to him? He's done nothing but—god, he's done nothing but *care*. "You don't have to leave. I'm sorry, I'm taking it out on you because . . ." My laughter is a little phlegmy. Love that. "Because I hate myself, I guess?"

He turns around, surprised by *none* of this. Like I'm predictable. Or, at least, *predicted* by this man who shouldn't know the first thing about me.

I don't know what to say. So I ask, "Do you want to have sex?"

His smile is quiet. "With you. Yes. But that's my default setting, so don't read too much into it."

I lower my chin. "Maybe we should. It might take my mind off things."

"Yeah, it would. I'd make sure of it. The thing is, I'm not convinced that your mind shouldn't be *on* things."

"So I should just be this way? Beached in my own failures?"

His head tilts. "What constitutes failure for you, Scarlett?"

"I don't know, *Lukas*." I press my lips together. "You're sounding more like my therapist, and less like a fun guy who threatens me with ball gags when I'm mouthy."

"We've established that neither of us is into those, and that I have better uses for your mouth."

I flush. Glance away.

"What happened today?"

"Just . . ." I rub the heel of my palm against my eye. "My brain *won't* do that stupid dive. And the MCAT email—I can't open it. And my . . . my high school coach, his wife is an alumna, and *of course* this is the year she decides to show up. And I miss my stupid

dog." I'm being barely coherent. Lukas, however, nods like I'm painting a full, polychrome picture for him.

And asks: "Do you have a mental block?"

I hate that word. I hate how accurate and solid and *massive* it
sounds. "It's not like it's news."

"You never told me."

"Should I have disclosed it on the list? An asterisk between the
titty fucking and the STI part of the form? Why would you need to
know, anyway? Do you make a point of not associating with athletes
who aren't in the ninety-ninth percentile for their discipline?" I
wince, rubbing a hand down my face. "I'm sorry, Lukas. I'm not sure
what's wrong with me. Actually . . ." I look up with a sad smile.
"Maybe I'm just a total bitch?"

"Is it *all* dives? Or just the one you mentioned—inward?"

"I don't want to talk about it."

"Too bad, because *I* want to know."

I swallow a groan. "Maybe you could ask Pen? She'll explain."

"Why would I want to find out what's in *your* head from Pen?" He's
baffled, and I have no answer for him. "Has it been since your injury?"

I nod.

"The dive you were doing when you got injured, was it . . . ?"

I nod.

"No inward since then?"

I shake my head, and he must be satisfied with the information
he gathered, because he exhales sharply and sinks further into the
door, as if suddenly burdened with a heavy weight. His head tips
back, eyes toward the ceiling, and stays like that for a long while
before his gaze settles back on me.

I wait for him to tell me what I've heard a million times already.
*It'll get better. It's not your fault. There are things you can do to fix it.
Don't give up. I knew someone who knew someone whose block just
poof, disappeared. At least you are physically healthy. There, there.*

He doesn't, though. What Lukas fucking Blomqvist says to me, damn him to hell, is: "I'm sorry, Scarlett."

It's unprecedented. Destabilizing.

In the past year of self-loathing, training, practicing, trying, failing, trying again, visualizing, exercising, catastrophizing, *not* catastrophizing, resenting, fearing, pretending, demanding . . . In the past year, being *sorry* is simply not something that I ever allowed myself.

It just never occurred to me.

But now that the prospect of some simple, uncomplicated *sorrow* is here, glowing in my palm, I cannot deny it to myself any longer.

And that's how it happens: My face crumpling into something ugly and blotchy and wet before I can hide it into my own hands. The foul, guttural wail that tears out of my throat. I need—I need Lukas to leave right *now*, before witnessing the unattractive, flawed mess that I am. And I don't know how I find myself across his warm lap, the crown of my head lodged under his chin, one of his palms cupping my thigh while the other wipes back and forth over the elastic of my underwear.

A silent: *I'm sorry, Scarlett.*

I'm not tearing up. I'm not weeping softly. These are *sobs*. Bawling. Hitched, shivering breaths. My fingers fist in his shirt, cling to it like it's a religious doctrine. I'm hiccuping, crying my stupid heart out, loud and sloppy, and there's *snot* involved. But Lukas doesn't let go, not even when his phone buzzes several times, not even when my eyes run dry.

"Scarlett." His voice is a deep hum under the side of my body, full of things that make my heart ache.

This may be the most embarrassing thing that ever happened to me—and I've been publicly flunking dives for the past year. "I never cry," I say, sniffling, in lieu of an apology.

"Liar." He presses a kiss against my temple. "I've made you cry plenty of times."

"It's different—"

"Is it?"

"—and you just have a dacryphilia kink."

I feel his smile against my cheek. The bristle of his stubble scrapes my skin. "The fact that you know that word is proof of how well matched we are."

I let out a watery snort. Sure, we're both degenerates. But he's an Olympic multi-medalist, and I can't jump in a pool without having kittens. "You won't believe this, but I used to actually be a good diver." *I wasn't always at my worst, Lukas. A few years ago, I was someone worth knowing.*

"Why wouldn't I believe you?"

I shrug in his arms. His grip tightens, like he's no more ready to let go than I am. "Sometimes, I feel like my life is split in two. There was the first part, where I was in control, and was able to make myself do what needed to be done, and then . . . now."

His hand tilts my chin up to force our eyes to meet. "What's day zero? When you got injured?"

I nod. "There's no reason for me to be so hung up on it. I had surgery, and . . . I was so *lucky*. But instead of taking advantage, I can't even . . ." I free myself and hide my tear-smeared face in his throat. His palm lifts to cup the back of my head.

"What would you do, in the past?"

"Hmm?" He smells comforting and familiar, sandalwood and Lukas and *safe*.

"When you'd fail a dive, what would you do?"

"I didn't. I never used to fail dives. I used to be *good*."

He sits on this piece of information for a minute. "What about blocks?"

"What about them?"

"Is this your first?"

I nod. Leave it to me to start with a bang.

"They're not uncommon among divers, though."

"What do you mean?"

"Pen has had several since I met her—not as long-lasting as yours, but my guess is, they're pretty widespread. What about injuries? Did you have any before college?"

"No."

"So . . ." He brushes a lock of hair behind my ear, pulling my head back to look at me again. "To recap, on the day of your first NCAA final, you failed your first dive, and had your first significant injury."

"God, it was such a horrible . . ." I straighten in his lap, wiping my cheeks with the backs of my hands, feeling the same spurt of frustration I always experience. "It was everything, all at once. The night before my father contacted me to tell me he'd been following the NCAA competition online and was proud of me and—he's not *allowed* to do that, by *court* order. I tried to call Barb to figure out what to do, but she had patient emergencies, and I couldn't sleep and was so anxious—and then that morning, Josh, I mean . . . I'm glad he didn't just decide to *cheat* on me, but couldn't he have waited twelve hours to tell me that he'd met someone else—"

"Hang on," Lukas interrupts. His eyes are narrow slits, his tone low, a little dangerous. I realize that I've been rambling.

"Sorry, you don't have to listen to—"

"Did you just tell me that your boyfriend of . . . how long were you two together?"

"Three years?"

"Your boyfriend of *three* years broke up with you out of the blue, *right before* the NCAA finals?"

I swallow. Lukas seems angry, and I—I know, instinctively, he's not mad at *me*, but his displeasure is nonetheless unsettling. "He . . . I think things with this new girl he'd met had been heating up, and . . ."

"Right," he says. His tone is so deceptively mild, I shiver. "What

I'm hearing is that you had a near-perfect history when it came to diving. Within twenty-four hours you got dumped by your boyfriend and contacted by your abusive father. When the final of the most important competition of your college career came around, despite your state of mind, you went ahead and tried to focus. Under those conditions you failed a dive for the first time in your career, and *that's* when you became a failure?"

He says the last word like—like it's all in my head. Like I've been misusing it. Like I don't know what it means. So I retreat into myself, trying to poke holes in Lukas's story, in his retelling of the worst day of my life that *surely* cannot be an accurate summary of what happened.

Can it?

"Why are you so reluctant to talk about that day?" he asks.

"I'm not."

"And yet I had to pry the story out of you. We've discussed your injury, your relationship, your father. But you never told me, 'My pieces of shit of a boyfriend and father and their piece of shit timing upset me so much, I severely injured myself to the point that I could barely move for weeks,' and—did he visit you?"

"My father?"

"Josh. Did you see him after your injury?"

"We haven't really talked since the breakup. He's in Missouri, and—"

"Scarlett."

I give up and admit, "No, he didn't," even though the tears once again streaking down my face would have been answer enough for Lukas—who cradles both my cheeks and presses the top of his forehead against mine.

"Scarlett," he says again, his voice completely different—kind and caring and full of all the things, all the redos, all the truths I know he'd give me if only it were in his power. "I'm going to tell you something, okay? Something I don't talk about. And after I do . . . we don't have to bring this up ever again. But I need you to understand. Okay?"

I nod. My head rubs against his, bone under skin under skin under bone. His freckles blur together, pretty on the bridge of his nose.

"My mom died when I was fourteen. We all knew it was coming, but we thought we had more time. The doctor said . . . What matters is, it happened while I was gone. When the phone call came, I was in Denmark, not close enough to make it home in time. It was devastating for all the reasons you can imagine, but it also messed up my relationship with swimming. By that point I was good enough that the Olympics seemed like a guarantee, but after my mom died . . . I didn't *want* to win, I *had* to. It went from dream to necessity. Because if I'd done something as egregious as being absent on my mom's last day, for something as trivial as a swimming competition, then swimming *had* to be the most important thing in my life, right? It was the only way I could make it make sense. The only way I could forgive myself."

He holds my face and my eyes, and the way he says this, it's so . . . so *Lukas*—at once earnest and measured, sad but patient, head and heart. *Unfazed*, Pen had called him, but the truth is altogether different: Lukas works *hard* to hide what's underneath the surface, and not acknowledging his efforts seems like a terrible disservice.

"I *had* to win, and suddenly, I *couldn't*. In the span of a few weeks, I gained seconds on every single race. There was no physical reason for me to be so slow. I told myself that I just needed to get through the first few practices, the first few meets. But it never got better. I messed up the Olympic trials. And everyone in my family— they meant well, but their advice was 'Don't give up.' 'Stick to your routine.' 'Fake it till you make it.' Even my dad, even Jan . . . they were kind and patient, but I needed to take a step back and they didn't *get* it.

"The only person who truly understood was an American girl I'd met at a competition a few months earlier. We'd kissed once, stayed in touch. She wanted to be my girlfriend, and I liked her, but I didn't get the point of a long-distance relationship, especially at our age. But there I was, needing to take a step back from the pool, and the only person validating that was Pen. She'd call me and text me and was so easy to talk to, before I knew it she was giving me the tools to communicate to my trainer and my family that I needed to stop swimming for a while. That I might never go back. I didn't have the words, but she helped me find them.

"And I did step back. The Olympics happened, and I didn't watch them. I traveled. Spent time with friends. Visited Pen and decided that after what she'd done for me, I never wanted to *not* have her as my girlfriend. Above all, I let myself mourn my mom, and acknowledged how fucked up it was that for some twist of fate I hadn't been able to say goodbye. And when I felt ready, I went back to the pool. But only after I'd proven to myself that I didn't *need* to swim to be whole." His thumbs wipe my cheeks, once again drenched in tears. "I didn't go back because it was expected, or because I wanted to make someone proud. I did it because I didn't *have to* win anymore. I *wanted* to."

"So, you're saying—" A shameful, mortifying hiccup. "That I won't be able to do inward dives again until I—" Another. "Dive only for myself?"

His muttered "Fuck, no" has me laughing through my sobs. "I'm not a psychologist. I have no idea how to fix a block. You divers do things I can barely fathom, and what works for one athlete is trash for another. But." He kisses a hot tear from my cheek. "I think letting yourself be *sad* would be a great start."

"But I—"

"You don't have to be angry at your ex or at your father. *I'm* angry enough for you. But you need to acknowledge that what happened to you last year was terrible, that it gave you pain, and that you deserve time to heal in more ways than just the physical."

"But what if I never . . . What if I don't . . ." I sniff, unable to put thoughts into words. "What would I even be, without diving?"

A hushed, barely audible Swedish word, exhaled into my hair. Lukas pulls me deeper in his lap, and my skin sticks against his. "It'll be okay, baby. No matter what happens, you will still be *you*. No matter what happens, you will be okay."

"But what do I do in the meantime?"

"In the meantime . . . just cry it out." He sighs deeply, and the swell of his chest, the gravel of his voice, his hands stroking my hair, are as comforting as any perfectly executed dive. "I'm here, okay?"

I hope he's right. Because I don't know how much longer I cry on his shoulder—but I do know that once I cannot bear it anymore, I fall asleep in his arms.

# CHAPTER 41

I COME TO WITHOUT TRANSITIONS—SEAMLESS, ASLEEP TO awake, lost to lucid, burning with a very specific need.

"Lukas," I immediately whisper.

He's unresponsive, heavy biceps folding me into him. A hand cups the back of my head. The thick denim of his jeans is rough between my bare legs.

"Lukas." He's an annoyingly deep sleeper. I jostle in his arms, hoping the commotion will do the trick. All it accomplishes is a small frown, and him pulling me closer.

"Lukas!"

Nothing.

I roll my eyes, contemplate the lengths that I will go to wake him up, and decide that they are *very* long: I tilt my head, open my mouth, and bite into his triceps like it's an Iowa State Fair corn dog.

I expect him to yelp. Instead he slowly opens his eyes, buries a yawn into the bottom of my throat, kisses the very same spot, and asks, "Is it morning already?" Bleary lidded and confused, he's just . . . *adorable.*

Whatever. I'm allowed to think that the guy with whom I'm having power-exchange sex is *cute*. It's fully within my rights. "I want to go to the aquatic center."

He frowns. Lets me go long enough to retrieve his phone from his pocket, which lights up with more unread notifications than I've had all month. He ignores them, unalarmed, and instead squints at the numbers.

"It's one twenty-three a.m."

"Oh." I deflate—then reinflate when I remember: "You have keys, though. Right?"

His skeptical "Yes" is more question than reply.

"Can you let me in?"

He slow blinks at me. "Scarlett—"

"I never get to—you're right. It's for other people. It's always for others—Coach Sima, all the trainers I've had since I was a child, Pen. I feel guilty about disappointing them when I fail a dive. And it's hard to shut them out, because they're *always* around when I'm practicing." They have to be—it's regulation. Unsupervised training is forbidden. The risk of injury and drowning is too high. "What you said about doing it for yourself, about having to prove something—"

"I'm *not* going to let you dive alone, Scarlett."

"You can be there."

"I'm serious. If we get to Avery and you decide you don't want me around, I'm not leaving."

"It's fine. You can stay, because you don't count."

"I don't count," he repeats. Stony faced.

"No, because you don't care."

"I don't care." He sounds like the word *displeased* was invented for him and only him, and I don't understand why—until it occurs to me how he's interpreting my words.

"Not because—not in that sense!" I'm hot with frustration and embarrassment. "What I meant is, you care about me being *well* more than about me being *good* at something—anything. And when you're around I don't feel as anxious or scrutinized as I do with—"

He interrupts me with a hard, quick, somehow *encompassing* kiss. When he pulls back, his mouth twitches into that little smile that makes my heart gallop, and orders, "Grab your parka. Nights can get cold."

◆　◆　◆

Lukas wraps an arm around my shoulder, and even wearing a jacket, I still freeze my ass off as we walk through campus, shocked by thermal excursion following a perfectly nice fall day. In a T-shirt, he shakes his head in his most Swedish *I just caught you setting fire to a children's hospital* disappointment, and says, "Americans are so weak," before pulling me even closer.

Avery is well lit throughout the night (good), but when I dip my toe into the water, I find it so chilly, it belongs to Lukas's BDSM list (bad). I forgot to put on a swimsuit, but my sports bra will do. I take my clothes off and prep with a shower, setting the temperature several degrees hotter than usual to warm my muscles. I turn on the pool sprayers. I stretch a little, but I'm not stalling, or trying to put distance between me and the dive. I'm eager to climb the steps of the tower, and keep my surprise to myself when I realize that Lukas has taken off his shoes and is coming up with me, a tall, reassuring presence at my side.

"Springboard or platform?"

"Platform," I reply. It's how it started. First love, first heartbreak.

"Don't you have to put that thing on your body before diving?"

"The what?"

"That stuff you guys are always putting on your legs?"

"You mean, the stripper pole wax?"

He stops to give me a wide-eyed look. "You put stripper pole wax on your shins?"

"It's a grip aid. Divers use it to hold on to their legs, strippers use it to hold on to their poles. Have you ever seen strippers do their thing?"

"This feels like a trick question."

"They're *elite athletes*. In great shape." I plant my hands on my waist. "Did you really not know what it was?"

"Pen uses tape spray."

"Right. Well, I prefer the stripper stuff."

"You prefer the stripper stuff," he repeats, toneless.

My eyebrow quirks. "Are you surprised?"

He puffs out a small laugh, and mouths something that sounds more admiring than weirded out (was it *troll* again?), but I'm too busy hauling my ass ten meters high to investigate.

I'm a little more wet than I like to be when I dive, but I forgot to bring a shammy. I take my position at the edge, savoring the familiar ruggedness of the floor, letting my heels poke past the rim. "Any last words?" I ask Lukas.

It's nice that inward dives start facing toward the diving tower. Nice that his face can be the last thing I see. His amused frown. The way he crosses his arms. "Is there something I don't know about this pool?"

"What do you mean?"

He shrugs. "Does it have its own Loch Ness Monster? Piranhas? That Amazon River fish that swim up your pee hole to raise their babies in your genitalia?"

"I . . . do they actually exist?"

"Two out of three."

"I sure hope you have scientific evidence on the Loch Ness Monster." I sigh again. "So, no last words?"

"Scarlett, I'll talk to you in five seconds. What 'last words' are you going on about?"

I smile, because he's right. I'm going to try an inward dive, and if it works, great. If it doesn't . . . nothing hangs on this specific dive, does it? Actually, nothing hangs on *most* dives. If I'm honest, nothing hangs on my overall ability to dive, either.

It's true. Whether I manage to do this or not, when I get out of the pool, I'm still going to be *me*. And Lukas . . . Lukas is still going to be here. And admitting it to myself is such an odd relief, I find myself laughing.

And laughing more.

And some more.

It's *not* a hysterical cackle. I'm *not* deranged. But for the first time in what feels like a century, with Lukas standing in front of me, with the water ten meters underneath and the cold biting into my skin, diving seems *fun* again—and lifting my arms, bending my knees, taking off just high enough to manage a pike . . .

It just works.

Second nature.

Like it used to be.

And I'm almost sure . . .

It's a bit of a blur, but I think . . .

I may be wrong . . .

I punch out of the bitter chill of the water to meet the bitter chill of the night air, fluttering my legs to keep afloat. "Lukas?" I scream, sputtering, dragging locks of untied hair out of my eyes, fixing the bra riding half off my tits. I tilt my head up, and he's already there, peeping from the edge of the platform. "When I entered the water, was I facing the tower?"

He presses his lips together. "Hmm."

"Or the other way?"

"Let me think."

Oh, for fuck's—"Remember when I entered the water!"

"Hmm."

"Was my face looking at you?"

"Your face?"

"Lukas, I swear to god—"

"Scarlett," he says, in that tone that's final, that makes me feel like he's hearing me and he's got me and he's there. That tone that makes me go silent. "I learned what an inward dive is after the first time you mentioned them to me. And I know one when I see it."

I blink up at him, my lashes clumped with water and chlorine and something else.

"You mean . . ."

"I mean." He smiles, lopsided. "You did it."

# CHAPTER 42

I T TAKES ME SURPRISINGLY LITTLE TO CONVINCE LUKAS TO JOIN me in the pool. He throws his jeans and T-shirt from the platform, and says, "I've never done this. Any advice?"

I think about it. "Make sure you jump into the water."

"Great tip."

A moment later he dives in feetfirst, oddly elegant, managing something that's almost a rip entry.

Show-off.

I'm ready to yell at him for being *good* at *things*, but he doesn't reemerge for a *long* while. In the dim lights the water is opaque, and I grow anxious. I'm about to dip my head back in, when a tight grip sharks my ankle, pulling me underwater. I thrash and paddle and even try to pull Lukas's hair, but he doesn't let me resurface.

"I hate you," I splutter afterward, arms circling his neck. The water remains stomach-turningly cold, but Lukas's body is a block of heat.

"Of course you do." He wraps my legs around his waist.

"I thought you were dead." I shake the water out of my face. "Could already hear the Swedish king bitching over the phone."

"Did we not go over Sweden's government structure?"

"Can't recall." I unsheathe my best Swedish impression. *"I understand our national treasure died on your watch, ja? We have lost our golden porpoise, and it is all your fault, ja?"*

"Whatever just happened with that accent is a violation of NCAA bylaws *and* the Geneva convention."

"Take me away, Officer."

His eyes are black and golden, warm despite the temperature. He grins—a rare, unrestrained smile, in which his happiness is not just hinted at, something I have to dig for.

"I did it," I whisper. Just to hear it. Just to remind myself.

"You did." He tilts his chin up and kisses me, thorough, his lips cold and chlorine-flavored, my hair a sodden curtain sticking to our cheeks. It lasts a long time.

Way too damn long. "Lukas?"

"Huh?"

"I can't feel my face."

He laughs. "Weak Americans."

"Unlike the Swedes, who on the day of their birth are tasked with swimming from fjord to fjord to honor their Viking ancestors."

He moves us toward the deck, treading water with no effort. "Actually, we only have one fjord in Sweden."

"But the rest is accurate?"

"Naturally."

"We really need to get out. I doubt the Avery family had this in mind when they bankrolled the aquatic center."

His laughter is a hot huff against my ear. "Plus, we need to check those MCAT scores."

"What—why do you even *remember* that?"

"Because I listen when you talk. You're on such a brave streak, you can open one little email."

I groan into the curve of his shoulder. "Just let me have this moment."

"You're still going to have this moment."

"It will be *tainted*."

"You don't know that."

"I—should we go to sleep? I have practice tomorrow morning."

"Me, too. Let's just accept that we'll be asked to leave the team and make the most out of tonight."

We laugh. He kisses me. I kiss him. It becomes something heated and deeper and—

"MCAT," he reminds me. I feel the shift of his muscles as he lifts me to sit on the edge. The chill pebbles my skin, teeth instantly chattering.

"I really do hate you."

"I know." He pushes himself out effortlessly. "Your loathing cannot be contained. Troll."

"Okay, why do you keep calling me—"

Another lingering kiss, and a couple of minutes later, I'm in the men's locker room.

It's the exact copy of ours, no messier or more foul smelling. Lukas cracks open a locker, pulls out a towel, and dries me, thoroughly, and himself, quickly. He puts one of his hoodies on me, and I savor the way it hangs softly past my thighs. "Hand me your phone," he says.

"Actually, can we go to my locker and get a scrunchie?"

He knows exactly what I'm doing, but he's willing to let me stall one more minute. In the women's locker room, he watches me patiently as I detangle my hair, then asks, "Your phone."

"Maybe we should go? You shouldn't be here. Stanford Athletics might send you back to where you came from. Where you'll enjoy all the skiing and upwards of seven herring-themed meals per day."

"Scarlett."

I sigh, and we sit next to each other on the uncomfortable wooden bench. I pluck at the fray of his well-worn jeans, half baking the idea to distract him with sex, but he traps my hand in his and doesn't let go.

Instead, he holds out my phone.

"Why do I have to do it right now?" I whine.

"Because I'm leaving tomorrow night."

I jerk back. "You're leaving?"

He nods.

"What . . . for how long?"

"Ten days."

"*Ten—*" I gasp. "Why?"

"Nordic Swimming Championships."

"In Sweden?"

"In Estonia."

"Is it . . . a big deal?" I've never heard of it.

He shrugs. "Moderately. But most of the Swedish Olympic team will be there, and after we'll go on a training trip."

Is Coach Urso okay with that? Lukas's professors? The Stanford chancellors? "Did you clear it with everyone?"

"Nope. Better to ask for forgiveness than for permission." My eyes must be saucer wide, because he adds, "Yes, Scarlett. Everyone has known for months. They expect me to put swimming for Sweden over swimming for Stanford."

I guess it makes sense. "Are you friends with the rest of the team?"

He nods. "Basically siblings, really. We've been around each other for decades. Anyway"—he points at my phone with his chin—"if it's bad news, I'd rather be here. With you."

So difficult, pretending that his words don't make my stomach flutter. "To pat my back?"

"If that's what you want, sure."

I tear my eyes from his, and they catch on his sleeve. I've seen his tattoos so many times, touched them, dug my nails into them, gripped them when I felt like I needed something to hold on to or I'd dissolve into nothing. But I've never asked him about them.

*It*, more precisely. There are a lot of interlocked parts, but they all work together to form a coherent landscape. With my eyes first, then my fingers, I trace the spruces and oaks and pines, blackbirds and sparrows, snowy patches and rocks.

"What is this?" I shake my head and correct myself. "*Where* is it?"

"My hometown."

"I thought you were from Stockholm."

He lifts his most *I know you bookmarked the bio section of my Wikipedia entry on your Chrome browser, on Safari, and maybe even on Internet Explorer* eyebrow.

I roll my eyes. "If I were the current record holder for the one hundred freestyle, you'd know where I was born, too."

"You were born in Lincoln, Nebraska, on August thirty-first. And yes, I did grow up in Stockholm, but my mom was from Skellefteå."

I try to shape my tongue around the name. Instantly give up. "That sounds like . . ."

"Say, 'A piece of IKEA furniture not even the Swedish king would be able to assemble,' and I *will* throw you back into the pool."

I smile and bump him with my shoulder. "When did you get it done?"

"Eighteen. My brothers have similar ones, too. According to my father, after Mom died we took the easy way out and decided to get tattoos instead of dealing with our feelings."

"That's a serious accusation."

"Right? But on the upside"—he holds out my phone—"you get to book a despair tattoo if you don't like your MCAT score."

"Oh, god—fine, *fine*." I laugh softly, shaking my head, tapping at my email app.

Then stop to say, "You don't have to, you know?"

"Hmm?"

"Just . . ." My throat feels too full. "I appreciate this. The way you care. That you want to be my friend. But I don't want you to feel like you have to be my emotional support. I've been a . . . a wounded *bird*, stealing your hoodie, while I should be some kind of black-laced, collar-wearing, sultrily submissive—"

"Scarlett." He looks at me like he's having fun. "I don't think you get it."

"I . . . maybe I don't."

"You and I have an agreement, don't we? And the agreement says that until you say *stop*, I can do what I want with you. Even if it breaks you into pieces. Even if it makes you cry."

I nod.

"I love that you opened up to me," he says, pressing his mouth into the side of my head. I feel his inhale, and something sweet and thick drips inside me, warms me in my very core. "But they're sides of the same coin. I get to take you apart and split you open—but if anything else, *anyone* else makes you feel sad, upset, cracked, I also get to be the one who puts you back together. Until you say *stop*. You get it?"

I wish I could see his eyes. I wish my world was more than his stubble brushing my temple, the scent of sandalwood and chlorine carving its way in my brain. "I get it." I just *do*.

"Good girl," he murmurs, kissing my cheek. And then: "Now open that fucking email."

I laugh, and laugh, and laugh some more while the score report loads, and—

I blink. I'm unable to process what I'm seeing.

"Oh my god. Is it . . ."

There's a five. And a two. And a six. Three numbers that together make another number, one I should be able to make sense of, but it's high, so high, so much higher than I expected . . .

"Congratulations." A low, scratchy voice. Another kiss in my hair. Around my waist, a strong arm pulls me into warmth.

I whip my gaze up to Lukas's, dizzy. "You knew," I half state, half accuse.

He says nothing. His lips twitch.

"How? How did you know that it would be good? Oh my god—did you hack my email? Is it because I made my password kink related?"

He looks intrigued. "Tell me more about this password of yours."

"How did you know?"

"I didn't."

"You *did*."

He shakes his head. "I just know . . . you." His thumb smooths the furrow in my brow. "I've worked with you on the bio project. Spent time with you. I've—"

"Fucked me?"

He smiles and pushes back a lock of my hair. "I know that you are a perfectionist, and studied to the point of being overprepared. And that you're anxious, which clouded your perception of your performance. Above all, I know how much you want to get into med school, and I'm starting to suspect that you might be unstoppable—"

Lukas has more to say, but I don't let him finish, and reach up for a kiss. My phone clatters against the floor with a dull thud, but I don't care, arching upward to get closer to him, exhaling in relief when he lifts me to straddle his thighs.

This is *not* the way it usually goes. He's the one who initiates, and we both vastly prefer it that way. But for a few short moments, it's nice, being the one with the upper hand. Setting the pace. Feeling the restraint in his hard muscles as we approach the point where he'll make me feel good. And I'll make him feel good.

Except—I pull back, a hitch in my breath. "Sorry. Sorry—but you and Pen . . ."

Lukas blinks, lips stung, eyes glassy.

"Are you . . . are you two still having sex?" I swallow at his confused silence. "I know it's not my business, and you and I—but when she called you last week, I thought . . . And Pen is sleeping with other people, and you and I are not using condoms, so—"

"Scarlett. It *is* your business." His hand rises to my cheek. It always does, when he wants to make sure that my eyes won't leave his. "Last week I helped Pen because she's my friend, and she was stranded, and she didn't know who else to call. But I haven't touched her since we broke up. And I have no interest in having sex with anyone but you. Haven't in . . . a while."

I'm relieved in a way that I don't want to examine. "If you change your mind . . ."

I cut off because of the way he's slowly shaking his head. He clearly cannot fathom changing his mind, and I—can't breathe. His firm, determined look feels so much like a promise, it sucks all the air out of me. But it doesn't matter, because now he's the one kissing me, and we're back on the trodden path.

"I'm not sure that you get it, Scarlett," he says in my ear, and it happens so quickly—one second I straddle him, the next I'm kneeling on the floor, his clothes between my knees and the linoleum. My elbows brace on the low bench, and only one person can control where and how I move.

Lukas. Behind me.

"Actually, I *know* you don't."

"I—"

"I'm starting to suspect that you don't understand a single fucking thing, Scarlett."

There's something like barely restrained fury in the icy pitch of his voice. Fear rolls into me, and I respond like a fine-tuned instrument. I'm already *so* wet, it's embarrassing, and he can tell. He yanks my panties down, hands sliding under his hoodie to tighten around my waist with bruising force. The hot imprint of his cock presses against my skin through his jeans.

"Remember what you asked me earlier?"

"I don't—" I choke out, then stop. But it's fine, because he doesn't want an answer. His hand wraps around my mouth and I moan against it. I can't breathe. I feel dizzy. I want more of this.

"I walked into your room, and you looked at me, and you said . . ."

His hand loosens, and I take in a big gulp of air. "I don't *know*. I don't *remember*."

"You asked if I was there for a pity fuck," he whispers in my ear. His anger is terrifying. "And I let it go, because while you may think I'm mean—" His thumb and index fingers find my nipple and pinch it, pushing hot liquid into my abdomen. "I'm actually nice, Scarlett. And you weren't doing great. Now, though." He must have unzipped, because I suddenly feel the scalding length of his cock on my lower back, in the crease of my ass. "Does this"—he rolls his hips—"feel like a pity fuck to you?"

"*No.*"

His hand travels around my hip bone, then lower, softly tracing just outside of my cunt. "Look at you. Soaked. I fucking love it." He sucks a kiss into my jaw, a scrape of teeth, and then . . .

With an echoing sound, his other hand slaps against the right side of my bottom.

Lukas lets out a low, guttural grunt.

My mind goes completely blank.

"What do you do if you want me to stop, baby?"

I'm trembling. My ass cheek is hot, pain and pleasure radiating from where he hit me. He kneads the soft flesh, the fat, the muscle, and I—I *thought* I knew what being turned on meant, but I had no idea.

"Scarlett." Another slap—less firm. To get my attention. "What do you do if you want me to stop?"

"I—I say *stop*."

"Good girl. Should I stop?"

I shake my head like my life depends on it, wondering if I've ever wanted anything *more*. But his palm hits once again, and I cannot think, just feel, experience how *good* it is, the burn and the pleasure mixed together, the perverse, satisfying feeling of knowing that right now I'm as much the center of Lukas's universe as he is of mine.

"I don't fuck you because I pity you. But why *do* I fuck you, Scarlett?"

Slap.

"B-because—"

His teeth scrape against my jaw.

Slap.

A precious, first Communion kiss on my cheek.

Slap.

"You don't know, do you?"

His hand returns to my cunt, and this time it parts me. "Christ." His hot cock throbs against my hip, and I cannot help myself.

"Please," I beg.

"Please, what? You could come just from this, couldn't you? From me playing with your nipples and your ass. You want to be roughed up, don't you?"

I nod frantically.

"Hmm." His finger dips into my opening, and it's so close to what I need, so *close.* "Not yet, sweetheart. Not until my cock is at least halfway inside you. Why do I fuck you, Scarlett?"

I don't know. I whimper, tears flooding my eyes.

"I'm going to hurt you once more. Once more, and then I'm going to get inside you. Okay?"

"'Kay."

It's the hardest yet, and I'm crying because of how good, how wrong, how perfect it feels. His large hands cup both cheeks of my ass, slowly massaging them, healing me and hurting me more. His thumb slides between them, catching against my hole, lingering and pressing there for just a second, and he must feel the sudden tension, hear the alarmed hitch escaping my mouth, because what he says over my shoulder is "Next time we're on a bed."

It's not a question. He's informing me. He's *telling* me what he's going to do with my body, and I—"Please."

"Please, what?"

"Please, please, *please*—"

"Not until you tell me why I fuck you, Scarlett."

My cheeks are covered in tears. I try to squirm, but my hips are imprisoned in Lukas's hands. "I don't know. I don't *know, but I—I need you to*—" I'm babbling. I'm not proud of it, but I can't help myself. And Lukas . . . Lukas says something in Swedish, something frustrated and resigned, and then the blunt head of his cock is right there, pressing against me, too big.

I sigh in relief.

He nestles inside, less of an inch. I grip the edge of the bench to avoid coming. "I fuck you—" He pushes deeper. "Because—" Deeper. "It's all I want to do—" *Deeper.* "From the moment I wake up." He hits a *spot*, and . . . I hope he's halfway inside, I really do, because I'm already coming, clutching around the too-big, hard width of him, flutters I cannot help. It's so intense and shuddering and good, I'm lost to everything but my pleasure, and I almost don't hear the rest of what Lukas whispers in my ear.

"I fuck you because you're the most perfect thing I've ever felt, Scarlett."

The last thing I see before I close my eyes is Pen's locker, her name in white and green against the cardinal red metal.

# CHAPTER 43

THE FOLLOWING MORNING, WHEN I ATTEMPT ANOTHER IN-ward dive from the springboard, my core twists itself into some backward career-ending abomination.

Guess What Dive Scarlett's Body Will Come Up with Instead of the One She's Supposed to Do has been a recurring segment in my practices, but this time I did not expect to fail. In fact, I'm so virulently outraged at having *once again* fucked up, I inhale about a liter of chlorine.

"*Fuuuuuuuuck*," I scream underwater. The cutesy, almost cartoonish bubbles that spill out of my mouth only heighten my fury.

But when I resurface, coughing and sneezing and generally miserable, no one pays attention to me. Coach Sima is doing dryland with Pen. The assistants are focused on the twins practicing at one meter. Not a single glance slides in my direction, and in all honesty . . . why would it? *Congrats on your one thousandth missed dive, Vandy—here's a cake made of Swiss chard and anchovies!*

I suspect that their expectations of me have been permanently downsized. After all, I haven't told Coach that last night at 2:00 a.m. I managed an inward dive. *Oh, that's amazing, Scarlett! In which facility did that happen?* he'd unavoidably ask. I'd be left with the choice of throwing Lukas under the bus, or pretending that I'm a patron of the Palo Alto public pool.

But it doesn't matter, does it? It's not about what others think. What's important is how *I* feel about my own mistakes, and that's where I sense something new.

I'm not as mortified as I used to be. I am . . . combative. Determined. Ready to be over this.

Last night didn't heal my mental block, but I shed some helplessness, and that seems as big a win as the Powerball.

I think of texting Lukas, to inform him of this new step in my recovery journey. He seems fascinated by the workings of my slightly dysfunctional brain—maybe he plans to go into psychiatry? But he's on a plane, forty thousand feet on top of the Eiffel Tower, a neural network haphazardly drawn on the back of his hand. Likely watching reviews of cleaning supplies.

Do flights to Tallinn enter the French airspace? I could google and find out. Alternatively, I could just do my damn German homework.

On Sunday, instead of spending the day getting ahead with homework, I do something groundbreaking: celebrate my MCAT results. Pen and I eat industrial amounts of ice cream and walk around campus, taking in the homecoming alumni crowd, mildly befuddled by their unwavering support, wondering if there's something wrong with the school spirit part of our brain.

"You get letters from the alumni office, like, once a quarter," Pen says, holding my hand as we crisscross through the throng.

"I know."

"And they offer you the privilege of giving them *money*."

"I know."

"On the basis that you have already given them money for *four whole years*."

"I *know*."

"Absolutely bonkers."

It's just a regular Sunday. Nothing special happens. There are no milestones or achievements, nor do I go to sleep secure in the knowledge that I've achieved perfection. And yet it's a really, *really* good day.

On Wednesday, Sam is back, sounding nasal and clogged, like a virus is holding on to her for dear life. "So, your first big meet of the year. Would you like to tell me what happened?"

"Sure. From the platform, I dove well enough for the armstand—got eight point five . . ." I stop.

Do the scores really matter?

And the meet . . . does the *meet* matter?

I clear my throat. "Actually, could we talk about something else?"

Her eyes widen. "Yes, of course. This is your time, Scarlett."

"Okay. Thank you. It's . . . about my accident, mostly. I wasn't strictly *lying* when I told you about my injury, but I did omit a few things." She waits patiently, without looking mad or betrayed. It's encouraging. "I had a boyfriend at the time. On the morning of the NCAA finals he called me to break up with me. And the day before I received an email from my father."

"Your father? I thought he was . . ."

"Controlling. Abusive. Yeah."

She doesn't yell at me that I should have told her sooner—just studies me calmly, head tilted, no judgment. Like Lukas does. Like it's fine that I mess up. Like it's acceptable for me to be a constant work in progress.

Scarlett, beta version.

"I told myself that this stuff had nothing to do with diving, and that you didn't need to know. But I realize now that it's all connected. And the more I think about it . . . Do you remember when you asked what I was afraid of?"

She nods.

"I think I've figured it out. And it's not to be injured again."

"What, then?"

I grip the soft end of the armrest. "I'm afraid of the unpredictability of existing. I'm afraid of not being able to control the direction of my life. I'm afraid that no matter how much I plan, I won't be able to avoid hurtful and sad things. But above all . . ." I take a deep breath and laugh softly, because what I'm about to say is ridiculous, even if it's true. Even if it's *me*. "Mostly, I'm afraid of attempting something and not being perfect at it."

Sam nods. Smiles. And I realize that she knew this all along.

Later that afternoon, during practice, I manage two terrible inward pikes.

# CHAPTER 44

**N**OVEMBER STARTS AS A FANGED, BLOODCURDLING NIGHTmare.

"Novembers always do," Victoria tells Pen, the twins, and me in the athletes' dining hall—to which she's not supposed to have access. Every time someone swipes her card, we hold our breaths like a new rover is attempting to enter Saturn's orbit. "All the meets, the traveling, then Thanksgiving, and right after, Winter Nationals. I feel like I'm forgetting something—oh my god, classes. Yikes." Her cast has come off, and she seems to have discovered her true calling: affectionately berating us for every tiny synchro mistake. "You guys are gonna do great," she adds magnanimously. "Your hurdles are starting to look less like you come from different galaxies. Pen has been doing the correct number of twists. Vandy can inward. Rejoice!"

She's right. I've been consistently producing inward dives, if only mediocre ones.

"Problem is, you're still anxious and not approaching the dive with a clear mind," Coach Sima told me. "You're not failing them, though. Been a long time since I took math, but a four point five is still better than a zero." For him, the relief of me doing the bare minimum is too strong to fuss over the minutiae.

It's something Sam and I have been working on. "In some situations," she told me, "done is better than perfect. Not always. But when you're on the trampoline—"

"Springboard?"

"Yes, so sorry. When you're on the springboard, you can ask yourself that question, and make your own choice."

Our first away invite of the year is a two-day triangular up in Pullman, against Washington State and Utah. By the time it ends, I'm shell-shocked, wondering if I've traveled in time to two years ago.

"Wait, let's take another selfie, I look like I'm possessed by the spirit of a Georgian dandy in that one," Pen says, angling her phone. Later, while I'm supposed to be packing up in the hotel room, I waste entirely too much time studying the photo—our wide smiles as we toast our medals.

We placed third in synchro from the platform, and second on three-meter springboard, after the twins. Pen won the individual platform, and I finished third.

It was a small meet. Few competitors. The other programs are not as strong as us. Except for Fatima Abadi at Utah, who was a junior world champion but is out sick. I've been keeping the degree of difficulty for my inward dives as low as possible, a pike and a tuck, and they still felt tricky, but . . .

I could list a million reasons why my wins at this meet are not a big deal, but they are a precious reminder that *this* is what diving used to feel like. Exciting. Fun-scary. Challenging.

I let myself fall back on the mattress, smiling at the ceiling, and when I cannot hold in the happiness anymore, I kick my legs until I'm out of breath.

And then I get a text from Lukas. Congratulations.

I touch the word. Swipe over it with my thumb like it's flesh and blood. It's been nearly ten days since I last heard from him.

I've felt his absence more than I thought possible.

SCARLETT: Thanks!

SCARLETT: I owe lots of it to you. And the very illegal thing you did.

LUKAS: Letting you into the pool?

SCARLETT: I was trying to be secretive, in case one of us murders someone and our texts get subpoenaed.

LUKAS: In that scenario, nighttime pool usage is the least of our problems.

SCARLETT: Yeah, good point.

SCARLETT: Heading for the airport to return to California. Gotta go!

LUKAS: Be good. And slow down with the murders.

I wonder when he'll fly back from Europe, and where he'll go after. Swimming and diving, men and women, sometimes are the same team in name only. There are schools in which the female team is stronger; others where diving is little more than an afterthought. When it comes to meets, we rarely travel together. The men's swimming schedule is probably somewhere on Stanford's website, but if Lukas wanted me to know where he is, he'd tell me.

Not that I have time to think wistfully of him. Traveling has a domino effect that never fails to shrink my heart: classes, labs, tests to make up for, which means that every meet is sandwiched by days stacked back-to-back. Moving as a team requires more social battery than I could ever scrounge up, even if the Gravelines power plant were to relocate inside my chest. Last but not least, I always, *always* get the cruds.

"Have you considered purchasing a new immune system?" Maryam asks when she catches me sniffling in the kitchen.

"Too expensive," I mutter, pouring hot water into the Pipsqueak travel mug Barb got me for my birthday.

"I think Aldi sells 'em at a discount. Even a used one would be better than what you're working with."

I give her the finger and step outside. It's windy and foggy, and the prospect of practice in preparation for the *next* away meet, in less than eight goddamn days, turns my will to live into a raisin.

I must not be the only one. When I get to Avery, Pen and the twins seem delighted by the sight that greets us.

"How did they even . . ." Bella looks at the dozens of seagulls that have taken residence in the diving well. "You know what? Doesn't matter. Coach, what's going on?"

Coach Sima ambles toward us. "They're sanitizing everything, but apparently there are so many droppings, only a monster would force you to dive in these conditions."

I tilt my head. "Did you ask if you could force us to dive in these conditions?"

"Yes, and you know what I was told. No practice today."

"Oh, no," Pen deadpans.

Coach Sima glares. "Strength training's still on, smarty-pants."

We glance up at the platform, which appears to have become the vacation home of a family of seagulls. A quiverfull one.

"The heroes we need," I say.

Pen nods. "But not the heroes we deserve."

Pilates indoors feels like a decadent step up from freezing my ass in the air. I'm jackknifing my way into oblivion when I overhear Pen chatting with Monroe, one of the swimmers.

"Where the hell is Lukas?" he asks. "I thought he'd be back by now. I owe him ten dollars."

Pen laughs. Clearly, the rest of the team still doesn't know that they broke up. "He got back a few days ago, but immediately left for Seattle. Med school interview."

"No shit?"

"He should be back tomorrow."

I force myself not to wonder why *she* knows, and I don't.

It's because they're still friends. Best friends. Or because *Pen* didn't chicken out of texting him every night for the past two weeks, typing and deleting and retyping until she fell asleep. The problem is, his list covered stuff like orgies and pony play, but offered no insight on whether I should contact Lukas if I simply *miss* him. I don't want to overstep and ruin our arrangement. And Lukas . . . I have no clue what *he* wants. All I know is that he hasn't been texting, either.

"Jesus," Monroe says. "And then he's heading straight back out to UCLA for the quadrangular meet?"

"I think so, yeah."

"Ballsy. Can't believe he's applying for med school during an Olympic year."

"Kinda pointless, honestly. Even if he gets accepted, he's going to defer. He might as well have waited, but hey. He loves to torture himself."

He does, doesn't he? And yet later, in the locker room, I find myself asking her, "Is he really going to defer?"

"What?"

"Lukas, I mean." He never mentioned it to me. Then again, when would he? In between bouts of helping my therapist fix my post-traumatic issues? Or while defiling poor Dr. Smith's pristine cancer research lab?

*What about while you two were getting busy on top of me?* The bench in front of my locker asks. It's been calling me a slut for two weeks.

*You know what you did.*

I turn away.

*First you disgrace me, then you ignore me.*

Jesus.

"Yeah," Pen says. "He physically can't go to med school *and* still pursue swimming at the elite level."

She's right. I'm not sure why it never occurred to me. Maybe it's because *my* intention has always been to quit diving after senior year, but . . . he's a much more successful athlete.

"Don't you miss Lukas?" Bree asks Pen. "He's been gone for a while. I'm still trying to figure out how to deal with Dale spending Thanksgiving in Iowa."

"I'm used to it. We were long-distance for so long. And we text." Pen shrugs, then grins at me. "What about you, Vandy? Do you miss Lukas?"

I choke on my coconut water, and Pen starts patting my back with unnecessary force and glee.

"Why would Vandy miss him?" Bella asks.

"It was just a joke," Pen says. "No reason."

Twenty minutes later, I'm threatening to stab her with a dining hall spoon. "Seriously?"

"Come on." She lowers my weapon with her fork. "It was hilarious."

"Was it."

"For me, anyway. You should have seen your lustful little guilty face."

"Lustful."

"Or panicked. Mostly panicked. Don't worry—any day now, Lukas and I will bite the bullet and tell the team that we broke up."

I scoop up four peas, shaking my head. "Any news about Hot Teacher?"

"Yes, actually." She plays with a sticker peeling off her water bottle. "He asked me to spend Thanksgiving with him."

My eyebrows shoot up. "Like, with his family?"

"He doesn't have much of one. And mine barely remembers that I exist, so they wouldn't even notice if I didn't go back to New Jersey. Theo said we could just rent an Airbnb and chill for a few days, and . . ." She shrugs. Not very nonchalantly.

"It sounds like you're considering it?"

"Well, I *like* being with him."

"Is this . . ." I glance around, shaping my question. "Does it feel like it's becoming serious, between you two?"

"I . . ." She stares at her plate. "We just have lots in common. It's a nice change of pace, because of our shared interests. And the sex is amazing. And he's so easy to talk to, and very affectionate, and really into me, you know? Luk was . . . I mean—it's a personality thing. His range of emotions is kinda narrow, so . . ."

*Are we speaking of the same person?*

But she's known him for seven years. If one of us is wrong about Lukas, that has to be me. Right? "Do you and Theo talk about the future?"

"A bit. Sometimes. He knows that I'd like to dive professionally. He wants to be an academic, but he's so supportive." She flushes a little, but there's a giddiness to her I never noticed before. And it's possible that I'm a little giddy, too, because in a scenario in which she's happily and openly dating Theo, she wouldn't care that Lukas and I might evolve into . . .

It doesn't matter.

In November, Pen and I spend most of our free time together. Meals, homework, a game night at Victoria's. We take the train and go to San Jose for a concert. I invite her over, and she's once again exposed to Maryam ("Absolutely fucking terrifying"). Our next dual meet is in Minnesota, and we wipe the floor with the other team.

"That inward right there?" Coach tells me after my last voluntary dive. The temperature in the pool is lower than I'm used to, and my skin is bumpier than a chicken's.

"I know, I didn't get high enough, but—"

"No, Vandy. Look."

I turn to the scoreboard. *Seven. Seven. Seven point five.*

"Holy shit," I whisper.

"Language," he chides. "But yeah, holy *fucking* shit."

We're not scored individually, but the result sheet is right *there*, and my name is listed right after Pen's. For springboard synchro, we're only three points behind the twins. It's mostly because Bella's back has been acting up, but still.

My German test makeup exam is scheduled for the day we get back. After flash-carding throughout the dual meet, I'm optimistic in a reckless, if resigned, way. Afterward, with the sun already set and the lack of sleep making my head heavy, I walk to Dr. Carlsen's office.

"The part about Gibbs sampling here?" I tap at my paper on his desk, perhaps a little too forcefully. "You docked off two points and told me to double-check my rate of convergence. Which I did, and I was correct, so—"

On the margin, Dr. Carlsen scribbles, *Otis. Triple check your double-checking requests.*

"Thank you," I say, satisfied.

He sighs and sits back in his chair. "You're welcome. Unfortunately," he adds dryly, "your grade is already the highest A I've ever given in this class."

"It's a matter of principle," I explain primly. "I'm sure you understand."

He seems pained. "I do, and it's making me reconsider several things about myself."

"I think our profound respect for computational biology should only be cultivated."

He *almost* cracks a smile—the closest I've seen him to showing emotions that don't fall under the umbrella of irritation or contempt. It's *petrifying*. "Dr. Smith tells me your work on her project has been invaluable."

"Really? I feel like I've been so busy with meets and practice, I don't get to work on it as much as I'd like."

"Right. You said you're an athlete." He glances at my Stanford Swimming and Diving hoodie. "Swimming?"

"Diving."

"Had a fifty percent chance."

I make a sympathetic face. "And you got it wrong."

"Try not to enjoy it too much."

"I am. Desperately."

Another sigh. "Ol—Dr. Smith mentioned that you're applying to med schools."

"Yup. Well, not yet. But soon."

"If you need a letter of reference . . ." he says. And doesn't finish the sentence, which is unlike him and a little befuddling. I blink owlishly, hoping he'll explain himself, wondering how I'm supposed to read his mind, when suddenly—

I gasp. "Wait. For *real*?"

"Provided that your performance in my class remains up to par. And that you do not reveal objectionable support of superseded pseudoscientific theories."

"Are you referring to homeopathy?"

"Of course."

"Please," I say flatly.

He nods once. "Excellent."

I walk through the semi-deserted, pre-Thanksgiving campus, wondering how far a rec letter from Adam Fucking McArthur Fucking Carlsen could get me here, at Stanford. Or anywhere in the country. In the world? Maybe there's a med school on one of Neptune's moons. I should look into that.

Maryam is already in Florida with her family. Her note on the kitchen table reads *i left some food for you in the fridge*, but when I open it, all I find is our usual array of sauces and condiment bottles— and a gold medal. The Post-it stuck to it reads *sike! how does it feel to be the roommate of the number one wrestler in the whole world?*

I immediately text her.

SCARLETT: You mean, in a single dual meet and in your weight category?

SCARLETT: Either way, my answer is: it would feel better if you'd gotten me food.

MARYAM: New phone who dis

Our last practice is on the Tuesday before Thanksgiving, and I book a flight to St. Louis for that night. The USA Diving Winter Nationals are going to start next week, and I seriously considered not going home—stay on campus, have a lonely turkey sandwich and some cranberry juice, and spend the holidays practicing. But last week Sam asked me, "Do you really think it's what's best for you?" and the answer seemed so simple.

I miss Pipsqueak. And Barb (though not as much). "I just . . . how will I know if I'm cutting myself too much slack?"

"Oh, Lordy." Sam actually laughed—a foreign sound I'd never before encountered despite our many hours together. "You've got a ways to go, Scarlett."

Lukas returns from an away meet that Tuesday. I haven't seen him in person in almost a month, and . . .

It's odd, being aware of him. Noticing. Just a little while ago, he and I were strangers. But now he's a presence and an absence in my life, at once ghostly and bulky.

I spot him poolside, talking with one of his coaches, Pen's arms slung around his waist. I *see* him, but I have no *right* to go to him. Or do I? We never agreed to anything more than kinky sex. All I can do is shake off the heavy weight in my stomach and climb the diving tower. Stare at the water where we kissed in the silent hours of the night, while everyone else slept. Rise on the tip of my toes for my best inward dive yet.

After, it's hugs with the twins in the locker room, wishes for safe travels, and the faint trepidation of knowing that we'll next see each other in Tennessee, for the Winter Nationals. I step briskly out of the aquatic center, already dreading the shitshow I'll find at the airport.

"Scarlett."

It hits me hard when I turn around: Lukas, and his post-practice tousled hair, the rapidly fading freckles, the way he slouches against the wall of Avery and yet remains graceful. A million other trivial, mesmerizing things.

"Are you waiting for . . . ?"

"You," he says.

My stomach opens like a sinkhole. "Oh. Hey."

"Hey."

I hang back for a second, my instincts confused, oscillating wildly. *Run away. Run to him.* As usual, he takes charge. Comes closer till I need to tilt my head to look him in the eyes. Smiles. Something faint and small, but no less committed for it.

"That email Olive wrote," he starts. "About presenting at that bio conference."

"Ah, yes! I was going to ask if . . . we should do it?"

He cocks his head. "Are you asking? Or telling me?"

"I . . ." I snort a small laugh. "Actually, I don't know. What do you think?"

He shrugs. "I did something similar last year."

"And?"

"It was boring."

"Oh. No, then?"

"But with you, it would be fun."

My heart races. "It would look good on med school applications, right?" I add quickly, to put a shield between myself and my enjoyment of his words.

"Probably."

"Then let's do it." I smile. He doesn't. A cluster of water polo players walks past us, and we fall into a silence that's not quite as comfortable or familiar as I'm used to.

And then we start talking at the same time.

"Do you wa—"

"I'm go—"

We both stop.

"You first," he says.

"Nothing much. I'm headed for the airport. Going home."

He nods. "I guess I won't need to ask my question, after all."

*Do you wa—*

*What were you going to ask, Lukas?*

*Do I want . . . what?*

I should demand he tells me. Instead: "Are you doing something fun on Thursday?"

He frowns. "Thursday?"

"Thanksgiving."

"Ah, right. I always forget that you Americans celebrate that."

"Yup. Mid food and colonial violence. It's our thing." I shift my backpack from one shoulder to the other. "How did your competitions go? Are you officially the King in the North?"

"I've never heard anyone phrase it like that, and now I'm wondering why."

"A missed opportunity. Any new records?"

"Nope." He lifts his hand, showing me his skin. "My good luck troll's stamp had already faded by the time I was competing."

I frown. "What's a good luck troll?"

"You know. Those little creatures who watch over us and bring good fortune."

"I most certainly do not know of . . ." I laugh. "Oh my god, is *that* why you've been calling me troll?"

He says nothing. Just looks at me warmly, fondly, and I glance away—but when I turn back, he's still staring. A little differently from earlier, more intense, inquisitive, and it makes me bold. "Too bad we're not overlapping longer."

He nods. "Yeah. Too bad." He seems briefly impatient, lips pressed together, fingers twitching. Like he wants to reach for something, but knows he can't. "After the holidays, then." He looks around, and I wonder if what's going through his head is the same as mine.

*What if we moved closer? For just a second, what if we kissed? Would anyone see? Would anyone care?*

In the end, it's Lukas who lifts his hand and reaches up to push a lock of damp hair behind my ear, letting his thumb brush against my cheek once, for less than a second.

His hand drops back to his side. I cannot breathe.

"Safe travels, Scarlett," he says hoarsely. His pupils are blown wide. "Keep in touch. If you want to."

I can feel my pulse. Pounding in my cheeks. Spreading across my abdomen. "Bye, Lukas."

I don't turn around, not even when I hear Pen's voice greeting him. But his face sticks behind my eyelids long after I land in St. Louis.

# CHAPTER 45

THE CLAIM TO FAME OF THE USA DIVING WINTER NATIONALS is one, and one only.

"It's the qualifier for the world championship," I tell Barb over a plate of microwaved leftovers. It's a treasured yearly tradition: me, (re)explaining the basics of competitive diving; her, treating everything I say as though it's new and highly intriguing information.

"It's not my fault," she whines. "Do you know how many bones the body has?"

"Two hundred and six."

"Precisely. And I have to know them all—there's no room in my chubby little brain to retain any other knowledge. Plus, you know how I feel about sports."

"They're a crime against couches."

"Exactly. Come on, tell me again about this convoluted rigmarole that you have to go through to launch yourself off a cliff."

I sigh, but Pipsqueak is in my lap, snoring softly, displaying her pudgy belly. It's hormonally impossible for me to feel anything but joy.

"In three days, I'm going to the diving Winter Nationals qualifiers, in Knoxville. If I qualify—"

"Which seems likely?"

"I'm optimistic. If I qualify, I move on to the diving Winter Nationals. Which start in *five* days, at the same pool in Knoxville."

"And what's our goal at the diving Winter Nationals?"

I love the royal *we*, especially considering her hard stance on athletics. "As I mentioned, that's where people qualify for the World Aquatics Championships."

"That sounds like a big deal. Wait, did you already go to one of those?"

"Only junior ones. Montreal and Doha. You accompanied me to both."

"Told ya—chubby. *Little*."

"World Aquatics are going to be next February in Amsterdam. Every country gets to enter only *two* athletes for every event, which means that if I place first, or second, I'll get to go."

"Hmm. And how likely *are* you to place first or second?"

"I try not to think about it too much, because otherwise I'll just work myself into a panic and move into a system of caves with a nice bat family, *but*." I tap my fingers against Pipsqueak's tummy. "My strongest event is the platform, and I'm *basically* a shoo-in. Not that I would ever place first—Pen's better, no doubt. But I'm certain to place second if a couple of things happen."

Barb's eyes widen. "And what are these things?"

"Okay, first"—I lift my index finger—"Fatima Abadi from Utah needs to withdraw from the competition for an urgent, but ultimately inconsequential, family matter. Then"—middle—"Mathilde Ramirez should injure herself. Nothing bad, maybe a mild sprain that'll heal right away? Just something that'll last long enough to sit out Nationals. After that"—ring—"I'm going to need Akane Straisman, Emilee Newell, and C. J. Melville to leave the discipline altogether. Maybe they could fall madly in love and elope? Move to a cabin in the woods and live their cottage-core dreams? I'm flexible when it comes to—"

"I get it, I *get* it." Barb rolls her eyes, but she reaches out to me. My fingers twine with hers. "What you're saying is, unless I'm willing to break my Hippocratic oath and shank a handful of young women, I shouldn't buy nonrefundable tickets to Amsterdam?"

"Pretty much. But it doesn't matter," I hasten to add. "It's not black or white, you know? Winning or losing. As long as I can do my best and be proud of my performance, I don't care."

"Whoa. Who are you and what have you done to my step-daughter?"

I laugh. "There is a little bobblehead living inside my skull. She looks just like my therapist and *looooves* to remind me that if I don't redefine my concept of failure, I'll die of acute ventricular tachycardia before turning twenty-five."

In fact, plastic Sam is my main companion for the first two days of the qualifiers. I'm in Knoxville alone, because Bree, Bella, and Pen already have their spots. I have acquaintances from the junior varsity circuit, but for the most part I'm on my own, and don't mind. I qualify for all my events easily, acquaint myself with the diving well, rest.

No pool is like another: The way the water looks from above; sounds and temperature; where the judges sit, hostile, merciless. Every springboard has a fulcrum that needs to be adjusted. Want a stiffer, easier-to-control board? Move it forward. Love to be propelled into the sun by a massive rocket of elastic energy? All the way to the back. It all needs getting used to, and I'm glad for the opportunity.

The night before Winter Nationals start, I get an unexpected invite to dinner. "Vandy, we're tired of hotel food—want to get Chinese with us? There's a cheap place three minutes away."

It's Carissa Makris. I know her from my recruiting trip to the University of Florida—the team she ended up joining. We were shuttled around together and got along well enough to stay in touch afterward, but I think she hoped to have a college buddy, because after I told her I'd be going to Stanford, she never contacted me again. At the time she was mostly a springboard diver, but she's made a lot of progress on the platform. And now, after three years of ignoring my existence, she's inviting me to dinner. "Oh. Really?"

"Come on. We'll be back early." She runs a hand through her dark curls and grins. "It's gonna get so crowded here tomorrow, we'll be eating stacked in each other's laps."

Chinese *is* my weakness, so I head over with her and five other girls from Florida, and have lots of fun. We complain about FINA, NCAA, USADA, about our respective institutions and coaches, about swimmers, about the aches in our joints, about the academic work we'll have to make up for.

"I was there when you got injured," Carissa tells me later, while the others are getting soft serve and it's just me, her, and Natalie, her synchro partner. "I teared up. True story."

"She did," Natalie confirms.

"It looked so painful, and it could have happened to anyone."

I fold my napkin into little triangles. "Yeah, it sucked."

"I'm glad you're back on."

"My friend up in Pullman," Natalie adds, "said you are at the top of your game."

Compared to last year, when there was *no* game, for sure. "At this point, not hitting my head against concrete would be a raving success."

They chuckle. "So, you're doing synchro?" Carissa asks.

"Yup, with Penelope Ross."

"Ah, right." Natalie nods, but I get the discomfiting impression that she already knew that. "Won silver for the three-meter spring-board at the NCAA last year, right?"

"And a gold for the platform."

"Right. Well." Carissa steeples her hands, elbows braced wide on the table.

All I can think is: *There it is. The true reason for this dinner.*

"I'm not one to beat around the bush, Vandy. I like you. You've never shown anything but good sportsmanship. I remember you at the Olympic trials, four years ago, you know? You didn't make the team, but I thought, 'She's got something. She's good.'"

"Thank you," I say, instead of pointing out how slightly patron-izing this sounds. We're the same age. Carissa was at those trials, too, and placed lower than I did.

"I'll just say it straight to you. Pen Ross? You need to watch your back with that one."

Whatever I expected, this was *not* it. "What do you mean?"

"Plainly, she's a backstabbing bitch. Back in Jersey I dove in the same club as her, and she was universally despised. Ask *anyone*. She may be the next big thing in diving, and she may have grifted Stan-ford into believing that she's not a sociopath, but I know better. And you should, too."

I try to digest Carissa's words, trying to reconcile what she just said with my own experience, but my brain instantly rejects it. In the last few months Pen and I have been growing closer, and . . . "I don't like this."

"Being stuck with Pen Ross?" Natalie snorts.

"Pen is a friend. Nothing in her behavior has ever suggested what you're saying."

"How many years have you known her?"

"About three."

"I more than double you, then."

"Still, I can't imagine that through the thick and thin of three diving seasons she wouldn't have let slip this humongous harpy personality you speak of." I shake my head and scoot to the side of the booth, ready to walk back to the hotel.

"Hey," Natalie calls, "we're just trying to be nice here. Nothing to be mad about and lots to be grateful for, so—"

"Let her go." Carissa stops her with a hand on her shoulder, her eyes never leaving mine. "Vandy . . . just watch your back, okay?"

♦  ♦  ♦

When I show up to the platform prelims, I discover that C. J. Melville is out due to injury. My gasp is loud, but submerged by everyone else's shocked noises.

"Is it bad?" Bree asks. "Was it karma?" C. J. has been universally considered The US Diver for the past six or seven years, but has an interesting reputation. *Less than nice*, some say. *Mean as a banshee*, most say.

Personally, I've had enough experience with the way not-beamingly-outgoing women tend to be written off as bitches to mistrust the rumors.

"No idea," Coach says, "but she was as good as guaranteed to take up a world championship spot on most events, so that ups y'all's chances by . . . fifty percent? That sounds right."

I frown. "Actually, the math isn't—"

"No one likes a know-it-all, Vandy."

Pen pats my knee.

*What did you do?* I text Barb—who has, I'm informed, notifications silenced. Probably busy buying crowbars to off the rest of the competition. Or in surgery. Who knows.

"Of course," Coach continues, "C. J. doesn't compete in synchro, because of her . . ."

"Distaste for anything that houses a soul?" Bree offers.

"Sure, let's put it like that. But Madison Young, who was at TAMU till last year, is disqualified. Not sure why."

We all fall silent. There's usually one reason for people to be disqualified, and I can't picture Madison taking stimulants and screwing up her career. "And Mathilde Ramirez is coming off last month's injury."

Pen and I exchange a glance. "All of this is . . ."

"Convenient?" she finishes.

"I'm just glad you didn't make me say it."

She laughs. "By the way, Luk asked me to give you something."

My eyes widen. "Lukas?"

"You forgot it at his place, or something?" She wiggles her eyebrows at me. I glance around, relieved to find that no one is paying attention.

"I never forgot anything at his . . ." Oh my god. Is it my underwear? Did he give Pen my *dirty underwear*?

"Here you go."

She hands me something soft and colorful, then turns to reply to something Bella asked. It's for the best, since I think I might be shaking, and blood pounds in my temples, and my chest is suddenly red-hot.

Because in my hands there's a tie-dye shammy.

💧 💧 💧

We all progress easily to finals, but Bella's back is not getting better, and she misses qualifying. She's a good sport about it, but Bree must notice something I don't, because she looks at her sister with a worried expression and disappears with her for a couple of hours. It's a hectic competition, with simultaneous and combined events and little buffering time. We're all exhausted by the end of day one.

Carissa is diving, too. The first couple of times her name is announced, I sneak glances at Pen for signs of discomfort, but she seems indifferent. *One-sided feud,* I decide. *Likely jealousy.* I put the whole thing out of my mind. I don't have the constitution for drama, not if it includes me or people I care about.

My dives are a mixed bag: I mess up an entry like I'm Flipper's fucking blowhole, but my pikes are *tight.* It makes me proud—not that I dove well, but that I manage to dust myself off and put my mistakes behind me. *Not perfect* can still be *good.* What a mind-altering thought, huh?

In the locker room, I zip up my hoodie and turn to Pen. "I need a snack, but do you want to practice synchro after?"

"Isn't the pool closed?"

"Dryland, I was thinking." I hold the door open for her as we head out. "Mostly, for the running approach—"

"Look what the hyena dragged in."

We halt. Carissa stands in our path, staring daggers at Pen. Natalie scowls at her side, channeling the henchman of the scariest lunch-stealing bully at the playground.

"Carissa." Pen's face is polite and pleasant, but . . . different, too. "We have to go. Sorry about—"

"Ruining my life?"

A beat of silence. Pen's voice takes a conciliatory tilt. "This is not the time, nor the place."

"There is no time or place, is there? You got what you wanted, and we all have to get over it." She tries to shrug, but it doesn't work, like a chip is physically tilting her shoulder.

"Carissa, I—"

"I don't wanna hear it." Last night I thought she was bitter and angry. Today she can't conceal the hurt in her words. "I just wanted to let you know that you're *not* forgiven." She turns on her heels and walks away, Natalie's arm slung over her shoulder, pulling her closer as if for comfort.

I turn to Pen, at a loss for words, and find that she's already looking at me.

"Scarlett," she says, voice trembling. "I need to talk to Lukas. Right now."

# CHAPTER 46

**W**E GO TO MY ROOM AND CALL LUKAS FROM MY PHONE.
I wonder if I should text him a heads-up—*I know this is weird, pls don't send me to voicemail, neither of us selected phone sex or long-distance role-play on the list, I'm aware.*

"He won't pick up," Pen tells me, dejected. "I just remembered. He's at the US Open. The two-hundred-meter freestyle finals are happening right now."

"Oh." I wipe my palms down my joggers and sit next to her on the mattress, unsure what to do. It takes me almost an entire minute to gather the courage to cover her hand with mine. "I'm sorry about Carissa. If there's anything I can do . . ."

"I can't believe she actually *talked* to me this time. Shit." Pen rubs a hand down her face. "Vandy, I need to explain some stuff to you."

"She warned me about you last night," I blurt out. Possibly the wrong thing to say, given Pen's instantly betrayed look, but I need to come clean. "She was high on the spewing and low on the specifics. Just said you're a . . . well, a bad person was the gist of it."

"Why didn't you tell me?"

"Honestly?" I shrug. "I didn't believe her. What she said made no sense, so I shelved it as bullshit. It didn't even occur to me that you might want to know, and I'm sorry I—"

Pen's arms wrap around my neck, holding me so tight, breathing is not the piece of cake activity it used to be. I hesitantly hug her back. A moment later I feel her tears against my cheek.

"I'm sorry. It's just—" She pulls back with a sniffle, wiping the back of her hand on her face. "She's poisoned so many people against me, and the fact that you didn't even hesitate . . ."

My heart squeezes. "I'm sorry she cornered you like that. Maybe we could report her?"

"No." Pen shakes her head. "This goes way back, Vandy."

I nod. "You don't have to explain anything to me. I support you no matter—"

"But I want to." She takes a deep breath. "Carissa and I went to the same diving club in central Jersey, and I cannot remember when we stopped liking each other, or pretending to like each other, or why by the time we were fourteen we were in an all-out conflict. Maybe we were young and competitive? I'm not proud of the way I acted at the time—I'd gloat when I won, seethe when she did. That cringe stuff you think back on and want to drown yourself over?"

I nod, highly familiar. Children can be mean. Athletes can be mean. Mixing the two together . . . an unstable equation.

"Her mom was the director of our diving club. Coach. Former diver. She had a knack for teaching, but over time she went from being passionate and supportive, to verbally abusive. She'd constantly yell terrible things at us, *including* her daughter. And the younger kids . . . she terrified them. Shamed them about their weight, forced them to train in bad weather, said all sorts of toxic stuff. And I was the one who reported her."

"Oh." Shit.

"An investigation was opened. She was suspended. It was for the best, but Carissa remained in the club, and decided that I'd ruined her mother's career, maybe even her *life*. And the rest of the club . . . they *knew* that the report wasn't false, but she managed to spin the narrative that I'd overreacted out of jealousy, and either they believed her, or they pretended to." Pen wipes her eyes. "It was miserable. The bullying. The things they said behind my back. To my *face*. I wanted to find another club, but there was *nowhere* with a reasonable commute. My parents didn't care. And Carissa and I were in the same high school. She spread rumors about me, turned friends against me. Not everyone believed her, but it was so hard, going to a party and not knowing if people . . ."

"Would throw a bowl of soup at you?"

She laughs, watery. "Were there many soup-involving parties at your high school?"

"Wouldn't know, as I was never invited to one. But I think it'd be a winning idea."

Her amusement lifts some weight from the room. "My junior and senior years were hell. And if not for Lukas, I'd have been totally alone. But he'd call to remind me that I wasn't an unlovable piece of shit, and . . ." She sighs deeply. "And then there's the part I hate the most. Stanford was Carissa's dream school. But when Carissa contacted Coach Sima to express her interest, he noticed that she and I had been in the same club, and asked me about our relationship. I was truthful, and he decided not to pursue her."

I scratch the side of my head, taking it all in. "I still don't think any of this is your fault."

"I know. It's just . . ." She tips her head back, staring at the ceiling, her eyes once again overflowing. "I hate it. Knowing that she's here, and still resents me is just . . . Lukas is not around, and I feel so alone all over again, and—"

"You're not, though." She looks at me, and I squeeze her hand. "I'm here. I may not be Lukas, but I'm your friend. And if Carissa makes a single wrong move, I'm going to—to *glower* at her, and hiss—"

"Hiss?"

"It's a very effective defensive behavior within the animal kingdom. The point is, I'm on your side. I hate bullying, and people who intimidate others. I've always been on the fringe of every team. You made me feel welcome from the start. I trust you, and you can trust me."

Her tears spill over. "Are you sure?"

I nod just as Lukas's name flashes on my phone. I quickly accept the video call.

"Scarlett?" He must have dialed me back the second he got out of the pool, because he's still dripping. He looks, at once, surprised, pleased, and worried. "You okay?"

I remember what he said about his mom. *The phone call came.* "Yeah, everything's okay." I angle the camera to include Pen. "Just, Carissa—"

"Nothing," Pen says from beside me. Her cheeks are still shiny, but she turns to me. I do the same, and notice her smile. "I had an . . . issue. And wanted to talk to you. But as it turns out, Vandy helped me through it, because she's an amazing friend. And I don't deserve her."

My heart swells. I feel . . . chosen. Worthy. "That's nice of you to say, because I live in fear of you seeing through my daily charades and realizing that I'm so numbingly boring, dentists inject me into gums before root canals."

"What? You're not boring at all," she says. And there's an echo—because Lukas said the same thing, at the same time. He looks confused by the whole thing. Might still be panting from his race.

"Did you win?" I ask.

He shrugs, because *of course* he did. And doesn't even look smug about it. "Is everything okay? Do you need me?"

I get the impression that the question is for me, but it's Pen who shakes her head and says solemnly, "It appears that your presence will not be required, after all."

He lifts an eyebrow, puzzled but not displeased. "Okay?"

"Basically, I'm the new and improved version of you," I tell him with my most self-satisfied smile, which makes his own lips quirk.

"And here I was, thinking you were a troll."

Pen looks confused, so I squeeze her hand again, and we change the subject.

# CHAPTER 47

THE WINTER NATIONALS LAST FIVE MORE DAYS, EACH WITH highs and lows.

During the springboard final, neither Pen nor I qualify for the world championship—but neither does Carissa, who's on track for the gold until she flunks an entry so bad, chestnut-backed chickadees in the Pacific Northwest must have felt the spray. I've produced way worse dives, and when it comes to enjoying someone else's screwups, I don't have a single toe to stand on, but just this once I allow myself some gloating room.

"We should celebrate," I whisper at Pen during the award ceremony. Coach Sima turns back with a worried look, like maybe I forgot that *not* being on the podium is a bad thing, but Pen leans her forehead against my shoulder and wheezes for five minutes.

Everything okay? Lukas texts me that day.

SCARLETT: Yes. Pen's doing much better! We're about to start some synchro prelim.

LUKAS: And?

And?

SCARLETT: Would you like a picture of the dive sheet?

LUKAS: How are you, Scarlett?

There is no reason for this simple question to make me blush. Must be the heat of the pool. I'm no longer used to diving indoors.

SCARLETT: Fine?

LUKAS: Is that a question or an answer?

SCARLETT: Not sure.

LUKAS: Think it through, then.

The second day, I wake up to an email from my favorite German insomniac, Herr Karl-Heinz.

*Scharlach,*

*Look at you go!*

It's an A. On my exam. "In your face!" I scream—in absolutely no one's face. "I did it! I did *it*!" I text Barb a screenshot. Then Maryam. Then—why not?—Lukas, who says, Swedish better be next.

I don't know why, but it makes me kick my feet.

On the third day, after a long, hushed conversation with her sister, Bella decides to withdraw. "My back's just too . . ." She shakes her head.

Coach Sima sighs, patting her shoulder. "Not your fault, kid. Stop by PT, okay?"

Watching the twins leave the pool is heartbreaking. Because of Bella's injury, and because of the wistfulness in Bree's eyes as she looks back at us. Pen and I finish fifth on the board synchro, as good as we could have hoped considering the competition, but it's hard to celebrate when Carissa and Natalie take the gold, which means they'll be heading for Amsterdam.

We don't stay for the award ceremony that follows the event, even if it's terrible sportsmanship. Instead we head for the locker room and quickly shower. We're out before most of the other divers arrive, and because the universe punishes athletes with the aforementioned sportsmanship, we cross paths with the two people we care to avoid.

"Hey, Vandy," Carissa says. "I'll see you tomorrow at the platform synchro finals. And"—her eyes flit to Pen—"take what I said to heart."

"You need to stop," I tell her, squaring my shoulders.

"Stop what?"

"Being rude to Pen."

Her face hardens. "You know I'm doing you a favor, right?"

"Actually, you're just harassing us."

"Yeah?" She takes a step closer. "If this is how you thank me, I hope you get to reap the consequences of your stupidity."

I smile sweetly. "And *I* hope you get explosive dysentery in the middle of a somersault dive." I brush past her, Pen on my heels. It's probably the most out-of-character thing I've ever done, said, or thought. But Pen is at my side, gripping my arm.

"That may have been the sexiest thing that ever happened to me."

Oh? "Well, I'm no hero, but . . ." I pretend to dust myself off and she laughs.

"Even better than when she saw me and Lukas hold hands the first time. I swear, her face shattered in a million plankton-sized pieces. Clearly, you and Lukas are my knights in shining armor." We enter the elevator, and her eyes narrow on me. "You *are* quite similar."

"Me and Carissa?"

"God, *no*. You and Lukas."

I laugh. "Believe me, we aren't."

"You are both reserved. You get intense about the people you care about. You're single-minded, and have a solid core of strength and self-confidence. You hide your sense of humor from most people, but are hilarious. And of course you're both into . . ."

"Kinky BDSM stuff?"

"I was going to say science-y shit. But that, too."

I shake my head. "I'm not confident at all. Up until two months ago, I could barely dive."

"Confidence is not about being able to do shit, Vandy. Confidence is showing up, and trying, and not giving up because deep in your heart you know who you are and what you're capable of."

Is that right? I have no idea. *I do want to be like Lukas*, I tell myself later that night, in bed. Somehow, it's a good thought to settle on. It feels less messy than wanting to be *with* Lukas.

The following day, during the platform synchro final, Pen screws up her takeoff and sprains her ankle.

"It's not bad. You'll be like new in a week or so," the doctor tells her.

Her eyes light with hope. "Can I continue competing—"

"Today and tomorrow? Absolutely *not*."

It's disappointing, but we're both relieved that her injury is minor.

"No podiums," Coach Sima tells me, Bree, and Pen on the last day. I'm waiting to be introduced for the individual platform final, and they're here to support me. "That's not ideal, of course." His lecturing gaze meets each of ours for a socially cruel length of time. "On the plus side, the whole team qualified for the Olympic trials. Though your three-meter dives *badly* need work, Vandy."

"There isn't enough *room*," I mutter sullenly into my PB&J. "It's my least favorite, anyway. I feel like I'm jumping off a gangplank."

"Any more back talk?"

I lower my gaze and stay silent, but thirty minutes later and four dives into the platform finals, I'm wondering if Coach is eating his words. Because my scores are, incomprehensibly, hovering very close to the podium.

"It's really just the four of you," Pen whispers at me while I try to keep warm between dives. "I mean, Akane Straisman is way too far ahead and she's going to take gold, and unless Emilee Newell's bones turn into glow sticks, she's gonna take silver. But bronze is either going to be you or Natalie." Carissa's henchman. "You two have been switching third and fourth place the whole time."

"I don't know what I want the most—to get a medal, or to stop Natalie from getting one."

Pen wraps her palms around my shoulders and squeezes with all her might. "Pick one, Vandy. Because I want to buy you a bronze medal's worth of drinks tonight."

"What's your last dive?" Bree asks me.

"Armstand double one and a half."

"Oh my god!" Pen gasps. At my best, this dive is my masterpiece. Anything less than that? An utter shitshow. And there are so many places for it to crumble to dust. But this is Pen, of course. And she's amazing. And instead of telling me what could go wrong, she hugs me. "It's my favorite dive of yours!"

"Mine, too!" Bree bounces on her feet. "This is fucking *fate!*"

I keep that with me. Even after Natalie dives and I do the math on the score I need to get the bronze, even as I climb up the stairs, even when I'm drying off with my tie-dye shammy, so similar to the one I lost two years ago—the one I barely recall mentioning to Lukas.

*He* remembered, though.

I look at it, smile, and throw it off the tower. And when I rise into an armstand, I don't think about what could go wrong. I don't think about perfection. Instead, I focus on the people out there who enjoy watching me perform the dive. When I take off, when I'm in the air, when I enter the water and then exit it, I hope they'll have a good time. And when I'm barely out of the pool and they're already there, wrapping their arms around my drenched body . . .

"You did it! You did it, you did it, you—"

"You have ten points over Natalie!"

"It's bronze! It's certain bronze, 'cause there's only Emilee left, and she's already ahead of you! Bella's gonna cry so hard when I—" Bree cuts off abruptly. "Oh my god," she says, her tone chock-full of shock. She's looking past my shoulder.

"Are you okay?" I ask.

She opens her mouth. When no sound comes out, she points at the scoreboard behind me.

Emilee dove. The competition is over. And . . .

"I think Emilee Newell's bones must have turned into glow sticks," Pen whispers. Because all of her scores are unexpectedly low—so low, she's fallen to third place.

Which means . . .

Coach appears out of nowhere, holding out the tie-dye shammy. "Well, Vandy," he chokes out, "I hope you have a valid passport."

I guess I'm going to Amsterdam.

# CHAPTER 48

I T'S A BLESSING AND CURSE," COACH SIMA TELLS ME WHILE I wait to be called on the podium. "It'll be only five months before the Olympics, three months before the trials—you're going to be exhausted, Vandy. And the coaches have not been selected, so you could end up with Mr. Resting Fish Face, that new guy at UCLA . . ."

I barely listen. He's right, but I need fewer warnings, and more silence to process the fact that I started this season with a mental block the size of a manatee, and now . . .

I'll be representing my country at world's.

The enormity of it is staggering.

"Emilee Newell is a better diver," I murmur on the plane. "She just made a mistake. I don't deserve to take her spot."

"What was that?" Pen asks, taking out an AirPod.

I shake my head, but once we land I'm relieved—even more so when Maryam's not home, and I get to be alone.

Someone wants to interview me for Stanford's student newspaper. There is an article with my name on ESPN.com. The school's athletic director personally emailed to congratulate me. USA Diving sent a nine-hundred-item pre-championship to-do checklist, and added me to the Tier I High Performance squad. I am assured by multiple individuals that USA gear is forthcoming.

It's Saturday night, but we have a three-day break from practice, and I plan to shut myself in my room, relax, and panic in peace.

And then I get Lukas's text.

LUKAS: Are you freaking out yet?

I burst into laughter.

SCARLETT: Since before the podium.

LUKAS: I could tell from the live stream.

*He watched the live stream.*

Pen invited me to some big swimming party. I considered going, mostly to see Lukas, but I'm too exhausted. I shower, put on pj shorts and a tank top, and when I hear a knock, I groan. It's probably the super. I hate the super. He talks for hours, and—

I pull back from the spy hole with a gasp. Tear the door open.

"Lukas?"

I'd forgotten how tall and broad he is. Or maybe I'm just barefoot. I don't know, because it's hard to focus when he's looking at me like that, the ghost of a smile brushing his mouth and sitting around his eyes, two mastodonic paper bags in one arm. "I figured you'd be out of food," he simply says.

*Oh my god.* "I . . . thank you."

The counter is next to the door. I take the bags from him, set them there, and turn around, expecting to find him engaged in his favorite ritualistic behavior—taking off his damn shoes. But he's closed the door and just stands there, looking at me like . . . like in this moment in time, contemplating doing anything else is beyond his ability.

I smile up at him. "This smells amazing. Is it Chinese?"

He nods.

"It's my favorite. Had I mentioned?"

Another nod.

I landed in the state less than two hours ago, and he came to see me. He brought me milk and bread and coffee. Fresh produce. My favorite dinner.

My throat is full with this knowledge. I take a step closer, pushing up on my toes. "Thank you for remem—"

Suddenly, I'm off the floor, pressed between Lukas and the door, my thighs wrapped around his torso.

"—bering."

He kisses me hard, immediately deep, as if to lick the word out of my mouth. "Scarlett," he says, a raspy rumble that comes out of his heart via his throat, and maybe it's the desperate sound of it, but a second later we're grinding on each other, his hips pushing into mine, his palms frenzied, impatient, changing trajectory, squeezing, and—

My hands dip between our bodies and begin unbuttoning his jeans. He kisses a humming, inviting sound inside my mouth. When I reach inside his boxers and close my fingers around him, he groans like he is in physical pain, pressing his hips into my touch. He's hot and already fully hard. I smear the head with the wetness I find on the tip and circle once, twice, three—

He stops my wrist with a displeased grunt. Pushes my hand away. He takes his cock out, shoves my shorts to the side, finds me bare and wet, and—

"Fuck," he mutters. He slides one finger inside me while thumbing my clit.

It's so *good*, I cannot believe I managed to do without him for over a month. I squirm against his touch and slide my hand back around his cock to do the same to him.

Lukas *growls*. Grips my wrist again, and this time pins it next to my head. "I think you forgot who's in charge."

"I haven't." It comes out as a whine, and earns me a near-painful bite at the base of my jaw. I hate myself for the way I can't stop writhing against him, but I'm not sure he's in control of himself, either. And I *know* that he isn't when I feel him nudge against my opening right there, against the door, when beds, couches, a table exist.

Thing is, I don't think he can wait to be inside me. Because he is guiding me down onto his cock right now.

The first few inches glide in all at once. I close my eyes, let out a small, breathless whimper of adjustment, arching to make him fit.

"Lukas," I moan.

It's smooth sailing—until it's not. His eyes on me are wild and soft. "You are very beautiful. Have I told you?"

No idea. I can't even remember my own name. "I . . . maybe?"

"I was watching you dive the past few days." He starts moving, and I whimper into his neck. It's as always, with him. A little painful. Unbelievably good. Annihilating the possibility of any other thought. "And I was thinking . . ." A particularly hard thrust, and he stuffs himself deeper. His mouth exhales against mine. An almost kiss. "I swear, Scarlett. I think about the ways I've fucked you all the time. Replay them in my head so much, I'm afraid they'll wear off."

One more inch. He's just big enough that this is never going to be easy. The pressure of him, impossible to breathe around. I feel feverish, too hot, pliant, and it's just *nice*, the way he holds me and fills me. Concentrating on his words is more effort than I can spare.

"But I can't remember whether I told you how beautiful you are. And it's been driving me crazy."

Deeper still. For a split second, it's too much, and I almost push him away. Then it passes, and . . . "Oh my god, Lukas." I think I could—it's insane, I must be losing my mind, but I think I could easily come just from the drag of him inside me. I roll my hips, trying to get closer, but the hand under my bottom stops me. My other wrist is still pinned to the wall, and I let out a restless groan. "*Please.*"

"Hush." He kisses my cheek calmly, like his cock is not throbbing inches deep inside me. "Did I?"

"W-what?"

"Did I tell you how beautiful you are?"

I'm fluttering around him, ready to burst. I think—I remember—I'm almost . . . "Yes. Yes, you did."

His mouth twitches in satisfaction. "Good," he says, pulling out and then filling me again. "My brilliant, beautiful girl."

He fucks me like he's thought of nothing but this since the last time we touched. We both come like avalanches in less than a minute.

◊  ◊  ◊

"Isn't there a party somewhere?"

Lukas gives me his best *Why would that matter?* look and spoons an indecent pile of fried rice on my plate. "More?"

I shake my head. I should feel embarrassed at the way I have to lean against the counter, boneless and dripping, cotton-brained and flushed all over. I can't, though, not when he moves around my kitchen like he's been cooking in it for months, not with the lingering glances he sneaks at me every few moments.

He takes both our plates to the table, and must notice my post-orgasm uselessness, because he returns to pick *me* up, his palm firm under my ass, my legs wrapped around his waist. He's a wonderful means of transportation—safe, timely, comfortable. I want a yearly pass.

"I was going to let you eat first," he says, taking a seat next to me. "Couldn't, though." He shrugs and dives into his rice.

"Is this an apology?"

"Come on, Scarlett," he chides. "You know it isn't."

*Good*, I think.

"Now that I got a better look, it's not as bad as I thought," he adds.

"What?"

"Your apartment. I expected muddy shoe prints and sentient mold." He glances around like a judgmental landlord. "This is livable."

"High praise."

"Moderate praise. I might still do some breaking and entering while you're at practice." His gaze warms. "How do you feel?"

"You know when something that's unexpected but good happens? You should be happy about it, and you *are*, but also terrified, and the anxiety drowns everything else?"

"According to my psych prof, winning the lottery is one of the most stressful things that someone can experience."

I tap my index finger against the table. "That's exactly what I feel. Like I won the lottery. On average, Emilee was a million times better than me—"

"A million."

"—but because of one mistake, *I* get to represent my country. Seems like bullshit."

His hand reaches to cover mine, and I stop fidgeting. "And you think that whoever perfected the national team qualification process over decades never considered similar scenarios?"

"I'm sure they did. But in my case—"

"If the situation were reversed"—his fingers twine with mine—"would you think that *you* deserve to go to Amsterdam?"

"I . . . no, but—" Lukas's eyebrow quirks and I fall silent—which seems to please him a little too much. "I hate that smug 'checkmate' expression."

He smiles like he could not give less of a shit. "You're beautiful when you dive."

I flush. Look away. "Yeah, you mentioned."

"That's not what I mean. I always respected divers, but never found real pleasure in watching them." His eyes are dark in the dim kitchen light. "Until you."

It feels wrong and forbidden. The obvious question—*What about Pen?*—lingers between us, unasked.

Or maybe it doesn't. Because part of me is starting to wonder if their relationship was more about two young teens being alone against the world and swearing mutual protection, than about romantic love. But it's a dangerous path to take, muddied by wishful thinking and a question I'm not ready to ask myself.

*Why do I care, anyway?*

"I know you're anxious about competing," he says. "But selfishly, I'm glad you'll be at the world championship with me."

My heart beats louder. Quicker. "Maybe we could . . ." I stop.

"What?"

"I was going to say, maybe we could visit Amsterdam together? But you're best friends with the entire Swedish delegation, and the king will be there—"

"Like I said, Sweden's a democracy—"

"You flamed-pants liar." I lean forward, elbows on the table. "I checked Wikipedia. You *do* have a king."

The buzz of his phone interrupts us. *Penelope*, the name on the top of the screen reads. Then texts pop up:

PENELOPE: Luuuk!

PENELOPE: Come on, we're having so much fun!

PENELOPE: Where are you?

He turns the phone face down and pushes it to the side. Unobtrusive. A silent *it's just us.*

"Our king, as I'm sure your sources mentioned, has no political power or relevancy." He inches closer, too. I want to free my hand and trace that perfectly slanted jaw. "What else did you find out about my country during your countless hours of research?"

A lot, actually. Since I can't seem to stop myself from reading up on it before bed. It's like I'm planning a trip. "Let's see. That you guys have a word for when your hair is all messy because you just had sex."

His mouth twitches. "True. *Knullrufs.*"

"And also a really tasty-looking nuclear-green dessert that I'd do unspeakable things to try."

*"Dammsugare."*

"Is it good?"

"Are glycemic comas part of your kink portfolio?"

"Hell yeah."

"Then it's good."

I laugh. "I learned about . . . *lagom*? Am I saying it right?" He nods, and I continue. "It means 'the perfect amount.' Not too much, not too little. The idea is that society is like a team, resources should be shared equally, and people should be humble."

He looks intrigued, like I've found a deep cut.

"And it can come with some downsides. Like with the law of J . . . ?"

"Law of Jante."

"Law of Jante, correct," I say haughtily. Lukas laughs softly. "People shouldn't brag about their accomplishments, or think that they are special, which can make it hard for them to celebrate their successes." Lukas has once again gone unreadable. "Reminds you of someone, huh?" I ask, injecting just a hint of challenge in my voice, thinking of everything he is, everything he does, everything he never speaks of.

And maybe he gets it, at least a little bit. I watch him trace the inside of his cheek with his tongue, mull it over, ponder options, until he says, "I had my first two acceptances."

My heart stops. It seems so early, and—he's talking about med schools, right? Oh my god. This is . . . "Where?" I ask, treading cautiously.

"Penn. Emory."

I nod slowly, to avoid spooking him.

"Emory offered a merit scholarship," he adds.

"Full?"

"Yes."

It's *fantastic*. More than that. It's the best news ever, and I want to explode out of my chair and scream my excitement, but something that passes between us in subtexts, well underneath the frequency of words, tells me to just stay *calm*.

"I haven't told anyone yet," he says.

*Oh, Lukas.*

I don't know what I'm allowed to say, but I can't stave off this happy, bursting feeling. So I stand. Make myself at home on his lap. Wrap my arms tight around his neck. And once I'm sure he won't bolt the second I open my mouth, I whisper in his ear, "I'm *so* happy for you." The words are low and hushed and a little sacred, even though we are alone.

*It's just us. You're safe with me.*

His arms lock around my waist, hands splayed open over my flanks and ribs. It's not until much, much later that I hear him murmur, "I'd love to see Amsterdam with you."

# CHAPTER 49

I END THE AUTUMN QUARTER WITH ALL AS, AND NO, I DON'T care that English composition and German come with a small dash right after the letter. The plus that Dr. Carlsen tacked to my comp bio grade offsets at least one of them. In my heart, if not numerically.

"Will this ruin your GPA?" Maryam asks.

I credit the work I've been doing with Sam for my unbothered "It'll lower it by a decimal point, which is *fine*." Maryam is on my shit list, even more so than usual—has been since the night I returned from Tennessee, when she barged in on Lukas and me doing the dishes, drunkenly threatened to call the landlord if a single sex noise made it to her ears, and then absconded to her room with *my* fried rice.

"Sorry about her," I told Lukas while getting ready for bed, handing him the still-packaged toothbrush from my last cleaning.

"I'm a Swede. We handle bluntness well."

I fully planned to make a camgirl-worthy number of sex noises, just to annoy her, but fell asleep while Lukas brushed his teeth, and woke early the following day as he slipped from under the sheets.

"Practice," he said, pressing a scratchy kiss into the corner of my throat. "Go back to sleep, Scarlett."

I next see him when we meet to update Zach on our progress. I get to the library ten minutes early, but show up to the study room *late*—because Lukas finds me in the lobby, grabs my wrist, drags me into one of the single-person restrooms, and spends a pornographic amount of time with his head between my legs. His tongue is flat against my clit, his shoulder broad under my thigh, and . . .

He doesn't let me come.

"Please." My chest is heaving. "*Please.*"

He presses one last, feathery kiss against the top of my cunt. With horror, I watch him rise to his feet and lick his lips. He gently pulls up my joggers and wipes a solitary tear off my cheek.

"Go in first," he says. He pats my ass lightly, like I'm an unruly pet in need of guidance, to treat with a firm but affectionate hand. It's extremely condescending. I should *not* be turned on by it.

"But I want to—"

"No, Scarlett." He doesn't sound particularly authoritative about it, because there's no need for posturing. He's *that* confident.

I swallow. Ask, petulant, "Why don't you go first?"

He points at the front of his pants.

"Oh."

What's remarkable is how otherwise unaffected he looks. I'm about to either shatter in a million pieces, or thaw into a syrupy puddle—jury's deliberating.

"I could sneak into the next-door bathroom and make myself come," I threaten resentfully.

"You could," he acknowledges. "But you won't."

"I—you have no idea what I'm going to do."

His smile is . . . really sweet, actually. And so is the way he pushes my hair back from my forehead before pressing a kiss in the middle of it. "You'll do what I say, and we both know it. Or at least, *I* know it." All my frown does is coax him into smoothing the little vertical wrinkles between my eyes with the pad of his thumb. "You're fucking adorable, Scarlett." He tilts my chin up. Another kiss, this time on the tip of my nose. "It makes me want to *wreck* you."

The following hour in the study room is misery. I try not to fidget, especially while Zach asks me questions about my plans for the holidays, whether I'll stay in town, *hit me up if you want to get coffee.* His words drift in and out, devoid of meaning. I show my neural network, still fever hot and breathless.

"The accuracy is thirty percent higher than what I got," Lukas says, wholly focused on the data. "Scarlett, that's a masterpiece." He sounds impressed and happy that the model I created exists, and I wonder whether the bathroom ever happened. Maybe I hallucinated it. I was never about to come. His grunts were never muffled into my cunt. Healthcare professionals will come to take me away.

But the meeting ends—*You have my number, right, Scarlett? Yup, Zach. Thanks for everything and happy holidays*—and Lukas heads straight for the bathroom. I follow him, just a step behind. Don't wait for the door to close to snarl, "I can't—"

He presses me against it with a hard push, his body hot against mine. "I don't know why it's such a turn-on that you're so much smarter than me, but every time we have a project meeting, I have to go home and jerk off until my dick is raw."

"I'm not that smart—"

"Shut *the fuck* up, you brilliant, beautiful genius." He kisses me deep and hard, first on the mouth, then lower, and he must know that I'm stretched to the brink, because he doesn't tease. He bites. He licks. He sucks. In less than twenty seconds, my orgasm is ripped out of my spine, and I crush my moans against my own palm.

"Thank you," I pant when I can talk. His face tucks against my belly, a sweet, delicious sting. "Thank you, I—"

He's not done, though. Barely started. He buries his mouth in my cunt and licks it all up, humming his approval. It starts again. Finger in his hair, I try to push him away, but he won't quit, and I come and come until I'm pleading with him to give me a break, and he just rumbles, "You can bear it for one more minute. One more. For me."

I can, and it hurts in the sweetest possible way. When he's done, I expect him to turn me around and bend me over. Instead, he remains on his knees, presses his unshaved cheek against my hip, inhales my scent, and starts moving his arm in rhythmic strokes.

It takes a moment for the meaning to sink in. "I—I . . . Lukas?"

He kisses my abdomen and looks up at me, eyes infinitely blue. "I can . . ."

His arm doesn't stop moving. "Can?"

It's not the way it usually goes, between us. Me, offering. Him, asking. What I like is when he *takes*, and what he likes is . . . to watch me squirm. "Can what, Scarlett?"

I look down at him, still winded.

"Come on, sweetheart. Use your words."

Why is it so weird to say? "I can—I *want* to go down on you."

He thinks about it. An intriguing but not-too-tempting offer. "But that's not what *I* want." And yet, he rises to his feet and pushes me down on my knees. I open my mouth, willing, *eager*, and—

He presses it closed with a thumb under my chin. "I said no," he reminds me, mild, almost bored, but tilts my face upward, like it's something beautiful he wants to memorize, and continues stroking, his rhythm sustained.

"This is nice," he says, voice raspy and focused. Cheeks flushed, a dull red. Hair dark, haloed by the ceiling lamp. The shift of muscles and veins and ink on his strong forearm. "It's like when I'm home, masturbating, thinking about you. Isn't it?" His thumb sweeps over my cheekbone. "Which is every time."

His hand slows down, like he wants to pace himself, but speeds again when I wet my lips.

"That okay with you? The filthy stuff I think about doing to you while I make myself come?"

I nod. The movement has my mouth brush against the underside of his cock, and his breath hitches sharply.

"I knew you wouldn't mind. Being my precious toy. My girl. Mine to use. Mine to fuck. Mine to destroy and to fix."

Another eager, wholehearted nod. It's *all* I want. For him to tell me what to do, and to take care of me.

"Christ. I can't believe you fucking exist, Scarlett." His thumb slides into the corner of my mouth, prying it open, and I offer no resistance. When the head of his cock shoves inside, heavy on my tongue, he's already coming. His eyes stay open, even as his entire body shudders and a deep grunt explodes out of his chest.

I swallow what I can. What's left, I lick off his fingers. "Perfect," he repeats over and over, kissing my face, eyelids, mouth. The praise feels as good as the orgasms did.

# CHAPTER 50

N MID-DECEMBER, THE SWIM TEAM LEAVES FOR A SWANKY ALL-expenses-paid training trip to Hawaii. Diving stays behind, and recriminating words like *second-class citizens*, and *redheaded stepchild* are thrown about.

"Less bitching at me, and more taking it up with the athletics department, okay?" Coach Sima mumbles. "And Ross?"

"Yeah?"

"You *are*, in fact, redheaded."

By the time Lukas returns, I'm already in St. Louis.

Hope you manage to get to Stockholm all right, I type—then delete it, because . . . I don't know why. But the following day, I see three dots next to his name, and it occurs to me that maybe I'm not alone, in all this *not knowing*.

"Are you *crying*?" Barb asks when she picks me up at the airport, watching me roll on the floor as Pipsqueak licks my face. Being reunited with her heals my wonky shoulder, my congenital inability to eat spaghetti without a spoon, my fifth-grade cystic acne.

"Shut up," I tell Barb. "It's just . . ."

"What?"

I shake my head, burying my nose in Pip's fur. She badly needs a bath. "She's so *beautiful*."

"Can't deny that. I would, however, like to point out that *I* did not receive a hug, or even a half-assed hand wave."

I lift my eyes to hers, and my chest squeezes a little bit tighter. It's good to be *home*. "I dunno, Barb. You're just not as cute."

"What every woman wants to hear from her adult daughter." She hands me the leash and points at the exit. "Let's go. Gotta hit Schnucks before the carnivorous amoeboid alien gets there in all its cosmic horror."

"The what?"

"Holiday grocery crowd, Scar."

Christmas is quiet and lazy, good food and movies and naps, just the three of us, just the way I like it. Barb is, miraculously, not on call. Pip snores softly and farts loudly. I'm full and happy and maybe a little reckless, because I snap a picture of the holiday spread and send it to Lukas with the caption Fika?

The reply is, as usual, instantaneous. That's a meal.

SCARLETT: How do you even know that?

LUKAS: No coffee in sight.

I add a Pac-12 mug to the side. Better?

LUKAS: Still a meal. With an empty mug next to it.

SCARLETT: Are you the fika police?

LUKAS: Unlike you, I speak Swedish.

SCARLETT: I'm tired of this gatekeeping.

Two minutes later, my email pings with a message. Someone gifted me a yearly premium subscription to Duolingo. Lukas must not know my middle name, because he went with *Scarlett Troll Vandermeer*.

Most likely, he's perfectly aware that it's Ann.

SCARLETT: The passive aggression!!!

LUKAS: Nothing passive about it.

I want to ask him how he's doing. If he's freezing his ass off. How many hours—minutes, milliseconds—of sunlight he gets. But my bravery runneth dry, and the *not knowing* is back with a vengeance, so I download the damn app and begin my Swedish journey.

In the following days, though, Lukas starts sending me pictures.

Jan, cross-country skiing, smiling broadly at the camera.

His niece and nephews, baking with a striking blond woman.

A tree branch crystallized in ice.

The most beautiful lake I've ever seen, surrounded by snow-covered trees that remind me of the ink on Lukas's arm.

I reply with snippets of my own time at home—the Arch in downtown St. Louis; the diving well where I used to train; Pip rolling over, tongue out; the mischievous grin on the face of Cynthia, our elderly neighbor who came over for tea and slipped an inch of whiskey into our mugs.

With anyone else, I'd feel self-conscious about the small banality of my life, afraid of letting slip how uninteresting I am. But my sexual relationship with Lukas is so fundamentally based on brutal honesty about our wants and needs, it bleeds into every aspect of our interactions. Second-guessing my worth hardly ever occurs to me.

If he didn't enjoy sex with me, he'd amend the list.

If he didn't like my pictures, he'd leave me on read.

So it continues. A cat's tail peeking through two inches of snow, like a shark's fin. Barb's office at the hospital, her lab coat draped over a chair. Ice-skating. A cronut.

Sometimes, we say nothing. Sometimes, we ask questions. (Is that a wolf? Was he just outside your door? We went to Gävleborg and tracked it. Oskar's a pro.) Sometimes, I laugh at us. Shouldn't we be exchanging nudes and flowery masturbation recounts? He should tele-dom me. Order me to suck his cyberdick. And yet, the only parts of our bodies that travel across the Atlantic are my dimple, from the day Pip wouldn't stop licking my cheek, and the long-fingered grip on the rod he uses for ice fishing.

I write new drafts of my med school essays, and shadow Makayla, my favorite of Barb's colleagues. "You should do an internship here next year," she suggests. "Maybe in the spring quarter? Would look amazing on applications."

The inevitable happens at Costco, two days before New Year's Eve. Barb and I are debating whether it'd be amoral to pass up on a stellar deal that would provide Biscoff to the next four generations of Vandermeers (or, more likely, to the two of us, for the next week) when someone calls our names.

It takes me a minute to place Josh's mom's face, and another to realize that he's standing next to her. Barb and Juliet have, unfortunately, always liked each other, and when they start chatting, Josh moves closer to me.

"Hey, Vandy."

"Hi." I expect my heart to speed into a race, but my sympathetic nervous system must be on a *fika* break.

*Did I use it correctly, Lukas?* My smile softens into something sincere.

We catch up for a few minutes. His classes. Mine. *Still premed? I changed my major four times. I play the bass in a band. Is it true that you're going to the Olympics? Ah, world's. My bad. Still awesome.*

Then, out of the blue: "I missed this."

I blink up at him, trying not to think about the many ways he feels so . . . insubstantial, now that I'm used to Lukas. It's not a fair comparison. "Yeah."

"I wasn't sure if you'd be angry."

*You could have asked*, I think.

"We should get together sometime. Aurora wouldn't mind, and . . . I care about you," he adds.

Something inside me switches on. "Nice way of showing it," I say. His stare is confused. "What do you mean?"

"You didn't act like someone who cared about me."

"Vandy." He has the audacity to look hurt. "If you think our breakup was easy for me—"

"You can't control who you fall for. You *can*, however, decide not to break up with your girlfriend on the day of her NCAA finals."

He sighs. "I'm sorry about that. I was so busy with . . . It didn't occur to me. I didn't even remember until Jordan told me that you got hurt."

Jordan. Former classmate. Josh kept custody of her—and everyone else—in the split. "So you knew I was injured, but never reached out?" I think I got him, because his eyes are wide and his skin too pale. God, what a waste of time. "Listen, we haven't talked for the past year and a half. I don't know you anymore. And it wouldn't have worked out, anyway." I can say this with the utmost certainty now. "But here's a reflection prompt: if it never occurred to you that you could have acted less selfishly, maybe you're not the nice guy you think you are."

Later, in the car, Barb doesn't bring up Josh, but she does ask me if I'm seeing someone.

"There's this guy." I drum my fingers at the base of the window. "He's . . ." *Great. Perfect. My friend's ex. I like him. He likes me, too, I'm sure. Not just because of what we do. Maybe there's something here. But what if there isn't? I should ask him. It makes my stomach hurt.* "It's needlessly convoluted."

"Sounds like a rom-com premise."

I shrug. "We're just having fun."

Her eyebrows lift.

"Oh, shut up."

And *lift*.

"You're terrible," I laugh.

"I just hope you have fun safely, consensually, and contraceptively."

"You're a physician. You *know* that's not a word."

"All *I* know is that I'd be the best step-grandmother in history."

"You would."

She was, after all, an excellent mom. Busy, for sure. Scatterbrained. But that never mattered. After Dad, what I needed wasn't someone who'd come to my meets, memorize dives' names, pack me nutritious lunches. *Vandy's mom is a little absent, huh?* I once overheard, bored parents gossiping in the stands. But that was dumb. Barb was there when I needed her, always, without me having to ask, ever. She put me first in any meaningful way. Reminded me that adults could be trusted, that they didn't have to be scary and unpredictable—they could protect and nurture and allow freedom.

*Well, she's not her* real *mom. Vandy calls her Barb.*

I remember being eight, scolded by Dad for introducing Barb to a teacher as my mommy. Sent to bed without dinner. Sneaking downstairs for a glass of water. A conversation in the kitchen.

". . . don't see the problem, Alex! I'm committed to her. I'm not going anywhere. If she wants to call me Mom—"

Dad's response, in the tone that made my guts churn and my skin goose bump. Not being hungry anymore. Crawling back upstairs and drinking from the Dixie cups in the bathroom, the ones Barb had bought for me to rinse my teeth.

She is, indisputably, the best thing that ever happened to me. I wondered for years why she kept her married name after the divorce, and at eighteen I realized that it wasn't because it was Dad's—but because it was *mine*.

I turn to her and say, "You can just say *grandmother*, you know?"

"Mm?"

"If I ever have a kid—which for the purpose of this conversation would be grown from the mitosis of cells scraped from my cheeks, since I conduct myself *very contraceptively*—they wouldn't call you *step*-grandma."

"I know, honey." She lets go of the steering wheel and wraps her fingers around mine. Barb and I rarely do this. Have moments. *Sap.* "They'd be required to call me Dr. Vandermeer, of course."

I snort and pull my hand away.

That night I stream a movie, and send Lukas a picture of my computer screen. I get a reply when the credits start rolling—eleven for me, 6:00 a.m. in Stockholm. Yup, I can calculate the time difference like a pro by now.

LUKAS: I knew it would come to this.

I laugh.

SCARLETT: "This" being me watching Midsommar?

LUKAS: I should have taken preventative measures.

SCARLETT: Mandatory follow-up question: do you actually celebrate Midsommar?

LUKAS: Yes.

SCARLETT: And do you . . . ?

LUKAS: Go out of town to dance around the maypole, play sack races, eat pickled herring? Yes.

SCARLETT: Interesting.

LUKAS: Just ask about the sex rituals, Scarlett.

SCARLETT: I don't want to be culturally insensitive, but I need to know if they happen.

LUKAS: How disappointed would you be if I said no?

SCARLETT: Immensely.

LUKAS: Problem is, we mostly celebrate Midsommar with our extended families. Siblings. Parents. Grandparents.

SCARLETT: That's too kinky even for me.

LUKAS: Figured. You should come visit next summer. See for yourself.

SCARLETT: You're luring me there with the promise of depraved sex rituals, while planning to use me for depraved human sacrifices.

LUKAS: It's a real invitation. Ideally you should come when Jan's here.

SCARLETT: Why?

LUKAS: Keeps telling everyone how amazing you are. Pulling up videos of your dives to show every Blomqvist in a thirty-kilometer radius.

SCARLETT: You need to stop him.

LUKAS: Why? I like watching you.

It's not normal, the speed of my heartbeat even though I'm lying down. I'm an athlete in peak physical condition, goddamn it.

SCARLETT: He probably thinks we're dating. We should set the record straight.

LUKAS: Or maybe we should just start dating.

I stop breathing. Freeze. Did he really—

LUKAS: I checked. This year Midsommar overlaps with the US Olympic trials, and as much as I want you in Sweden, I want you to come to Melbourne with me more.

I force my heart to slow down. My head to stop spinning.

SCARLETT: You're optimistic, huh?

LUKAS: I've just seen you dive, Scarlett.

LUKAS: Come after the trials. Taper here. You'll love the quiet. And the hikes.

I fall asleep with my phone in my hand, and dream of the midnight sun.

# CHAPTER 51

IN JANUARY, LUKAS IS ACCEPTED TO STANFORD MED.

My reaction is . . . complicated, but only because he tells me while we're in the middle of fucking.

He and I have done some irresponsible stuff since our arrangement started, but this tops it all. I blame it on how busy we've been with travel and meets, and on the fact that the extent of our January encounters amounts to passing each other in one of the hallways at Avery, the always crowded one right outside of the PT room.

I don't say hi.

He doesn't smile.

His fingers brush against the back of my hand, though, and for the next twenty minutes I feel like the air is thinner than on a Tibetan plateau.

In those weeks, our closest interaction is a plastic bag I discover outside my locker, full of the green sweets I mentioned to him before the holidays.

*For real fika*, the note reads. I devour them, thinking of him during every bite.

At the end of the month, both the University of Arizona and

Arizona State teams come to Avery for a four-day invite. The after-party is at Kyle's house—which is, shockingly, also Lukas's.

"I'd heard rumors," Victoria says, walking up the driveway. "But I dared not believe them. Thought my sickbed was playing tricks on me. But no—Scarlett Vandermeer actually goes out. Color me shocked *and* pleased."

"Vandy *likes* parties," Pen tells her. "She just . . ."

"Likes her bed more," I finish.

"I'm just making an appearance," Pen whispers in my ear a minute later. "And then I'm skedaddling to Hot Teacher's place."

They've been inseparable for all of January. I even met him, with Pen introducing me as "one of my closest friends, Theo," which had me *so* happy. We had lunch together, and they couldn't keep their eyes, and hands, off each other. Meanwhile, I couldn't stop thinking about Lukas.

*What if he and I* really *started dating?*

*Would it be against girl code?*

*Would you even mind?*

Most of the crowd, and it's a *big* crowd, is out in the garden. Victoria disappears into her flirtation with a Montenegrin swimmer who looks uncannily like Michelangelo's *David*. Pen is best friends with everyone, and is seamlessly absorbed by gaggle after gaggle. I wander around, am polite when a male U of A diver chats me up, but I'm looking for . . .

Lukas spots me through the windows and immediately extracts himself from the conversation he's having with Johan and a couple in ASU tees. I meet him in the kitchen, and I want to touch him so bad, my blood fizzes like champagne.

He looks at me like a bird of prey. Focused. Acquisitive.

The U of A diver excuses himself.

"I cannot believe you allowed this," I say. "Who's going to clean this mess?"

"Not me." He drains the last of his beer and sets it on the counter. "Detailed contracts were drawn."

"You're the least fun roommate, aren't you?"

"I'm the roommate who lays down the rules." He stands over me. "Let's go upstairs."

It's the closest we've gotten to sneaking around, except that Lukas is not the kind of man to keep his head less than high. Five minutes later I'm inside his room, and he's inside me.

"I fucking missed this," he tells me.

I'm on top, but have no delusions about who's in control. I have to take several deep breaths, because it's a new position with Lukas. He drags my hand to my abdomen and covers it with his own, pressing down. Through my flesh, I can feel the faint outline of him, spearing inside me. "This." He kisses my shoulder, and I feel his cock twitch, like he needs to get deeper.

"A little more," he says, thrusting up, pulling me down. "Just a little. Be a good—fuck, *yes*, that's what I'm talking about."

Once he's in all the way, my thighs spread wide to make room for his hips. I feel like I'm being split open. He lets out a pleased, guttural sound. One of his hands closes around my waist, the other cups my ass, and then he moves me—up, and up, and then down again, eyes flicking between mine and the bounce of my tits. Then he lets go and says, "Stop."

I do. He's inside me to the hilt, and I can barely breathe around him.

"Come here." He hugs me closer. His hand splays on my back and pets me, a soothing vertical motion that lulls me into a floating, dreamlike headspace. He plays with my nipples, pinching them hard enough for me to moan in the right amount of distress, the one that'll make him harder and me wetter. I try to roll my hips, but he won't have it. "I don't think so."

It dawns on me then, what he's planning. The wait ahead. I

whimper, and he clicks his tongue soothingly. "It's okay, Scarlett." It's the permission I need to bury my face in his neck and complain. I kiss him there, licking the salt off his skin, a couple of whined *pleases*, a handful of truly pathetic tears, a hard bite on his trapezius that he barely notices. He comforts me through it, tormentor and savior, and once I've exhausted myself, he settles me down in his arms.

Music vibrates through the walls, drowning laughter and chatter. I feel like an object, created for him. By him. Did I exist before the first time he fucked me? I have no memory of it. Do I exist when we're not together? I'm just a toy. His favorite. Irreplaceable.

And that's when he speaks about Stanford's acceptance. How he couldn't wait to tell me. How dark Sweden is this time of year, but every message from me felt like a little burst of sunlight. He tells me what he'll show me when I visit in the summer, and that he doesn't want us to be apart for as long as we have been in the last couple of months, because it feels "cruel, Scarlett, to know that you exist, but I can't touch you and fuck you and be with you. You get it, right?" And after minutes or centuries of this, he finally takes pity on me. "You are so sensitive—you'd come if I moved just a little. You'd come for me, wouldn't you?"

I would. I nod.

It takes one thrust, and that's it for me. Maybe two more for him. We both come silently, clutching each other through shudders and twitches and aftershocks that never seem to end, and when the sweat is cool on our bodies and I can breathe again, I say, "Lukas?"

He nods his head into my throat, like he doesn't trust his vocal cords.

"Sometimes I'm afraid that this is the best thing I'll ever have. For the rest of my life."

He sighs, and murmurs something in Swedish that my Duolingo app has yet to cover.

Downstairs, the party trudges on.

⬥  ⬥  ⬥

I wake up alone in Lukas's bed, to a handful of noises coming from downstairs—like someone's gathering trash or washing the dishes.

*Well, shit.*

The weather's gray and dull, but it's already midmorning. If Lukas's roommates are up, getting out unseen is going to be difficult. Impossible, since I'm not willing to dive out of a second-story bedroom and into a dumpster full of beer bottles.

I clean up quickly, slide my jeans up and my shirt down, and make my way downstairs, as inconspicuous as possible. I stop in the hallway to the kitchen, listening for voices, wondering if I should just go back to Lukas's room until the coast is clear.

". . . was asking after you," Hasan is saying.

"She has my number," Lukas replies, unconcerned.

The rustling of plastic bags stops. Someone kills the faucet. "You told me a couple months ago that you guys broke up, but last night you went upstairs with Vandy. I wasn't sure if I could tell Pen, or . . ." Hasan sounds puzzled.

"You can. Pen knows about it."

The garden door opens. Kyle comes in, muttering something about being too wasted to remember who threw darts at the fence, but Hasan ignores him. "Okay. So, if she ever asks again . . ."

"What are you guys talking about?" Kyle interrupts.

Hasan sighs. "Just Sweedy's love triangle with Pen and Vandy."

Kyle whistles. "Dude, you're doing *Vandy*?"

"There are no secrets," Lukas says, once again pretending Kyle doesn't exist. "Whatever Pen asks, you can answer sincerely."

"Okay." Hasan. "That's a fucking relief, because I'm shit at lies."

"Dude," Kyle groans. "How did you manage to bag Vandy?"

I tense. Wait for Lukas's response, but it's Hasan who says, "Kyle, what kind of question is that?"

"Others tried. In vain. *I* tried. Maybe I shouldn't have given up?"

"Bro, did you just say you shouldn't have listened when she said no?" Hasan sounds pained.

"All I'm saying is, I kinda thought of her as off-limits—"

"She is." It's Lukas's usual, laid-back tone, just a brush of tension sitting at the edges. I wonder if Kyle notices. "To you," Lukas adds, which feels a bit like a threat.

Kyle, though, is still drunk. "I'm impressed. She's seriously cute. The dimples are cute. The little gap between the front teeth is cute. Her t—"

A glass is set on a surface. None too gently. "Consider carefully whether you want to finish that sentence, Kyle."

My cheeks are on fire. There's a pause—in which, I'm sure, Kyle's life flashes before his eyes. "You know what? I have no desire to." He clears his throat. "What about Pen? Pen's supercute, too. Always liked her. And if you're not dating her . . ."

"Be my guest."

"Got it. Pen, green light. Vandy, death wish."

"You know, Kyle," Hasan interjects, "you don't have to hit on *every* woman you're introduced to. They'll experience fulfilling lives without your clumsy presence in them."

It feels like a now-or-never entry point, so I walk into the kitchen as casually as possible. "Hey."

"Oh." Kyle has the decency to flush a little. "Hey, Vandy?"

I smile at him. Tight-lipped, because I'm suddenly self-conscious about my teeth, and I wore braces way too many years for that. *The dentist said my wisdom teeth would descend and push the front together* is on the tip of my tongue.

Whatever. My teeth are fine. *Cute,* even.

"Hey, Vandy," Hasan says, a bit awkwardly.

Lukas just drops the red Solo cup in his hand into a garbage bag, comes to me, takes my face between his hands, and kisses me.

It's slow. And thorough. And surprisingly public. I can practically *hear* Hasan and Kyle look away.

"I, um, have to go," I say at the end.

"I'll walk you home."

"Actually, I want to make a stop before. I'd rather go by myself." It's a lie, but I'm rattled. Overhearing people talk about you is like being pinned to the vivisection table while med students take notes on your organs. I need to be alone for a minute.

"I'll still—"

"And the thing is," I add, walking backward, "the idea of you helping them clean even though you don't have to, just because you won't know peace until the house returns to its state of asepsis? Kind of a turn-on for me."

Hasan and Kyle cackle. I wave goodbye. When I open the front door and turn around, Lukas is staring at me with an odd smile.

# CHAPTER 52

ISHING CARISSA EXPLOSIVE DIARRHEA MAY HAVE BEEN A poor idea. When Team USA meets in Houston ahead of the world championship, I'm given the cold shoulder by the other divers so openly, I almost expect to be bullied at recess.

Oh, well.

I didn't come here to make friends, I guess. Not to make enemies, either, but I'll deal. Your pal can really hold a grudge, I text Pen. It's making me sad that Kyle, or any other swimmer from Stanford, didn't manage to qualify.

PENELOPE: Oh, you have no idea.

PENELOPE: Want me to make a sock puppet account and add to her Wikipedia that she has a foot fungus?

SCARLETT: Let me think it through.

The coach may be in on it. Mei Wang is legendary, and I consider begging her to sign my shammy, but she stares at me a little too intensely, and her handshake gives me a metacarpal fracture.

We fly out in advance, to combat jet lag and get in a few days of on-site training. Team USA is huge, well over two dozen athletes, most of whom ignore me. But the Swedish delegation is already in

Amsterdam, and I text Lukas as soon as I'm done pressing my nose to the bus window and basking in the beautiful architecture. His reply is instantaneous, like all he does is wait around with his phone in his hand, waiting for *me* to contact him.

LUKAS: What hotel?

SCARLETT: Motel One. You?

LUKAS: Same.

SCARLETT: Who are you sharing with?

LUKAS: No one.

Oh, come on.

SCARLETT: Did the King of Sweden pull some strings?

He sends me a picture of a handsome middle-aged man.

SCARLETT: Who's that?

LUKAS: The Swedish Prime Minister.

SCARLETT: I heard he's just a puppet for the King. Anyway, I'm sharing with Akane.

LUKAS: 767

SCARLETT: 235843

LUKAS: ?

SCARLETT: Are we just sending random numbers?

LUKAS: It's my room. Come see me tonight.

Akane is quietly terrifying. Small and wiry, with long, dark hair, full but unsmiling lips. She's in her late twenties, on the older side for a platform diver, especially one as good as her. All I know is that she trained at Cal, has a child, and enjoys minding her business. The reason we've been paired is that Emilee, the good friend she usually rooms with, didn't qualify. Because I fucked her over in the clutch.

If a vengeful angel of death has to stab me and stuff my corpse in a plastic bag, so be it. Still, as I roll my suitcase into the hotel room, I cannot help some trepidation.

"Don't look at me like that," she orders, severe.

"Like . . . what?"

"Like you're afraid I'll bite your head off while you're asleep. It's not your fault if you dove better than Emilee."

"Technically, I didn't—"

"You dove more consistently."

I've never felt less inclined to contradict someone. I really *do* respond well to a firm hand.

"So, you're this year's pariah?"

"Looks like it." I clear my throat. "Is there always one?"

"It's a small sport." She shrugs. "People have history."

I sigh. "I kinda walked into my pariahship. I'm not very good at these kind of games."

Akane studies me with stern, wide eyes, and says, "There's hope, then."

"Hope?"

"For the two of us to get along."

◆   ◆   ◆

The pool is bright, warm, and clean—the trifecta. I practice during the time slot assigned to the US, pleased to notice that I can spot the water easily and the platform doesn't feel weird under my feet. Some do, and careening off them at twenty miles per hour is terrifying.

Coach Wang, who wants to be called Mei, stops me on my way out.

"Vandermeer, come here." God, she's intimidating. "Your forward." She lifts a tablet and shows me my most recent dive. I had no idea she was TiVoing. I fully expected to be ignored in favor of more promising athletes. "You see how you washed over?"

I nod at the slo-mo replay. It's not a disaster, but also not world championship material. "You come out a little too early, that's why. Here." She shows me the error twice more. Each time I cringe harder, till I'm ready to throw my body out of the window for the carrion birds to feast upon. "I think I can correct that," I tell her.

Tomorrow I'll do better.

But Mei looks at me like I'm a pimple, newly sprouted on her nose. "Why are you standing here like a lamppost, then? Go back up. Fix your dive."

Wincing, I haul ass.

Go back up.

And fix my dive.

We repeat the process for three more dives. She tells me what parts look "uglier than starvation," gives me precise corrections, and shows me how improvement can be driven by tiny adjustments. "This pike? There's half a dozen points here."

I nod, bewildered.

"You know," she tells me. "I'd written you off."

"I . . . excuse me?"

"I remember you from Junior Nationals. Even told a couple scouts to check you out. But then you got that injury, and I thought you were over." Her eyes eviscerate me. I'm a salmon, and she's carving my spine out. "But you're not bad. Even better, you're good at taking directions. Where are you training?"

"Stanford. With—"

"Sima." She nods. "He's good. Some things, though, even a good coach stops being able to spot. A second pair of eyes is always useful." I nod, until she starts looking at me like I'm a wart again. "Are you gonna stay here all day? Training slot's over. Beat it."

I vow to learn to tell whether I'm being dismissed.

◆　◆　◆

The event mascot is a horrific seahorse with piercing blue eyes. I walk in desperate search of a snack station, trying to avoid his too-long snout. Athletes move in packs, wearing their countries' colors, and I feel weird wandering alone. I'm about to take a shuttle back to the hotel, when I come across a basketball-court-sized room, sectioned in different areas.

"There's one for each country," a volunteer tells me before glancing at the badge hanging from my neck. "US is over there."

I glance at our table, where Carissa and Natalie are eating yogurt. No, thank you.

"What about Sweden?"

It's in the opposite corner. I walk, taking in the different languages around me, till I find it. There appears to be no strife among the Swedish team: they stand around their table, playing ball with something that looks like a protein bar.

I instantly spot Lukas, even though everyone in the delegation is as tall as him. His hair is a little shorter than when I walked out of his house a week ago, but he's still himself. Still handsome. Still mi—

"Scarlett?"

A second later he's in front of me. He reaches out to touch me, but I feel myself inch back a little, even through the flutter in my chest, the prickling heat in my throat.

I'm not sure why. Maybe it's just too overwhelming and too soon, having him near me after the gaping void of his absence.

He gets the memo. Of course he does, dialed in as he is. "I thought you'd rest at the hotel." His blue and yellow compression shirt does great things for his eyes.

"Our coach doesn't believe in rest. She's probably wondering why I'm not running laps."

He smiles, wider and so much more boyish than usual. So *happy* to see me, I'm a little floored. "How's your pool?" I ask, to distract both of us.

"Only used the warm-up one, but fine. The diving tower?"

"A problem, actually."

"How so?"

"I've been looking for something to complain about. Lay the groundwork for what I'll blame my future failed dives on. Can't find anything, though."

"A tragedy."

"See, you get it."

He stares, smiling. I stare, smiling. Maybe no one would catch a single, tiny hug. A small kiss. My hand in his.

"Hi." A man appears at Lukas's side—wearing the same shirt, built like him, dark skinned. His smile is warm. "Wasn't your hair red last time we met?"

My heart capsizes.

"Different person, Ebbe."

"Oh, *shit*."

"This is Scarlett Vandermeer. Scarlett, Ebbe Nilsson."

Ebbe shakes his head. "*And* an idiot."

"Don't worry about it. Pen and I don't look too different."

"That's probably a lie, but thank you. USA, right?"

"Yeah. Lukas and I are in school together. We . . ." We? Lukas watches me, entertained, like he'd be fine if I said, *Responsibly practice BDSM together.* "Collaborate on a biology project," I end weakly. Big middle school science fair vibes. "I was looking for food, actually. Where did you get your, um . . ."

"Ball?" Ebbe asks.

"Precisely."

"Come with me." Lukas's fingers wrap around my upper arm. "I'll walk you to one of the stations." We're on our way out when someone yells something at him, which starts a quick back-and-forth in Swedish that ends with laughter and "*Vi ses.*" It was on my app, but I can't recall the meaning.

"What was that?" I ask. His teammates seem to be studying me.

"They wanted to know whether I'd join them for dinner."

"And? What did you tell them?"

He guides me out, fingers pressed against my upper back. My world coalesces to five points of contact. "I told them that I had better things to do."

◊ ◊ ◊

I can tell from the way Lukas touches me that he's becoming impatient about the long bubbles of time in which we are apart.

It's possible that I am, too, but *he* is in charge. *He* sets the rhythm. *He* is the one who fucks me standing up, my pants pulled down and my back pushed to the wall as soon as we're inside his room. I'm not at my most lucid, but I estimate it lasts about three minutes. We both come, but he doesn't stop. When he slips out of me, it's like being thrown into a freezing lake. Then he turns me around and shoves me face down on the bed.

"I need a minute to—"

"Nah." He pushes inside me in one thrust. I'm as wet as I could be, but he's Lukas, and it's not easy to let it happen. "I'll fucking tell you what you need."

He's been rocking inside me for about fifteen seconds when I come again, a rush of heat spreading through me, my cunt clenching in tender little pulses. I can't stop. Can't get myself together.

"You're *made* for this, aren't you?" His fingers fist at my nape. They take several turns in my hair, until it's wrapped around his hand, until I feel the brush of his knuckles against my scalp with each tug.

"A beautiful thing. Made for me."

I nod, and it pulls at my skin. Then he's moving inside me deeper than before, deeper than ever, and the achy spot he presses against feels like the origin of all pleasures and pains.

"Shhh. You have to be quiet." I realize that I've been making wretched little noises. "I know, baby. I'm right here. Just breathe for me, it's okay." I hide my face in the pillow. It smells like cotton and laundry detergent and Lukas. "Be a good girl and bite into that."

Afterward, when the sun sinks and the shadows lengthen, I lift from the me-shaped spot in his arms, and press a kiss into the sweat gleaming at his temple. *Gross*, I tell myself, salt clinging to my lips. Except, it isn't. I'm not capable of perceiving Lukas and his body as anything but *good*.

"Should we stop having sex?"

His look is mystified. Offended, too.

"I mean, doesn't it interfere with athletic performances?"

"Is that a thing in diving?"

"No, but I'm not an endurance or speed athlete. *You* are."

His fingers caress my hair, gentle. His touch always matches what I need. "We're here without practice, classes, and all the shit that constantly pulls you away from me. I'm going to take advantage. If that costs me a race, so be it."

I laugh, but my heart doubles in size. "I'm serious."

"Me, too. I'm making an informed choice. Plus, half of the people here are fucking each other." His palm is warm against my cooling cheek. "Move your stuff in here."

"What?"

"Stay in this room. With me."

"I . . . mine's only two floors down."

"Too far."

"Why?"

"Scarlett." He drags me down to him. Kisses me slowly, lingering, like getting enough of this, of *me*, is a concept not translatable in his language. "You know why."

"I . . . really don't." My cheeks are aflame, as always when I try to lie. Except that I'm not. I don't *understand*, and that's the truth.

He nods. Patient. Kind. Serious. "Okay. We're at a major competition. I won't ask you to have this conversation right now." *What conversation?* "But if you're ready, I can tell you why I want you here."

My heart slams against my ribs. I glance away—an automatic

gesture, like I'd avert my eyes if a car came crashing toward me on the highway.

"Tell you what." Lukas sighs, but not in frustration. His thumb sweeps under my cheekbone. "Let's take it day by day. You're always welcome, here, with me." He pulls me all the way over his body, toes against his shins, chin on his pecs. Skin to skin, it's almost shockingly intimate, even after all the filthy things he and I have done. He's so solid, he could be my life raft. Already is, maybe. "What time are you training tomorrow?"

"Early morning. Why?"

His fingers skim to my lower back. "Because we have plans."

# CHAPTER 53

AMSTERDAM IS BEAUTIFUL. THE FOOD IS GOOD. DUTCH PEO-
ple are nice, even when we don't speak a word of their language and are so immersed in talking, we wander off and get lost.
At the end of the day, in the clunky rise of the hotel's elevator, I
cannot remember what we discussed. Everything. Nothing. Both.
All I know is that Lukas took my hand sometime after lunch, and
hours later I'm still holding his index finger. That he got a phone call
from his team, asking if he wanted to join them, and told them he
was busy. What's the last time I spent a day like this, turning completely *off*? Not worrying about events, classes, whether Pipsqueak
is holding a grudge over me being gone?

"I need your help tonight," he tells me. His fingers play with
mine, relaxed, like I'm an extension of his body.

I give him my flirtiest *Is that what we call it nowadays?* smile.

"I really do need—"

The elevator stops. A giant suitcase appears, followed by a tall,
dark-haired man who instantly hugs Lukas. "Hey, mate!"

Lukas laughs. "Only you would show up the day before prelims."

I may not follow swimming, but I do follow *Lukas*, and I

recognize this guy. Callum Vardy. Australian. Big butterfly sprinter. He and Lukas seem more than circumstantial friends.

"Your family's here?" Callum asks.

"Nah. They'll be at the Olympics. I quote: 'Can't come see all your little races.'"

"Christ, they sound like mine. And you . . ." He turns to me. His eyes are, frankly, ridiculous. So green, they might be responsible for the deforestation of eastern Madagascar.

"I'm not Pen Ross," I hurry to say.

"I know, love." He seems entertained. "Pen and I go way back." His eyes flick to Lukas's, and then to where his hand is once again holding mine. "We know each other . . . well."

He and Pen had sex—that's what he means. I'm sure of it. I glance at Lukas for any tells of jealousy or irritation. Find only amusement.

"So . . . ?" Callum asks. His eyes travel from me to Lukas, asking a question I cannot interpret. Lukas immediately shakes his head.

"No."

"You sure?"

"Very."

"What can I do to convince you?"

He smiles. "Absolutely nothing."

"Too bad." The elevator pings and the doors open. "Well, this is me. Let's get a drink after the finals, since you two are no fun."

He disappears into the hallway, and I spend the rest of the ride trying to formulate an appropriate question, but I have *nothing* when Lukas hands me a can of shaving gel and a razor. "Can you do my back?"

"I'd forgotten you guys do that!"

"Only before big competitions." The absence of body hair and dead skin cells can apparently snip a few hundredths of a second off a race.

"Who shaves you, usually?"

"Gösta does my back and neck, and I do his." I give him a blank look. "Gustafsson? He's in our medley team."

"Is there a specific way I should do it?"

"As long as you don't saw off my arm, you can't be worse than him. Or me."

"How can you be bad at shaving?"

"I'm okay doing my face. But the rest . . . there's so much fucking hair, Scarlett."

"Aww. Poor, innocent, seven-feet-tall baby."

"I'm not seven—"

"Hyperbole. Get in the shower, Bigfoot," I order.

He raises a surprised eyebrow, but I don't back down. "Seriously, I'll make you as smooth as a nineteenth-century brothel's satin sheets."

"Graphic."

"The king will make me a knight of the Swedish empire."

"Like I said—"

"But you gotta shower first. Open up those pores."

He inches closer, looming, and pulls me in the shower with him.

Twenty minutes and some fooling around later, I straddle him while he's face down on a towel on the floor, and start the long process of de-yetifing him. It's fascinating, having him at my mercy, unusually passive and relaxed. Taking care of *him* for once. "Your thighs are currently smoother than the Danish electoral process. Gösta could never."

"You're killing it with the rhetorical figures."

"With the shaving, too." I work in silence, thinking, churning. Then: "Did they date?"

"Who?"

"Callum and Pen."

He laughs. "They didn't."

"Turn around, I need to do the front of your legs—thanks. So they . . . had a thing?"

"Sex, yeah."

"Oh." When, though? The timeline doesn't add up. "Were you guys ever in an open relationship?"

"Nope."

"Then when did she—" I drop the razor. "Did the three of you . . . ?"

"Yup."

"Oh . . . wow."

Lukas props up to his elbows, clearly finding my shock diverting. "For someone who'd be A-OK with me tying her up and keeping her in a closet for an undetermined length of time, you're easily scandalized."

"You're right. Why am I being a prude?" I massage my temple. "I'm just surprised."

"Why?"

"In the list, you said that . . . you weren't that interested in threesomes."

He sits up in a flurry of golden skin and abs. "I'm not."

"Pen is?"

He nods. "It was a couple of years ago. When we saw each other a handful of times a year it was hard to tell, but once we were living in the same city, we realized that our sex life wasn't great. We tried stuff."

"With Callum?"

"Among others."

Others. "How many?" His eyes lift to the ceiling in concentration—like he's counting. "That many, huh?"

He shrugs.

"I have a lot of questions about the logistics."

"I see."

"All of them inappropriate. None of them my business."

He smiles. "Let's hear them."

"How did you choose . . . ?"

"It was mostly Pen who . . ."

"Spearheaded the project?"

He snorts. "She'd find someone. Ask me if I agreed. Come to me when the plans were made. Some guy who was in her class. Tracy— he used to be on the team? Backstroke? Callum. Others."

"Always guys?"

He shakes his head. "It was pretty even."

"Did you . . . ?"

He nods.

"And?"

"It was fun. Good, even. Though I'm not as attracted to men as I am to women."

"Tragically straight?"

A soft laugh. "Or thereabouts."

I pull up my legs and prop my chin on my knees. *How did I never hear about it?* Then again, who would tell me? "I might need a list of the Stanford people involved, or I'll be wondering every time I talk to someone. The twins. Billy the maintenance guy. Coach Sima. Dr. Smith."

He bites the inside of his cheek. "None of them, Scarlett."

I sigh. "You know, I wish I was more like the two of you."

"In what way?"

"You're just . . . rational. Never jealous. I don't think I could . . . share."

"It's not that simple at all, Scarlett."

I shrug, forcing myself to move on from something that could get very sad, very fast. "Break's over. Before the pores close, we—"

His fingers close around my wrist. "I asked for you."

"What?"

For a few moments, his jaw works. "Every single person Pen and

I had sex with was her choice, and I was okay with it. But when you joined the team, I asked her if she could approach you."

"I . . ." My cheeks glow, on fire. "Why?" But I remember something I haven't thought of in months: Pen's words at Coach Sima's barbecue. *I know you think she's hot. You said so.*

"You were beautiful, but that wasn't . . . You seemed so quiet and reserved. We have this saying in Swedish, 'In the calmest of waters . . .' I couldn't stop thinking that you were hiding something. That there was a secret in there, something everyone else was missing. And . . ." A silent laugh. "I was right. It was there. Same as mine." He looks at the slowly setting sun. "So I asked Pen about you. It was the first time I did anything like that."

"And?" I'm surprised my vocal cords still work.

"You had a boyfriend, and that was it. But she didn't forget. She knew I found you attractive, would tease me about it, in her way. That's what she does with people she loves."

I feel a little numb. "Is that why she threw me at you at Coach Sima's house?"

"Maybe. Or maybe she was just drunk."

I nod, realizing that I *really* don't want to talk about this any longer. "We should finish the shaving. Okay?" I force a smile. "Let me make you smoother than a saxophone solo."

Lukas mutters something that sounds like "This needs to stop, Scarlett," but before lying back, he pulls me down and kisses me.

I kiss him back, and it's unlike any other time.

# CHAPTER 54

**I**T'S NOT A GOOD YEAR FOR USA DIVING.

Hayden Bosko, our three-meter hopeful, loses hope somewhere around her fourth dive and limps to a tired sixth place. Carissa and Natalie don't even make it to the synchro finals. Peter Bryant forgets the concept of rip entry while in the air, and Akane, our only medal, pulls off a bronze by the skin of her teeth. And then there's me.

BARB: Maybe you're not on the podium, but you are officially the ninth best platform diver in the world. Isn't that good?

It doesn't *feel* good, not as half a dozen sports journalists who'd rather be on the NFL beat ask me, "What went wrong, Scarlett?"

*Everything*, I want to scream. Instead I clear my throat, and say, "Lots of tiny mistakes that added up." It's true. No earthquakes, just aftershocks. I smile and repeat what the media specialist taught us. "I'm really happy to be here."

But I'm *not*. "What a waste of time," Akane mutters back in the hotel room.

"I fucking hate it."

"Wanna join me in my feel-like-shit ritual?"

"What's that?"

We spend an hour watching amateur diving fails, and when Akane falls asleep, I head upstairs. Nine months ago, I wasn't sure I'd ever dive competitively again. I have no reason to be this frustrated with myself. "Why am I so furious?" I ask the second Lukas opens the door, brushing past him.

"What happened to your back?"

"What—oh." I guess he can see the bruises under my tank top. "Nothing. I screwed up the fulcrum, smacked during my lead-ups."

"What the fuck, Scarlett?" He turns me around to examine the purpling edges.

"It's fine. It was during warm-up, it's not bad—"

"This *is* bad."

"It was from the board and—" I whirl around, surprised by the worry in his eyes. "I should be happy, shouldn't I?" My cheeks feel wet, because my fucking eyes are leaking. I wipe at them with my palms. "'Just happy to be here.' That's supposed to be my motto."

He crosses his arms. Gives me a long, assessing stare. "Where else are you hurt?"

"Just that and the back of my thighs, but—"

"Take off your clothes and get on the bed. Face down."

"I don't—"

"Scarlett."

I obey, and squeeze my eyes shut. When he starts rubbing bruise-relief lotion into my skin, my tears overflow anyway.

"You don't have to—I have some in my room, too."

"But you didn't use it. Because you felt like you didn't deserve it."

I turn my head. "How do you—"

"I know you, Scarlett. Come on. Breathe in, breathe out."

It takes me a while to calm down. "I used to feel sad when I lost. I don't understand where all this . . . this *fury* comes from."

"You used to be in survival mode. You just wanted to compete again." His hands are warm and gentle. "Now you know what you're capable of, and you're angry you didn't perform accordingly. It's a good thing—within reason."

I bury my face into the cotton. "Why do you sound happy about it?"

"I like you like this."

"When I am become Death, Destroyer of Worlds?"

"Yup. Fighty." He presses a kiss against my nape, lingering, rubbing his nose through the baby hair. "It's healthy, Scarlett. Take the anger and use it as fuel."

He's right. He's always right. Also, he's medaled in all his races so far, but has to take care of me, a loser. How does he not feel impatient with me?

*He told you to do it*, a voice reminds me. He asked me to go to him when I'm falling apart. And he's so *good* at putting me back together, patching me up like a too-worn shirt, weaving me into my original shape. Even though my rough days at the office cannot possibly be relatable to him. "Is it weird for you? When others lose?"

He laughs. "You think I never lose?"

"I *know* you don't. You are forty-five gold medals in a trench coat. You got into med school. There are fancams of you on the internet."

He snorts. "I tried training backstroke and longer butterfly distances, and never qualified for shit. I had to come to the US for college because the Karolinska Institute didn't accept me. I tried building a neural network, and the accuracy was abysmal compared to yours. And as you know, my girlfriend of seven years broke up with me because of how not fun I am."

I try to turn around, but he doesn't let me. "I have fun with you," I protest.

"That's because you are a kinky little troll. Which is, incidentally, how I will re-save you in my contacts."

I laugh. "No! I mean, yes, but also—I have fun with you even when we're not . . ."

"Fucking?"

"Indulging in our paraphiliac inclinations. And I have fun when we're just hanging out. Maybe it doesn't mean much, coming from someone who according to Dixon Ioannidis from ninth grade has less personality than a sourdough starter, but I *like* you." I suddenly feel warm. I've said too much. "And I'm sorry Pen broke up with you."

"I am very much not, Scarlett."

Even *warmer*. "And I didn't know about the backstroke. Or the school. And your model wasn't that bad."

He moves down, to the backs of my thighs. "Now you're just lying."

"Yeah. It was a shitbowl."

He finishes with a chuckle and goes to wash his hands. When he comes back, I'm putting on my top. "Maybe it's for the best," I say.

"What is?"

"The butterfly thing. That stroke feels like lots of unnecessary work."

He pushes my hair back and picks me up. I respond instinctively, letting my legs wrap around his waist, holding tight onto his neck as he moves us to the balcony. The sun just finished setting, the air is chilly, but he wraps a blanket around me as we stare at the pretty skyline. It feels like something out of a fairy tale.

"Doesn't butterfly make you want to just flutter kick your legs?" I ask lazily.

"It's illegal."

"Would they arrest you?"

"Execute me."

"Intense." I burrow into him. "What's your favorite stroke?"

"Free." On the back of his hand there are remnants of the models I've been drawing every morning, soft kisses and hushed *troll*s whispered low into my hair before we make our way to the pools. He strokes patterns on my arm, and I nuzzle my nose against his neck. "You can't mess free up. You can get to the end of the race however you want."

"Really? What about sculling?"

"That's fine."

"Windshield wiping?"

"It'll take a while, but yeah."

"What if I break into backstroke?"

"Fine."

"I just wait for the currents to drag me."

"Also fine."

"Doggy paddle?"

"Sure."

"Can I do it naked?"

"*I*'d enjoy it."

I smile into his neck. "See? I just do."

"What?"

"Have fun. With you." His arms tighten around me, just a little, just a second. "Can I tell you a secret?"

"Sure. You already know all of mine."

"It's . . . I don't want to make you uncomfortable. I'm not going to turn into a stalker or anything like that, so don't worry."

His laughter is quiet. "Scarlett . . . you have no idea."

It's encouraging. So I make myself blurt it out: "Sometimes I think that it would be nice, if you and I ended up in med school together."

He says nothing. Just leans back to catch my eyes, and in the light that seeps through the balcony doors, he seems so . . . so intense and present and focused on what I just said, I almost want to take it back.

But I power through. "We'd make a good team. For study groups and stuff. I'm not even talking about . . ." *Sex*, I cannot bring myself to say.

Although . . . why not? He and I go so well together, in so many ways. Would Pen even care? She's with Theo. Lukas likes me, maybe even as much as I like him. Yes, we agreed on *just sex*, but things have obviously evolved. He talked about *dating*. Is there any reason for us not to continue on together? The prospect of him disappearing from my life tears through me with such violence, the only person who could sew me back together is . . .

Lukas.

With whom, I fear, I might be a little bit in love.

It's a gut-punching realization. I'm ready to panic, but Lukas stops me with a single word.

"Yeah?" His voice is hesitant, a little rough. Like my words grated against his vocal cords.

*Lie*, I order myself. *Swallow it back.* But I can't. I don't *want* to. "Yeah."

And maybe it's fine. Because he kisses me, something never-ending and supple and so, *so* sweet, it feels like being in the air. Hovering above the water. Running off a platform with the certainty that a good dive is there, ready to spring out of my muscles.

"Except." He pulls back, more composed. "You're a junior. In this scenario, I'm ahead and you're shamelessly using me for tutoring."

I press a kiss against the corner of his mouth. "Firstly, I do not need the tutoring of someone whose neural network has chance-level accuracy."

"Savage." His smile swells under my lips.

"And, Pen told me you're going to defer your acceptance, which means that . . ."

I stop. Lukas is shaking his head. "I'm not."

"You're . . . not?"

He folds a lock of hair behind my ear. "I'm starting med school this fall."

"Oh. Maybe I misunderstood."

"I'm sure that's what she told you. But I have no intention of postponing."

I nod. "Well, you have great time-management skills. M1 work-load is tough, and you'll have little time for caribou watching and other famed Swedish pastimes, but if anyone can keep up with a training program while learning how to dissect cadavers—"

"I won't."

"Lukas." I cup his cheek, not wanting to break his heart. "Corpse stuff is mandatory in US med schools."

He laughs. "I'll be fine with *corpse stuff*. It's the swimming that I'll avoid."

My hand drops in his lap. "What?"

"These Olympics are my last."

"You're joking, right?" But he's not. It's in his eyes, the confident air of someone who has made peace with his choices. "You're one of the best swimmers of the century. Everyone agrees."

"Eh, century *just* started."

"You hold several *current* records." He shrugs. The movement vibrates in my bones and tendons. "You probably have a *decade* ahead of you."

"A decade of what?"

"Of . . . becoming faster. Winning."

"And then? Three, five, ten years from now, there'll be better tech suits, better nutrition, better and smarter training. A bunch of talented kids will show up and wipe the ground with us and . . ." He shakes his head. Not bitter, just accepting. "I can't find it in me to give a fuck, Scarlett. The idea of being faster than them doesn't mo-tivate me to swim repeat one hundreds, or to endlessly debate one up versus two downs. There's no endgame."

"But . . . what about the glory?"

"What about it?"

"I don't know. You have fans. People love you. The *king* loves you!"

"The king's elderly and has no idea who I am, thank fuck. And this shit, it's not the kind of love I'm interested in, Scarlett." He says it so pointedly, into my eyes, it could almost be a jab, but . . . not quite. "Being respected as a swimmer is great. But I don't want to make that my identity any longer than I already have. I've been telling this to Pen for years. She just thinks I'll miss the attention and pull a Tom Brady."

I'm not so sure. Lukas is single-minded, yes, but I can see him apply that drive to many other parts of his life. "You won't," I say.

"What?"

"Change your mind."

"I don't think so, either. Wanting a gold medal, a record, it's a great dream. But it's not mine anymore."

I tilt my head. "What's yours, then?"

His smile is crooked. "For a while, I thought I needed to have some over-the-top goal, something comparable to the Olympics, but . . ." He stops. Runs his thumb over my lower lip. "I want to spend four years in med school, fully knowing that it'll be hell. Do a fellowship and a residency. *Corpse stuff*, sure. I want to travel to places that don't have a fucking pool. See my family more than once a year. Sleep in. Go on hiking trips. Stay home for long weekends and have morally bankrupt amounts of sex with someone I'm in love with. Kinky, vanilla, I want it all. I want to adopt rescue animals with her. I want to take care of her, and watch her be cold in Sweden, and marvel every day at how much smarter than me she is, and . . . Scarlett." His thumb swipes under my eye. "Why are you crying?"

It's a lie. I want to deny it. But my cheeks are blotchy and hot. There's a terrible, scalding thing inside me that threatens to explode all the way out, and all I can do is hide my face into his throat. "I don't know."

His hand is heavy on the back of my head. "Are you sure?"

I'm not. But I nod, and even though his sigh tells me that he sees through my half-truths, he still hugs me like he'll never let me go.

# CHAPTER 55

**M**EI TAKES ME ASIDE BEFORE THE FLIGHT HOME, EYES ALL business. I brace for a lecture on the ways I disappointed her, but she surprises me.

"Here's what I'd do if I were you, between now and the Olympic trials. Stop wasting your time on the springboard."

I blink. "I . . . what?"

"No offense. Actually—full offense. Take this as the harsh reality check it's meant to be." She shrugs. "Unless the Three Wise Men visit you bearing gifts of gold, frankincense, and a spanking new hurdle, you're not going to win three meters. The ten-meter platform? When you're good, you're *fantastic*. But you make too many mistakes, and there's only one way to beat that out of yourself." I'm so terrified that she'll bring up corporal punishment, the conclusion is almost underwhelming. "Train smarter. Be more selective. And you could stand to lose a couple degrees of difficulty."

I scowl. "My degrees of difficulties are already lower than before my injury—"

"Guess what? You have a different body now. Stop living in the past. You're less flexible but have better control. What you need is *consistency*."

I hate that there's no magic button, no sleight of hand except for hard work. I still thank Mei for everything she's done, which is a lot.

"And, Vandy?" she calls after me.

I turn around on my way out.

"Send me your TiVos if you need pointers. I love telling people what they're doing wrong."

♦ ♦ ♦

Lukas wins three golds, a silver, and two bronzes.

The airport in Amsterdam is leather-market crowded, and his fingers hook into the belt loops of my jeans to keep me as close as possible. With the aquatics-loving population denser than usual, people recognize him every ten steps. Other athletes, but also a couple of families, and a group of American girls who look at him like he *is*, in fact, an underwear model. He's pleasant about it, but I can tell he hates it, so while he's at the ticketing desk, I buy him an orange Netherlands hat and the douchiest pair of sunglasses I can find.

I snicker at his *Are you for fucking real?* frown. Hoot at the challenge in his expression as he puts both on, and snap a picture to add to his contact.

"You have me in your phone as Lukas Penelope?"

"Oh, yeah. I wasn't sure how to spell your last name. There are some backasswards *q*'s and *v*'s in there."

He gives me an unimpressed look and holds out his hand, demanding, so I give him my phone.

"Write your name, though, not dumb stuff. Maryam checks my notifications if I leave my phone out. She found out that Barb had broken up with her boyfriend before me."

"What's dumb stuff?"

"I don't know. Sex god. Master. Daddy Dom."

His mouth twitches. "Can't hide from the truth, Scarlett."

"I hate you."

"Of course you do." A kiss, warm against my forehead.

My ticket was for basic economy, while Sweden sprang for one of the fancier sections that live between first class and the plebs. I don't know how Lukas pulled it off, but when we board, I find myself miraculously seated next to him. I lean against his shoulder and half nap, half watch *The Office* while he reads a book in Swedish. His hand never leaves my thigh.

"Stay with me tonight," he asks when we land. Except that it's not a question. We're jet-lagged and exhausted, and I'm still a bit fucked out from last night, but I nod, and my heart cartwheels at his pleased smile.

We've spent the last ten days together. Why not one more?

When we get to his house, all the lights are off. "Where are Hasan and Kyle?"

He shrugs. Before he can stick the key into the hole, the door springs open. *"Surprise!"*

The loudest voice is Pen's, but the entire swimming and diving team is here, clapping and cheering, startling my half-asleep brain. Some bass-heavy music is switched on, and a blue and yellow balloon lands at my feet. The homemade banners are a particularly tasteful touch.

CONGRATS!!

FUCK YOU SWEEDY IT SHOULD HAVE BEEN TEAM USA

PLS BREAK A LEG BEFORE THE OLYMPICS WE LOVE YOU

And my personal favorite:

U GUYS ALREADY HAVE IKEA AND LIVABLE WAGES,
LEAVE US SOMETHING

Lukas reads them with a deepening scowl, then crosses his arms. "Really?" Judging by the roar of laughter, his stern tone is a hit. Pen presses a giggly kiss into his cheek, and I clench my fist. There are high fives and backslaps and lots of *congrats, man, bro, dude*, a glass of something pushed in his hand. Before Hunter whisks him away, Lukas turns back to me with a wistful look. I cannot help a smile.

If people think that it's weird that we appeared together, no one mentions it. Maybe they assume I knew about the surprise. Maybe I'm just invisible. Pen, the twins, and Victoria give me long, warm hugs. We've been texting back and forth in the team group chat, but I hadn't realized how much I missed them.

"Was Europe cool?" Bree asks. "Were there lots of castles?"

"Um . . . not that I noticed."

"What about shoe cobblers? Horses? Carriages?"

Victoria pats her back. "Babe, it's not the Oregon Trail."

I can barely keep my eyes open. I drift away as soon as the opportunity arises, brushing past people mainlining beer. What day of the week is it? "Have you seen Lukas?" I ask Hasan, who points to the ceiling.

"On the phone with his dad."

I find him sitting on the edge of his bed, right as he hangs up. "Hey." Being with him is a second wind.

"Hey." He reaches for my wrist and pulls me between his legs. "Thoughts on how to get rid of them?"

"Hmm." I pretend to think. He runs his palm over the back of my thigh. "Do you have a turnip cart on hand?"

"Nope."

"Then I'm not—"

"Hey, you." We turn, and Pen's at the door.

Instinctively, I try to put some distance between Lukas and me, but his grip tightens. "Hey," he says, relaxed, like this is not weird, and we aren't doing anything wrong.

And we *aren't*.

But it *is*.

Pen's eyes travel over the place where our bodies make contact, but her smile betrays nothing. "Do you need a ride home?" she asks me.

I freeze. Do I? I assumed I wouldn't, but . . .

"She doesn't, Pen."

"Okey dokey. Luk, can I talk to you for a minute?"

"Sure, what's going on?"

"Alone," she adds.

His eyes narrow, but I take a firm step away.

"Let's talk tomorrow," Lukas tells her. Not a suggestion. "Scarlett and I—"

"It's okay. I need to use the restroom." I smile, too, and exchange another hug with Pen on my way out.

"So happy that you're back," she whispers.

"Me, too."

The door closes behind me, and I tell myself that there's no reason for the nausea floating in my stomach. They're friends. Lukas has made it clear that he's no longer romantically interested in her.

I snake my way through the crowd, but there's lots of alcohol flowing, and no one notices me. I'm zonking out. Swaying. When I close my eyes, waterfowl honk into my ear.

It's shitty, leaving a party without telling anyone, but I call an Uber. In the back seat, I shoot Lukas a quick text, and that's when the floor flips out from underneath me.

His renamed contact reads LUKAS SCARLETT.

# CHAPTER 56

I'VE BEEN HOME FOR ABOUT AN HOUR, SHOWERING AND UN-packing and scowling at the chore chart Maryam crafted in my absence, in which all activities are magically listed under *my* name, when I hear a knock.

Lukas stands tall in the doorframe, hands in the pockets of his jeans, dark circles covering his freckles. Serious and tired and silent.

I don't know what to say, so I stay quiet.

There's no reason for him to be here.

No reason for me to let him in.

No reason to take his hand and guide him to my bedroom.

No reason for any of this, but still I burrow into the curve of his throat, and fall asleep with his scent in my lungs after just a few seconds.

# CHAPTER 57

THIS WINTER QUARTER I'M TAKING THE LIGHTEST POSSIBLE academic load, to offset training and championship season travel, which is all going to happen between the end of February and May.

Pac-12.

Zone E meet.

If I qualify: NCAA.

It should feel overwhelming, but on the first practice after Amsterdam it just . . . doesn't.

"I didn't medal, which is disappointing," I tell Sam during our catch-up session. I'm over my block, and there is no overt reason for me to continue therapy, but talking to her helps me put everything into perspective. "But I'm not going to let it define me. I'm excited about the season. I'm ready to be as strong as I can be."

Sam smiles, which will never *not* look weird. "I'm very happy for you."

"Sorry about Saturday night," Pen tells me later in the locker room. "I felt bad about kicking you out. I just needed to talk to Lukas."

"Everything okay?" I ask, even though I'm not sure I want to know. The three of us, our relative positions, the sum of our degrees . . . I don't want it to feel like a love triangle. And I don't want to be left out when it flattens into a line.

"Yeah, I just needed him to know . . ." She looks vaguely upset, so I take a seat next to her. "It's Theo. Hot Teacher."

"Oh."

"He broke up with me, Vandy." Her voice cracks a little in the end. I stare, not quite processing.

"He . . . what?"

"He said that—I don't know, something about how we needed to take a step back, because he wasn't sure that we worked together, and that sometimes I felt too *young* for him, and . . ." Her eyes are bright with tears. "I mean, it's fine."

She looks anything but fine. "I'm so sorry, Pen."

"I cannot believe that he just decided that it was over and left, like I'm a SoulCycle class. We spent Thanksgiving together. I met his sister and his friends, and he got me a necklace, and . . . I was at his place every weekend, Vandy. We did so many things, and now . . ." She shakes her head, somewhere between pain and anger. "Anyway. It's over. I wanted to tell Lukas because . . . well. He's still my oldest friend."

My heart beats in my stomach. "And what did he say?"

"Nothing much. Said it was Theo's loss. Patted my back. Told me I'll find someone new soon. Nice, but distant. After Theo, I'd forgotten how cold he can be. Honestly, sometimes I wonder how Lukas and I even managed to get together to begin with, all those years ago."

Because he's *not* distant. Or cold. "Have you ever considered . . ." I start.

"What?"

I gather my words. "He mentioned what you did for him when his mother passed. And he helped you out with Carissa."

"Yeah?"

"Is it possible that you two mostly bonded over your respective trauma, and then entered a romantic relationship on the wave of that, without . . . ?"

Her eyes search my face for so long, I start wondering if I've overstepped. And maybe I did, because she lets out a small laugh, a little watery, and asks, "Are you saying he didn't love me?"

"No. I know he did. And he still cares about you. I just wonder if . . ."

*If he didn't love you the way you want to be loved.*

*If that was so painful, you decided to tell yourself that Lukas simply isn't capable of deep romantic feelings.*

*If maybe you only know certain little parts of him, and completely ignore the rest.*

*If you still see him as the fifteen-year-old boy who needed you when his mom died, and never realized that he's grown into a different person.*

*If what's between you two was more about mutual protection.*

"If?" she prompts.

"If maybe the transition to romantic love was a little rocky for the two of you."

"I mean . . ." She purses her lips and shrugs. "I know Lukas well enough to know that it's not the case. I know what we had. But in any case, I think that bonding over trauma is still a nice way to fall in love and build a future. More valid than sharing the same sexual fetishes."

Her tone is gentle—and a punch to the stomach. I blink at her, trying to parse what she just said and decipher the way she intended for it to land. Whether I should be offended. "I . . . excuse me?"

"Oh my god." Instantly, her eyes widen and her hand closes

around mine. "I didn't mean it like . . . I promise it wasn't a jab! There are lots of valid ways to fall in love, that's it. I'm *so* sorry."

I nod, relieved. Pen just got dumped. She's emotional. I *know* she didn't want to be hurtful.

But then she adds, "I'm just wondering if I made a mistake, that's all."

"A mistake?"

"By breaking up with Lukas. I mean, he and I have been through so much, and he *gets* me, and . . ." Her head cocks. Her eyes on me are almost pleading. "Are you two . . . It's mostly sex, right? You're not officially dating."

It would be an indisputable lie, to say that what's between me and Lukas is *mostly sex.*

However. As much as it hurts to admit: "We aren't officially dating."

Not that it matters. I don't need a stamped certificate to know that Lukas cares deeply about me, and that what we have is real. The problem is, Pen's relief at my words is so obvious, I doubt that right now she'd be capable to accept any of that.

She's hurting. I'm her friend. I can keep the truth to myself for a little longer. Put her first, just for a while.

"He's right, by the way," I say, squeezing her hand back.

"Who?"

"Lukas." I smile. "It *is* Theo's loss."

She lays her head on my shoulder, and I do my best to joke and laugh while walking to dryland training. Once we're there, I excuse myself and go find the coaches.

*It will be all right*, I tell myself.

Pen feels rejected, maybe for the first time in her life. She's fragile, and needs her friends' support. She doesn't love Lukas. Lukas doesn't love her. That relationship is over.

It's just not a good time to point it out.

And I have more important things to worry about, too.

"Coach Sima?"

He doesn't look up from the piece of paper he's reading. "Yeah?"

"I'd like to discuss the possibility of making some changes to my training program."

# CHAPTER 58

*D*O YOU HAVE TO BE KIDNAPPED FOR IT TO BE STOCKHOLM syndrome?" I ask. "You shouldn't, not if the guy you fell for *against your will* is Swedish."

Sam seems unimpressed with my mastery of psychological constructs. "Does being in love with Lukas make you unhappy?"

"No. Just . . . guilty."

"Because of Penelope?"

Her name has been coming up a lot during my therapy sessions. "Yeah."

"And Penelope's well-being is important for you?"

"Of course. She's the closest thing to a best friend I've had in . . . ever."

"She hurt you, though. The other day."

"She didn't mean to. She was just . . . careless. Because she is hurting, too."

Sam nods. "Is she the reason you've been avoiding Lukas?"

"I haven't—"

"How many times have you two met since Amsterdam?"

I lower my eyes. Too few, and only because of me. In fact, my excuses have been so laughable, I *know* Lukas doesn't believe them. Study group. Paper due tomorrow. Exhausted.

LUKAS: Just come over to spend the night. I sleep better when you're around.

SCARLETT: Why?

LUKAS: Because I know you're safe.

LUKAS: And you smell good.

LUKAS: And you're soft.

I should change his name in my contacts. I know how to spell Blomqvist, and it hurts to see what he wrote—sharp kitten claws digging into the squishiest parts of my chest. But.

"I caught Pen sobbing in the locker room, this morning," I simply say.

"That is sad. But as we discussed, her relationship with Lukas is unlikely to productively resume, while *your* relationship with Lukas—"

"I *know*. But it's temporary. She feels so alone, and the possibility of getting back with Lukas is . . . an illusion she clings to. I can't shatter it by spending time with him under her nose."

"Is a lie this big really kinder than the truth?"

I sigh and rub my face. This won't last long. Pen will feel better soon. I just need to wait it out. Curl into myself like a pill bug. Focus on training—exclusively ten meters.

Coach was initially reluctant, but begrudgingly came around on the condition that I keep on practicing three-meter synchro with Pen.

"It doesn't have to be forever," I told him. "But Mei said that—"

"Why do I feel like a cheated husband?"

I try to keep a straight face. "Because Mrs. Sima has taken up with the landscaper?"

"Because my diver came home smelling like another coach!"

"That's not true."

"Mei is your favorite. You *stan* her."

I wince. "Did your son teach you that word?"

"Don't change the subject."

But if Coach Sima knows what I used to be capable of before my injury, Mei has a better idea of what I'm capable of *now*. And it works: endless repetition, constant corrections, infinite fine-tuning. I become, if not better, more confident, and the focus helps drown out the noise in my head.

"He's back," Maryam says into my room on the following Saturday night.

I look up from my neurobiology homework. "Who?"

"The *Love Island* contestant."

"What?"

"The heartthrob with the accent."

I blink. "Lukas?"

The deep "Yup" coming from behind her squeezes my stomach like it's a washcloth.

"I'm not sure whether I'm being flattered," he says, closing the door, "or torn to shreds."

"With Maryam? The latter. Always."

"I introduce myself every time. She could just use my name."

"Nah, not her thing."

He stands over me and I'm breathless. Even more when he bends down to kiss me, one hand on the back of my chair, the other on the desk. He's a blanket of heat and comfort. I lean into his lips because I can't help myself, then clear my throat.

"I'd love to hang out, but I have to finish my quiz."

He nods, ever understanding. And says, "Action potential, sodium, amygdala."

"What?"

"The answers to the three questions you have left." He crosses his arms and looks down at me like he's never, not once, fallen for someone's lie. "What's going on, Scarlett?"

"Nothing. Why?"

"Why?" He huffs, amused. "You're not good at this, no more than I am."

"At what?"

"At playing fucking games."

He's right. It's why we like what we like, and each other. Structure. Negotiations. Agreements and predictability. "I'm just catching up with schoolwork. We're so close to Pac-12—"

His fingers pinch my chin like I'm a child, leaving me no choice but to meet his eyes. I don't know if I can stand it. It's that pressure again. A constant threat of tears. "I left this place two weeks ago. You were happy and fucked out and half in—" He breaks off. A muscle in his jaw twitches. "Are you okay?"

I nod, but can't bring myself to say a single thing.

"Hey," he tells me, tone shifting to real concern, searching, weighty. "You don't have to pretend. You don't have to come up with some bullshit excuse. It's just me."

It's true. This is Lukas, and he loves the truth. I can vomit out whatever's in my head and he'll accept it—and doesn't that make it even worse?

I'm being strangled. Cannot breathe. Have to slow myself down. "Pen is . . . not doing well."

"Right. Pen and her fucking delusions." His tone terrifies me—icy. Angry. A dangerous machine he could use to excavate the beating heart out of my chest. "Did she ask you to take a step back?"

"No."

"No." The word is, at once, out of his mouth before I'm done answering, and spoken in the most unhurried of ways. "All on your own, then."

"She's my friend." I run my palms down my bare thighs. "I don't think she could handle that you and I . . ."

"You and I?" His smile is a little cruel. "Come on, Scarlett. What are *you and I* doing? Are you ready to finally say it?"

I stare down at my legs, hoping the words will roll out easily when I'm avoiding his eyes. But no. "Until she feels better, maybe we should pull back. Or focus more on the . . . physical part of our relationship."

Lukas doesn't answer, not for a long stretch, and when I give up and tilt my head up at him, his gaze is cataloging, all-seeing. "Now?" he asks.

"What?"

"Do you want me to fuck you while pretending that you're not the person I feel closest to in the whole fucking world *now*, Scarlett? Or another day?"

I don't know what cuts deeper—the words, or the chill in his tone.

"I . . . if you want to, now, we can—"

"I want." He sounds mocking, even a little contemptuous, but his hand is gentle enough as he pulls me out of the chair. "Am I allowed to kiss you?" His smile is bitter. "Would that be unfair toward Pen?"

He's angry, and anger doesn't go well with power exchange. I just have to decide whether I care. "Of course you can kiss me."

But he doesn't. He pushes me onto the bed, belly down, and his strength vibrates throughout my body. And we haven't even started.

Or—*I* haven't. Lukas has pulled my shorts down to the bottom curve of my ass. I didn't bother with underwear after my shower, and feel the heat of skin against mine. His fingers tangle in my hair, lifting my head until his other palm is right in front of my mouth.

"Get it wet."

"I—what?"

His grip tightens on my scalp. "Since when do we ask questions, Scarlett?"

Oh my *god*. "I—I'm sorry."

A hard slap on my ass. "If I tell you to do something, you just fucking do it. Lick it." He's rough, which addles my brain. I'm so turned on, I can feel the smear of it between my thighs. I part my lips, running my tongue up the center of his palm. "Again."

I repeat it four, five times. When he deems his palm wet enough, he pulls back, and then I feel the thick denim, the rhythmic bump of his knuckles against the soft part of my bottom, the sticky wetness of his skin dragging over my lower back. He's just jerking off. Using my body—barely.

I'm at his disposal. Any disgusting thing he's ever thought of, he could do with my blessing, but he doesn't take advantage. It's detached like this, like I'm a canvas, nothing more than a picture he found on the internet, some faceless, nameless girl he doesn't care about and never will.

His grunt when he comes is familiar, embedded in the back of my brain. I squeeze my thighs together and my eyes shut, hiding my face in the cotton sheets.

A dip in weight, the bounce of the mattress. *He's leaving.* My heart sinks for a flurry of reasons that have nothing to do with the fact I'm this worked up and he won't make me come. Then his shirt hits the floor, and relief floods over me. He presses a kiss between my shoulder blades, long and lingering, a stark contrast to the clinch of his hands around my waist as he arranges me. His fingers dip in the come at the base of my spine, and he asks, "You know what I like about fucking you?"

I shake my head.

"You'd let me do anything, wouldn't you? You trust me *that* much. You're just that perfect."

It's Lukas who's perfect. Who knows how to push my boundaries but never cross them. To make me hurt just enough to feel good.

Maybe we're just perfect for each other.

*More valid than sharing the same sexual—*

"What do you say if you want me to stop?" he asks. But I'm distracted. His hand slides down my back, between my ass cheeks, smearing his come against my hole.

My breath catches and I squirm. I thought he'd leave me like that, a fair punishment for my lies, but instead a single finger presses inside me, foreign and new.

I tense. Gasp in fear and hunger. It's all messed up, blended together in my heart and in my belly. The fullness aches, a slick, perfect burn.

"Lukas, I—" I've never done this. He knows it.

"Scarlett." He's immensely displeased. "What. Do. You. Say?"

"*Stop.*" He rewards me with a *good girl* that makes my cunt flutter.

He's gentle, but not too much. He makes the head of his cock slick with his own come, and it takes him long enough to fit it in that I'm a puddle underneath, trembling and clutching at the sheets and forcing myself to breathe around him.

"Okay?"

I nod, overwhelmed. He's not all the way inside. Without real lube, even *with*, I'm not sure he'd manage. He parts my cheeks, rubs against the place where his cock stretches skin, and lets out a husky, surprised grunt, like he didn't expect to enjoy it *this* much.

"I want to take a picture of this."

I twist my hips, searching for something—not sure *what*. It's too much. No room. I shudder. One of Lukas's palms plants on the side of my head, and I turn into it, rubbing into the tendon of his wrist, pressing a simple kiss on his skin, because—he could *really* hurt me. Split me and make me bleed. The thought is as much a turn-on as knowing that he'd rather slash his own arm off than harm me.

That's where it lives, my love for him. In the space between the things he *could* do, and what he *chooses* instead. Care, swallowing

violence, swallowing care. Over and over again, until it's all exqui-
sitely tangled up together.

"But I don't need a picture, since I'm never going to forget this."
He presses maybe a fraction of an inch deeper. My breath hitches.
"It's okay. You're okay," he says, a comforting hand up and down my
back. Somehow, his words make it true. "A little more. You were
made to be fucked by me. Is it too much?"

I nod.

"Liar." His laughter is low and gentle against my skin. "I'll give you
more. Since you want it so much." He knows my body better than I
do. When to stay still. How long till the burn fades. All my tells.

He knows me. I know him.

*Than sharing the same sexual—*

I let out a single, pitiful sob. A warbled *sorry* that has nothing to
do with what's happening.

"Baby." Another kiss. On my cheekbone. "It's okay if you want to
cry. It hurts, doesn't it? It all hurts so fucking much, huh?" He
sounds like I'm gutting him with a rusty knife—because it has
nothing to do with his cock sinking into my ass.

What *really* hurts is pushing him away.

The balcony in Amsterdam.

His name in my phone.

Self-professed belonging.

"Lukas." Despair and heat spill into me.

"Sweetheart. I'm here to pick you up," he whispers. "Fuck you
into a thousand little pieces, and then put them back together. You
don't *need* me to do it, but it's what you want, isn't it? For me to fix
you?" It's horrifying, the truth of it. Even more so when I feel his lips
against my ear, a whisper rolling out of his mouth. "You want to
come, baby?"

I nod. I'm almost there, and yet a million miles away.

"I could make you wait for it. I could force you to tell me all the things you cannot say." His hand slides between my hip bone and the mattress. "But I won't. You know why?" He finds my swollen clit. Index and middle fingers draw circles around it. A tap that makes me shiver. "Because I know all of them already."

A wet explosion in my brain. I burst just like that, wedged between his hand and his chest, clenching around his cock until I'm so narrow, he almost slips outside of me. His groan rolls through me—*There you go, such a good, beautiful girl*—and when I'm mellow again, he orders, "Be nice and quiet while I finish, okay?"

He can't manage proper thrusts, but he drags his movements out anyway, like he doesn't want this to end. I lie patiently, loving every second of it—being his, being used, being wanted, it's all a contented, indistinguishable hum reverberating inside my body. His pleasure makes him speechless, a handful of noiseless grunts and foreign words and my name, hands gripping my breasts and teeth holding my neck. He throbs and jerks, and then we lie there, waiting, catching our breaths.

Then he lifts my hips up, knees wide on the bed. I feel his gaze on me, studying, memorizing, and I'm about to beg him to stop, when his mouth is suddenly *there*, tongue lazy and broad against my clit, painful bites where my ass joins my thigh. Orgasms sweep over me, and I'm sobbing, choking on my own cries. He's the one to push my face into the blanket and remind me that I have to *hush, c'mon, Scarlett, just bite here* and *you're fucking ruining me*, and then I'm coming again.

I'm outside my body. It's the best and worst thing I've ever felt. I space away. Perfect. *Perfect.*

Afterward, he disappears in the bathroom, door open, not bothering to turn on the lights. I watch him, boneless, sweat slowly drying on my spine. When he comes back to clean me up, little tears pebble under my eyes, and he wipes them away with his thumb. Tucks me into bed. Doesn't join me.

Instead he crouches by my pillow, holds my hand to his lips, and asks, "What are you scared of, Scarlett?" His eyes look . . . sad, maybe. I'm not sure. Traces of emotions crease the corners.

"Everything."

A deep sigh. "When it comes to what matters, you're fearless. Try to remember that, okay?"

I make no promises. Instead, I snooze. Dip in and out of sleep, but Lukas stays there, watching me, for what feels like a long time. Then he presses a kiss against my forehead, turns off the light, and lets himself out.

The following week, Pac-12 starts.

# CHAPTER 59

**P**AC-12 SWIMMING AND DIVING ARE SEPARATE EVENTS, ONE
after the other. Lukas and I are out of town at nonoverlapping
intervals: while he's flying back from Seattle, I'm waiting for one of
the assistant coaches to drive me to the airport, trying to decide
what polish to pack in case I get time to do my nails.

However.

"I think the guys' plane just landed," Pen announces while we're
waiting at SFO, sitting up in a burst of excitement. "The gate's five
minutes from here—shall we go say hi?"

"Yes!" Bella says, followed by Bree's blasé, "Sure."

In a plot twist rom-com writers can only aspire to achieve, Bree
and Dale broke up over a yet-to-be-revealed conflict, while Bella
and Devin are still dating. Once again: so many questions, and absolutely zero way of asking them in a tactful way.

Pen's eyes meet mine in one of the many *I guess we cannot spec-
ulate about this now, but boy, will we be discussing later* looks that
we exchange on a daily basis. "Let's go."

"Should we bring our bag?" Bree asks.

"Good question." Pen turns to me. "Do you mind keeping an
eye out?"

I shake my head, pretending it doesn't make my stomach feel like it's full of metamorphic rocks. When the girls return, I don't ask who they met, or how it went.

♦ ♦ ♦

It feels a little like the first meet of my career.

Weird, when I've recently returned from a world championship, but my mindset has evolved more in the last few weeks than in the previous three years. New, more intentional choices. No perfect-or-nothing mentality. My brain, finally able to go quiet.

When I started out the academic year, my dream was to qualify for the NCAA tournament. *I'll have done good if I manage*, I told myself. *And poorly if I don't.*

I'm not sure I still believe that. In fact, I'm certain that I don't need to qualify for anything to consider this year a success. "The real NCAA qualification spot was the mental health we gained along the way."

"What did you say, Vandy?"

"Oh, nothing." I finish warming up my quads and smile at Pen. "Ready?"

We place first in the ten-meter synchro event.

"This is the best day of my fucking life," Pen whispers after we step on the podium. It's not hard to hear her, even over the applause. She cries. I cry. We take a million selfies. Tear up some more. Sandwich Coach Sima in a giant hug. Celebrate with the twins, who got bronze on the three-meter synchro. FaceTime Victoria and tell her that it's all due to her training. Have ice cream. Pass a shop that says TEMPORARY HENNA TATTOOS and . . .

"No," I say.

"We have to."

"No."

"Yes, Vandy."

"No."

"It's a sign. It's destiny. God and our ancestors and Emily Dickinson want this from us."

"We can't."

"Not only we can, we *must*."

We settle for two divers entering the water side by side, and the words DIVING BESTIES underneath, on my right and Pen's left shoulder. The employee, a teenage boy who'd rather be playing *Fortnite*, looks at us like we're the least cool people he's ever encountered. He's not wrong.

It's not until later that night, when we're brushing our teeth next to each other, that I notice something weird.

"Pen?"

"Yeah?"

"How do you spell *bestie*?"

"B-E-S-T . . . Oh, shit."

The following day, Pen wins the platform gold, and I take the bronze. We do all our pool deck interviews together, our new DIVING BEASTIES tattoos on full display. I am so happy, I need to take a minute alone in the bathroom to relearn how to breathe and iron my cheeks out of this unsustainable, too-wide smile.

The following week, at the Zone E meet, we both qualify for the NCAA.

# CHAPTER 60

*U*NKNOWN: I see you've been following my advice.

I stare at the text, trying to recall the *Beware of scams and phishing* email Stanford sends every quarter.

UNKNOWN: It's Mei, by the way.

I laugh. Save her contact.

SCARLETT: I have. Thank you so much.

I chew on my lower lip before adding: Is it okay if I send you a couple of TiVos? I'm not super happy with my armstand.

MEI: I thought you'd never ask.

♦ ♦ ♦

The men's swimming and diving NCAA championship is separate from the women's portion, because . . . I have no idea. But I'm glad that in two weeks the men will fly to Atlanta, and in three weeks the women . . . won't.

For the first time, the women's tournament will be at Avery.

"The *luxury* of it." Pen sighs. "No new pools. No jet lag."

"No having to put on compression socks for a flight."

She studies me, narrow eyed. "You use compression socks?"

"You don't?"

"How *old* are you?"

"Shut up."

She shakes her head. "At least I know what to get you for your next birthday."

The lead-up to the NCAA hits different—electric, a center of gravity, ready to gather the crackle of energy accumulated during the season. Divers don't normally take breaks before big meets, and aside from reducing strength training, our routine doesn't change. The twins, though, didn't make the cut for any NCAA event, which means that their season is over, and their presence at practice is optional. It's just Pen and I, and while the number of times we get our bodies wet is well into the triple digits, our tattoos persevere. At least two journalists have commented upon them. In written pieces. That can be read on the internet. By any individual.

I quietly pray that med schools are too busy to google prospective students.

There are so many parties, I lose count. Over thirty swimmers have qualified for the NCAA championship, and they're all in taper.

"A tapering swimmer's a dangerous thing," Pen tells me when she comes over to get some help for her programming class. She has been feeling much better—because of our wins, and because time does heal all wounds. This morning, when Theo texted her to congratulate her, she rolled her eyes and blocked his number.

"How so?"

"So much time and energy on their hands, all of a sudden. Lukas goes nuts. He'll pace. Gaze longingly at the pool. Wash his hands a lot. Wake up earlier and earlier. You know, the perfectly normal acts of a totally non-deranged person." She shrugs. "Anyway, I gotta go. There's a party tonight. This rower I like will be there."

After she leaves, I manage to hold off for about half an hour. *I'm texting Lukas to check on him,* I tell myself. Because of what Pen said. Because he checked on me over and over when I needed him. Plus, Pen seems to be over the idea of getting back with him.

More simply: we've both been competing out of town for the past two weeks, and I miss him.

SCARLETT: Are you tapering?

LUKAS: And I hate it.

His reply is instant—so odd, for someone who barely checks his phone when we're together. Maybe he's bored. Clawing at the walls. Eager for distractions.

I can't picture it. I run my finger over his photo—Netherlands. Sunglasses interrupting freckles. That indulgent lift at the corner of his mouth.

SCARLETT: Pearls to swine

LUKAS: No idea what that means. Not flattered, though.

I feel almost drunk. Remarkable, the energy that sparks from two texts after such a long stretch of nothing. Tech bros should harness it for their cryptocurrency-mining endeavors.

SCARLETT: Want company?

LUKAS: Not particularly.

LUKAS: Would love to see you, though.

The power requirements of the world's water desalination plants are *met.*

SCARLETT: Where?

LUKAS: Maples.

I think of Maples as the basketball stadium, but an informal volleyball game is going on. Both teams are mixed, three men and three women, with no referee. A handful of spectators scatter on the bleachers. Lukas sits next to Johan, talking with a tall, blond girl in a Stanford volleyball jersey.

Johan notices me first, and waves. The others turn, too—the girl with a curious expression, and Lukas . . .

Lukas.

I stop right next to him, trying not to stare like he's a piece of avant-garde performance art. "Practice game?"

"More for fun, really." The girl's accent is as faint as Lukas's.

"Scarlett," he says, "this is Dora."

We shake hands. She smiles. "You're the diver, right? Premed?"

"Yeah."

"It's good to finally meet you. I've heard so much about you."

"Oh." I dip my hands in the back pockets of my shorts. "Same," I say, just to be polite.

Both she and Johan laugh. "That's nice of you," she says, "but I doubt Lukas talks about me that much."

"Dora, maybe Lukas was secretly in love with you all along," Johan offers, which has her laughing even harder, and Lukas giving an amused reply in Swedish, a short back-and-forth. By the time Dora returns to the bench area, I'm wondering if I've been summoned here to be the butt of a joke I can't even understand.

"Hi," Lukas says, moving his water bottle to make room for me.

"Hey." I take a seat, leaving a few inches between us. His arm, though, snakes behind my back, loops around my waist, and pulls my flank flush against his. Then he lets go.

"You seem—" I break off. Clear my throat. "Less inconsolable than I was led to believe."

"Inconsolable?"

"Pen mentioned that tapering messes with you."

He gives me an odd look. "How so?"

"Increasingly intense handwashing. Lots of early mornings."

"I wash my hands a lot to avoid getting sick—standard guidelines before big meets. And I wake up early because the championship will be on the East Coast."

"Oh. What about the rumored yearning glances at the pool?"

"I don't know. Were you in it?"

Blood sweeps up, into my cheeks. I lower my eyes to my knees.

"Not yet, huh," he says cryptically. "Too bad."

"Congrats on Pac-12," I rush out. As good a topic as any other.

"You, too."

I smile. He does, too. And then tells me, "You looked happy. Not as anxious. During the competition, I mean."

"Thanks. I actually came out a tad too quickly in one of my voluntary dives, and any other time it would have completely thrown me off, but I was able to trick my brain into—" I glance away. "Sorry. You didn't ask for an unabridged recount of my mental state."

"Scarlett." A heavy weight on my knee. His hand, warm and rough. "I did ask. And it was nice to see you up there."

It's like the contents of my rib cage are being wrung out. I almost, *almost* cover his hand with mine. Stop myself. Take a deep, inconspicuous breath. "So, since when are you guys volleyball fans?"

"Since the party we were at got very boring," Johan says from the other side of Lukas, who drinks from his water bottle and then offers it to me. I take a sip, even though I'm not thirsty.

I missed him.

So. Much.

"That guy over there?" He points at a tall, dark-haired man on the court. "He invited us."

"And the game had the advantage of not taking place in a frat house," Johan adds.

The name on the back of the shirt reads *Torvalds*. "Another Swede?"

Lukas nods. "We've infiltrated every sport and branch of government."

"Uh-huh. Are you and *Torvalds* related?" I ask jokingly.

"Yeah, he's my cousin."

My eyes bug out. "For real?"

"No."

I huff.

"He's *my* cousin, though," Johan says.

"Wait. Really?"

They both snort at my gullible American soul. I deserve it.

"Do you guys have a Swedes' club? With your secret language?"

"You mean, Swedish?"

"Yup. Do you meet for *fika* every day? Screen Americans for potential Midsommar human sacrifices?"

They laugh. "I'll be right back," Lukas says. The game is at a break, and he heads down to the side of the court to talk with Torvalds the Cousin.

"Lukas is right about you," Johan tells me.

I turn, alarmed. "Whatever he told you, he lied."

"He just said that you're funny."

"Oh. Then maybe he didn't lie."

"And that you were out of his league."

I blink at sweet, baby-faced Johan. He's what, two years younger than me, tops? But so naive. "When did he say that?"

"When I asked him if you two were dating, outside of Avery. Months ago."

What? "Are you sure that—"

"Let's go."

I look up. Lukas holds out his hand. "Where?"

"Home."

I sneak a glance at Johan. Should we leave him here, all alone? Should we be talking so openly about . . . Well. The Swedes are not easily fazed. "Mine or yours?"

He shrugs. I take his hand. Johan seems unsurprised by this turn of events and waves goodbye.

"Is he going to hate me because I stole you?"

"Nah. His boyfriend's playing."

"Ah." We exit the court, still holding hands. This is . . . more public than we've agreed on. But if Pen is at a party with some rower, maybe she's okay with them finally announcing their breakup. Plus, it's just the two of us. I can't find it in me to pull away, not even when he gently eases me into the wall and bends down to kiss me.

He tastes like beer and himself. Smells less like chlorine, more like soap. His shoulders under my hands, the scratch of his cheek against mine, it's all so fiercely familiar, it could be the stairway up a diving platform.

"You know," he says against my lips, "I wanted to be righteously angry at you. I told myself I wouldn't be with you until you were ready to be honest." I don't ask about what. It would be supremely dishonest. "But I'm just so fucking *happy* to see you, Scarlett. I can't be mad at you, when every time I think about you I am reminded that you exist."

I don't think he's joking, but I smile anyway. "I'm glad you're not angry," I say, pulling him down again, deepening the kiss until he's licking into my mouth and I'm arching into him. The heat and comfort and joy that come simply from being *close* to him rip through me, burn in my stomach. He tries to ease back, but I can't let him go, not after so long without him.

"Fuck, Scarlett." He groans, like my inability to unwrap my arms from him physically devastates him. "Not here."

"Why?" I protest.

And maybe there's no good reason. Because he looks around and finds a door. It's a meeting room that smells like lemon and disinfectant. There are chairs, a whiteboard. One of those insipid inspirational quotes Stanford loves to paste all over athletic facilities, something about pain and discipline and regret. I read the first half while Lukas wedges a chair under the doorknob, but he's already kissing me again, lifting me on the closest piece of furniture—a podium.

My hands run to the fly of his jeans.

"You can't just—I can't fucking do this," he says.

I manage to undo a single button, but he stops me with his fingers. I'm forced to look up. His eyes are a dark, relentless, vaguely desperate blue.

"This is so much more than sex," he tells me. "It was the first time, and sure as hell is now."

I stare at him, breathing heavily. Find something in his face that's half plea, half determination.

"I need you to admit it, Scarlett." His voice is a low, resolute rumble. "I need you to *not* leave me alone to face this."

I'm going to burst into tears. They are lodged in my throat, behind my eyeballs, and I have to swallow past their sharp heat before I can say, shakily, "From the very start, I . . ."

It's good enough for him—but it changes everything. His urgent, frantic kisses melt into slow, reverential trails over my shoulders, cheeks, eyelids, collarbone. His hand closes against my breast, grazes my nipple. He says my name, over and over. I say his. My shorts and underwear are pulled down, gently, and he doesn't have to check whether I'm ready to take him in.

It just works. He sinks inside, little by little, inexorably. It's so good, so alarmingly exquisite, I let the tears flow. He licks them up and buries deep, husky sounds into my skin. In and out, full and empty, and it's so easy. We've been leading up to this for the past eight months. Every time we met, fucked, spoke, touched, looked, texted—every time I thought of him, it was all for the sake of a perfect moment.

In some shitty multimedia room in Maples Pavilion.

I let out a hushed, watery laugh. He shakes his head and continues to move, slow, good, as good as always, maybe even better. But new. "I fucking can't with you," he says, before kissing me like he *can*, with me.

"Lukas." I exhale in the cotton of his shirt. My arms, around him. He's not holding me down. This is vanilla. We're both out of control. It's me and him, suddenly *equals.*

"Slow down," he asks, instead of making me. "Just a little. Or I'm going to come, and it's going to be over, and I don't want that."

We stop, and kiss, soft and open mouthed. We start again, and then it's me who's going to—"A minute. Just a minute. Please." His hips rock into me. Stop. We laugh in each other's mouths. We break away, breathless. We make it last as long as we can. We arch into each other, clutch and grope, but never too hard. He sighs. I cry.

It feels good. Him and me. Like something else altogether. Not less or more—just unexplored, but suddenly accessible.

"I want to do this with you every day and night for the rest of my life."

I nod, still full of tears. *Me, too*, I think. *Me, too.*

"Let me say it," he demands. "I want to say it. Just once."

I know what he means. I cannot take it. I bury my head in his throat and shake it, because I *cannot.*

"Scarlett," he pleads. "Let me tell you, please."

*Pen*, I think. There's Pen. And everything else. The future. The past. What if he says it, and then I lose him. What if I fail at this, too? How will I bear it, then?

He's so deep inside me, my entire body trembles with it. "Please," I beg. "Don't."

"The thing is." His forehand drops against mine. "I don't know if I can keep it in."

"I just—I—"

He grunts in frustration, but then says, "Hush. It's okay, baby." He moves a little faster, a little harder, cupping the back of my head and leading it to the spot at the base of his throat, holding it there like he wants to protect me from something, and a moment later the shudders start, and my cries are muffled into his body, and I'm coming like a dam breaking, and Lukas—

He says it.

Just, not in English. Slow, musical sentences. Words, repeated over and over. I'm awash with them as he comes inside me, his broad shoulders shaking under my arms. And yet, I have the luxury of pretending that I cannot understand him.

I cry anyway. After, he kisses my tears dry, and he's not angry, or impatient, or anything but reveling.

"I'm sorry," I say. "I just . . . I need to . . . I need to square out a couple things. Make sure Pen is . . . before I can . . ."

He nods. "I know." He pulls out of me, and I gasp at the sensation. He kisses the intake of breath off my mouth. "It's okay. We're going to figure it out. I l—" He huffs a small, rueful laugh, catching himself. His hand touches my cheek, and then he straightens my clothes, scattering kisses on me like breadcrumbs. "Let me take you home and—"

Buzzing startles me. Lukas finishes zipping up my shorts and pats the pocket of his jeans, looking for his phone. "Pen?" he asks, a tinge of impatience in his tone. There was no ringtone, which means that he must have deactivated the emergency bypass.

He tenses. Pen's sobs are so loud, even I can hear them, and he's saying things like *Calm down*, and *Where are you?* and *Slower*.

"Come on." He tells me after hanging up, taking my hand. "We need to go get her."

# CHAPTER 61

I'S A WEIRD SETUP, PEN AND ME IN THE BACK OF THE CAR WHILE Lukas drives. I'd throw out a joke about his Uber driver career, but humor would no more benefit the situation than picking up a serial-killing hitchhiker.

"I didn't do it." Her sobs have slowed to quiet sniffles. "You believe me, right?"

I squeeze her hand tight. "Yes, of course." The more I think about it, the surer I am. Pen is no fool and she certainly wouldn't jeopardize her NCAA eligibility by taking banned substances.

"When did you get the AAF?" Lukas asks.

"The what?"

"The notice of adverse analytical finding," I whisper.

"Right, duh. Sorry, I had a shot on an empty stomach. I feel like a boulder just dropped onto my head." She rubs her face. "Half an hour ago. I was at that party with Vic, but couldn't find her, so I took out my phone to call her and . . . the athletic director emailed me and Coach Sima. It's from the Pac-12 sample. Not even a random test!"

Lukas nods. "When was the previous time you got tested?"

"Five, six months ago? Diving nationals."

"And your diet hasn't changed? No new prescription medications? Drug use, vitamins, supplements?"

Pen gasps. "Lukas, you know me."

"I know very little about your daily life, by now." He says it without inflection, but it ticks her off enough to twist her hand out of mine. She leans forward, gripping the headrest of his seat.

"My brain hasn't turned into clam chowder in the past year. I know how easy it is to get a positive doping test. I would not take unregulated substances without running them by the team physician."

He nods, unfazed by her defensiveness. "What are you positive for?"

"I didn't—" She slumps back, bare arm brushing against mine. "Anabolic steroids? Where the fuck would I even get *those*? Do they think I'm cooking meth in my laundry room?"

"And this was the A sample?"

"Yeah. Jesus. I don't even—what's going to happen now, Luk?"

"Back when they tested you, they took a B sample, right?"

"Yeah."

It's a process all DI athletes are intimately familiar with. Chugging down gallons of water to pee in front of some lady who needs an unobstructed view of me filling a plastic beaker has been part of my life for years, and I barely register the unpleasantness. Every time, we're asked to fill two bottles. The A sample is used for testing. B is frozen. If the A sample comes back positive, B is used for retesting when the athlete contests the results.

I've heard of a few people having to go through that, but they were always grapevine stories. Some cross-country junior. A diver who graduated before I joined the team. Friends of acquaintances. Famous athletes in the news. This just feels . . . odd.

"The first step is asking for a retest," Lukas says calmly. "And maybe a lawyer—"

"A *lawyer*?"

"I'll ask around. What did your coach say?"

"He hasn't replied. Even if we ask for a retest, the NCAA championship is coming up. Will it get done on time? Or I could be disqualified, and—" She breaks off, fat tears sliding down her face, and I pull her into me.

"You have a window of twenty-four hours to ask for a retest, right?" Lukas asks.

"Yeah."

"Is Stanford taking care of that, or should we?"

"They will."

"Okay." Lukas nods, and the knot of tension in my chest slowly loosens. It's the way he lays it all out—plans, timeline, to-do list. "For now, don't worry about it. You have not taken steroids, there's something else going on, and we'll get to the bottom of it. Focus on sobering up. Sleep on it."

"I'm not going to be able to sleep until this mess is over." Pen wipes her eyes. "How am I supposed to function while I wait? What am I even going to *do* if I can't dive?"

"I'll take you home and—" He stops when I catch his eyes through the mirror and shake my head. I can only imagine how scared Pen must be. We athletes build our whole identities around competing, and I know firsthand how destabilizing having it ripped away can be. It's clearly already messing with Pen's head, and I definitely don't want her to have to deal with it on her own.

"I don't think you should be alone," I say. "Why don't you stay with me for a few days?"

Her eyes are wide. "Really?"

"Of course. We can watch TV. Hang out."

"But don't you have a twin bed?"

"You can sleep in it, I'll take the couch."

"I don't want to put you out like that. Isn't your roommate a total bitch?"

I wince. "She definitely tries."

"Don't worry about it, then. Luk, can I stay with you? Hasan and Kyle won't care."

I freeze. So does Lukas. His eyes find mine again, and the fear of what might happen if Pen is left alone has me quickly nodding.

"Yup," he says, eventually. I don't think he's pleased, but Pen can't tell.

"This is such a relief." She snuffles, tearful. "Luk, do you happen to have—"

He's already holding a box of tissues out to her. Five minutes later, they drop me off at home.

♦ ♦ ♦

Victoria declares, "Ah, yes, the three forms of torture. Nail pulling, waterboarding, and waiting for a WADA-accredited lab to do what they're paid for."

Coach Sima side-eyes her, but there's a grain of truth in that. The procedures for retesting are soul-suckingly lengthy, even sped up to give Pen her fair shot at the NCAA.

Morale is six feet under. The days crawl, high-strung. Assistant coaches mumble among themselves, stop when I walk by. I catch one of the water polo players peek into Pen's locker, hoping to find a stash of syringes and hormone vials. On Tuesday, after I mess up a running forward and get a mild concussion, Coach Sima tears into me about being irresponsible—and then gruffly apologizes when the doctor sends me home with orders to rest.

"Pen is heroic," I tell Bree on Thursday, watching Pen do a perfect reverse two and a half. She's been holding her head high, showing up for practice, giving her best.

"No shit. I'd be a bug drowning in puddle water."

I put myself in her shoes, and cannot imagine functioning as well as she does.

We are together a lot—practice, meals, study hours. Whatever time is left, she spends with Lukas. He and I have agreed that Pen needs us, and that she shouldn't be left alone.

And yet.

*Jealousy*, I remind myself, *is ugly.* Envy, uglier still. All the more when it's directed at someone in need. Pen is my friend, and I'm proud of Lukas for being solid and dependable, for accompanying her to the doping lab to witness the opening of the B sample, or to listen to a lawyer "exploring options." He makes sure that she's sleeping and eating and staying healthy. If his support of an ex in need were half-assed, I'd respect him much less.

Still, I miss him.

When we text, it's mostly about her. Is she okay? Need anything? I'm dropping her off at Avery. Okay, I'm here.

When he leaves for his NCAA championship in Georgia, Pen moves back into her apartment, and so do I. We share her small bed, laughing at the way we kick each other during sleep. We avoid compulsively checking our emails. We watch Lukas being his obnoxious, winning self.

"Just another day at the office," I muse, watching him hoist himself out of the pool, a handshake and half hug with the Cal guy who came in second. Water slushes down his tattoo, over the tech suit. He leans in to listen to Coach Urso list the things he did wrong, even after winning a race. He barely even smiles. When he does, it's not *real.* I know the difference. "He dominates his sport so much, and yet cares so little."

Pen scowls. "He makes everything look breezy, but when he was younger and having issues . . . you weren't there, but I saw how much it fucked with his head. He *does* care."

I used to assume that Pen was familiar with the depths and shallows of Lukas, and knew things he wouldn't show *me*. Now, I realize that her perception of Lukas is stuck. A sixteen-year-old boy, instead of the man he has become.

That night, my phone vibrates. Everything okay?

Pen breathes softly next to me. Yup. She's sleeping.

LUKAS: You?

SCARLETT: Not sleeping.

LUKAS: But are you okay?

SCARLETT: Yeah.

Shadows of tree branches mottle the ceiling.

SCARLETT: Lukas?

LUKAS: Yes?

SCARLETT: Congrats on winning your last race in the US.

LUKAS: Thank you, Scarlett.

# CHAPTER 62

CAMPUS IS OVERTAKEN BY ATHLETES.

For a couple of days, the diving well—*my* diving well—is off-limits to us locals, as divers from other DI schools familiarize themselves with it. It's a monkey paw situation: I was *so* envious of the swimmers for their tapering holidays, but I find that idleness doesn't suit me much. I still show up at Avery, for dryland and some light PT.

It's where I learn that Lukas is back. I see him in one of the offices, talking to the athletics big shots who only show up when we win something, and my heart flutters in my throat. The happiest hummingbird to ever fly.

*Later. I'll text him later.* I force myself to leave, remind myself that he's busy, but while heading to the dining hall, I hear running steps behind me. A hand closes around my upper arm, and he's there.

I'm bursting, with . . .

It has to be love. It's expansive and all-consuming and full and joyous. Hungry. Thick. At once heavy and light. Everywhere and golden. It's *him* and *me* and the myriad of little strings that tangle us together.

I grin, and my happy smile seems to disorient him. He reaches up, brushes my cheek with his thumb, says my name so low, even I can't hear it. Then he pulls back with a slight frown.

"When did you get back?"

"This morning." A step closer, towering over me. "We need to talk."

I frown. "Is she okay? I thought she was with Coach Sima."

"Who?"

"Pen."

"This is not about Pen." His hand is still around my arm. "It's about you having a concussion and not telling me."

"How do you know?"

His eyebrow lifts.

"It wasn't a big deal. I was cleared the following day. And you were splashing around the East Coast. Winning shit. Übermensching."

"You need to tell me these things."

"What things?"

"*Everything.* You need to . . ." He inhales. Looks away, then back to me. "I want to know this stuff."

"Why?"

"Because it's about *you.*"

Another spill of heat. My stomach is made of butterflies. "I'm fine," I reassure. Grasp his hand lightly, a silent apology, a promise that *I'm safe*, and he sighs deeply. Looks down at me.

"We do need to talk, Scarlett."

We do. Still. "It's just a bad time. She needs us more than . . ." More than what? More than I need him? More than he needs me? Is it even for me to say?

No, judging from the way his jaw shifts back and forth. He bends down to kiss me, short, hard, like he means to leave an imprint. Little does he know, it's already there.

"As soon as this is solved," he warns.

I take a deep breath. "As soon as this is solved, and the NCAA is over."

The following morning, one day before the competition is due to start, Pen receives an email from Stanford's athletic director.

The initial lab results were a false positive.

◆ ◆ ◆

The NCAA tournament has no synchro event. "Which sucks," Pen tells me, "since we'd just hit our stride."

"Right?" Even though, in the privacy of my own head, I do love the idea of only competing in one event, my best, on the last day. "I'll be there on the second day, though. For the board stuff."

"To hold my shammy?"

"And send you rip vibes."

Avery is pure chaos. Every time a race starts, a stadium-like ruckus rises from the competition pool. Tickets are sold out, and access to the stands is prohibited to non-holders. To support us, the men's team resorts to watching events from the sidelines and the entrances to the lockers, clustering, making bets, producing bombastic noises whenever Stanford is adjudicated any number of points.

"It's because they placed fourth at their championship," Shannon informs me. She's one of the captains of the Stanford women's team. I get plenty of mass emails from her, but I cannot recall if we've ever talked before. "How they could *not* place first with Blomqvist on their team, I have no clue."

"Who won?" Boy, I really should care more.

"The men's? Cal. But *our* main rivals are Texas and Virginia. Can you dive better than them?"

"I hope so."

Her *not good enough* scowl reminds me why we never hit it off. "It's okay. My horse is Penelope Ross."

But perhaps it shouldn't be, because Pen is not having a great championship. During the prelims for the three meter, she nearly doesn't qualify because of a wrong twist. Later, in the final, even without failed dives, her form is . . .

"That was so *good*," Rachel says after Pen's back two-and-a-half pike that just . . . isn't. Dives are to non-divers what wine is to me: it could come from a cube, or from the cellar of an impoverished French baron whose family fell upon hard times. I'd have no way of discerning.

"It wasn't bad," Bree says between claps.

Hasan frowns down at her. "But?"

"Was missing a bit of height," she offers.

A bit of a balk, too. The scores appear on the board, and I grimace. She finishes in fifth place, which is below expectations considering last year's medal.

"It's the doping scare," she tells us later, when we debrief in Coach Sima's office. "Messing with my head. I couldn't find my groove."

"Doesn't matter," Coach tells her. "What's done is done. Don't dwell on it. Tomorrow's platform, you're the favorite. Onward."

"Yup. Onward." She sighs and turns to me. "Is Lukas around? Was he watching me dive?"

"I'm not sure." I haven't heard from him since before the competition.

"I saw him at the swimming events," Bella says. "I think he has to go to those, since he's one of the captains."

And yet. The following morning, Pen and I get through the platform preliminaries without issues. When I return for the final, late in the afternoon, Lukas is there. I'm so distracted by my phone, I almost crash into him.

"What are you staring at?"

"Barb sent a video of Pipsqueak saying good luck."

I show it to him. To his credit, he looks immensely charmed.

"You like dogs, right?" I ask.

"Is it a deal-breaker?"

"I'd never thought about that, but . . . yes. It is."

"I love dogs. I'm just not sure Pipsqueak qualifies."

I'm considering whether letting her rip off Lukas's face is a legitimate defense of her honor, when Maryam texts, I'm in the bleachers. Look for me. I glance up, squinting at the stands. There are no signs of her—Sike, she texts a minute later—but I spot a familiar face.

"Lukas?"

"Mm?"

"Is that . . . ?"

He follows my gaze. "Yup. Sure is."

"Is Dr. Smith into diving?"

"She once asked me how it was different from swimming, so I doubt it. I think she might just be here to support you."

"That's very . . ." I cut off. A fainting couch moment comes over me. "Lukas?"

"I'm still here."

"Do you know who Dr. Carlsen is?"

"Comp bio guy?"

"Yup."

"I took his class last year. Why?"

I point at the spot in the stands when Dr. Smith leans her head on Dr. Carlsen's shoulder. His hand is wrapped around her waist, and he seems less than enthused to be here. Then again, it might be an improvement from the quiet wrath that's his default state.

"She mentioned a husband," I say. "Is she . . . openly cheating on him?"

"Olive?"

I nod, flabbergasted. But Lukas's mind doesn't seem to be half as boggled as mine. In fact, he's fighting a smile.

"Scarlett, I think Dr. Carlsen *is* the husband."

I stare, uncomprehending. "No."

"Yeah."

"No."

He bites the inside of his cheek. "Honestly, I see it."

"No."

"They complement each other. And they do have several publications together."

"No."

He laughs. "Are you okay, sweetheart?"

"I'll never be okay again."

"What are you guys talking about?"

I whirl around. Pen is behind us, already wet in her suit. "Nothing. Just, this professor we were doing this research—"

"You need to go shower, Vandy. It's about to start."

"Right. Thanks." I leave with one last, wistful glance to Lukas, and feel his eyes on me as I move away.

The final begins ten minutes later.

# CHAPTER 63

I'S AROUND THE THIRD DIVE THAT I REALIZE THAT I'M HAVING the best competition of my career—and it has surprisingly little to do with the scores.

I'm light in the air. My limbs find their path to good form. Above all, I'm able to clear my mind. I'm ten feet above the world, and no one else exists. It's me and the water. Sam's voice in my head reminds me: *Your brain is not a muscle, but sometimes you can use it as one. Train it for competition as well as you train any other part of your body.*

Pen, too, is in much better shape than yesterday, and breezes through her dives. Her first voluntary has a higher degree of difficulty than I've ever managed in competition, and I gasp when she performs it with minimal errors. Her second is an inward—a work of art, and it makes me so delighted, I hug her. I'm giddy about how well it's going for us, and that's why I don't fully grasp the implications of it until the end of the fourth round.

I'm in first place. Pen trails after me by a couple of points.

"If either of you fucks up the last dive," Coach Sima threatens, "I swear I'm selling you to the woodspeople."

"No pressure, though," Pen mutters.

"Yes, pressure. So much pressure."

But it doesn't frazzle us. Or at least, not me. My last dive is an inward two-and-a-half pike, the same dive that fucked up my life two years ago to this day, and it's . . .

Good. Not *perfect*, but good enough. I know this the second my hands knife into the water. I know it without reading numbers. It's a knowledge that comes from someplace inside me that didn't exist a few months ago.

Pen's turn is after mine, and she dives well. The cameras follow me around. Athletes rehearse their last dives, get last-minute tips from their coaches, jump in place to keep warm. I dry off my suit, put my sweats back on, and look at the list of names on the board. The competition is not over yet.

My phone pings with a text. Smile.

It's Mei. She probably meant to send this to someone el—

MEI: Watching the live stream, and you need to SMILE.

SCARLETT: What?

MEI: You just won the NCAA.

I glance at the rankings, and she's right.

I'm going to finish first.

I need . . . a minute.

To comprehend the enormity of it.

I slip inside, past the pack of swimmers watching the competition. Their chins are up, to the platform. They don't pay attention to me as I make my way into the belly of Avery, a quick turn, a slumped back against the wall, eyes screwed shut till little bursts of gold appear.

I cannot wrap my head around it. The person I was two years ago. How alone I felt. Scared of being too much, of not being enough, of being imperfect. Surrounded by *impossibles*. And now I dove, and—

"Scarlett."

I blink. Lukas is there, smiling at me. A *real* smile.

"Crying again, I see."

I hadn't even noticed. "I . . ."

"I know." He comes closer, palms above both my shoulders. Kisses the tears off my cheeks. "It's okay," he murmurs. "I'll put you back together."

My fingers fist into his shirt. "It's just . . . a lot."

"I know." Another kiss, gentle against my lips. "Scarlett. You're brilliant. You're perfect. And I—"

An outraged, teary voice swallows the rest of his words. "Are you two *for real*?"

# CHAPTER 64

*L*UKAS DOESN'T TURN AWAY FROM ME. DOESN'T LEAVE. Doesn't pull back.

I know he heard Victoria's question, but he seems unwilling to let it dictate his movements. A statement, perhaps:

*We're not doing anything wrong.*

*I'm happy here, the way I am.*

*Go away.*

I respect that. But I'm not certain it's the best course of action, so I press a palm to his chest to push him away.

It does nothing. Lukas kisses me one more time at his leisure, lets out an aggravated sigh, and takes a step back.

Victoria, I notice when I can finally look at her, is flanked by Bree, Bella, and . . .

Pen, of course. Four pairs of wide eyes and four dropped jaws, all ranging from affronted, to disbelieving, to shattered.

"What are you doing, Vandy?" Bree asks. She sounds like I just threw her grandfather under a tractor.

I'm considering how to reply when Lukas says, "Tell her, Pen."

Pen, though, isn't listening. She's pale, trembling next to Victoria, and zeroes in on me with an expression I can't decipher, to ask, "Did you just want to be *me* all along?"

Betrayal—that's the expression. And she stares like I'm the one doing it. To her. "I . . . what?"

"Because it feels like that, Vandy." Tears start running down her face. "Are you in your *Single White Female* era?"

"Enough," Lukas says. His hand is on my shoulder, warm and grounding. "Pen, they are Scarlett's teammates, too. If you won't tell them what's going on, I will."

"What *is* going on? The boyfriend and the gold medal that were mine a year ago are now hers. That's what."

Lukas exhales, impatient. I'm afraid of what could come out of his mouth. Of the impact it might have on her.

"I know you're hurting, Pen," I interject, steadying my voice. "But you're still a silver medalist. And Lukas . . ."

"What about Lukas?" Vic asks, inching closer to Pen. "Because from my side it feels like he could have at least ended things with Pen before—"

"Pen and I aren't together," Lukas interrupts her. "Haven't been for months." He turns to Pen. "I went along with what you asked and kept our breakup a secret, because Scarlett knew, and she was the only one who mattered. This is where it ends, though."

"I don't think we should be here, guys," Bella mutters. There must be a general agreement, because all three of them shuffle away, Vic with a final squeeze of Pen's arm.

"You should go, too, Pen," Lukas says once they're out of earshot, not unkindly. "We'll discuss this when we've calmed down—"

"Do you realize how painful this is?" She shivers and wraps her arms around her waist, still wearing her wet suit and nothing else. "To see you like that, with my best friend?"

"You have no right to this reaction. You have known about me and Scarlett for months. In fact, you pushed us together."

"But it was just—you were hooking up, it wasn't—"

"Pen, when you broke up with me, I was clear that I considered my commitment to you over. I told you I'd be there for you as a friend, but you knew from the start that I wasn't going to treat my relationship with Scarlett like a way to pass the time."

"But I'm the one who broke up with you! A few months ago, you and I were still in love and now—what, you're in love with two people now?"

"No, I'm not."

It drops between the three of us like a body in water. Perfect rip entry. No splashes or noise, just a terrible, deafening silence. And when it has sunk deep enough into Pen's brain, she turns to me. "You just . . . took everything from me. Thank you, Vandy."

I shake my head. She's being unfair and irrational, and I know I should be furious at her, but she's so obviously heartbroken, I can't find my anger. "I know this is hard to hear, but . . . neither the title nor Lukas were yours to be taken," I say softly.

"You have to stop, Pen." Lukas's hand tightens on my shoulder. "She's your friend, and you're hurting both of you."

"She *was* my friend, and—" She points at Lukas with trembling fingers. "I *forbid* you to fall in love with her."

"Pen. I already have."

"Oh, yeah?" She laughs, bitter and a little mean. "Vandy must have not gotten the memo, because she looks pretty fucking shocked by this piece of news."

Lukas doesn't glance at me, but his throat works with his swallow. "She wasn't ready to hear it yet. This is none of your business."

"How can it *not* be my business? You're my boyfriend and my best friend!"

All of a sudden, it's too much for me. "I need us all to take a minute, and . . ." I wipe my cheeks with both palms, overwhelmed. "Pen, you . . . I'm sorry, but you're being unfair. And Lukas, I . . ."

I turn and slide away, toward the locker room, toward the nearest exit. By the time I've turned the corner, Lukas has already caught up. He stops in front of me, blocking my path, hands rising to cup my cheeks.

"Scarlett. Don't."

"I . . ." We are in the same place where I ran into him and Pen arguing last September, at the start of school. A cruel joke, that's what this is. "I can't go to the award ceremony."

"Fuck the ceremony. I'm here. Stay with me."

I shake my head. My tears scatter. "I should have told Pen about us. The second things started changing, I should have . . ."

"Scarlett, you said it yourself. Pen is being irrational. She needs to get the fuck over herself."

"But I wasn't truthful. Sam said—I should have been honest. I wasn't, and now she's unhappy. I did this to her—and to you—"

"To me?" He smiles, amused. "What have you done to me? You made me happier than I've ever been, Scarlett, that's all." He tilts my face up, until our foreheads press against each other. "Pen is not heartbroken. She's not in love. This is just possessiveness. She's lashing out because she lost two of her favorite toys, and she wants someone else to hurt as bad as she does. And I—I've been trying to tell you how I felt for months. And I know it's hard to hear, I know this stuff doesn't come easy to you, but it's out there now. You don't have to be terrified of it anymore. I love you. I'm in love with you. And you're in love with me. We can say it."

"Lukas."

"I have been in love with you for so long. And I won't stop. I know it."

"Lukas—"

"This is it, for me." He presses a kiss against my cheek. "Remember back in the fall? When I was being a total asshole, trying to prove to myself that I could exist without you? I can't, Scarlett. I *can't* be without you. And for the first time in my life, I don't care. I think of you all the time, and I want to make plans with you, I want to talk about the future, and I'm fucking *happy* about it—"

"*Stop.*"

It's the word—our word. The one I never used. And Lukas recognizes it, because he immediately straightens.

After a beat, he even manages to let go of me.

"You said that if I said *stop*, you would stop. And I'm asking you to stop now. I—this is too much. That's my best friend. And my team. And you are my . . ." The words start shaky and die in my throat. I cannot even think them. "I'm asking you to give me a minute to figure this out. Okay?"

I watch him watch me for long, long moments, his need to respect my boundaries at war with his need for *me*, the determination in his eyes that doesn't quite hide the pain.

His heart may be as cracked as mine.

"You know it, don't you?" he asks.

"What?"

"From the very start, you had all the power. From the very start, I was in the palm of your hand."

I did, I think. I definitely do now. "Yes."

He smiles, but it doesn't quite reach his eyes. "As long as you are aware, Scarlett."

I don't even have to run from him, because he's the one to leave. He kisses my forehead and turns around, and then I watch him walk away until he's just a fuzzy figure, blurred by my tears.

# CHAPTER 65

**I**'M NOT A COWARD.

Or maybe I am.

Am I?

"I'm not saying that you are. Or aren't," Barb muses, eating a bite of mac and cheese I made from scratch like the ingrate she is. "Like Ludwig taught us: some questions don't need to be solved, but dissolved."

"I don't recall meeting anyone named Ludwig."

"Wittgenstein. Renowned Austrian philosopher."

I sigh. "I knew it wasn't the bones that took up space in your head."

"Perhaps it's aphorisms." She licks her spoon. "The point is, Ludwig wouldn't want you to keep wondering whether you did the right thing by leaving California. You should simply dissolve the problem and accept that you did what you needed for your peace of mind."

"Are you sure that's what Ludwig would want?"

"Of course. He personally told me. He always cared so very much about your well-being."

"He did, didn't he?"

"Plus, you're doing your internship with Makayla here in St. Louis."

True, technically. I just hadn't planned on peacing out of California the day after the NCAA.

On a needlessly overpriced flight.

Without saying goodbye to anyone.

Leaving uneaten groceries in the fridge.

I've been home for nearly ten days, and it took me about half of that to explain to Barb why I turned up on her doorstep with no warning at all.

The rest has been spent trying to sort out my feelings.

"You've always been slow at that kind of stuff," Barb says now, over the bowl of mac and cheese for which I bought expensive pecorino. Using *her* money. "But take your time. It's not like there's a strapping Swedish lad with a Stanford Med acceptance waiting for you."

"My feelings for Lukas are—that's not the problem."

"What's the problem, then?"

Right. What *is* the problem? "Do you think that . . . Do you think that a relationship that started so messily, and with so many hiccups, and hurting other people, can have a happy future?"

Barb smiles. "I think every relationship is the same."

"Which means?"

"You won't know until you try."

A few days ago, I started receiving the first tentative texts from my teammates. Are you okay? (Bella) If you need someone to talk to, please know that I'm here. (Bree) Hey—what I said was messed up. I didn't have all the facts, or any, and I still decided to run my mouth. I'm sorry. (Victoria) Not to mention, the constant email communication with Coach Sima.

*My cardiologist has advised me not to involve myself in drama, and I know the season is over and I have no right to make demands of your time. I am, however, sending you a picture of me receiving your gold medal. Please come collect it at your earliest convenience.*

*I am proud of you.*

*The things in your locker are now in a box in my office.*

*PS: Stanford placed second.*

And:

*I understand that this is a delicate time for you, but I cannot stress enough the importance of signing up for the Olympic trials. You are already qualified. This needs to be done as soon as possible.*

And:

*I hope you took a (well-deserved) break, but you better be practicing again now.*

He's lucky, because I am—though it has little to do with the trials, and everything with the fact that diving is, once again, my happy place. I spend long days interning at the hospital, then go to my high school club, where I train mostly on my own. No objectives, just vibes.

"It's truly incredible, how much you have improved," Coach Kumar tells me. "Such good work, all around."

And yet, as the days go by and I give myself enough time to think, I'm not certain that it's true. In the past year I've become a better diver, sure. But what about the rest?

*The near career-ending injury I described*, I write in the millionth draft of my med school essay, *played a big role in my decision to become an orthopedic surgeon, but no more so than my step-mother. She is the single most influential figure throughout my life, the person who rescued me from an abusive situation when it would have been much easier to simply rescue herself. Thanks to her, I know what courage is, and* . . .

Okay. The last sentence requires work. If I was courageous, I'd be with Lukas, wouldn't I? If I was courageous, I'd go back to California and confront Pen.

On an impulse, I open a blank Word document.

*Dear Pen,*

*I should have been more transparent about my feelings for Lukas, and for that I am sorry. You fucked up, too, though. I get that you're hurting, but maybe you shouldn't have made a scene and stolen my gold medal moment, especially after what happened to me at my last finals. Maybe what you said about Lukas and me bonding over sex was insulting. Maybe you shouldn't have treated Lukas and me like windup toys. Maybe you don't get to make us kiss and then break us apart. Maybe you cannot be the center of everyone's world. Maybe I want for Lukas to be the center of mine.*

I don't send it. However, I ruminate over that for the following day, until in the middle of an armstand, my feelings are finally sorted out.

Anger and disappointment toward Pen and the way she acted. And toward Lukas . . .

In the locker room, I pull up his number to—I'm not sure. Call him. Text him. Send him an *I fucked up* Memoji. Then I see the location under his name. "Shit," I say.

Almost immediately, an idea buzzes through me.

I dial Barb.

"Yup?"

"First question: Would it be okay if I took a break from my internship?"

"Um . . . sure? You've already done way more than you were supposed to, so I can't see Makayla complaining about it. Plus, you *are* a nepo baby."

"I prefer 'legacy artist.' Second question: Can I borrow some money?"

"Borrow? You mean, you'd later return it?"

"Probably not."

"Hmm, I *want* to say yes, but I feel like the wise thing would be to first ask: How much money?"

"I'm not sure. Enough to fly to Sweden."

The noise she makes is so triumphant, I have to move the phone away from my ear. "Scarlett, baby, *finally*. Mi bank account es su bank account. Within reason."

I head out of the swim club, googling flights *without* reason (sorry, Barb), trying to figure out what's the earliest time I could leave if I first stop home to grab my passport and a pair of clean underwear, until someone stops me with a hand on my arm.

"Vandy?"

When I look up, I find Penelope Ross.

# CHAPTER 66

KNOW YOU DON'T OWE ME ANYTHING," SHE TELLS ME THE SEC-
ond we're sitting together in the park across the club. No benches
are devoid enough of bird shit to meet our lofty standards, so we say
a little prayer about the weight limit and settle on the swings, like
we did last summer in Coach Sima's yard, where it all started. Pen's
head hangs low, carefully studying the groove her shoe carves in the
sand. "Maryam said you weren't in California. And I remembered
you were still sharing your location, and . . ." She shrugs. "I could
have called. But I decided that behavior as horrendous as mine deserved a grand gesture."

I consider myself a nice person, but I'm not even tempted to
deny it.

"You don't have to accept any apology. I just wanted to look you
in the eye when I said . . ." She seems to realize that she's not, in fact,
looking me in the eye, and lifts her head. "I'm sorry, Vandy. I screwed
up, big-time. And I have no excuses."

I study her familiar, beloved face. She seems tired. Anguished.
In the gray of this cloudy day, her hair is duller than usual. "I never
tried to take anything away from you."

"God—I know." Her face screws up, like the memory of her

words pains her. "I know, Vandy. I know *you*. And even if you had been trying, neither Luk nor the NCAA title were *mine*. The things I said . . . I was out of my mind. I could tell you where I was at, but I wouldn't want you to think that I'm trying to find excuses for my behavior—"

"Tell me. Because I've been trying to wrap my head around what I did to deserve to be treated that way, and—"

"Nothing." She reaches out to grasp my hand, and glances away when I instinctively pull back. "I knew you and Luk were seeing each other, but . . . for years I had to pry personal information out of him with a crowbar half the time, and you were not the type to do that. I figured your relations would just be sexual, and never progress. And honestly, while I was seeing Theo, I barely thought about you two, which is . . . not the behavior of someone in love." She rubs her forehead with her palm. "And you and I grew so close, and I couldn't believe how lucky I was. When you won Winter Nationals, I was genuinely happy. But then you went to Amsterdam, and Carissa took pictures of you and Luk together and sent them to me."

"Carissa?"

"She kept my number over the years, apparently."

"Jesus."

"Planning to use it for evil all along, I'm sure. She thought she'd caught Luk cheating on me with my friend and sent an entire fucking photo shoot of you guys playing tourist. He and I . . . we both realized years ago that we had little in common. He stayed with me out of gratitude because I helped him through the loss of his mom. And I don't think I ever admitted it to myself before last week, but I stayed with him because being Lukas Blomqvist's girlfriend felt like the biggest middle finger to every single bully who'd tormented me in high school." She shakes her head, like she's ashamed of that. "So when Carissa sent those pics, I told myself that I didn't care, but the way he looked at you . . . I don't think he's ever wanted anything or anyone the way he wants you. And that hurt, because I was with him for years. And then Theo ended things, and the false positive results . . . I realized how *alone* I was. You and Lukas were so supportive, but when I stayed with him, he slept on the couch every night, and I could tell that all he wanted was to be around *you*. He only became interested in conversations when you were mentioned. He'd walk me to practice just to find some hiding spot and watch you dive. It had never been like that between us. I started questioning my entire fucking life. And then . . . well, at the NCAA, I was the favorite, but *you* won. And Lukas was celebrating with you, looking so smitten.

"I was in pain, and someone had to be the villain of my story. But then my head cleared. You weren't there for me to apologize, so I started with Lukas, and . . . he laid out all the facts. Everything that I should have already known about him, myself, *us*, he packaged it for me to see clearly. How little we shared. We were the closest at sixteen—not when he moved to the US, not now as adults. When we were *children*. I never even cared about his dreams, and . . . we'd been codependent friends, but our romantic relationship was long dead even if we Weekend At Bernie'd it for years. Lukas was reliable, and I knew I could always fall back on him. He was—" She laughs. "He was my crash mat. And when I saw him kiss you, I felt like you were pulling him from under my feet. And it hurt five times harder, because it was *you*, and I'd never had a friend like you."

I snort. "Pen, you have so many friends. *Everyone* loves you."

"And they're great. But with you . . . it was always so easy. You never judged me or made me feel anything but accepted. And when I realized that I'd be losing both Luk *and* you, I lashed out. I acted like Luk was a sandwich, stolen by a seagull, and—"

"Are you saying that I'm the seagull?"

"I think so, yeah."

I fight a smile. "Wow. Thanks."

"Better than what *I* am."

"Which is?"

"The fucking villain."

I sigh. This time, I'm the one reaching for her hand—cold, rough, too-thin surrounded by mine. "I don't think anything is as simple as that. There were just . . . choices that we made. And consequences." I shrug. "I also made mistakes. I could have told you that I was falling for him."

"And I probably would have still been a bitch about it." She stands with a wistful smile. "I came here to apologize. What I said was cruel, and false. I stole from you the joy of your first gold medal. I want to make it up to you, but I don't know how. If you no longer want to be my friend, that's fair. And if you want to make me work for it, it's also fair. I will, believe me. If you want to think about it . . . take your time."

I nod. "Thank you." My stomach feels buoyant. For the first time in days, I'm not going to be swallowed by quicksand. "For telling me all this."

"Thank you for listening, Vandy."

I watch her step away, and when she's a few feet from me, something occurs to me. "Actually."

She turns around.

"Are you going back to California?"

A nod.

I stop fighting my smile. "I'm going to the airport, too. In case you need a ride."

# CHAPTER 67

J AN IS MY ACCOMPLICE, AND I'M PROUD OF MYSELF FOR RE-
cruiting him. Initially, I just hoped to get an address from him.
Then I found out that he was visiting Stockholm, and he became my
coconspirator.

"I have a hotel booked," I tell him when he picks me up at the
airport.

He looks at my face. Then at my backpack. Then at my face
again. "You travel very lightly."

"He might be angry at me," I explain. "We didn't leave off on the
best terms. I'm not going to stick around if he doesn't want me."

He laughs and puts my bag in the trunk, shaking his head
like I'm warning him about the dangers of chemtrails and mind
control.

Everyone around me talks in the same beautiful, singsongy way
I've come to associate with the Swedish language. The colors seem
more vibrant than back home, though it might just be because I
know that Lukas is nearby. And because, past 10:00 p.m., the sun is
still in the sky. "Won't go down at all," Jan explains.

It's early June, just like in *Midsommar*, and—

Wait a minute. "No human sacrifices, right?"

"What are you—oh. That movie?" He sighs. "Ari Aster has a lot to answer for. And Ingmar Bergman is *right there*. Anyway, how do you want to play it?"

"What do you mean?"

"You said you wanted a grand gesture. What's your plan?"

"Oh. Well. I guess I thought that flying over an ocean and a good chunk of land where toilets are holes in the ground and water is served without ice would kind of be . . . it?"

Jan is unimpressed. "But what will you do once you see Lukas?"

"Oh." Had I considered that far? No. Yes. I know that I'll tell him that I—

"Did you bring flowers?"

"I . . . don't think it's legal? Fragile ecosystems and such."

"Then are you proposing to him?"

"What? I'm *twenty-one*."

Jan shrugs. "When you know, you know. Did you learn a complicated TikTok dance?"

"Would he even enjoy that?"

"Who wouldn't?"

"I clearly didn't think this through."

"Well, you better fix that quickly," he says, pulling into the driveway of a red two-story house. The roof is pitched, and the green of the surrounding trees is almost cartoonishly bright. "Because we're here."

"Your father's home?"

"Yes. He's very excited about you coming, by the way."

"Oh, god. You *told* him?"

"Of course."

I cover my face. Pray for the car seat upholstery to wrap around me like a boa constrictor and release me from this ignominy.

"He's very happy. I told him you're smart and you like nature. He's glad you're Lukas's first girlfriend."

"I am not his girlfriend, and he dated Pen for *seven years*."

Jan shrugs. "Dad never met her, so he thinks Lukas made her up."

This is a terrible mistake. "It's nearly eleven. Is Lukas usually awake?"

"No, not usually."

Crap. "Then I should go to the hotel and come back tomorrow?"

"Well, he's not *usually* awake, but he clearly is tonight." He takes the keys out of the ignition to point at the house, and when I follow that line . . .

Lukas is leaning against the porch baluster, arms crossed on his chest. His usual barefoot self, but wearing jeans and a T-shirt—*not* pj's. He does not have the look of someone who just got out of bed. In fact, the curl of his mouth holds no trace of surprise.

He's been waiting for me.

"You told him," I accuse.

"I did not," Jan assures me, placid as usual. "Believe me, I would not get on the bad side of my future sister-in-law this early in the relationship." He slips out, and short of carjacking this vehicle and flooring it back to the airport, I have no choice but to do the same. But after a couple of steps I freeze, because Lukas is coming toward us, that half-smug, half-pleased smile still on his beautiful face.

He tells Jan something in Swedish that starts with *tack* (thank you) and contains the word *troll*, but despite my religious Duolingo sessions, I cannot follow any further. Jan grasps his shoulder as he passes by, and then turns around before entering the house. "Scarlett. *Lycka till!*" *Good luck.*

"Thanks," I reply, too weakly for the sound to carry. "I'll need it."

"No, you won't," Lukas says, clearly amused. "What did I tell you?"

"Many things." For reasons that probably only Sam could list,

I'm already crying. A couple of fat, lonely tears. "Which one are you referring to?"

He shakes his head. His fingers come up to dry my cheeks, and my heart swells so much and so fast, I feel as though I could take flight.

"In the palm of your hand, Scarlett. From the very start."

I screw my eyes shut at the sweet, bitter pain of his words. I have to wind down. Things to say. Peace to make.

"How did you know I was coming? Did Pen tell you?"

"You never stopped sharing your location with me."

"I know that. But still, you'd have to have *checked* where I was to . . ." Oh.

"I can't sleep unless I know where you are." His shrug is delighted. Unapologetic. "And during the day . . . I just feel better keeping tabs. Control, you know?" He leans in and presses a single, soft kiss to my hair, murmuring, "I'd say sorry, but you should probably just get used to the way I am."

My laugh is choked. Breathless. "So you just . . . know everything?"

"Not *everything*." He pulls back. Even the blue of his eyes is more vivid. "I know that you came here to see me—even though I did briefly wonder if you were just in the mood for *dammsugare*. I can only imagine the rest. That you're scared, for instance?"

"Petrified, more like it," I whisper. Another tear streaks down to my chin. "This is so messy."

"Falling in love?"

I nod. "And I did it so . . ." Deeply, desperately, fast. It's just pure violence.

"The ultimate loss of control, huh?"

I breathe deeply.

"But we've done this before," he points out, patient, almost detached. "You've given up control. You've trusted me to take over."

"And you never took advantage."

"Nor will I. What else?" He drums his fingers on his bicep. "I assume you want us to be together?"

I nod again.

"That's going to require some discussions. I have to make plans for my future. You have to make plans for yours. Let's do that together, okay?" It all sounds so simple coming from his mouth. The alphabet. The most basic of arithmetic. Us, being in love.

"What about med school?" I ask, trying not to sniffle.

"There are a couple of ways to deal with that." He's clearly considered this. At length. "I could see if the schools that accepted me are willing to grant a one-year deferral. That way we could choose a place we're both—"

"Lukas, no. You can't waste a year just for . . ."

"Scarlett." His fingers come up to my chin. Grab it gently, but tight. "The only time wasted is time we are apart."

My heart might beat out of my chest.

"I could also keep my commitment to Stanford, if you're interested in staying in California," he continues casually. "We'd be together next year, while you finish up undergrad. And I have no doubt you'd get in the following year."

"I just . . . I can't ask you to make life decisions based on me."

"That's okay, because no asking is involved. Scarlett, this is it for me. I'm in."

"But what if we start dating and we don't work out?"

He seems to find the question hilarious. "We've been dating for nearly a year in everything but name. We *work* together, in every possible way. Except the chaos you live in, but I can probably train that out of you. Punishments. Positive reinforcement." He pushes my hair back. "You respond well to that kind of stuff."

"But what if—"

"Scarlett," he interrupts, a little less restrained. "Listen to me.

The last few years, I did everything I could to be happy with someone else, and did *not* manage." His hand slides down my arm, slowly. Long fingers twine with mine. "And then I spent the last few months trying not to fall for you, and failed so fucking miserably that—" He shakes his head. "This is it. I'm not going to pretend otherwise. No more lies."

I frown. "Did you lie to me?"

"By omission."

"What did you not tell me?"

"How early I fell for you. How soon I realized it. The enormity of it."

I close my eyes, so overwhelmed, so intensely *full* of Lukas, that looking at him might be too much. "I thought you'd be angry at me. For being such a coward back at the NCAA."

"Difficult to be angry at someone when their actions hurt them as much as they hurt me."

I look away. Clear my throat. "Well, I . . . I guess we covered a lot of ground, but I should still say what I came to say. Which is . . . first of all, thank you. For the past couple of weeks. For giving me the space I needed to figure myself out and to get my shit together. I thought it was very nice of you to respect my wishes and . . ." His shoulders shake silently. "What?"

"Don't be *too* grateful." I'm being pulled into him. Thick arms. The width of his hand on my lower back. Lips to my temple, and his enveloping scent. "I have a plane ticket for St. Louis, two days from now. We're going to have to change that, huh?"

I bury my head into the familiar warmth of his throat. Feel his pulse, steady against my cheeks. "The US Olympic trials are next week," I say.

He nods. "Should we go? It's up to you."

That *we*. "I think I'd like to, yeah." I wrap my arms tight around his shoulders. "It would be nice if I qualified. I could go to Melbourne with you."

"You should come whether you qualify or not." His hand slides up my back. "I don't think I want to let you out of my sight again this summer."

There is no space between him and me. No air between the hot tension spilling in my stomach and the shift of his muscles under my hands. "I can't be like Pen."

"You never have been."

"What I mean is, I don't think I'd be able to ever live apart. And I'm . . . greedy. I wouldn't be able to be with other people, or handle an open relationship, or take breaks—"

"That's good. Because I know you think that I'm not capable of jealousy, and maybe I thought that, too. But if you were to ask me for any of those things . . . it would gut me, Scarlett. It would absolutely end me. And if it were nonnegotiable, if it were a condition to be with you, I'm still not sure I'd be able to say no."

His stubble scratches my cheek. "I'm so sorry I wasn't able to say it before, but . . ."

"But?"

I take a deep breath. Turn until my mouth is against the shell of his ear. Kiss him underneath it before I say, "I love you. So, so much. All the things you talked about in Amsterdam, on the balcony . . . I want them, too. With you. For the next million years."

"Million? Hyperbole?"

"Not this time."

His smile is easy. Quick. Wide. I don't see it, but it blooms against my skin. "Wow."

I pull back, puzzled. "Wow?" I just told him that I love him and he—

"You know what we call this?"

I shake my head. His fingers close around my waist, and he's picking me up, lifting me high, and it's my turn to bend down and kiss him, but before I manage, he whispers against my lips, "A Midsommar miracle."

# EPILOGUE

**A FEW YEARS LATER**
*Lukas Blomqvist, MD, PhD*

*H*E HASN'T SEEN HER IN TWO DAYS. SPOTTING HER ON THE other side of the hospital cafeteria doesn't count. Neither does waking up and finding her in his arms, eyes closed and breathing soft, too exhausted to even stir as he gets ready for his shift.

Sometimes, when she's in deep sleep, a thoughtful little frown furls on her brow. Lukas cannot physically get out of bed until he has smoothed it over with his lips.

He used to want to prove to himself that he could thrive, even without her.

He has given up on that. Now he just wants *her.*

▲ ▲ ▲

SCARLETT: I hate bones.

LUKAS: I hate bones, too.

SCARLETT: Why do you hate bones? Shouldn't you hate brains?

LUKAS: Bones steal you away from me. Brains keep me entertained when you're gone.

⠀⠀⠀◆⠀◆⠀◆

Carl XVI Gustaf starts rubbing against his shins the second he steps inside the kitchen, so Lukas glances at the magnetic board on the fridge.

*Katten åt*, it reads. *The cat ate.*

He crosses his arms. "I know she has already fed you."

*Meow.*

"She told me. She wrote it right there, on the board."

*Meow.*

"I'm not her. I will not be manipulated."

*Meooooow.*

He sighs and opens the treats cupboards.

⠀⠀⠀◆⠀◆⠀◆

He finds it at work, during rounds, while patting the pockets of his white coat in search of a pen.

The note reads:

*Whenever you open this, I'm probably thinking of you.*

⠀⠀⠀◆⠀◆⠀◆

Occasionally, someone brings up his previous life.

"Do you really not miss swimming?"

"Not really, no."

"Interesting. You know, there's an orthopedics resident here who used to be an Olympian a few years ago. Like in . . . Paris, I want to say?"

*Melbourne*, Lukas corrects in his head.

"Diving, I think. The one in pairs? She and her partner got a bronze medal."

*Silver.*

"Do you know of her?"

Lukas smiles. "I am familiar, yes."

* * *

They compare their schedules as soon as they receive them. Some months are better than others.

SCARLETT: How many times do you think we'll see each other in the next year?

LUKAS: At least one.

SCARLETT: Right, the wedding.

LUKAS: Two, if we can both make the rehearsal dinner and neither of us has to send a proxy.

SCARLETT: Sounds far-fetched. You must believe in fairy tales.

LUKAS: If trolls exist, anything can happen.

* * *

"This is Lukas, my best friend's fiancé," Pen says.

He cannot help a small smile.

"What?"

"The way you introduced me." Not her own ex. Not her own *friend*. It seems to occur to Pen, too, and her eyes widen. "Oh, shit, I'm so sorry. I promise I love you and stuff."

"And stuff."

"Come on. You know I would throw myself under a bus for you."

"You absolutely would not."

"Well . . . under a tricycle."

"Better."

"I *would* throw myself under a bus for Scarlett, though."

He can certainly relate to that.

* * *

He's listening to a talk on ependymomas when his phone vibrates.

SCARLETT: Premise: love being a doctor.

SCARLETT: Love corpse stuff.

SCARLETT: However.

SCARLETT: I cannot wait for next year when we're slightly less busy and can, you know.

SCARLETT: See each other.

*Scarlett*, he thinks. *You have no idea.*

᭥     ᭥     ᭥

He slips into bed after 3:00 a.m. He usually waits until he's warmed up to pull her closer. When she's the one to roll into him, though, all bets are off.

"Oh my god," she mumbles in his chest. "You actually *exist*. I thought I'd made up a whole Swedish fiancé."

He smiles into her hair, heart too big and too full. "Go back to sleep."

"Nooo. Don't wanna."

"Why?"

"Because."

"Because?"

"You're not going to be here when I wake up."

He smiles against her temple. "Baby."

"Yeah?"

"Remember how I covered Art's shift last week?"

"Oh, no. Are you covering another?"

"Nope. Art is covering mine. Tomorrow."

"What?" She pulls back. Her tired, dark eyes blink open. "It can't be."

"It can."

"*Surely* you must be on call."

"Nope."

"It's impossible. Check again."

He kisses her forehead. "Just sleep. I *will* be here when you wake up."

"But . . . what are we going to do with all that time together?"

"I was hoping we'd sleep in. Then go at it like animals. Then maybe a quick break at the pool? Then back home, more animal stuff."

"Oh my god, Lukas. What are we—a *couple*?"

"Let's not get ahead of ourselves."

A minute later she's asleep. The entire universe is here, in his arms.

# ACKNOWLEDGMENTS

As usual, it takes a whole metropolis! Infinite thanks to my therapist—and by therapist I mean my agent, Thao Le (you know what you do); to my editor, Sarah Blumenstock, and my babysitting editors, Liz Sellers and Cindy Hwang, who let me write the book I wanted to write (as opposed to the one I had, cough, *promised*; special thanks to Sarah, who endured years of daily harassment regarding sprayed edges; it pains me to say this, but blocking my number when you went on sabbatical was the right move); to my production editor, Jennifer Myers, my managing editor, Christine Legon, and my copyeditor, all of whom, I'm sure, had to read way more sex scenes than they signed up for when they started working in publishing; to my marketing and publicity team (Bridget O'Toole, Kim-Salina I, Tara O'Connor, and Kristin Cipolla), who have to deal with an increasingly unmarketable and unpublishable author; to my cover illustrator, Lilithsaur, my jacket designer, Vikki Chu, and my interior designer, Daniel Brount, for making my filthy book infinitely pretty.

Thanks to my foreign publishers, and in particular to Aufbau (Rollberto Rolando, Sara, Astrid, Andrea, Martina, Sophia, and honorary Aufbau employee Aleks; please note that I would *not* like to thank Stefanie for lying to me about someone's ability to speak English) and Sphere (Molly, Clara, Lucie, Briony, Lucy) for hosting me so warmly, allowing me to connect with amazing German and UK readers, and feeding me doner kebab and high tea.

As usual, thank you, Jen, for the invaluable beta read. To my friends, family, and to the fellow authors I've had the privilege of meeting during this journey: I love you. To all the booksellers, librarians, and readers: I'm not sure I deserve you, but please know that I am very, very grateful.

*Justin Murphy of Out of the Attic Photography*

**ALI HAZELWOOD** is the #1 *New York Times* bestselling author of *Love, Theoretically* and *The Love Hypothesis*, as well as a writer of peer-reviewed articles about brain science, in which no one makes out and the ever after is not always happy. Originally from Italy, she lived in Germany and Japan before moving to the US to pursue a PhD in neuroscience. When Ali is not at work, she can be found running, eating cake pops, or watching sci-fi movies with her three feline overlords (and her slightly less feline husband).

### VISIT ALI HAZELWOOD ONLINE

AliHazelwood.com
AliHazelwood
AliHazelwood

# LEARN MORE ABOUT THIS BOOK AND OTHER TITLES FROM *NEW YORK TIMES* BESTSELLING AUTHOR

# ALI HAZELWOOD

**SCAN ME**
or visit
prh.com/alihazelwood